C000215628

Modern
Scottish
Writers

Reading
Douglas
Dunn

Edited by
Robert Crawford
and
David Kinloch

Edinburgh University Press

© Edinburgh University Press, 1992

Edinburgh University Press
22 George Square, Edinburgh

Typeset in Linotron Garamond 3 by
Photoprint, Torquay and
printed in Great Britain by
The Redwood Press, Melksham

A CIP record for this book is available
from the British Library.

ISBN 0 7486 0369 7

The publisher gratefully acknowledges subsidy
from the Scottish Arts Council towards
the publication of this volume.

Contents

| | | *Preface* | vii |
| | | *Abbreviations* | viii |

| *One* | Biography | I |
| | Jane Stabler | |

| *Two* | 'There are many worlds': The 'Dialogic' in *Terry Street* and After | 17 |
| | Ian Gregson | |

| *Three* | Moving Towards a Vernacular of Compassion: *The Happier Life*, *Love or Nothing* and *Barbarians* | 32 |
| | Bernard O'Donoghue | |

| *Four* | Dunn, Larkin and Decency | 51 |
| | Glyn Maxwell | |

| *Five* | Dunn and Politics | 66 |
| | Sean O'Brien | |

| *Six* | Them and Uz: Douglas Dunn's Technique | 80 |
| | Dave Smith | |

| *Seven* | Writing with Light — *Elegies* | 94 |
| | Paul Hamilton | |

| *Eight* | Secret Villager | 108 |
| | Robert Crawford | |

| *Nine* | Dunn and Dundee: Dunn's Re-entry into Scottish Culture | 122 |
| | W.N. Herbert | |

| *Ten* | Telling Short Stories | 138 |
| | Anne Varty | |

Eleven   'The Music inside Fruit': Douglas Dunn and France   151
            David Kinloch

Twelve   Taking Exception: Douglas Dunn's Criticism   168
            Richard Price

Thirteen Bibliography   182
            James Kidd

                                                   About the Contributors 286

                                                                    Index 288

Preface

This is the first book-length study of Douglas Dunn's work. Its title is intended to indicate that it focuses principally on Dunn's published volumes, although many unpublished and uncollected pieces have been taken into account. *Reading Douglas Dunn* is designed to function as a critical introduction to the work of one of Scotland's foremost living writers. It makes available a substantial body of new information about Dunn's life and work, offering a variety of approaches. In editing this book, we intend to provide future readers with both commentary and factual material which will provoke further discussion of the work of a writer already admired throughout the English-speaking world. Not least, James Kidd's bibliography will be essential to future commentators.

We are grateful to Faber and Faber for permission to reproduce copyright materials in this volume. These are detailed in full on the 'Abbreviations' pages, which constitute a continuation of this copyright acknowledgement. Earlier work by several enthusiastic readers of Dunn's work, particularly the distinguished interviewer John Haffenden, has greatly facilitated the writing of the book. Douglas Dunn has been unfailingly helpful to contributors and editors alike, not least in allowing his collected, uncollected and unpublished writings to be quoted so extensively. The secretaries at the Department of English, University of St Andrews, have provided invaluable support to the editors, as have the Librarian and staff of St Andrews University Library, who have made it possible for James Kidd to compile his bibliography. To these and other individuals and institutions, including the editorial staff at Edinburgh University Press, the editors owe a debt of gratitude.

R.C., University of St Andrews
D.P.K., University of Strathclyde

Abbreviations

The following abbreviations of works by Douglas Dunn are used in this book:

A   Racine's *Andromache*, translated by DD (London: Faber, 1990)

B   *Barbarians* (London: Faber, 1979)

E   *Elegies* (London: Faber, 1985)

EL   *Europa's Lover* (Newcastle: Bloodaxe, 1982)

HL   *The Happier Life* (London: Faber, 1972)

IL   *'Importantly Live': Lyricism in Contemporary Poetry*, Dundee University Occasional Papers I (Dundee: University of Dundee, 1988)

LN   *Love or Nothing* (London: Faber, 1974)

N   *Northlight* (London: Faber, 1988)

NSP   *New and Selected Poems 1966–1988* (New York: Ecco Press, 1989)

OxPoe   interview with Bernard O'Donoghue, *Oxford Poetry* Vol. II, No. 2 (Spring 1985), 44–50.

PD   'Interview with the Devil' in Sean O'Brien and Stephen Plaice, eds, *The Printer's Devil* (Tunbridge Wells: South-East Arts, 1990), 12–33.

PS   *The Poetry of Scotland*, ed. DD (London: Batsford, 1979)

PT   *Poll Tax: The Fiscal Fake* (Chatto Counterblasts, No. 12), (London: Chatto & Windus, 1990)

SKP   *St Kilda's Parliament* (London: Faber, 1981)

SP   *Selected Poems 1964–1983* (London: Faber, 1986)

SV   *Secret Villages* (London: Faber, 1985)

TD   *Two Decades of Irish Writing*, ed. DD (Cheadle Hulme: Carcanet, 1975)

TM   *The Topical Muse: On Contemporary Poetry* (Kenneth Allott
      Lectures, 6), (Liverpool: Liverpool Classical Monthly, 1990)

TS   *Terry Street* (London: Faber, 1969)

Verse   interview with Robert Crawford, *Verse* 4 (1985), 26–34.

Viewpoints   interview in John Haffenden, ed., *Viewpoints: Poets in
      Conversation* (London: Faber, 1981), 11–34.

On these pages which constitute a continuation of the copyright acknowledge-
ments the editors would like to thank Farrar Straus & Giroux for permission to
quote from *Collected Poems* and *High Windows*, both by Philip Larkin; Peters
Fraser and Dunlop for permission to quote from *Northlight*; and Faber and Faber
for permission to quote from *The Whitsun Weddings*, *High Windows*, *Collected
Poems* and *The North Ship* also by Philip Larkin.

The editors would also like to thank Isabel K. McLean for her excellent index.

One

Biography

Jane Stabler

Douglas Dunn has spoken of being 'shackled' with subject matter, 'simply as a fact of who I am', but he has also described tradition as 'a reference library, a magic house . . . where I go for stimulus and solace'.[1] This dual response to the idea of home is evident throughout his work, and the extent to which his background has become a foreground is a question which still preoccupies him. Dunn grew up in what he calls 'a normal working-class' environment: his continuing artistic emphasis on the extraordinary resources of the ordinary lends his Clydeside childhood a significance – both mythic and mundane – which cannot be understated.

In an autobiographical essay in *Poetry Review*, Dunn admits how easy he finds it 'to emphasise a vague drift of happiness and infant excitements at the expense of what recollection understands to be true but privately dispiriting'.[2] With that caveat, Dunn's retrospective view of his childhood suggests that it was both happy and secure. He ensured his personal well-being, in part, by placing a high value on privacy and individual space. Dunn's reserve continued throughout his childhood when his twin obsessions were reading and running: even as a boy, he controlled his distribution of energy in physical and mental pastimes. Passionate involvement in these two isolating activities anticipated the way that Dunn was to train and guard his skill for writing verse. Although he chose to spend much of his time away from other people, his youthful pursuits did not prevent him from feeling part of a wider community. His cross-country running fostered an intimate knowledge of the north Renfrewshire countryside where his childhood (as opposed to Larkin's 'unspent' youth) was invested.

* * *

Douglas Eaglesham Dunn was born on 23 October 1942 and brought up in Inchinnan, a small community with both a rural and an industrial identity. Familiarity with the agricultural calendar and a pleasure in landscape are integral parts of his work, in which he makes frequent use of dialect names for wildlife and displays a quasi-mystical respect for trees. 'What is the larger conceiving force in a poet's imagination?' Dunn ponders while introducing the work of new poets from Hull, 'the phenomena of nature, and character, working against the background of a place, or a style of writing arranged from reading and original gifts? One can hardly exist without the other, no matter which part of the question you put first'.[3] His own recollections of his childhood show how these two forces merge.

Inchinnan was ten miles away from Glasgow and four from Paisley. From the south bank of the Clyde at the edge of the village, Dunn used to watch ships heading to or from the port of Glasgow. Shipyards on the north bank of the Clyde were then much in evidence, and the thriving industry of Clydeside extended into Inchinnan where India Tyres had offices and works. William Douglas Dunn was employed in this factory, and Dunn remembers with affection the distinctive smell of the 'gutty works' on his father's overalls. Dunn's mother worked as a housekeeper for a Catholic lady in the village who gave the young Douglas Dunn religiose books as presents. Dunn's mother was a devout Presbyterian, and many of her values became implanted for her son in the ideal of the well-kept house. An excerpt from his essay 'Little Golden Rules' reveals how the physical appearance of a house mattered to the poet as a boy in the way it embodied a matriarchal presence:

> I once knocked on the door of where a boy lived whom I sometimes played with. His mother asked me to come in. Clearly, my chum's mother was nothing like mine: the house was a foul-smelling scatter of dirty clothes, ripped furniture, greasy carpets, unwashed dishes, a real mess. Friends at Inchinnan lived in a farm cottage which was still without electricity. It didn't have an inside tap let alone a lavatory and a bath. But they were proud. Everything was spotless. I liked it there, the way the girls did the sewing, the cheerful decency of it, and I was heartbroken when they left, and angered when the farmer let the cottage go to rack and ruin, using it as a bothy for itinerant Irish tattie-howkers, that abrasive breed of strange people, with their unusually stubbly chins, their suspicious eyes, their frightened women, their tatters, their scowling children.[4]

Dunn emphasises the loss of domestic composure with a startling impression of evolutionary chaos. The essay was published in January

1983 and it evokes obliquely Dunn's horror of a home life gone to rack and ruin.

During his childhood, Dunn remembers that his own home contained very few books. His father seldom read but he believed strongly in education and taught his son to read by the age of four. Dunn was regarded as a precocious child and was given books by various aunts and uncles. Dunn's grandfather on his mother's side was a baker in Hamilton, a self-taught man who had gathered a substantial library. Dunn remembers that he was always closer to his mother's side of the family. He visited this grandfather most weekends and for longer periods during the school holidays. He had access to his grandfather's bookshelves, so that, although Dunn had little experience of children's literature (not reading *Peter Pan* until his teens and *Alice in Wonderland* until his twenties), he had read authors like Walter Scott, Robert Louis Stevenson and R.M. Ballantyne by the age of eight. He enjoyed the work of ancient historians, geographers and the miscellaneous prose and verse snippets from children's annuals. The first book Dunn purchased was a collection of Walter de la Mare's work which he found at a primary school jumble sale.

Both parents encouraged his bookishness but 'in a very neutral way', Dunn recalls; 'I certainly wasn't pushed.'[5] Reading was not encouraged on days when it was dry enough to play outside. Other enthusiams that Dunn inherited from his father were those of fishing and stamp-collecting. His earliest memory is being taken on the crossbar of his father's bicycle to fish at Linwood Bridge. Foreign postage stamps were regarded by Dunn as 'thousands of tiny windows on other places in the world'. While still at primary school in Inchinnan, he developed a faultless knowledge of the atlas which he associated with the origins of his stamps and the route marks of franking. He loved to identify in the atlas places which had furnished his collection, and in interview allowed himself to resample the sound of the names 'Solomon Islands, Comoro Islands, Barbados'.

The ability to apply himself to a subject both methodically and imaginatively also contributed to a prize-winning apprehension of the Bible. Dunn rapidly gained a reputation for feats of memory and erudition and his accumulation of general knowledge was sharpened by the unavailing attempts of teachers to catch him out. According to Michael Longley, most true poets relish making catalogues[6], and Dunn's classroom recitations of place names and biblical verse must have mingled the pleasures of incantation with the power of outdoing his contemporaries.

At the age of eleven, Dunn sat the Qualifying Examination which determined whether he should enter the junior or senior level of secondary education. This selection process was regarded by a certain sector of the Inchinnan population as a test of social standing. 'If you were intelligent enough,' Dunn remarked wryly, 'you went to the fee-paying school: the people who went there were not my friends.' He was admitted to the junior secondary school, Renfrew High, and was aware at the time of the social implications: 'even when you were young, you intuited that something stank about "the system".' This early experience of a spurious social yardstick encouraged Dunn's hatred of class-consciousness which he regards as a destructive English export: 'a rotten, rancid and disgusting thing in British society, not native to Scotland until someone put it there.'

Candour of speech and an identifiable morality were the native values of Inchinnan which Dunn appreciated:

> there was an open-heartedness about Inchinnan's colloquial, vernacular, no-nonsense style of life. People were direct and candid, amused, sometimes mischievous, speaking their minds on most issues, reticent about those subjects that decency dictated should be kept to themselves.[7]

The fabric of this community has been essential to Dunn as a writer and as a surprisingly conservative thinker: 'I take the side of what some would call the old-fashioned,' he asserted in interview, 'although I'd claim it to be native':

> No matter what people do to the land, it's indestructible, and for reasons about which I'm never sure, I find it necessary to be loyal to somewhere. Inchinnan, where I grew up, and here in Fife where I live, sometimes seem to me involved in my interior Third World, a different time zone from London, Paris or New York.[8]

When asked whether he had been aware of the mythical Clyde qualities of Calvinism, socialism and craftsmanship as a child and if these influences had fostered his growth as an artist, Dunn was cautious. 'I'd discount the Presbyterianism,' he said – at least half the population of the West of Scotland is of Catholic Irish origin. Presbyterianism, you don't think about that when you're young. The political thing, though, got to me a bit – I had an uncle who was a communist and he used to lean on the fireplace at Christmas and New Year; his opening sentence would be something like, "There will be no socialism in Scotland unless on the bayonets of the Red Army."' Dunn's father's sympathies were with the old Left, and Dunn says that he will never forget his father's expression during these family discussions. As for Clyde craftsmanship and its relation to his verse, Dunn explained, 'the qualities of something being well-made, these are things I enjoy in anything. I have linked it to "Clyde-built" — some Clyde-built ships were very badly built mind you. In its heyday the Clyde was the South Korea of its time. The connection doesn't seem to me fortuitous. Up until the 1930s — probably still — that part of Scotland is the Third World. Glasgow was the second city in the empire, *but* . . . '

The distrust of Glasgow came from Dunn's father, and it is an attitude which the poet doggedly maintains, despite the renaissance of the city. Dunn concedes, however, that his scope for book-buying was enhanced when at the age of fourteen he was considered old enough to visit Glasgow alone. There, in Grant's Educational Company and in McDougal's bookshop in Paisley, he remembers spending all his pocket money. Well ahead of his class in English at Renfrew High School, Dunn found mathematics, physics and chemistry burdensome and he found himself a source of amusement and anger to the teachers of those subjects. In his mid-teens (encouraged by his mother), Dunn considered the Presbyterian ministry as a career, but this aspiration ended at Camphill School when a new mathematics teacher (and former missionary) advised Dunn that his battle with the subject could be won if he worked harder and prayed more.

When Dunn moved on to Camphill Senior Secondary School, he 'affected a hysterically adolescent scorn for the subjects [he] would inevitably fail'. The fact that he had begun to write verse was a closely kept secret. There was nobody with whom he could discuss his reading or his writing. He cultivated an extrovert public profile which deflected attention from his private book-buying self. 'It was not,' Dunn stresses, 'a struggle between my temperament and those of my contemporaries . . . as it happens, my devotion to poetry was one I could not declare even to myself with a round, warm, full-blooded conviction until my late twenties.'[9]

In his sixth year at school, Dunn had given up the study of physics, chemistry and maths (which he had failed at Lower grade and was supposed to be resitting). He remembers his final school examination season as a 'careless session' of truancies when he would arrive at school to register an attendance and then depart alone for the Reference Room in Paisley Public Library, before visiting the grass running-track of the air base at Abbotsinch or the cinder track at Renfrew. These private trials of physical endurance balance the image of the adolescent who read Tennyson and Longfellow on the shores of Loch Lomond. At this time, Dunn was engrossed by his reading, but he did not seriously consider university entrance because of his lack of Higher certificates in compulsory sciences.

Instead of university, Dunn opted for a more direct route to the domain of the Reading Room and began to work for Renfrew County Library. He was stationed in various branch libraries, including a stint at Port Glasgow where he remembers he had lots of time to read. Dunn then entered the Scottish School of Librarianship. There, in contempt of the school authorities who had made it clear that he had fallen short of their expectations, Dunn passed all the examinations necessary to qualify as an Associate of the Library Association by the age of nineteen. It was not technically possible to become an Associate until the age of twenty-three. Dunn insists that it only took a few weeks of steady application (away from the jazz clubs) to pass his librarianship examinations. His easy passage through library school suggests that his failure in sciences was due to reluctance to expend any energy in that direction rather than an intellectual block.

In 1962, Dunn abandoned the local library circuit to work for the Andersonian Library in the Royal College of Science and Technology, which became Strathclyde University. He was, and still is, passionate about professional librarianship with its unique combination of solitary and social engagement. He summarises the vocation as 'a wonderful profession . . . dedicated to the organisation of books and knowledge for the greater benefit of the community'. At this time, he first encountered Irish poetry, and has returned either to the north or the south of Ireland nearly every year since. Dunn remembers finding Seamus Heaney's poem 'Mid-Term Break' in a journal there (*Kilkenny Magazine* 9, 1963) and thinking that it had been written by 'somebody from the past because it was . . . good'. Dunn's early visits to Ireland were made with Lesley Balfour Wallace, whom he had met in 1961. At the end of November 1964 they were married and, two days after the wedding, flew to America.

The Dunns went to Akron, Ohio, where Douglas had obtained a job at Akron Public Library. He was considered 'something of a library whizz-kid', and to work in the well-funded American libraries was an advantageous step in a librarian's career. In the States, Dunn asserted, 'public libraries were much better organised, much more professional, much more enthusiastic in the way in which they attempted to solicit the community to use their resources.' The Public Library at Akron had its own radio station where Dunn took part in programmes on books and interviews with writers.

Although they lived in America for fourteen months only, the place made a lasting impression. Dunn remembers the rural landscapes of Ohio and around Akron and a village called Peninsula where they used to spend weekends with Liz O'Kane. She had a poetry library from which Douglas could borrow freely, and her neighbours were like-minded people with experience of museum curatorship and an interest in sculpture. In Peninsula, Dunn beame involved in a creative circle of friends who read, wrote and conversed about poetry — 'they were the first genuinely cultivated people I had met.' Dunn was struck by what he called the 'variousness' of American life juxtaposed with the oddly familiar presence of the rubber industry in Ohio. He was fascinated when he encountered an elderly derelict called 'the Scotsman' who had been one of Hart Crane's early lovers. In an interview in *Verse*, Dunn gave details of his growing interest in American literature:

> Increasingly I think that the time I spent in America has been tremendously important to me as a poet and as a writer in general. I did a terrific amount of reading . . . a great deal of American fiction, short stories, novels, and masses of American verse . . . I think a lot of my attitudes and approaches towards the short story come from reading lots of American short stories at that time . . . Scott Fitzgerald's short stories were important to me, very important. The stories by John Cheever which I was able to read at the time. John O'Hara's earlier stories, Carson McCullers, Eudora Welty, Faulkner's stories . . . stories by some of the other great American fiction writers from Hawthorne to Poe up to the writers who were flourishing by the mid-sixties . . . Sinclair Lewis's *Main Street* made a terrific impression on me, and Sherwood Anderson's *Winesburg, Ohio* was another extremely important book to me. It still is. (*Verse*, 28)

The months in America were critical in a personal as well as a professional sense. The Dunns were involved in a car accident which killed a close friend and seriously injured another. Dunn recalls the eeriness of looking at a photograph taken at Niagara Falls a few hours before the crash occurred. A wary fascination with the way in which photography exactly holds the past shadows his writing and his approach to film work. Towards the end of 1965, before they could have recovered from that personal loss, Dunn was called up for the US armed forces. He was on an immigrant's visa because of Akron Library regulations and was therefore liable to the military draft. Selective Service No 33 113 42 904, Dunn attended the preliminary medical but, having recently experienced the trauma of loss of life, was not prepared to enter the shambles of the Vietnam War. He also opposed the conflict on principle. Douglas and Lesley left America two weeks after his medical. Not having enough money to fly back to Scotland, they crossed the Atlantic by ship in January 1966. Dunn allowed subsequent notices from the authorities to accumulate unanswered inside a copy of Robert Lowell's *Selected Poems*.

Back in Scotland, the Dunns lived with Lesley's parents in Giffnock while Douglas worked as Librarian of the Jospeh Black Chemistry Library at Glasgow University. In the vital literary atmosphere of America the previous year, he had decided that he wanted a university education, but the Scottish universities to which he had applied required an Attestation of Fitness. This would have meant resitting the subjects (including ironically, chemistry) that Dunn had failed at school. Certain English universities, however, were prepared to waive his shortage of certificates and, in 1966, Dunn was accepted to read English at Hull.

Dunn bought 26 Flixbro Terrace in Hull for £250 and sold it for the same amount two years later. It was the first house they had owned, and Dunn describes its location as a slum terrace:

> To use a phrase from Larkin's 'Large Cool Store', I was living in one of those 'low terraced houses' which were once so characteristic of Hull – red-brick, the colour of burnt carrots, many of them one up, one down; outside lavs; kitchens, where a proper kitchen existed, created by extending a cupboard-sized room into a coal bunker; damp; the staircase in the corner of the ground floor room so narrow and its turn so sharp you wondered how elderly people managed to clamber up it.[10]

Dunn was acutely conscious that Lesley's home had been determined by his decision to become a student. His keen awareness of personal responsibility was accentuated by the way that other students regarded him. Married, and several years older than the average first-year undergraduate, Dunn became a father-figure for his contempories who turned to him for advice about what Dunn grimaced at as 'their squalid sex lives and their disgusting addictions'. The age difference isolated him from fellow students, and he spent most of his time as an undergraduate reading hard for his degree and writing verse. In 1967, Dunn had a vacation job in the university library's cataloguing department. It was there that he first met Philip Larkin, who was to become the single most important influence on his career. Larkin was an incarnation of Dunn's ideal librarian-poet, but he had a reputation for not indulging chatter about poems, and Dunn did not discuss poetry with him until 1968 when Larkin approached Dunn to congratulate him on the manuscript he had submitted for a Gregory Award.

The money from the award allowed the Dunns to move house and rent a larger flat. In interview, Dunn lovingly catalogued the rooms of 134 Marlborough Avenue: 'there was a nice big sitting-room, a nice big bedroom, quite a nice hall – it was a ground-floor flat – and a very nice, conservatory-type extra sitting-room, very beautiful, a long room of glass you could use as a dining room; quite a nice kitchen, a great big walk-in cupboard. It was just perfect for two. The sitting-room used to double as my study; it was big enough for that.'

One Sunday, Philip Larkin made an unexpected visit to the flat to see if Dunn had written any more poems. Larkin had been on the Gregory Award Committee and had heard from Faber that Dunn's work was to be included in a new anthology. It was Lesley who overcame Douglas's reservations about inviting Larkin back for supper at a later date. Larkin's antisocial mannerisms were not evident in his treatment of the Dunns, with whom he sustained a quiet friendship. He became a frequent dinner guest and played a formative role in the production of Dunn's first collection of poems: it was Larkin who gave the book its title and who urged Faber to publish it. *Terry Street* appeared in 1969, the year Dunn graduated from Hull University with a first-class degree. He considered postgraduate research and (less seriously) the Presbyterian ministry, but a sense of financial responsibility for Lesley coupled with his long-standing commitment to librarianship led him to work as junior to Larkin in the Brynmor Jones Library.

The hours, Dunn recalls, were extremely demanding. It was not uncommon to work from 8.30 in the morning until 7 o'clock in the evening, sometimes the late shift until 10.00 at night and regularly on Saturday mornings. Lesley's hours at the College of Art where she was working for a degree between 1967 and 1971 were equally long, and Douglas found that he had little time or energy left for writing. 'I got fed-up,' he said, 'of having to turn down offers, mainly from Anthony Thwaite, to review for the *New Statesman* . . . I hankered after the opportunity to sit down and do some writing.' Larkin's attitude to the working hours of his staff was inflexible, and he proved obstructive when Dunn requested time off to give poetry readings. Larkin had little patience for much of the new poetry that was being published, and he disapproved of the idea of informal contact with an audience. It was Larkin's assumption that he was right and his contempt for other (popular) opinion that irritated Dunn: 'he really did think that he was doing me a favour by not giving me time off to go and do readings.' In an interview with a student magazine in 1987, Dunn expressed his reservations about Larkin's attitude to his audience: 'I don't buy it all; when he's writing his irascible, ratty, short-tempered poems, I find him vulgar.'[11] Larkin wanted Dunn to continue writing in the genre of *Terry Street*, but Dunn felt that he had progressed from that. It was a mark of

Dunn's growing confidence that, in 1971, he left the library against his mentor's wishes and determined his career as that of a full-time writer.

Between 1971 and 1981, Dunn produced *The Happier Life, Love or Nothing, Barbarians, St Kilda's Parliament* and edited anthologies of Scottish poetry and criticism of Irish writers, but he was also working with the pressures of review deadlines. Hull, he has said, 'was never home' (*PD*, 14). The chief reason for staying there was that it was an inexpensive place to live. The house in Marlborough Avenue cost £4 per week. For most of their time there, Dunn was not short of reviewing work. Ian Hamilton was in charge of the Poetry and Fiction section of the *Times Literary Supplement* for which Dunn reviewed up to four novels every week. He received £5 per 400 words, so four novels paid the rent and allowed them to live in reasonable comfort.

In 1972, the Dunns spent several months in France in a village called Tursac near Les Eyzies de Tayac. During this period, Dunn read Sartre, Camus, Nizan and Merleau-Ponty without adopting French existentialism. The Dunns both loved the hidden, sensual landscape of the Dordogne with its abundant wildlife and astonishing caverns, and they considered settling permanently there. For this to have been successful, though, Douglas would have had to teach, which would have meant living closer to a city. Besides this, by 1972 Lesley had a career in art galleries lined up. Balancing the decision to settle in Hull in 1966, the Dunns returned to that city, this time to further Lesley's career.

By the mid-1970s, Lesley was the Senior Keeper of the Ferens Art Gallery in Hull and Douglas was receiving commissions for radio and television work. In 1972–3, he began to publish short stories. Dunn had been writing prose compositions since his late teens, and described the art form to John Haffenden as a type of home: 'a little place where you can be absolutely yourself . . . a sort of haven, a sanctuary, a place without the burden of theory and criticism' (*Viewpoints*, 31). They had, Dunn remembers, 'quite a lot of money, but it was up and down'. In 1976, they were able to buy 3 Muirfield Park, Westbourne Avenue – the 'Butterfly House'. A shortage of review work in 1974 had forced Dunn to take up a post as Fellow of Creative Writing at Hull University. He also worked for the Worker's Educational Association, the Extra-Mural Department of the University and the College of Art where he provided courses on German Expressionism, the history of jazz and modern poetry. Dunn enjoyed this work and claims that he found teaching more rewarding than giving his opinion about new poems in the talking shops which developed in Hull throughout the 1970s.

Although Philip Larkin was perceived as the centre of this phase of prolific creativity, he did not involve himself in the task of advising

younger poets (Dunn was an exception). Larkin's reluctance to
participate in readings and discussions about poetry encouraged Dunn
to assume this responsibility. His role as chief encourager of young
writers was built from the mid-Seventies onwards when he was Fellow
in Creative Writing (1974–5) and did not change with the arrival of
Andrew Motion in Hull. Although Dunn remained a reclusive
individual, younger poets sought him out. He recalled his role as
mentor in the introduction to *A Rumoured City: New Poets from Hull*
which he edited in 1982:

> Many poets are approached by writers younger than them, or other
> aspirants, in the hope of hearing revelatory criticism, or even the
> secrets of verse. Neither expectation is ever satisfied, I suspect,
> although there is no harm in trying. Unsuited by inclination or
> temperament to behave like Svengali, my own mind has changed
> in these critical sessions as often as my original point of view was
> accepted. Sulks, silences, loggerheads, insults, manic arias,
> surprise, delight, approval, disapproval – these are among the
> characteristics of the candid literary talking shop. (p. 12)

The charged literary atmosphere fostered the work of Ian Gregson,
Tony Flynn and Genny Rahtz, who were postgraduate students at Hull,
and Margot Juby and Tony Griffin, whose work Dunn saw regularly.
He was also in the company of Sean O'Brien, Douglas Houston, Peter
Didsbury, Tony Petch and Frank Redpath. Tom Paulin was in his
second year at Hull when Dunn was a finalist. Among the public houses
where writers met were The Queens, The Polar Bear, The Avenues, and
The Bull, which was the venue for readings organised by Dunn. He
remembers how simply by word of mouth there would be an audience of
one hundred for poetry readings. Robert Lowell and Ted Hughes visited
Hull in the Seventies, and during these years Dunn also met Michael
Longley and the Scottish poets Norman MacCaig and Stewart Conn.
Drama and the visual arts were thriving in Hull; there was the residue of
a strong jazz scene from the 1950s and 1960s and plenty of what Dunn
calls 'characterful' people like Ted Tarling who was a jazz musician.
Dunn had learnt to play the clarinet and the saxophone in his teens, and
jazz was an enthusiam he shared with Larkin, although Larkin's
increasing deafness made him prefer jazz through earphones rather than
live performances.

Dunn's distrust of Hull as a place rendered his friends and his home
life more vital: 'When I lived in Hull I made such a fetish of the house I
lived in. I don't think friends and neighbours would have known it but
I didn't go out much. I was almost agoraphobic' (*PD*, 14). Late in

1978, Lesley was diagnosed as having cancer. After what seemed a successful operation, the illness recurred and was diagnosed early in 1981 as terminal. She decided that she wanted to die at home, and they remained in the Butterfly House. During her illness, Dunn began work on *The Telescope Garden*, his radio play about the life of Thomas De Quincey. For Dunn, De Quincey's household wrecks offered a powerful imaginative correlative for his own fears. As a writer, he was a mysterious figure because so many of his papers vanished as he abandoned rooms across Edinburgh and Glasgow. In 1980, Dunn travelled to Dove Cottage in Grasmere to look at manuscripts in De Quincey's handwriting, but he only completed the play after the death of his wife. *The Telescope Garden* explores the mental landscape of a man who wrote to keep the creditors at bay, but it also hauntingly evokes the idea of a human relationship that can transcend death. In 1980, Dunn's father died, and Dunn had to rehearse the terrible process of clearing away personal effects and seeing how a whole life shrinks to a few objects. He remembered the contents of his father's tallboy: 'there was a copy of Burns, one of those editions illustrated with engravings, from which the hard covers had been torn off by a child – me. He had a family Bible, and there was a textbook on rubber technology, and a file of technical journals. That was his library. On top of the pile were the shoes in which he'd danced at his wedding.'[12]

Lesley was an atheist and she offered a schooling in how to die tidily. She gave away her clothes and possessions, asked for cremation and requested that no monument or tombstone should be left. 'Her unselfishness harrowed me', Dunn stated.[13] His anger and helplessness at her suffering were, however, modified by the experience of nursing her: 'before she died, her patient and beautiful example helped me to realise that I was waging war against life as much as death, and that, as a poet, life was the side I was supposed to be on.' Lesley died in March 1981 aged 37. 'No one,' Dunn continued in his article on bereavement, 'should need to be reminded that grief is an intense and extreme state of mind. For weeks it excludes all else.'[14]

As *Elegies* reveals, Dunn turned in towards where Lesley had been and invested their house with the heightened moments of their relationship. He experienced the disabling guilt that is felt by those who survive a partner, and worried over husbandly failings and a sense of his responsibility. Alasdair Macrae recalls that afterwards, Dunn spoke of the way events could be generated from within rather than being caused by an external force. A greater individual involvement than we might wish to believe, Dunn asserted, makes it necessary, at certain times, to scrutinise one's whole life. He now plays down the hold of his mother's religious beliefs, but in 1981 Dunn's Presbyterian background complicated his instinctive response to write *Elegies*:

> for months I thought that it was an unwholesome thing to do, that it wasn't something I should write. Like most people who are brought up as Presbyterians, when it comes to death and loss and things as intimate as that. I'm highly schooled in reticence. So I felt that I was in a sense blowing my cover, being indiscreet, shamefully so, and that was an inhibition; but at the same time I had to write these poems, and it took me quite a while in consultation with friends who are poets to clear my mind. (*Verse*, 31)

Dunn continued to compose the volume of *Elegies* in the autumn of 1981 when he started to work as a writer-in-residence at Dundee University, a move that Lesley had encouraged. As a place to live in, he claims, Dundee was marginally worse than Glasgow. He hated his accommodation there. It was a ground-floor flat, sub-let to the university, without any curtains, so he had to get dressed and undressed in the hall. 'It was very cold,' he said, 'and very, very sparsely furnished and I wasn't in the state of mind to do anything about improving it.' Dunn kept the old house in Hull and travelled back to it as often as possible during his term of employment at Dundee. When the writer-in-residence contract expired in July 1982, Dunn returned to Hull, where he finished *Elegies* in his old study. The poems were a tribute to Lesley and a painful and necessary revision of his life with her. Dunn's friends in Hull and Scotland were supportive, but it was Lesley Bathgate, an art student at Dundee, who released Dunn from his brooding self-immolation. They first met in April 1982, and the impact of her personality on Dunn's life and work has been decisive. Lesley's name was a catalyst which allowed Dunn to believe again in the future:

> Although it was not what I expected, it turned out that I met someone who excited in me more than a fit of passion. It may sound crude, but I do not know how love can be described if it is not a comprehensive feeling that surpasses physical desire and includes it. [15]

Dunn sold the old house in Hull at the end of 1983. In January 1984, Lesley and Douglas moved into a flat in Castle Street in Tayport while looking for a house of their own. It took several months to find a house with a room large enough to contain all of Douglas's books. In May 1984, they moved to their present home in Tayport. Braeknowe is a gracious house with a spectacular view of the Tay estuary. In the autumn of 1984, Dunn worked as the writer-in-residence at the University of New England in Australia. This term initiated a series of West and East European tours which Dunn made with other poets from Scotland and England in the late 1980's. In 1989, Dunn returned to America, where he visited New York, San Francisco and Minneapolis with Michael Longley.

The publication of *Elegies* in the spring of 1985 made Dunn famous in England, but his commitment to Scotland was underlined by his marriage to Lesley Bathgate in August 1985. In the same year, he was appointed as the lead book-reviewer for the *Glasgow Herald*. 'Earning a living from writing in Scotland is a lot harder than in England,' Dunn admitted in 1990 (*PD*, 20). Between 1986 and 1990 he held down writer-in-residence posts at Dundee Central Library, Duncan of Jordanstone College of Art and St Andrews University. Dunn believes firmly in this method of earning a living:

> the writer passes on experience and knowledge of literary crafts and skills. In return, the writer is left with the rest of the week free to get on with the making of poems, novels, stories or plays . . . To be a writer-in-residence is to play a minor role in preserving literature and, in Scotland, sustaining the country's cultural identity.[16]

Dunn's father had always had a relaxed attitude to money, and Dunn admits that he began to enjoy the financial insecurity of being a full-time writer in Hull. This perspective has changed with the births of two children in 1987 and 1990. The presence of Robbie and Lillias, Dunn says, has made him more concerned about the future, but it has also enabled him to discover his own childhood. Lesley works as a wood-engraver and Douglas considers that he now shares her miniature way of looking at landscape with the children's way of seeing things for the first time. The creative and domestic home life which informs *Northlight* has intensified Dunn's realisation of the ordinary as a source of epiphany.

In 1991, Dunn was appointed as Professor of English Literature at the University of St Andrews. He is adamant that although he has given up book-reviewing, his new responsibilities will not interfere with his writing. 'When you've been writing as long as I have, you know how to look after yourself, how to protect whatever gift you've got and you don't let anything get in the way of it.' Finally he was asked if his remark that the better community was in the future still stood: 'That has to be true because it has never existed yet. If there is such a thing — it's tomorrow.'

NOTES

1 *Viewpoints*, 29 and Douglas Dunn, interview in *Very Green* 1, Spring 1986, 11.
2 Douglas Dunn, 'Little Golden Rules' in *Poetry Review* 72:4, January 1983, 5.
3 Douglas Dunn, ed., *A Rumoured City: New Poets from Hull* (Newcastle: Bloodaxe, 1982), 11.
4 'Little Golden Rules', 6.
5 Douglas Dunn, interview with Jane Stabler, 22 May 1991. All unfootnoted quotations from Douglas Dunn in this chapter are taken from this interview and a subsequent one conducted on 29 August 1991. I would like to record my gratitude to Douglas Dunn for taking time to establish the accuracy of information given in interview.
6 Introduction to Louis MacNeice, *Selected Poems*, ed. by Michael Longley (London: Faber, 1988), xvii.
7 Douglas Dunn, foreword to *Inchinnan Past and Present* (Inchinnan Community Council, 1990), 3.
8 *Very Green*, 12.
9 'Little Golden Rules', 8–9.
10 Douglas Dunn, *Under the Influence* (Edinburgh University Library, 1987), 9–10.
11 Douglas Dunn, interview in *Rumblesoup III*, May 1987. 22.
12 Douglas Dunn, interview in 'Profile', *Glasgow Herald*, 4 March 1991, 9.
13 Douglas Dunn, interview in *Acumen* 13, April 1991, 19.
14 Douglas Dunn, 'Regained: the light behind grief's dark veil' [editorial title], *Glasgow Herald*, 24 September 1985, 9.
15 See note 14 above.
16 Douglas Dunn, 'Art of being a writer in residence' [editorial title], *Glasgow Herald*, 25 April 1987, 9.

CHRONOLOGY

1942	Born in Inchinnan, 23 October
1946–59	Inchinnan Primary School; Renfrew High School; Camphill Senior Secondary School
1959–62	Library Assistant, Renfrew County Libraries
1961	Scottish School of Librarianship
1962–4	Library Assistant, Andersonian Library, Glasgow
1964	Marriage to Lesley Balfour Wallace
1964–6	Assistant Librarian, Akron Public Library, Ohio
1966	Librarian of Chemistry Library, University of Glasgow
1966–9	University of Hull BA in English
1968	Gregory Award

1969	*Terry Street*
1969–71	Assistant Librarian, Brynmor Jones Library, Hull
1971	Began freelance and review work for *TLS, New Yorker, Encounter*
1972	*The Happier Life*; residence in France; Maugham Award
1974	*Love or Nothing*; ed. *A Choice of Byron's Verse*
1974–5	Fellow in Creative Writing, Hull University
1975	ed. *Two Decades of Irish Writing*; *Experience Hotel* (verse play performed at The Humberside Theatre); *Early Every Morning* (screenplay BBC TV)
1976	Faber Memorial Prize; ed. *What is to be Given: Selected Poems of Delmore Schwartz*
1977	*Running* (screenplay BBC TV); *Scotsmen by Moonlight* (radio play)
1979	*Barbarians*; ed. *The Poetry of Scotland*; *Ploughman's Share* (television play)
1980	Death of father
1980	*Wedderburn's Slave* (radio play)
1981	Death of Lesley Balfour Dunn
1981	*St Kilda's Parliament*; began writing for *Glasgow Herald*
1981–2	Writer-in-Residence, Dundee University
1982	Hawthornden Prize; *Europa's Lover*; ed. *A Rumoured City: New Poets from Hull*; ed. *To Build a Bridge.*
1984	Writer-in-Residence, University of New England; *Anon's People* (screenplay)
1985	Marriage to Lesley Bathgate; *Elegies*; *Secret Villages*
1985	Death of Philip Larkin
1986	Whitbread Award; Faber *Selected Poems*; *The Telescope Garden* (radio play)
1986–9	Writer-in-Residence, Duncan of Jordanstone College of Art and Dundee Central Library
1987	Birth of Robbie Dunn
1988	*Northlight*
1989	Writer-in-Residence, University of St Andrews; *New and Selected Poems 1966–1988* (US edition); *Andromache* (radio broadcast)
1990	Birth of Lillias Dunn; Cholmondeley Award; Racine's *Andromache*; *Poll Tax: The Fiscal Fake*; ed. *The Essential Browning*
1991	ed. *Scotland: An Anthology*; Professor of English, University of St Andrews.
1992	*The Faber Book of Twentieth-Century Scottish Poetry*

Two

'There are many worlds': The 'Dialogic' in *Terry Street* and After

Ian Gregson

Douglas Dunn's assumptions when he wrote *Terry Street* were, according to his own accounts, very much realist in kind. In his interview with John Haffenden, he says:

> In Terry Street, everything was there to be seen, and what I saw and experienced recommended itself to me in the form of a poem.
> (*Viewpoints*, 16)

He also speaks, in this interview, of the influence on him of American social realist novelists 'like Sinclair Lewis, Anderson and Dreiser' (*Viewpoints*, 15). And in the introduction to his work which he wrote for P.R. King's *Nine Contemporary Poets*,[1] he says that the programme he set for himself included the injunction 'do not invent when reality is good enough and lying to hand for the making of images' (King, 222).

There is, throughout these early poems, an attempt to evoke the objective conditions, the material circumstances, of the street's inhabitants. 'Winter' is the most extreme example of this – objective to the point of minimalism, it acquired a certain noteriety when the book was first published:

> Recalcitrant motorbikes;
> Dog-shit under frost; a coughing woman;
> The old men who cannot walk briskly groaning
> On the way back from their watchmen's huts.
>
> (*TS* 27)

People are reduced here to the noises they make, realism tilting towards naturalism. The most specifically human characteristic, recalcitrance, is attributed to motorbikes. The reference to dog-shit insists aggressively on the importance of recording things as they 'really' are.

Dunn's emphasis is similar when he talks about the formal aspect of *Terry Street*, referring to the need to make the form respond to the subject matter, to prevent it from imposing anything too rigidly poetic. In his piece for P.R. King, he says: 'Metre sometimes feels too specific, too much of an instrument for the exclusion of uncertainty. For that reason, I keep my options open.' Writing more specifically here about 'A Removal from Terry Street', he refers to the variety of iambic pentameter the poem employs and suggests how the experience he was describing adjusted the form by insisting on its own particular life:

> I suppose it was the weight of observation and narrative and the presence of people and objects – 'Four paperback westerns' and 'Two whistling youths' – which made it unnatural or undesirable to sustain the iambic rhythm of the classic English line throughout. (King, 224)

The realism of *Terry Street* is certainly effective in evoking a particular place (a small, run-down, working-class street in Hull) at a particular time (the late 1960s). However, to be more thoroughly understood, this realism itself needs to be accurately located – placed in its literary moment, its complexity becomes clearer. Its dominance in the 1960s owed much to the legacy of the Movement's empiricism, its appeal to consensual attitudes of unpretentious common sense, its use of English understatement. Most relevant to Dunn was the influence of Philip Larkin, who helped and encouraged the younger poet.

However, the realism of the Movement was complicated by its relationship with modernism. It is simplistic to refer to a Movement 'reaction' into an anti-modernist poetic because there are modernist elements, in a deflected form, in Movement poems. Larkin, in particular, established his own largely realist poetic through a continuing dialogue with modernism. This is made clearer by his recent *Collected Poems*[2] where his confrontation, in his juvenilia, with a number of modernist influences (Yeats, Eliot, Auden, even Dylan Thomas) is revealed as relevant to his mature practice. The process by which he absorbed these influences and overcame them – partly through the counter-influence of Hardy – can be observed there in detail.

What this book reveals is that the potency of Larkin's anti-modernism arose from the way his poems learned – through their contact with Yeats and the others – to take modernism into account in the act of opposing it, apparently to review its arguments and then refute them. Frequently there is a modernist scepticism about language implied in his poems that immunises his realism against charges of naïveté. Larkin's words often call attention to themselves – by being suddenly colloquial or recherché or by employing exaggerated sound effects — to show that he does not think they are a clear medium. Vagrants in 'Toads Revisited' turn 'over their failures/ By some bed of lobelias' (Larkin, 147); the moon in 'Sad Steps' is a 'Lozenge of love! Medallion of art!' and evokes 'wolves of memory! Immensements' (Larkin, 169). Larkin makes frequent use, too, of the montage effect he learned from Auden, placing separate scenes or actions on top of each other as a way of evoking a whole society. So in 'MCMXIV' (Larkin, 127–8), montage is used to summon up the innocence of pre-1914 England.

However, the smart manoeuvre Larkin learned — and developed with increasing sophistication — was to assign these modernist elements a subsidiary place in a dominantly realist context, thereby subjecting them to a kind of repressive tolerance. *Collected Poems* shows how Larkin learned to do this. The process was lengthy but there were sudden advances. Certainly there is a gulf in quality between the last of the juvenilia, 'Who whistled for the wind, that it should break' (Larkin, 311) — afflatus subverted by flatulence — and the first mature poem 'Going' (Larkin, 3). Here, Larkin imagines a 'real' person in a 'real' situation, and he does the same a few months later (September 1946) in 'Wedding Wind' (Larkin, 11). In these poems he initiated his maturity by starting from premises opposite to those of his modernist precursors, for whom 'reality' is always something to be put in quotation marks, and whose poems create their own, sometimes hermetic, contexts.

In the late 1940s and early 1950s, he evolved a poetic whose first concern was to establish a consensus with his readers based on shared experience — but that this poetic evolved through a dialogue with modernism can be seen clearly in his most important poem, 'The Whitsun Weddings' (Larkin, 114–16). This amounts to a realist rereading of *The Waste Land*'s fertility metaphor. What does all that Jessie Weston stuff really mean to someone living in industrial mid-twentieth-century England? Something like this: numerous couples heading on the same train toward their wedding nights in a London 'spread out in the sun/ Its postal districts packed like squares of wheat,' and

>   all the power
> That being changed can give. We slowed again,
> And as the tightened brakes took hold, there swelled
> A sense of falling, like an arrow shower
> Sent out of sight, somewhere becoming rain.

So the realism Dunn inherited was one that had been powerfully reinstated but had nonetheless acquired, in the process, an element of self-questioning. This was increased because it was linked with that form of modified Imagism which characterises much poetry of the mid-1960s and after, which is present, for instance, in the early poems of Seamus Heaney, with whom Dunn has declared an affinity (King, 227; *Viewpoints*, 33) and especially in poetry associated with *The Review* and then *The New Review* (magazines in which Dunn frequently published) — the poetry of Ian Hamilton, Hugo Williams, et al. So, Dunn describes the shaping forces of his early work as 'inhibitions', and they share much in common with the precepts of the Imagist manifestoes:

> never speculate on infinity from insufficient evidence; maintain a moderate degree of clarity, at least; do not invent when reality is good enough and lying to hand for the making of images; show more than you tell; do not push subjectivity too much into the foreground of the poem . . . But I suppose that, like other poets of my generation, I found it easier to know what I should not do, and strenuously difficult to discover a *positive* programme of aesthetic values. (King, 222)

These anxious imperatives have a complex ancestry. Their prescriptions for poetic technique are closest to Ezra Pound's 'Don'ts',[3] and their mistrust of 'infinity' and 'subjectivity' are most closely related to the anti-Romantic theorising of T.E. Hulme,[4] which injected a realist element into Imagism. On these points, however, the Movement, which was supposedly anti-modernist, unconsciously echoed Hulme, who was one of the founding fathers of Anglo-American modernism, and the mistrust of invention is a Movement rather than a modernist characteristic. Here, again, realism and modernism have an uneasy and complex relationship.

Moreover, up to a point, Imagism can be employed as a realist device:

In small backyards old men's long underwear
Drips from sagging clotheslines.
The other stuff they take in bundles to the Bendix.

There chatty women slot their coins and joke
About the grey unmentionables absent.
The old men weaken in the steam and scratch at their rough chins.

Suppressing coughs and stiffnesses, they pedal bikes
On low gear slowly, in their faces
The effort to be upright, the dignity

That fits inside the smell of aromatic pipes.

(TS, 15)

The precision and vividness of this are achieved through a number of characteristic Imagist techniques. There is the use of framing devices – repeatedly things are depicted inside other things: underwear and clotheslines in small backyards; the other clothes in bundles, and then, like the chatty women, in the Bendix; coins in slots; old men in steam; and, more problematically, dignity inside pipes. Combined with this there is the use of juxtapositions which combine with the framing devices to pinpoint the images like lines on a map: underwear with clotheslines (vertical against horizontal, soft against hard); women with old men (chatty and active against silent and passive); steam with chins (soft against hard – but also here some consonance of colour, echoing 'the grey unmentionables'); coughs and stiffnesses with bikes (human frailty against mechanical hardness); low gear with the effort to be upright (low against high; fixed, disinterested object against struggling person).

These Imagist techniques work in a realist way to depict objects and evoke scenes. However, they also produce a characteristically modernist effect in the way they defamiliarise the old men – in particular, there is an anti-humanist tendency in the way the old men are so persistently regarded through objects associated with them, so that there seems a danger of all humanity being drained from the poem. But Dunn defuses this by drawing on a further modernist aspect of Imagism – the way that its insistence on isolating objects draws attention to its own artificiality, its self-consciously aesthetic rendering of mere fragments of reality. So the narrowness of focus and the obsession with objects in the lines quoted produce an awareness of how much is being missed out and a paradoxical reaction in the reader who supplies the missing subjectivity. The danger that the old men are being reified heightens the sense of their humanity.

In early Douglas Dunn, then, as in Larkin, there is an equivocation between modernism and realism; in the younger poet, however, it is much less clear which is to be ultimately preferred. The evidence of individual poems suggests a preference for realism. In 'The Patricians', Imagism falters in the face of the human facts: 'the dignity/ That fits inside the smell of aromatic pipes' is a deliberate breach of Poundian decorum in the way it mixes abstract and concrete, and it does so with the clear implication that there are aspects of these old men that cannot be defined objectively, a humanity that evades the series of metonymies which has been imposed on them. Early in the poem, the old men's subjectivity seems to be as much of a grey unmentionable as their underwear: but the entry of 'dignity', followed by the ambiguous 'hearts', makes it rise increasingly to the surface:

They live watching each other die, passing each other
In their white scarves, too long known to talk,
Waiting for the inheritance of the oldest, a right to power.

The street patricians, they are ignored.
Their anger proves something, their disenchantments
Settle round me like a cold fog.

They are the individualists of our time.
They know no fashions, copy nothing but their minds.
Long ago, they gave up looking in mirrors.

Dying in their sleep, they lie undiscovered.
The howling of their dogs brings the sniffing police,
Their middle-aged children from the new estates.

                                        (*TS*, 15–16)

The 'anger' and 'disenchantments' of these 'individualists' are in stark
contrast to the way in which the start of the poem claustrophobically
frames the old men; the bald statement of these feelings embarrasses
such oblique Imagism. More than this, it hints at political implications
in that modernist technique – a sense that it colludes with the anti-
humanism 'of our time'. Against his own stated poetic principles, Dunn
here has pushed subjectivity very much into the foreground of the
poem. The result is to insert a second voice into 'The Patricians' which
speaks for the taciturn old men and thereby allows them to step,
momentarily, out of the Imagism that frames them in the poem and
which has become, from this perspective, the equivalent of the politics
that frame them in their actual lives.

This second voice grows especially intense when the poet refers
explicitly to his own response. Earlier in the poem, he has been a
detached observer, but, when the feelings of the old men are
mentioned, he insists on the way they affect his own, and does so the
more strikingly by introducing, for the first time, an image from
outside the immediate scene: 'their disenchantments/ Settle round me
like a cold fog'. This fog contrasts with the steam that weakens the old
men and also with the Imagism of the poem's first half – for it lowers
visibility and softens edges. This voice, then, speaks a different
language from the first and is saying something much more difficult
which baffles boundaries and distorts clarity and definition.

What happens at this point in 'The Patricians', moreover,
exemplifies something crucial about *Terry Street* as a whole, something
which makes it more modernist than it at first appears. For what
happens when this second voice enters the poem is that the poet's
subjectivity meets that of the old men, and *Terry Street* as a whole is set

as much in the metaphorical ground of intersubjectivity between the poet and the other Terry Street inhabitants as it is in the literal ground of the street. And this metaphorical ground is unstable and shifting: a cold fog forms where two states of mind meet.

In his interview with Douglas Dunn, John Haffenden suggests that the posture he adopts in *Terry Street* 'is that of the spectator', and the poet replies:

> Not just a spectator, but something of an outsider, because I'd never lived in a district like that before. And I was also a Scotsman among a universally English population. And I came from a messily semi-rural kind of background, and this, Terry Street and Hull, were quite different. (*Viewpoints*, 15)

As well as this different background, Dunn brought to his observation of the street a better education than the street's other inhabitants, and in particular a poetic sensibility which would allow him to have 'such a vision of the street/ as the street hardly understands'.[5] But Dunn also identifies with his fellow residents – his own background was working-class and the sense of belonging to this class has been one of the most important subjects of his poetry.

As a result, the angle of vision is always shifting in *Terry Street*. Connected with this, there is a characteristic movement from vision to feeling as already pointed out in 'The Patricians', as though the poet grows self-conscious, at a certain moment in the poem, about being a mere observer and withdraws into himself or, more often, moves outwards and looks through other people's eyes. There are suggestions of one of Dunn's most important influences at such moments, that of Randall Jarrell, especially in the treatment of women, though Dunn does not use dramatic monologue here.

'Young Women in Rollers' (*TS*, 29–30) starts, in the characteristic way, with description, but then reveals that this method is not as impersonal as it looks by showing the objects of observation reacting to the observer, who first of all is generalised; the young women 'call across the street they're not wearing knickers,/ But blush when they pass you alone'. This already indicates that the observed gets altered by the observer; but the next move is more radical still:

> This time they see me at my window, among books,
> A specimen under glass, being protected,
> And laugh at me watching them.
>
> (*TS*, 29)

The anxiety, implicit elsewhere, that the act of observation coolly dehumanises the observed is made explicit here as the observed do as they are done by. The clinical treatment that Imagism's hard impersonality imposes on what it observes is visited upon the observer as he becomes 'a specimen under glass'. The poem dwells on mutual incomprehension. Pop culture governs the outlook of the young women, and they mock the poet by minuetting to the Mozart playing on his radio. But then a change occurs like a brief dissolve, analogous to the fog in 'The Patricians' — the poet's gaze (brought once again into the foreground) softens:

> I can see soot,
> It floats. The whiteness of their legs has changed
> Into something that floats, become like cloth.
> (*TS*, 30)

This brief withdrawal into daydream arouses a warmth towards the young women. There is obviously a sexual element in this, but more importantly it reduces the importance of surface appearance — it prepares for the whiteness of their legs to fade into the background (to be removed as clothing could be removed). What moves, once again, in its place into the foregound is the intersubjectivity between them and the poet:

> I want to be touched by them, know their lives,
> Dance in my own style, learn something new.
> At night I even dream of ideal communities.
> Why do they live where they live, the rich and the poor?
>
> Tonight, when their hair is ready, after tea,
> They'll slip through laws and the legs of policemen.
> I won't be there, I'll be reading books elsewhere.
> There are many worlds, there are many laws.
> (*TS*, 30)

Just as elsewhere in *Terry Street* Dunn thinks of the inhabitants occasionally as 'we' — as in 'Ins and Outs' (*TS*, 28), which lumps the poet and the other residents together from the perspective of the dustmen — but usually as 'they', here he moves backwards and forwards between identification and distance. The consequent instability produces some self-consciously non-realist writing — wistful, baffled idealism and then comic surrealism. This anticipates much in Dunn's later work, for what it involves is his sense of how deeply politics penetrates into people's emotional lives and simultaneously his regret at how restrictive this is — his wish to evade it carries the implication that the happiest life would be apolitical. The fantasy of the young women slipping 'through laws and the legs of policemen' arises from a rebellion against the fixedness of social boundaries; stylistically it is a revolt against both Imagist and realist decorum and restlessly insists that both the poet and the young women have dreams – for one line at least, they share a dream and unite to subvert authority.

However, it is the belief expressed in the last line which has proven crucial to Dunn's poetic career. If 'There are many worlds', then the realist reliance on consensus and common sense is misplaced; realism assumes that there is a single stable world which we all inhabit – if this is not the case, then realism simplifies our experience. And it has been this sense that there is a plurality of worlds which Dunn has most consistently explored. In particular, he has set out to demonstrate that there is an official world-view – a dominant ideology – which deliberately misses too much out. An important part of what Dunn achieves in *Terry Street* is to dwell on lives which are too conveniently overlooked; there is already here a political anger that all such people, and not just the old men in 'The Patricians', are 'ignored'.

What Dunn's poems repeatedly do, as a result, is to bring voices, points of view, and consequently worlds into juxtaposition. They oppose the dominance of official culture by drawing attention to the world of the 'ignored'. This theme is adumbrated in *Terry Street* through a concern with silence – actions and objects figure much more than speech which has, anyway, according to 'The Clothes Pit' (13), been altered by 'pop rhetoric', and the young women in that poem dream of 'an inarticulate paradise'. This theme is made more explicit in 'The Silences' (32) where the people of Terry Street are described as 'like a lost tribe', who are 'a part of the silence of places'.

Increasingly, though, Dunn became concerned with the dialects of the working-class tribe, with its concern to express itself in speech and writing. 'The Student' (*B*, 19–20), for example, is the dramatic monologue of a member of a 'Mechanics' Literary Club' who studies Tacitus, describes reading as 'this grip/ Of mind on mind' but worries that literature may be 'a life proved much too good/ To have its place in our coarse neighbourhood'. In 'An Address on the Destitution of Scotland' (*SKP*, 19–20), Dunn says his 'eyes are heavy now with alien perspectives', describes the 'lunatic aroma' that arose when he worked as a boy on the land as 'Tasting of dialect and curses', and refers to an 'outcast silence' and 'song in the speech of timber and horse'. And 'Tannahill' (*SKP*, 52–6) is about the Scottish poet of that name who was 'a competent weaver [who] wrote songs and began to pick up the threads, so to speak, of Burns's work' and who 'committed suicide in

the River Cart . . . drowned himself with his poems, and they were
fished out of the water the following morning (*Viewpoints*, 25–6):

> You clutched the papers of your tongue:
> Gone, gone down, gone down with a song.
> Pity the mad, darkened with wrong.
>   Home Lycidas,
> You died in the dish-cloth Cart, among
>   The ugliness.
>
> And in the morning schoolboys came
> To fish for papers, speak your name
> And take their landed catches home,
>   Dried on the gorse;
> Aye, Tannahill, boys caught your poems,
>   Lost, watery verse.
>
>   (*SKP*, 55)

So this concern has acquired wide historical and geographical scope
and is best described in the terms used by the Soviet critic Mikhail
Bakhtin: Dunn, like Bakhtin, indicts the 'centripetal forces in
sociolinguistic and ideological life . . . [which] serve one and the same
project of centralising and unifying the European languages'; he attacks
also the

> victory of one reigning language (dialect) over the others, the
> supplanting of languages, their enslavement, the process of
> illuminating them with the True Word, the incorporation of
> barbarians and lower social strata into a unitary language of culture
> and truth.[6]

Throughout his work, Dunn has opposed the monologue of official
discourse and ideology with an insistently 'dialogic' poetic – much
about Dunn's world-view can be better understood if this Bakhtinian
term is applied to it. *Terry Street* is concerned above all with a dialogue
of consciousness and worlds, though in the case of this first book it is a
question more of inner speech which, given the book's objective Imagist
premises, takes the paradoxical form of silence. In 'A Window Affair'
(*TS*, 33–4), for example, the poet's world encounters the 'world of foul
language' of a woman who lives in a house facing his; but it is the
distance between them that is stressed – 'She was far away',
'Untouchable', and so it is implied they never speak but share instead an
inner dialogue, the 'love of eyes and silence'. So, in a way again
characteristic of *Terry Street*, the focus is on seeing rather than speaking,
and here the unsatisfactoriness of this reaches a climax as the poet gets
terminally impatient with it and decides to leave. This practical

decision echoes a poetic one – this is the last of the 'Terry Street Poems' and represents an abandonment of the silent imagist gaze in which 'I grasp only the hard things, windows, contempt'.

Consequently, Dunn is increasingly less tied in later poems to the need to be objective, to be realist and Imagist. He increasingly allows his own subjectivity into the foreground in dialogue both with objectivity and with the subjectivity of other people. The surrealism which is confined to single lines in *Terry Street* ('They'll slip through laws and the legs of policemen' etc.) is allowed much more scope in poems like 'The River Through The City' (*HL*, 13), 'The White Poet' (*LN*, 52–5), 'The Deserter' (*SKP*, 72–5) and *Europa's Lover*. Dunn's project in poems like this is the opposite of Larkin's in 'The Whitsun Weddings' and elsewhere: Larkin was concerned to ward off modernist instability by incorporating it into an English realist world-view and so safely domesticating and stabilising it. Dunn's surrealism deliberately offends against the realist mode whose dominance Larkin helped to establish – where Larkin's was a conservative dialogue with modernism, Dunn's is a subversive dialogue with realism.

The political implications of this are clear – Dunn's mature poetic is dedicated to undermining a conservative world-view whose appeal to consensus is actually a complacent suppression of alien perspectives. This is why Dunn has, as Haffenden puts it, 'denigrated common sense':

> I'm a Francophile, I don't believe in common sense; it's an Anglo-Saxon virtue. Scotsmen, like Frenchmen, don't believe in common sense, we believe in intelligence. (*Viewpoints*, 30)

Dunn's Francophilia is discussed later in this book by David Kinloch. It is worth describing here, however, how Frenchness is used in 'The Deserter' to insist on the bizarre horror of political life in the twentieth century: ideas from Robert Desnos are drawn upon to suggest that the powerful are like brutal but ghostly tycoons, while the weak are bewildered and lost – one 'A widow in her wedding-gown [who] gets into the wrong train' (*SKP*, 74), the other a 'deserter [who] parleys with sentries who don't understand his language':

> a man,
> Unarmed, talks with another five who hold their guns
> On him. This conversation is composed of cloth,
> Of buttons, stars and boots. Of wood. Of steel. Of wire.
>
> (*SKP*, 72)

Dunn is protesting here, as he did in 'The Patricians', against that reification which is the deadliest enemy of the dialogic – for in these

lines brute objects have taken the place of dialogue. The deserter is
being treated as Bakhtin says Dmitry is treated in *The Brothers
Karamazov*:

> All who judge Dmitry are devoid of a genuinely dialogic approach
> to him, a dialogic penetration into the unfinalised core of his
> personality. They seek and see in him only the factual, palpable
> definitiveness of experiences and actions, and subordinate them to
> already defined concepts and schemes . . . the major emotional
> thrust of all Dostoevsky's work, in its form as well as its content, is
> the struggle against a reification of man, of human relations, of all
> human values under the conditions of capitalism.[7]

Outside these surreal poems which explicitly adopt an exotic
perspective, Dunn insinuates the dialogic into official monologue by
using a more familiar English idiom and subverting it from within. In
this way, the formal structure of poems like 'In the Grounds' (*B*, 15–16)
becomes what Bakhtin calls 'a hybrid construction':

> an utterance that belongs, by its grammatical (syntactic) and
> compositional markers, to a single speaker, but that actually
> contains within it two utterances, two speech manners, two styles,
> two 'languages', two semantic and axiological belief systems. (*DI*,
> 304)

That is, poems like this adopt the compositional appearance of poems
belonging to an English aristocratic tradition, but they speak, as they
do so, in an alien accent, which that tradition has previously
marginalised and suppressed:

> Barbarians in a garden, softness does
> Approve of who we are as it does those
> Who when we speak proclaim us barbarous
> And say we have no business with the rose.
>   (*B*, 15)

In this way, the poem inserts an alien voice into a monological form, as
these 'barbarians . . . hurt a truth with truth, still true/ To who we are'.
This is a profoundly political act because it opposes the tendency of the
dominant ideology to appropriate language to its own single-minded
ends, 'to impart', as Bakhtin says,

> a supraclass, eternal character to the ideological sign, to extinguish
> or drive inward the struggle between social value judgements
> which occurs in it, to make the sign uniaccentual.[8]

Such a political treatment of language is evident also in Tony Harrison's
battles against 'Received Pronunciation'.[9] However, the effect is especially powerful in Dunn's barbarian pastorals because they intervene in

such an ancient, and therefore seemingly 'eternal', tradition – that of the 'happy man' secluded in his highly cultivated garden, which stretches back to Horace and was employed in English by Marvell and Pope, among others.

Dunn's insistence that 'There are many worlds' can be seen as central to his work when it is put in Bakhtinian terms – for his poems show that it adumbrates a concern with the polyphonic multiplying of perspectives. It also indicates that Dunn's socialism is not of an authoritarian kind. In fact, it should be stressed that the dialogic in Dunn's work is not merely political; that it places the political world in dialogue with others. Part of the aggression in his political poems comes from a sense that it should not be necessary to write in this way. For instance, the opening lines of 'The Come-On' (*B*, 13) – 'To have watched the soul of my people/ Fingered by the callous/ Enlivens the bitter ooze from my grudge' – arise from a need to affront complacency and insensitivity, but they contain a self-conscious embarrassment at their own anger. Something similar is at work here to what Dunn describes motivating Larkin to become a different poet from the one he should have been:

> I think he might see himself as a traditional lyric poet who's got fucked up on the *realia* of his particular moment of the twentieth century, which has ruined the nature of his lyricism. (*Viewpoints*, 33)

There are lyric elements in Dunn also. It is clear, for example, that he is attracted to pastoral – even in his first book, the longing for grass in 'A Removal from Terry Street' (*TS*, 20) is understood and endorsed. But it is the nature of the political circumstances that has made him write barbarian pastorals rather than traditional ones.

It is in the nature of modern circumstances, too, that the writing of traditional lyric poetry has become less possible. Dunn's case indicates how the solo voice of the poet has been overwhelmed by the clamour of other voices; it is perhaps largely this that has caused the dialogic, which was previously much more the domain of the novel, to invade poetry. Bakhtin has described this process as 'novelisation', involving the features of the novel imposing themselves on other genres so that they become 'dialogised' and are permeated with 'an indeterminacy, a certain semantic open-endedness, a living contact with unfinished, still evolving contemporary reality' (*DI*, 7). This process has interwoven with others in the literary history of the past two centuries, but it can be observed quite clearly, for instance, in the effects of romantic irony in Byron's *Don Juan*, in the multiple viewpoints of Browning's *The Ring and the Book*, and in the use of free indirect speech in Eliot's *The Waste*

Land. Dunn himself seems to refer to a possible Jamesian input into Imagism when he speaks of the need to 'show more than you tell' (King, 222) and so puts a novelistic gloss on his updated 'Don'ts'. Moreover, the effects of novelisation are apparent in contemporary British poetry in the narrative effects of poets as diverse as James Fenton, Carol Ann Duffy, Iain Sinclair and Glyn Maxwell; in the dialogic juxtaposition of perspectives in Craig Raine and Christopher Reid; and the semantic open-endedness of post-modernist poets like Paul Muldoon, John Ash and Peter Didsbury.

There is also circumstantial evidence, also, to indicate the influence of the novel on Dunn's sensibility. He has said

> I would very much like to do a novel; I've tried and done several drafts, all of which by my standards amounted to drivel. (*Viewpoints*, 31)

So, too, in a poem like 'The Hunched' (*HL*, 38), Dunn's novelistic thinking becomes explicit as he talks about his spontaneous tendency towards sympathetic identification with others — 'They will not leave me, the lives of other people./ I wear them near my eyes like spectacles.' Like a novelist, he tries on other people's perspectives, wants to see what the world feels like from their angle.

However, whether or not Dunn ever publishes a novel, his poems demonstrate what increased resources the novelised poet can call upon when compared with the lyric poet. When it came to writing *Elegies*, for instance, Dunn was very much helped by techniques he had evolved by then for introducing a dialogic interplay of perspectives. Baktinian theory stresses that the self cannot be understood without the other, as Tzvetan Todorov has said in his book on Bakhtin:

> we can never see ourselves as a whole; the other is necessary to accomplish, even if temporarily, a perception of the self that the individual can achieve only partially with respect to himself.[10]

In the case of love and death — the central themes of *Elegies* — the relationship between self and other is obviously paramount, and this collection is so powerful because of the way love and death are constantly reassessed by the movement from the poet's perspective to that of the dying wife and back, and into that of friends and even casual bystanders. There was a precedent for this in poems like 'The Haunter' by the profoundly novelised poet Thomas Hardy, but the poems in *Elegies* are more open-ended than Hardy's; there is much more suggestion in Dunn's poems that the single perspective is vulnerable, open to question. 'There are many worlds', and that of the dying is only one of them and mingles frighteningly, grotesquely but also matter-of-factly with that of the living. Such mingling of worlds produces both mutual bafflement and potential enrichment; it is edgy but fraught with imaginative possibilities.

NOTES

1 P.R. King, 'Three new poets: Douglas Dunn, Tom Paulin, Paul Mills', in *Nine Contemporary Poets, A Critical Introduction* (London: Methuen, 1979), 220–43. This piece is henceforth referred to as King in references incorporated in the text.

2 Philip Larkin, *The Collected Poems*, edited, with an introduction, by Anthony Thwaite (London: The Marvell Press and Faber and Faber, 1988). Further references incorporated in text.

3 Ezra Pound, 'A Few Don'ts by an Imagiste', *Poetry* March 1913, 200.

4 T.E. Hulme, 'Romanticism and Classicism', in *Speculations* (London: Kegan Paul, 1936), 113–40.

5 T.S. Eliot, *The Complete Poems and Plays* (London: Faber and Faber, 1969), 23.

6 M.M. Bakhtin, *The Dialogic Imagination*, edited by Michael Holquist, translated by Caryl Emerson and Michael Holquist (Austin: University of Texas Press, 1981), 271. Henceforth incorporated in text as *DI*.

7 M.M. Bakhtin, *Problems of Dostoevsky's Poetics*, translated and edited by Caryl Emerson (Manchester: Manchester University Press, 1984), 62.

8 V.N. Volosinov, *Marxism and the Philosophy of Language*, translated by Ladislav Matejka and I.R. Titunik (New York: Seminar Press, 1973), 23. Bakhtin is now generally regarded as the author of this book.

9 Tony Harrison, *Selected Poems* (Harmondsworth: Penguin Books, 1984), 122–3.

10 Tzvetan Todorov, *M. Bakhtin: The Dialogical Principle* (Minneapolis, University of Minnesota Press, 1984), 95.

Three

Moving Towards a Vernacular of Compassion: *The Happier Life, Love or Nothing* and *Barbarians*

Bernard O'Donoghue

Since Yeats first made it a practice, we have come to expect individual volumes of short poems each to have its own coherence that stamps it as a stage in the development of a poet's career: that it will be something more than a gathering of the poems written since the last volume. The reception, for example, of Seamus Heaney's individual volumes constantly manifests this expectation. It has accordingly become normal for the poems in Selected volumes to retain the assignation to the separate collections in which they first appeared.

This expectation is particularly crucial in Douglas Dunn's work. As with Heaney and Muldoon, his *Selected Poems 1964–1983* (1986) marks off, both in the Contents list and in the text, where the original volume divisions came. One striking exception makes its point precisely by departing from the assumption that this organisation prevails: the 1981 'Envoi' which imprecates after his wife's death:

> A curse on me I did not write with joy.
>
> (*SP*, 20)

This poem is placed in the *Selected* among the poems from *Terry Street* (1969), at the temporal point when Dunn was culpably failing to write with joy, rather than at the point when the poem was written. Dunn exploits the formal assumption that the book will be organised chronologically according to the component volumes. This departure only works if such an assumption is taken to be the norm.

Dunn's seven-volume corpus has tended to be dominated by two books (though the others were far from unnoticed: three of the five were Poetry Book Society Choices). *Terry Street* made a major impact as a debut in 1969, and *Elegies* in 1985 was the Whitbread Book of the

Year. The exceptional subject of *Elegies*, the death of Dunn's first wife, gave it a prominence beyond its place in the sequential development of the poems. Its subject also gave it a narrative status which is very unusual in modern poetry, where the writing can be taken as unquestionably autobiographical, unmediated by the use of a persona. The inevitable effect of the prominence of these two volumes was to reduce the reader's awareness of the intervening four, the first three of which are my subject here. Yet they are of crucial importance for an understanding of how – both in technique and in chosen subjects – the poet of the tight community of *Terry Street* was able to tackle triumphantly the vast and psychologically demanding programme of *Elegies*.

It was observed from the first that *Terry Street* was given a rare intensity through its clarity and singleness of vision. Dunn tells us (*Viewpoints*, 17) that it was written very quickly and that Philip Larkin recommended its division into two sections, of Terry Street poems and others. The coherence of this division was not the only factor in the book's integrity and singleness of purpose. The observing eye in it is remarkably unwavering. In several later poems, Dunn has used photography as a metaphor for the observing poet, usually to draw attention to the limitations of the camera as a mechanical recorder. Its failure to sympathise or to understand what it sees – a failure which must to some degree infect the poet through the metaphor – is suggested forcefully at the start of the poem 'I am a Camerman' from *Love or Nothing* (though the poem goes on to make a different point):

> They suffer, and I catch only the surface.
> The rest is inexpressible, beyond
> What can be recorded. You can't be them.
> If they'd talk to you, you might guess
> What pain is like though they might spit on you.
>
>   (*LN*, 41)

Such a failure of sympathy is certainly not one that the reader of *Terry Street* feels, even though we can see detachment there. But it is something which inevitably concerns a poet of such social awareness as Dunn. When John Haffenden suggests mildly that the treatment of drunks in the poem 'Midweek Matinee' (*HL*, 35–6) might be accused of 'disdainfulness' (*Viewpoints*, 22),[1] Dunn is quick to 'dispute' the charge by observing that the drunks in the poem are accurately represented, going on to remark uncharacteristically that he is always impressed and moved by 'the sight of such low deprivation, the sight of people having reduced *themselves* to it as much as having been reduced to it by other things' (*Viewpoints*, 22). This is perhaps more remarkable for its honesty than for the judgement of the 'cupboard Calvinist' Dunn calls himself (*Viewpoints*, 28); but in the context of this concerned poet, it is disconcertingly detached.

Dunn offers another reason to have reservations about the photographic method of poetic observation: 'perhaps my imagination wasn't being tested as much as it should have been' (*PD*, 13).[2] Throughout his career, Dunn has debated the relative demands on him of the artistic imagination and social responsibility. Ultimately he sees no irresolvable conflict between them, but it is a conclusion that he does not reach by any facile short cut. The problem in *Terry Street*, as the poet himself sees it, is not so much that the observer's eye is cold as that it is mechanical: the creative imagination is not actively enough engaged. The pictorial titles of some of the poems make this clear: 'Men of Terry Street', 'Sunday Morning Among the Houses of Terry Street', or 'Landscape with One Figure'. There was a contemporary vogue for poetry titles taken from paintings (for example *Man Lying on a Wall* by Michael Longley, another semi-classical poet whom Dunn admires), a practice which Dunn is exploiting subtly here. Such titles evoke paintings like Lowry's which are, so to speak, two-and-a-half-dimensional. Much of the critical interest in Dunn's next three volumes is in watching the rather painful and uneven process by which the extra half-dimension is supplied.

Although he is a very striking case, Dunn is by no means untypical of his era in his sense of the conflicting imperatives of public responsibility and the imaginative integrity of the artist. Its most famous playing-out was in the revenant sections of Heaney's *Station Island* where the ghost of Joyce tells the poet:

> You lose more of yourself than you redeem
> doing the decent thing.[3]

The demands of public responsibility are a crucial matter for the Irish poet of this era (indeed ever since Yeats), as Dunn himself observes in his introduction to *Two Decades of Irish Writing*.[4] But it has been much on the minds of Scottish writers too. For example, Sorley MacLean comments in the Introduction to a recent collection of essays on Norman MacCaig that 'lack of the "exultations and agonies" of the corporate struggles of humanity is a defect in the glorious totality of [MacCaig's] poetry'[5] (a somewhat ungenerous criticism, one might feel, of a man who was a conscientious objector). This illustrates forcefully the political imperative in Scottish poetry where it is arguably even more of a burning issue than in post-1960s Northern Irish poetry. The burn is slower but more constant.

It goes without saying that this criticism does not apply in any way to Douglas Dunn, the author of 'Barbarian Pastorals' and the fierce broadside on the poll tax, *The Fiscal Fake*. In any case, the issues of politics and of decency are dealt with elsewhere in this book. But the issue is important in placing the three volumes I am concerned with. *Terry Street* was a very propitious start; but in some ways it was not entirely the book Dunn wanted to write. Its photographic over-objectivity left unsatisfied his ambition towards both the imaginative and the socially conscious. It was also, as Dunn has repeatedly said, a crucial qualification that it was set in Hull, not Scotland. In this respect it is a very unusual book; it is hard to think of another such close focus on a parish which is not the writer's native affiliation.

A stylistic by-product of what Dunn seems to find limiting in the procedure of *Terry Street*, and a contributory factor to the two-and-a-half-dimensional feeling, is the rather dead hand of the neutral observer's present tense (a common phenomenon in poetry of that era), often placed with a temporal reference.

> They come in at night, leave in the early morning.
>
> (*TS*, 17)

Already some expansion on this standpoint is evident in *The Happier Life* (though the much smaller representation of this book than any other in the *Selected Poems* suggests that Dunn himself has contributed to the general critical view that it is a less impressive volume than *Terry Street*). Many of the awkwardnesses in *The Happier Life* seem to me the result of attempts to change the aspects of *Terry Street* with which Dunn had become dissatisfied. The first lines of 'The Hunched' are a brilliant, despairing statement of the observer's dilemma as he bids for imaginative liberation:

> They will not leave me, the lives of other people.
> I wear them near my eyes like spectacles
>
> (*HL*, 38)

(which is a close echo of John Montague's great opening, with the same implication that this is a dominating subject: 'Like dolmens round my childhood, the old people').[6]

What Dunn's two lines express so brilliantly is the paradox of minute observation: sympathy is suggested by the fact that the observed lives are 'near' the eyes. But spectacles promote clarity of vision by mechanical means, so this observer is at once close and analytically

businesslike. It is a paradox of engagement and distance that is worthy
of Swift.

In more explicit ways, this volume gives rein to more overt
expressions of social sympathy. *Terry Street*'s politics tended to be
negative, in a vein that can undermine itself by coming too close to
contempt, in poems such as 'A Poem in Praise of the British' (*TS*, 60–
1). Now, in 'After the War', Dunn allows himself a positive
sentimentality. The games of the peacetime soldiers and of the children
playing at soldiers are not shared by one boy:

> But one of us had left. I saw him go
> Out through the gate, I heard him on the road
> Running to his mother's house. They lived alone,
> Behind a hedge round an untended garden
> Filled with broken toys, abrasive loss;
> A swing that creaked, a rusted bicycle.
> He went inside just as the convoy passed.
>
>   (*HL*, 49)

This beautifully observed picture of bereavement at the immediate level
extends out as a perfect metaphor for social marginalisation. But we
should note too that this third-person boy is 'one of us'; the gap between
observer and observed has been closed.

This progress towards a more involved poetic was not a smooth or
uninterrupted one. As Dunn strives to find a place for the imagination
where 'the lives of other people' will allow him freedom of movement,
some of the directions he explores are questionable. It is unfortunate
that one of the weaker poems in *The Happier Life* (one which does not
appear in the *Selected Poems*) gives the volume its title. It is a poem which
is untypical of the book's strengths, too, it should be noted: the
phantasmagoric poem 'Supreme Death', for example, is one of Dunn's
finest parables, with a perfect balance of formal restraint and
imaginative freedom. That balance is not found in the poem 'The
Happier Life' in which the formalities, especially the rhyme-scheme, are
too obvious:

> Wise apathy's a proper stance, aspiring
> To wry complacencies of the retiring.
>
>   (*HL*, 42)

The danger with Dunn's often-stated belief that formal finish is essential
to poetry, most recently asserted in his interview with *The Printer's Devil*
(*PD* 12–13), is that it can be interpreted as meaning that the more
formal the poetic structure, the further removed it is from prose. A

comparison of these two poems clearly belies this: the woodenness of the Drydenesque couplet here seems impossibly anachronistic, while 'Supreme Death' is a paradigm case of how a sense of formal freedom is essential to the impact of lyric poetry in our time. The operative word there is *sense*: the formal control which produces a poem of that kind is much harder to achieve than strict metres. As Dunn himself says elsewhere, anyone can write a Burns stanza; to write the Burns stanza like Burns is the problem (*PD*, 32). If it is done woodenly, any strict metrical form will seem an end in itself.

It may seem unconstructive to dwell on the negative aspects of a poem which, after all, Dunn excludes from the *Selected Poems* ('Supreme Death' *is* in the *Selected*). But it is important for an understanding of the positive movements through his career. After *Terry Street* he makes a brave choice: he turns away from a highly successful free verse – perhaps the most effective employment of it in that era – towards more classical forms. Classical forms were hard to resist in 1970, especially by a poet who was to a greater or lesser extent under the influence of Larkin. Moreover, some of Dunn's greatest successes, in *Elegies* for example, are implicitly dependent on a classical tightness, the 'ghostly voice' that Yeats said underlies a good line of poetry.[7] But when Dunn turns on principle towards stricter forms, the drawing-lines remain much too evident in some of the poems early on. There are other ways too in which the classical is not an entirely happy influence in Dunn's early-middle poetry: as in the couplet quoted above, it tends to lend itself to undue philosophising which, again, can seem disengaged. Dunn's classicism is beautifully attuned to his poetic purpose in an *Elegies* poem like 'Attics':

> A room, unutterably feminine,
> A room she dreamed, but painted by Gwen John –
> I see a white-distempered attic in
> Her mind, pastel, and faintly put-upon
> By men . . .
>
> (*E*, 24) '

This recalls the formally accomplished writers for whom Dunn has repeatedly declared his admiration: poets such as Mahon, Longley and John Fuller. The form is fully internalised and made natural to its purpose.

Thus far, in following the ways in which *The Happier Life* departs from the nature of *Terry Street*, I have given a very partial account of Dunn's second book. Its developments are a good deal more complex than I have yet suggested: for example, the language is odder and more

experimental than a concentration on its classical aspirations indicates.
The disorientated syntax of this passage from 'Creatures' in *Elegies* has
been much admired for the way it enacts disruption of life and
inarticulacy:

> we stood, our trust
> In lizards, settling birds, the impolite
>
> *Belettes*, the heavy hornets and the truths
> Compiling in our senses, plain, of this life,
> If inarticulate. I loved my wife.
>
> (*E*, 33)

This kind of constructive dislocation first appears in *The Happier Life*; an
example is the line in 'After the War' quoted above: "an untended
garden/ Filled with broken toys, abrasive loss" (*HL*, 49), where the last
two words are daring both in their relation to the syntax of the sentence
and in their phonological structure because the first syllable of the last
adjective *sounds* as if it is going to be the indefinite article. Dunn is a
master of such instabilities, which are first evident in this book.[8] Other
instances are the use of words in odd contexts: 'like handsome Deaths'
(*HL*, 37); 'the bad meanings we are' (*HL*, 53); 'Where the parties of
Saturday happen' (*HL*, 54); 'The other style are out in the country' (*HL*,
55); and the rhetorically more familiar functional shift, beloved of late
romantic poets, whereby parts of speech are changed: 'the tribes of
second-hand' (*HL*, 53).

Two last linguistic habits might be noted as Dunn moves out from
the single authoritative focus of *Terry Street*. The first is the relativising
device exemplified by the volume's title: happier than what? The
second, which relates to it as a move away from absoluteness, is the
preponderance of negativising constructions, especially the *un-* prefix in
this book.

The use of comparative (rather than absolute or superlative) forms is
particularly interesting in a writer moving from a single perspective
which he has come to find restrictive to a more equivocal one. This
interpretation of the comparative is confirmed by the beginning of the
last (and most interesting) section of the poem 'The Happier Life':

> The happier life – not found among the streets
> Where broken lives and other men's defeats
> Blow with the litter that encamps like squatters
> Up sheltered alleys in old business quarters;
> And just as seldom found in rural shires
> Of bumptious villagers or dreaming spires.

> The happy life is dreamt, just like the love
> Before the first, and is not quite enough.
> Insufficient perfections – what else is there?
>
> (HL, 45)

Fulfilment is not to be found with certainty in any order of society, just as the poem has said earlier 'Community's a myth' (sounding improbably like a proto-Thatcherite). The poem ends by saying that the poet is as right 'as minerals or rain'; that is, as inorganic rather than social processes. It seems at first glance an odd conclusion for a declared optimist to come to, but it is appropriate for the imagination that is fighting for autonomy but obsessed by 'the lives of other people'.

The crucial point here, which Dunn makes himself (*Viewpoints*, 23), is that, though in principle he is optimistic, his way of writing is the satirist's, the negative way (though it is worth noting in passing that this is the way not only of the satirist but also of the mystic). The most salient case of Dunn's negative method is the second linguistic practice I mentioned, the use of *un-* prefixes. It is a critical commonplace that *un-*adjectives are an effective way of expressing an opposite positive, by the rhetorical figure *oppositum*: 'no mean city'; Milton's 'reasons not implausible'. But Dunn's usages are more genuinely negative in polarity. The last poem in *The Happier Life*, 'The Hour' (HL, 71–2), establishes the volume-title as ironic and the book as a whole as pessimistic. This poem about 'The Sylvia Plath hour' (somewhat reminiscent of Ingmar Bergman's film *The Hour of the Wolf*) is built up of heavily-charged negative symbolism and grammar: 'Deaths of many babies'; 'Many unbirths in the frog-morning'; 'no shining'; 'no sky'; 'unlit outline of trees'; 'no world'; 'lifeless individuality'; 'no papers'; 'no Cross-Channel ferries,/ No banks and no bookshops' (though the last three are closer to the traditional use of *oppositum* in their stated positive opposites). This does not come unprepared for in *The Happier Life*; for example, the title-poem includes these lines:

> Mistakes, disaster, rotten circumstance
> Unpopulate the landscapes of Romance;
> Unmoral and unmanned.
>
> (HL, 44)

'The Hour' ends with an unmistakeable, programmatically negative declaration, against the objection that this poem 'is just negative', a product of a passing depression:

> Keep me cold. Keep me alive. Keep me.
>
> (HL, 72)

It is a fitting end to a volume whose best poems are 'Supreme Death' and the hauntingly desolate, empty 'Modern Love', and in which the poems end with such things as 'live in dirt', 'pernicious', 'my grey dirt in his heart', 'how tough love is', 'the most profound unhappiness', 'should this world fail', 'the rubble fields where once houses were', 'the silence after entertainment', 'there is nothing new', 'and nothing will change'.

This somewhat relentless itemising is justified, I think, in defining the spirit of the volume. It is notable, finally, that the more optimistic endings come in the earlier part of the book and rather get seen off in the course of it: the first poem ends 'it might grow', and the best-known line from the volume 'The music inside fruit!' comes early on, in 'The Musical Orchard' (*HL*, 20). What has happened between *Terry Street* and the second book is that the cold accuracy of exterior observation has been internalised, as the poet's focus turned inward to the imagination. The relative failure of commentators to stress this pessimism may be explained partly perhaps by an undeclared assumption that Dunn is, at least in part, 'school of Larkin'. There is a curiously Pagliaccian aspect to the reception of Larkin (and of the other Movement poets, to a lesser extent): because his grimness is expressed in humorous terms, Larkin's gloom is disabled by being treated as a tragicomic act. The full tragedy of poems like 'Aubade'[9] is rarely faced. There is no comedy in *The Happier Life*; but it may be that the association with Larkin blurred its pessimism. We might recall what Dunn wrote in his brilliant account of Berryman in *Encounter* in 1974: 'Alienated writers, i.e. all contemporary writers with a proper knowledge of what contemporaneity is, do not seek repose'.[10]

But Dunn, we must remember, is an optimist made pessimistic by external circumstance rather than by nature. *The Happier Life* does not sound like the book he wants to write any more than *Terry Street*. His third book, *Love or Nothing* in 1974, is different from its first causative word, 'For'. Immediately it is stamped as a more elusive performance with a speaking persona much harder to place. What does this 'For' resolve? What special knowledge is implied as the previous stage in its argument? Even if that first poem 'Little Rich Rhapsody' is not one of the weightier pieces in the book (it is not in the *Selected Poems*, though it *is* one of the thirteen poems by Dunn included by Motion and Morrison in their *Penguin Book of Contemporary British Poetry*),[11] its use to strike an unsettling opening note is very important, continuing on from the initial linguistic dislocations of the previous book. Lyman Andrews's declaration in his *Sunday Times* review has become well known (partly because it is on the book's cover), but there is much to be said for it: 'with this collection Mr Dunn steps into the ranks of England's major living poets' (though 'England's' might give us pause in the light of later developments). The most marked technical advance over the previous books is the way the classical formalism is now fully digested in the poetry, seeming (to borrow Andrews's words again) 'so guileless that it is with a shock that one realises just how formal it is'. The technical advance is most marked in what might be thought Dunn's first totally convincing long poem, 'Winter Orchard'. (I should add, since I am not discussing that volume here, that I think the longer poems in *St Kilda's Parliament* are entirely successful too; Dunn has had more success than most in the common attempt to revive the longer poem in the course of the past quarter-century.)

Dunn tells us that 'Winter Orchard' began with the literal observation of a shrivelled, undeveloped apple in his garden. It thus offers an interesting contrast in its 'Revenge of the unfructified' (*LN*, 13) with the happy, fulfilled apples in *Northlight*: 'Ripened, come autumn, into savoury/ Pleasures' (*N*, 23). The photographic observation of the shrivelled apple is now reached by a much more circuitous, metaphorical route, starting with suburban fog,

> A breath with industry on it.
>   (*LN*, 13)

What is successful in this poem is the contained classicism which seems to find an ideal equilibrium between general reflection and its source in observed reality.[12] In this way it invites comparison with the great semi-classical poem of the era, Derek Mahon's 'A Disused Shed in Co. Wexford',[13] an appropriate comparison here because the title-poem of *Love or Nothing* is taken from the poem 'Realisms' which is dedicated to Mahon. It is a poem crucially concerned with matters discussed here in connection with the previous books: the 'algebra of "sympathies"', and its compatibility with the wish to escape the demanding pieties of place which the poem concludes 'we never escape' (*LN*, 20). The poem's conclusion is teasingly equivocal (following further a direction I have traced from *Terry Street* to *The Happier Life*) on this matter of pieties:

> The existential clarity
> Of love and nothing, the peace
> Poets in patched trousers deserve.
>   (*LN*, 21)

It is hard to see what exactly is going on here: why is 'love and nothing' changed in the volume's title to 'love *or* nothing'? Do the ragged trousers of the last line deliberately belong to poets rather than philanthropists: that is, artists rather than the socially conscious? This may be even more fanciful; but does the word 'peace' in the context of existentialism evoke the peace which passeth all understanding? However they are read, the lines provide a decidedly open-ended conclusion.

The ways in which *Love or Nothing* continues the trends of the previous volume are fairly evident. But the differences are more striking than the similarities. The persona is much more various in these self-examining poems: the much-used term 'confessional' might be applied to them much more than to the earlier volumes. Where *Terry Street* observed and *The Happier Life* tended to generalise, observation here is worked into reverie, in apparently autobiographical poems such as 'White Fields', 'Boys With Coats' and 'Sailing with the Fleet'. At the risk of labouring my metaphor, there is certainly a third dimension here.

I have argued that *The Happier Life* becomes more pessiminstic in the course of its development; *Love or Nothing* develops in power and interest in its course. Some of the disengaged classicism survives in the earlier poems, and the formalism does not sit easily with the harsh, post-Larkin diction. Larkin is saved from the charge of sneering by his lugubriousness; the sneer is too willed a facial expression for him. But his language, which is anyway redeemed by a masterly lightness of touch, is dangerous to follow. It does not suit Dunn because his political concern is incompatible with the elegant distance of the Movement, as Motion and Morrison said of the poets of Dunn's generation.[14] For example, 'The House Next Door' is a self-declared fiction ('You made us up for money'), but the language remains uncomfortably distanced from the 'Old dears gardening in fur coats', who at the end benevolently order the poet around:

> And you shall drive our old crock down to the sea.
>
> (*LN*, 9)

Even the fine following poem 'Winter Graveyard' degenerates at the end into a diction that is excessively jagged:

> Rubbish of names under vomit of moss . . . .
>
> farcical monuments
> To sanctities not worth the enshrinement.
>
> (*LN*, 12)

At these splenetic moments, the language is also inclined to fall into a routine, slack diction, such as the 'farcical' in that line. Similarly, the anger at the deaths of the young men in the First World War is warranted, but undervalued by its expression:

> died abroad defending an Empire's
> Affectionate stability
> And an industry of lies.
>
> (*LN*, 11)

The other negative aspect of the language is an inclination towards grandiose vocabulary. It is evident to some extent in 'Winter Graveyard' but more damagingly in the eerie, mysterious poem 'Ocean' whose remote power is slackened by the attention-seeking word 'thalass-ocracies' (*LN*, 27). Not that the experimentation with such language is not ultimately productive: it is the source of such marvellous sentences as this from 'Home Again':

> A floral light
> Bleaches my eye with angelophanous
> Secrets.
>
> (*E*, 52)

But in 1974 Dunn's poetic technique is still being developed, and the perfectly counterpointed diction in the *Elegies* passage is often not matched. (Indeed it may be the one word 'thalassocracies' that is responsible for the absence of 'Ocean' from the *Selected Poems*.)

The principal imaginative liberation in *Love or Nothing* is seen in the language through which the newly-employed first person speaks. After the caustic satire of these early poems, the poetic voice gains conviction through unassertiveness. In 'Winter Orchard' itself, the judgemental is avoided through the use of non-finite, participial phrases; the first finite verb 'is' occurs for the central 'photograph' of the shrivelled apple at line 21. Thereafter there is a shift to the past tense, as the woodenness of the observing present is entirely circumvented. 'Realisms' too starts with a non-finite sentence:

> Poetry in a flap,
> Its paper efficiencies
> Thoth with an accent.
>
> (*LN*, 19)

The release of the imagination through this avoidance of the flat present, whether that of *Terry Street*'s instantaneous observation ('Because it's wet, the afternoon is quiet' *TS*, 29), or the Drydenesque classical generalisation ('Capitals were made for governments and love' *HL*, 42), reaps rich dividends in the 'autobiographical' poems following. At last in 'Renfrewshire Traveller' we reach a voice that is the poet's own – or at least a characterisation of the poet's own, returning to the Clyde in a 'spray of recollection'. One of the curiosities of *Terry*

Street, as of any photographic representation, is that it has no prehistory, because the poet has no roots there. The recollection in 'Renfrewshire Traveller' liberates a past tense that provides an extra dimension in poems such as 'Sunday' in which 'my mother took/ Flowers to her dead' (*LN*, 31), and the beautiful 'White Fields'. In this poem, after recollecting childhood experiences of being comforted by his mother, the poet builds to a classical generalisation which now *is* warranted through experience and made an active process rather than flat generalising by its angular syntax:

> White fields, your angled frost filed sharply
> Bright over undisturbed grasses, do not soothe
> As similes of innocence or idle deaths
> That must happen anyway, an unmoral blankness;
> Be unforgiving stillness, natural, what is:
> Crimes uttered in landscape, smoke-darkened snow.
>
> (*LN*, 33)

Here the deracination and the *via negativa* noted above ('unmoral' here again) work in a convincing context of meaning and return to be earthed in experience: 'Trains in my distance altered'.

These strengths are evident in the following poems too. At a stage in his life when Dunn was moving in a determined way towards writing fiction again (*Viewpoints*, 31), 'Sailing with the Fleet' sees the 'parked destroyers waiting to be scrapped' (*LN*, 36) as a relict of stories which the poet briefly imagines. In poems like this, Dunn is inventing (I think) a form of narrative that has become very popular and productive in the last twenty years, the invented fiction that offers itself as autobiography. And perhaps the most significant poem in this series is a manifesto of a new direction for Dunn's work, 'Clydesiders':

> My poems should be Clyde-built, crude and sure . . .
> A poetry of nuts and bolts, born, bred,
> Embattled by the Clyde, tight and impure.
>
> (*LN*, 37)

One of the qualities that Dunn admires in Seamus Heaney (it is the starting-point in his review of *North*) is Heaney's insistence on the poet's craft as comparable to any skilled tradesman's making.[15] The tools of the poet's craft — what Robert Lowell called 'Those blesséd structures, plot and rhyme'[16] — are brought to bear on the writer's experience as their material, so 'Clydesiders' ends following the poet's footsteps backwards:

> They'll follow to my life. I know they must.
>
> (*LN*, 37)

Although concern for the crafting 'blessèd structures' still occasionally threatens to usurp the central place in this volume, Dunn's concern to have the craft and the material in perfect equilibrium is clearly established in that *Encounter* review (contemporary with the publication of *Love or Nothing* in 1974). While praising Williams and Mahon, in a passing caveat Dunn expresses a wish for 'a more generously social understanding in them', and 'less value placed on the prestige of the delicate touch'. [17]

But, beyond the binary confrontation between social understanding and the delicate touch which gives tension to Dunn's writing from this period onwards, a new element gains prominence in *Love or Nothing*. In the Haffenden interview, Dunn speaks of his admiration for the French surrealist poet Robert Desnos (*Viewpoints*, 29). The poem 'The Deserter', which is subtitled *Homage to Robert Desnos*, appears in *St Kilda's Parliament*, but the inclination to write in a surrealist vein is evident is a series of poems towards the end of *Love or Nothing*. Why it was that Dunn felt, as he claimed in the Haffenden interview, that 'surrealist poems in rhyme and metre' were 'more characteristic of my imagination than *Terry Street* or *Barbarians*' (*Viewpoints*, 29), has always been thought something of a puzzle. Motion and Morrison see this inclination in Dunn as something that links him with 'the Martian school', [18] but that is different from surrealism. Though it shares with Martian poetry an obliqueness of viewpoint that surprises the subject by stripping it of its normal associations, Dunn's surrealism seems more evasive: a kind of holiday from responsibility. Certainly it is linked, as Motion and Morrison say, to the 'expansive fictionalising' [19] which I have noted in 'Sailing with the Fleet'. It is not one of Dunn's central preoccupations, but the surrealism and/or symbolism of poems such as 'The Concert' or 'The White Poet' are an important index of the pluralism in Dunn's technical and thematic concerns. In any case, his declared preference proves prophetically useful in some visionary poems about death and ghostliness, such as the 'angelophanous' quality of 'Home Again', in *Elegies*. The achievement of mystical authority in this poem ending 'And it is very strange and wonderful' (*E*, 52) derives from the surrealist side of Dunn, as well as from some of the technical habits I have mentioned: the enriched language ('Home again' begins 'Autumnal aromatics') and the *via negativa*, associated with mysticism. We might recall too these lines from 'Reading Pascal in the Lowlands':

> I close my book, the *Pensées* of Pascal.
> I am light with meditation, religiose
> And mystic with a day of solitude.
>
> (*E*, 45)

If Dunn's only concerns previously had been the totally secular matters of social responsibility and poetic form, *Elegies* would not have been able to reach the metaphysical heights that helped to make it the foremost book of its generation.

However, *Barbarians* in 1979 was a marked shift towards Dunn's public manner and concerns, especially in the opening group of nine poems, 'Barbarian Pastorals', which (as Haffenden said) 'were as outspoken as [he's] ever been'. Dunn accepts that this is a more programmatic, campaigning volume, though the terms in which he concedes this made it clear that he does not entirely approve. 'In *Barbarians*, after I'd written the first couple of poems, I did realise what I was up to, and that wasn't nearly as natural and relaxed a performance as *Terry Street*; I did deliberatly organise *Barbarians*' (*Viewpoints*, 24). However, the resemblances to the themes of *Terry Street* are more striking than the departures from it, in the development of Dunn's writing. *Barbarians* is made up of three short groups of poems, a division which itself is only paralleled by *Terry Street* in Dunn's oeuvre. Only the first section has a title, 'Barbarian Pastorals', but the definitive qualities of the second section are also obvious: this section is made up of poems about Scotland, and the third brief section has poems that do not directly fit either of the two earlier categories (though it too has a tendency towards the political that is entirely compatible with them).

The reception of *Barbarians* has been dominated by the opening section of most outspoken poems. The nature of this section, 'Barbarian Pastorals', as Dunn's most politically outspoken writing is underlined by his telling Haffenden that three poems written after *Barbarians* belong to the group. He names two, which are among the most campaigning poems in the following volume, the less politically assertive *St Kilda's Parliament*, 'Tannahill' (*SKP*, 52) and 'John Wilson in Greenock, 1786' (*SKP*, 57–61). Judging by its subject and placing in *St Kilda's Parliament*, the third is probably 'Green Breeks' (*SKP*, 47). Haffenden suggests that the coherence in this group 'has to do with excoriating any section of society that condescends to any other section' (*Viewpoints*, 31). This maybe overstates the breadth of the constituency; the condescended-to sectors in 'Barbarian Pastorals' are workers, Scots and artists – a group whose limits are clarified by the addition of the extra three poems from *St Kilda's Parliament*.

It is interesting to ponder, though, not only the effect of adding those three poems to 'Barbarian Pastorals', but also the effect of subtracting them from the following volume. Dunn's remark that those poems should be in the first sequence in *Barbarians* and that he 'perhaps published the book too quickly' (*Viewpoints*, 25) has an air of getting the topic done with and out of the way: an obligation rather than a pleasure. Certainly the effect on the other sections of *Barbarians* seems liberating. The second section of that book is Dunn's most assured and diverse performance before *Elegies*. Here the personal context of the events, the aspiration towards the surreal, and the sense of social responsibility all work together in a series of formally lucid poems: the metrically adept but free 'Red Buses', the surrealist broadside 'Ballad of the Two Left Hands', the light philosophy of 'Lost Gloves'. These poems suggest comparison with the more developed (and mostly later developed, it should be noted) surrealism of another leading Faber poet, Paul Muldoon. For example, the way that hands (*B*, 41–3), gloves (*B*, 45) and 'arms that arm' (*B*, 44) are yoked together, not by violence but by a kind of exterior metonymic structure, is reminiscent of the way verbal themes (including hands, as it happens) run through a book like Muldoon's *Quoof*.[20]

Related to this is another feature of the poems in the second section of *Barbarians*: it is the period of his writing when Dunn's irony seems most assured. The jagged acerbities I noted in earlier volumes are gone. That rather aggressive touchiness was still evident in the opening poem of 'Barbarian Pastorals', 'The Come-on'. The poem faces a problem commonly encountered by the radical writer; other examples are Harrison, Paulin and Terry Eagleton in his literary broadsides. 'The Come-on' satirises the academic establishment for accommodating the refractory, radical writer by teaching him/her 'to tell one good wine from another'. This is fair as light satire but reductive in the more ambitious political context here. A more important problem critically is the satirist's difficulty of sticking to the satire's defined values. It is slightly disconcerting in the light of this poem to realise that the persona mourning Robert Lowell in the first poem of the third section of *Barbarians* is 'well-wined' in Cahors, or to recall 'the pleasant side of history' in 'Saturday' with its visit to friends in Kirkbymoorside,

> bearing a pineapple,
> Some books of interest and a fine Bordeaux.
>
> (*SKP*, 36)

Here the satirist is trapped by his own terms.

But this is untypical of 'Barbarian Pastorals' as well. From 'In the Grounds' onwards, Dunn uses his classical forms in ways which are entirely appropriate to his politics. The use of history is important here; 'Gardeners' and 'The Student' both have a historical setting, so that the parallels of Pomponius Mela and Tacitus seem less grandiose than they would applied to the poet's present tense. The imaginary, but politically recognisable, world of 'Loamshire' is placed in the year of the French Revolution, so that its classical formality and revolutionary message have a disinterested context that avoids the discomforts of 'The Come-on'. These lines, and their diction, would seem tub-thumping without the historical depth of the 1789 context:

> They call this grudge. Let me hear you admit
> That in the country that's but half of it.
> Townsmen will wonder, when your house was burned,
> We did not burn your gardens and undo
> What likes of us did for the likes of you;
> We did not raze this garden that we made,
> Although we hanged you somewhere in its shade.
>
> (B, 18)

The idiomatic flaws are interesting here, reminiscent of those of Keats in *Endymion*: 'the' omitted before 'half of it' and before the first 'likes' in the third-last line. It expresses admirably the impression of alienation in the language of the gardener, especially within the imperious form, the rhyming couplet. Dunn's classicism is now put to use.

The third section of *Barbarians* seems less assured again, but by now we recognise the open-endedness and equivocation by which Dunn's work develops. New forms and subjects are tried and slowly perfected. 'Stranger's Grief', the elegy for Robert Lowell, is perhaps too pure a form for elegy. As Dunn's great *Elegies* shows, it is a form that needs to risk embarrassment and to evoke a sense of loss by somehow getting on the reader's nerves. Especially coming after the dogmatic assertiveness of 'Barbarian Pastorals', the poems of this closing section are again too urbane. The Wyatt-like 'On Her Picture Left with Him' is a two-fingered exercise like some of Dunn's early metrical formalities. Apart from the balanced 'The Return', which closes the volume on a perfect note with his return to an earlier home, the most interesting and risky poem here is 'A Late Degree', which manifests a direct sympathy of the kind that ends 'After the War' in *The Happier Life*. 'A Late Degree' is a classic case of a poem that succeeds by taking risks, as in the slack diction of its opening:

> She stands there holding her valise
> Under the timetable for optional seminars,
> And is herself a bag, or so they say
> In our bullying, cruel vernacular.

> (*B*, 54)

The poem's catalogue of gaucheries proceeds through 'dim-witted wives/ Of his colleagues, who she always detested' to its calculated, powerful ending:

> Which is unbearably sad, unworthy of satire,
> For there is no vernacular of compassion.

> (*B*, 55)

Because there is no vernacular of compassion, a poetic expression of compassion is nearly impossible to achieve. But because of Dunn's dual devotion to social justice and imaginative form, his whole endeavour is to achieve it.

It is incontestable, I think, that, by the time of *Elegies*, that language has been reached, hard-won in terms both of experience and of craft. The virtue of *Barbarians* (which was perhaps the best-received of Dunn's books apart from *Terry Street* and *Elegies*) was that it brought all the poet's dilemmas into the open and worked them through. How far is it possible to satisfy the demands of social responsibility and the artistic imagination at the same time? What is the range of the term 'decency', with its etymology in classical decorum, in an unjust world? Dunn's post-*Elegies* writing has solved this problem partly by compartmentalising, so that his politics is expressed in the Chatto *Counterblast* and the poetry's imaginative artistry can be taken separately as a non-trivial issue. Dunn's view is that the language of compassion and of social responsibility has to be well-formed. But ultimately Dunn's argument, as in his recent essay 'Noticing Such Things',[21] is that there is no incompatibility here. Indeed the one is not perfectible without the other. The poet, as MacNeice says, is 'a specialist in something which everyone practises', that is, language; but the poet is also a specialist in the 'insatiable delight in life' which Dunn quotes from De La Mare.[22] The process by which the complex literary language to express this dual specialism is constructed can be traced through the various movements in form and subject through Dunn's middle-period poems, ready for consummate compassionate use in *Elegies*.

NOTES

1 The best discussion of this (as of many aspects of Dunn) is Alan
   Robinson, *Instablities in Contemporary British Poetry* (London, Macmillan, 1988), chapter 5, 'The Mastering Eye: Douglas Dunn's
   Social Perceptions'. This chapter is hereafter footnoted as 'Robinson'.
2 Cf. Robinson, 83–5
3 *Station Island* (London, Faber and Faber, 1984), 93.
4 *Two Decades of Irish Writing, A Critical Survey*, ed. Douglas Dunn
   (Cheadle Hulme: Carcanet, 1975), 2.
5 J. Hendry and R. Ross (eds), *Norman McCaig: Critical Essays*
   (Edinburgh, Edinburgh University Press, 1990), 4.
6 John Montague, *Selected Poems* (Oxford, Oxford University Press,
   1982), 26.
7 W.B. Yeats, 'A General Introduction for my Work' in *Essays and
   Introductions* (London, Macmillan, 1961), 524. Written 1937.
8 As one might expect from his title, the best discussion of this
   'instability' comes in Robinson's chapter, e.g. p. 88.
9 Philip Larkin, *Collected Poems* (London, Faber and Faber, 1988), 208–
   9.
10 *Encounter* XLIII, No 2 (August, 1974), 76.
11 *The Penguin Book of Contemporary British Poetry*, edited by Blake
   Morrison and Andrew Motion (Harmondsworth, Penguin, 1982),
   53.
12 For this more meditative view of the photographic lens, see what
   Dunn says in *PD*, 26.
13 *The Snow Party* (Oxford, Oxford University Press, 1975), 36–8. For
   his immediate appreciation of this poem, see Dunn's review in
   Encounter XLV, No 5 (November, 1975), 80–1.
14 Introduction to *Penguin Book of Contemporary British Poetry, passim.*
15 Dunn discusses Heaney's insistence on writing as 'craft' in the
   Encounter interview (XLV, No 5, 76).
16 'Epilogue' in *Day by Day* (London: Faber and Faber, 1978), 127.
17 *Encounter* XLV, No 5, 81.
18 *The Penguin Book of Contemporary British Poetry*, 18.
19 Ibid., 17.
20 *Quoof* (London, Faber and Faber, 1983), 11, 13, 14 (e.g.).
21 'Noticing Such Things' in *English Review* 2, No 2 (Winter 1991).
22 *English Review*, p. 14.

Four

Dunn, Larkin and Decency

Glyn Maxwell

Every poet, in every line, makes two things clear: how to write; how to live. Or, to borrow the formulation that so memorably concludes Philip Larkin's 'Talking in Bed' (*TWW*, 127)[1]: no poet writes any line that makes clear how not to write, how not to live. The furious silence of the poet in action, brows knit, mouth perhaps ridiculously set in a devil's grimace or child's gape, is the point of his existence, the speeches between which he merely pauses and senses: so, of course, in it, he does the best he is. For more is to be said, and he is not ready to stop. What are poems for? Poems are where poets live: where can they live but poems? This is a piece about two poets, Douglas Dunn and Philip Larkin, with some thoughts on the notion of Decency.

Decency: What is Decency? The Oxford English Dictionary has: '1: Appropriateness or fitness to the circumstances or requirements of the case; fitness, seemliness, propriety (of speech, action, behaviour). 2: Decent or orderly condition of civil or social life. 3: Propriety of behaviour or demeanour; due regard to what is becoming; conformity (in behaviour, speech or action) to the standard of propriety or good taste.' Decency.

Decency: what is fitting. The man and poet superficially regarded as the late century's stickler, as Dunn records, 'a deeply moral man, with very firm convictions on behaviour, propriety and considerateness',[2] the literary world's decent chap, the one of the boys – is the man and poet who did not, does not, fit, had no comfort or fellow-feeling to offer, neither had nor wanted a woman or kids, did not believe, could not hope, died expecting nothing for Man, and the worst for the world. The most frightened and frightening, most awfully isolated poet of the

century has become Oxford England's Good Old Philip. Decency and
Poetry, as we Oxford English know them, may prove to have difficulty
sharing a room, at least under those names.

When Larkin lived, he knew Dunn, who knew 'Larkin', as in knowing
'Shakespeare', or indeed 'Donne', as early as 1962. Five years later they
met. Dunn liked Larkin, though not his politics; he was consciously
influenced by him, but would later know what he didn't need; he got a
job in Larkin's library, but couldn't get him talking about poetry; and
Dunn's first book of poems, *Terry Street*, was pressured out of him by
time passed in the city that for both the true lover and casual observer of
twentieth-century verse has become the black-and-white film set
through which Larkin biked to the library in a jacket and tie.

He biked into the life of Douglas Dunn when the youngster down
from Renfrewshire was 'holding imaginary conversations with W.H.
Auden, Yeats and Eliot while walking to work'.[3] However distant and
uncommunicative the older poet may have seemed at first, he must have
come to sense that here was a soul kindred enough to his own to merit
rescue from behind those three great megaliths. After all, these lines:
'All the familiar horrors we/ Associate with others/ Are coming fast
along our way:/ The wind is warning in our tree/ And morning papers
still betray/ The shrieking of the mothers'[4] are not Auden's; nor these:
'And from the silver goblet of the moon/ A ghostly light spills down on
arched trees'[5] Yeats's. The Great Desk upon which groups of poems are
scattered to become collections was, though, in the case of *Terry Street*,
Larkin's.

> Feeling myself influenced by Larkin was disconcerting. He wasn't
> Scots — indeed, he was very, very English. I knew nothing of the
> scenes he wrote about . . . Nor, when I came to write my poems
> about Terry Street, in Hull, did I find myself able to use the
> melodiousness, or the best lyricism of his verse. What I was
> writing about, and where, dictated a looser kind of language, less
> metrical than Larkin's characteristic writing . . . What influenced
> me heavily was the up-to-dateness of observation in Larkin's verse.
> Rather like the sensation contemporary readers testify to have felt
> when faced with Auden's poetry of the 1930s, Larkin's poems of
> the 1950s and 1960s often feel as if they're addressing themselves
> to the moment, to the clock itself.[6]

Same years, same city: poverty, grime, envy, junk, the first crude forms
of consumerism, of mass exploitation: 'Cheap suits, red kitchen-ware,
sharp shoes, iced-lollies,/ Electric mixers, toasters, washers, driers — / A
cut-price crowd, urban yet simple, dwelling/ Where only salesmen and
relations come . . .' ('Here', *TWW*, 136). But how to write about

Here? How to live with Here? What sounds to emit when the heart and
the clock meet eye-to-eye in the suburban park or supermarket aisle?
What is the fitting resonse? Can the poet fit at all?

If to fit is to blend, become inconspicuous, part of what is there, all
we can watch is how spectacularly the poet tries, how completely he
fails, for it is impossible to overstate how isolated any poet is from the
world he describes, simply by virtue of his being the only one to
describe it, the one who turns life to his life, world to his world.
However many the apparent similarities, Larkin's Hull is Larkin's Hull;
Dunn's is Dunn's. Out of the white page of any place we never knew, in
the life before us, the life which can never be satisfactorily proved to
have happened, glitter the black marks of how it was, then, for a man.
The great men are those who make us believe it happened, because
that's how it does happen, and that's what it looks like.

Poets are of two kinds. The two kinds they are are thousands of
different two kinds (believers/knowers, reasoners/sensers, masters of the
old/glimpsers of the new, them/her, me/you), but the two kinds they
are at this moment on this page are Cities and Visitors.

In the City, there are Westminsters where laws are made,
Hampsteads and Morningsides where they are complained about but
complied with, and Sohos, Gorbalses, Town Halls and Inner Temples
where they are flouted, unheard-of, twisted or shamed. But there they
are, laws, so incontrovertible that one can prop the l to a capital and
shear off the s: it's the Law. Everything that passes in the City is viewed
from a central vantage with a fixed and sacred sense of right and wrong:
everything falls to ground somewhere, is a matter for agreement or
disagreement, applause or the police, the Keys to the City or the key in
the lock. Everything exemplifies a point by which the Elders of the City
hope to perpetuate their grip on it, their vision of that City as Life as it
should be: with them in it, running it, looked to, listened to.

The Poets who are more like this have a kind of fixed zodiac; they
work by certain stars. The clock can be heard almost throughout their
work: they prefer fixed forms, and they make points which they string
together by human detail. For our purposes: they have an opinion about
decency or morality, and it does not change. Herbert, Pope, Hardy and
Larkin are of this kind; John Donne's whole span is the best example: he
lived that early life all right, but he knew where it all fell.

The Visitor progresses through the City, but he is filled with more
Westminsters, Morningsides, Sohos, parks, depots, gases and wastes
than the greatest city, far more than he can understand or govern. What
he thinks about things in the morning by the river bears little relation
to how he feels in mid-afternoon upon the grand sunny park, not to

mention after three beers in a brassy darkened pub, walking back through drizzle to the filthy Zone 3 tube station, or, nearly asleep in the strange hotel, the luxurious loneliness.

The Poets who are more like this do what the weather hints to them, they use what is to hand, they cannot give the last word, they find it hard to close the lacquered lid on a poem because they have no idea what comes next, or how to react to it, or whether it is truly right or wrong. They are not ready for that, they probably never will be. They feel, but will not be final. They alter over months, not years. They look for some other City to visit. Visitors' Books contain the names Byron, Auden, Lowell and Dunn. We will follow Dunn through Cities he has Visited.

He arrives, a young university student, in the city of Hull, and rents a place in 'a slum street . . . off Beverley Road'.[7] It is 1966, which predates only *High Windows* among Larkin's collections, so that the world of 'Here' (*TWW*), 'The Whitsun Weddings' (*TWW*), 'Deceptions' (*TLD*) 'Mr Bleaney' (*TWW*), 'The Large Cool Store' (*TWW*), is precisely that into which this fresh poetic sensibility is thrust. And, thankfully, Dunn feels alien; like many a poet early on, his instinct is to write of where in fact he least belongs: to worry the sore. And in grey English Hull he is homesickened or otherwise hurt into the stuff of poetry. Looking back, he knows he then found his 'first serious opportunity for a subject'.[8] And of course what he found was himself, serious, alone, watching:

> This time they see me at my window, among books,
> A specimen under glass, being protected,
> And laugh at me watching them.
> They minuet to Mozart playing loudly
>
> On the afternoon Third. They mock me thus,
> They mime my softness. A landlord stares.
> All he has worked for is being destroyed.
> The slum rent-masters are at one with Pop.
>
> ('Young Women in Rollers', *TS*, 29)

Whatever liberation Dunn felt was represented by Larkin's choice of matters, his exemplary metrics, his lowered diction: the younger poet was, from the outset, setting off on his own. Hull, yes, a reading man's eye on the working class, yes, but that said, the whole dynamic of the poet/subject relationship: physically, culturally, with regard to tone, pitch, sympathy, vantage, is already different, has already travelled far from Larkin.

Dunn is, as we are as we read, 'among books', symbols of proper education, emblems of a middle-class 'decency' the poet knows to be far from its own capital: here books, Mozart, the Third, the poet himself,

'A specimen under glass', furnish a silent, painful alienation. Terry Street and *Terry Street* are likewise crammed with things; the educated, selective sensibility yearning to hone itself on Eliot and Yeats is baulked and bombarded by sheer clutter, things that are symbols of nothing but symbols of meaning nothing.

No trees in their autumn beauty but 'Recalcitrant motorbikes;/ Dog-shit under frost; a coughing woman;/ The old men who cannot walk briskly groaning/ On the way back from their watchmen's huts.' That is the whole of 'Winter' (*TS*, 27): all that can be added is a poet who sees nothing there to be added. Where Larkin's classic cataloguing of bleak (sub)urban reality slows concluding into a station:

> And past the poppies bluish nautral distance
> Ends the land suddenly beyond a beach
> Of shapes and shingle. Here is unfenced existence:
> Facing the sun, untalkative, out of reach . . .
> ('Here', *TWW*, 136–7)

Dunn's poems of Terry Street end only in gasps, sags or jumps of the spirits, glimpses, shards of light. Enisled in the bric-a-brac of lives so unembraceably other, he dramatises, over again, the distance between his life and the life he witnesses, the pain and meaninglessness of the space itself. Where he(re) is, he is invisible. Though he sees the pretty, worn-down young wife in the shop, senses 'The slow expanse of unheld breasts' ('Incident in the Shop', *TS*, 18), feels 'the draughts on her legs', knows that 'Under her bed, forgotten winter bulbs/ Die of thirst . . .' and look on as 'She buys the darkest rose I ever saw/ And tucks the stem into her plastic belt' – she does not see him; no more does the outwardly mobile man of whom he says 'I wish him well. I wish him grass' ('A Removal from Terry Street', *TS*, 20), nor the street's ignored, fading elders ('The Patricians', *TS*, 15–16). The young women in rollers, who laugh at him and 'mime his softness', are a rare example in the book of Dunn's subjects noticing him, as if the invisible man forgot to drink what makes him invisible; seen, he is ridiculed. He would prefer to vanish into this world:

> If I could sleep standing, I would wait here
> For ever, become a landmark, something fixed
> For tug crews or seabound passengers to point at,
> An example of being a part of a place.
> ('Landscape with one Figure', *TS*, 55)

Whatever the poet may believe about his goodness, his decency, the morality that embraces the many miserable lives with such bleak

tenderness, the facts of life there, here, reduce him to surges of feeling,
each one of which pulls him further away like an undertow — to lyricise
is to say 'so long', to idealise is to say 'not yet':

> I want to be touched by them, know their lives,
> Dance in my own style, learn something new.
> At night, I even dream of ideal communities.
> Why do they live where they live, the rich and the poor?
>
> Tonight, when their hair is ready, after tea,
> They'll slip through laws and the legs of policemen.
> I won't be there, I'll be reading books elsewhere.
> There are many worlds, there are many laws.
>
> ('Young Women in Rollers', *TS*, 30)

Larkin won't be there either: he will be travelling through his own City
on his train, he too a specimen under glass, though he is less inclined to
see it that way. When Larkin watches the day of 'The Whitsun
Weddings' through a pane, he too is invisible — not to us who know
that face, call up a distinct, comical, BBC/black-and-white image at the
words 'Struck, I leant/ More promptly out next time, more curiously
. . .' — but to his own subjects. In this sense, Larkin's people really are
subjects of his City, joined in his rhymes, not staring out of a stanza or
mimicking its movement like those women in Dunn. A lyrical taming,
controlling, is taking place here that Dunn did not feel was appropriate
to what he in his turn saw in Hull. Larkin

> saw it all again in different terms:
> The fathers with broad belts under their suits
> And seamy foreheads; mothers loud and fat;
> An uncle shouting smut; and then the perms,
> The nylon-gloves and jewellery substitutes,
> The lemons, mauves, and olive-ochres that
>
> Marked off the girls unreally from the rest . . .
> ('The Whitsun Weddings', *TWW*, 115)

In bright light and silence, people work for Larkin: it's the ultimate
Librarian's poem. He does not, like Dunn with his less rhythmical,
jagged glimpsing of the everyday, record what it is like to see and hear
life at the moment it happens, for remember that each suddenly-passing
detail of 'The Whitsun Weddings' is marvellous, and men looking out
of trains do not record marvels at that tempo; he perfects the experience
in silence, later. After a gap of time. And mind that gap, for into it falls
the shaping and turning of experience that misleads us into thinking
Larkin is very like a common, moralising man — that same gap that

Dunn, in *Terry Street*, is not prepared to caulk with approbation or censure, but only with a distant feeling of common humanity:

> Rain drying on the slates shines sometimes.
> A builder is repairing someone's leaking roof.
>
> He kneels upright to rest his back.
> His trowel catches the light and becomes precious.
> ('On Roofs of Terry Street', *TS*, 21)

The excellence of *Terry Street* is perhaps a kind of courage, the Visitor's courage not to internalise, announce, denounce, merely to do his best by how it looks. Larkin is widely and rather dimly celebrated for a quality of being 'unflinching' in the face of darkness and death, but when it comes to loud, staring, living reality, it seems to me that the younger poet is more commonly found without a pane of glass in front of his eyes. (Though glass is significant in Larkin: to say that he could see well only through glass(es) is not stupid. It's not that different from saying that Hardy could write good poems only in stanzas, Dickinson in quatrains, or cummings by fracturing syntax and grammar.) But it's Dunn who, at least in *Terry Street*, stands too close to the matter to sort or sift it morally, to draw conclusions. In 1981, he would add an 'Envoi' to the collection that ends 'A curse on me I did not write with joy', but one of the poems, 'Cosmologist' (*TS*, 62), already there, already did, and emphasised this wide gulf between the two poets, between fixity and uncertainty, between Place and Traveller.

'"Why can't you write like you did in Terry Street?"',[9] Dunn recalls Larkin saying to him many times, as the Scottish poet's career flourished clear of the word 'protégé'; and certainly by the time of *Barbarians* (1979) a cursory look at Dunn's themes, diction and standpoint makes the attitude unsurprising, but even in the next two collections, *The Happier Life* (1972) and *Love or Nothing* (1974), Dunn can be seen to be sharply diverging from what Larkin appears to have valued most in *Terry Street*. As Dunn himself saw it, 'it was probably Larkin's influence that convinced me that my poems of that time should take the form of testimony and, where I could manage it, of objective realism'.[10]

Decency, the civilised life, the right way to live in society, begin to be nagging questions in Dunn's work: for a Visitor, they always are, whereas the Legislators of Cities come to the page forearmed with at least one or two absolutes, points to get across. For the poems of outsiders in *The Happier Life*: 'Midweek Matinee', 'The Hunched', 'Under the Stone', Dunn speaks in a disturbing voice, a kind of common middle-class conscience merging indifference and gusts of deep-felt hatred, part satire, part confession:

> You are very bad, you are worse than civilised,
> Untouched by seriousness or possessions,
> Treading the taxpayers' roads, being found
> Incapable in public places, always hungry . . .
>
> If you have a sense of humour, I want to know.
> You claim the right to be miserable
> And I can't stand what you bring out into the open.
> ('Midweek Matinee', *HL*, 35–6)

Open wounds are the ends of so many Dunn poems: 'The River Through the City' (*HL*, 13) ends as no Larkin poem could: loud, unconcluded, with the poet still there: 'That's one old man who's nobody's uncle./ That's one fish you don't want with your chips./ Iron doors bang shut in the sewers.' Openness, raw stinking hurt, it's the poetry of questions, of the unresolved. Decency needs to come balancing to an end. Larkin asks himself questions in his poems, but if they are not resolved, they are so calibrated as to make them almost cancel out. One is left always with the sense that if you look carefully enough it is quite obvious what Larkin thinks, and you would be a fool to disagree. These questions are formal discussions in the chambers of that City: 'Is it that they are born again/ And we grow old? No, they die too' ('The Trees', *HW*, 12). Or:

> Therefore I stay outside,
> Believing this; and they maul to and fro,
> Believing that; and both are satisfied,
> If no one has misjudged himself. Or lied.
> ('Reasons for Attendance', *TLD*, 80)

This is the tone of an English decency, a narrow sense of proportion, measure: to draw to a close, to end with a rhyme, to fulfil the ancient expectations of hope that life is a solvable sum, that its truths have a tune. This is not at all what Larkin's City is or means, but most of its inhabitants just shop where they want to shop. As we see Dunn's career begin gradually to veer away from his first great influence, perhaps it is time to take a short, hard look at that influence, and ask the question that suddenly fits: why is a poet so howlingly dark and frightening, so utterly hope-negating, so fixedly unprepared to enjoy or partake of the very things we associate primarily with the happy life, the worthwhile time, so cherished? What on earth do we think he has in common with us? If we are not all Christians, husbands, lovers, agnostics or happy, surely we are not, to a man, celibate, dimly yearning, insomniac bookish loners believing in nothing but nothing?

What has Larkin to do with decency, in the popular narrow sense? Decent of him to write in rhyme, not smash things up like the other chaps? Decent of him to talk pub-talk? Decent of him to always be explicable, paraphrasable? Decent of him to keep his head down all his life? (One thing not to rock the boat, though, another not even to board it.) One can't help hearing his own words about the decent man, italicised, overturned: '*A decent chap, a real good sort,/ Straight as a die, one of the best,/ A brick, a trump, a proper sport,/ Head and shoulders above the rest;/ How many lives would have been duller/ Had he not been here below?/ Here's to the whitest man I know –/* Though white is not my favourite colour' ('Sympathy in White Major', *HW*, 168).

Larkin's poems are little to do with morality or decency, because he is not the kind of poet who fights towards an answer. He has an answer, and fights to live with it. He is, depending on your attitude to his attitude, beyond decency, or beneath it. Who travels to Larkin's City to know how to live? Who – honestly – wouldn't prefer to at least poke one's head round the door at Warlock-Williams's?[11] You might meet someone. 'They fuck you up, your mum and dad'[12] – do they? 'Life is first boredom, then fear'[13] – not so far, but well, I shall find out. 'Get stewed:/ Books are a load of crap.'[14] Aren't they just? 'Get out as early as you can,/ And don't have any kids yourself.'[15] Well, Larkin at his most camp, perhaps, making light of what is most important, but all those celebrated lines show the same thing, a huge sad ego contemplating the littleness of all else but its own end: the End justifies the Mean, as it were.

I think there are two Larkins: one great, one just superbly skilled. There is a Larkin whose poems disappear infinitely, over the edge of the page, over the garden wall, over the horizon; and one who first draws the black edge, then writes the poem inside. There are places in Larkin where mystery and the infinite blow a great blinding hole in the street. 'Water' (*TWW*, 93) is one, ending with these lines that seem to swallow up many of the poems of misery and mortality, in the process gulping down the old fools who use their chunks of Larkin to lob at lovers of Eliot, Auden, Dylan Thomas . . .

> And I should raise in the east
> A glass of water
> Where any-angled light
> Would congregate endlessly.

The terrible 'priest and the doctor/ In their long coats/ Running over the fields' ('Days', *TWW*, 67) represent another such moment, as do the ghosts of miners at the end of 'The Explosion' (*HW*, 175), who appear

'Larger than in life they managed' walking in the sunlight; there are many other points: the end of 'The Whitsun Weddings', where all the accumulated bountiful detail seems to whirr itself into an arrow-shower through a totality of joy that transcends the melancholy of the passenger; and in 'Dublinesque' (*HW*, 178), where he ends: 'A voice is heard singing/ Of Kitty, or Katy,/ As if the name meant once/ All love, all beauty' and surely realises that at that point that's precisely what it did, does mean. (I mean, what does 'Bleaney' mean?) And there is this: 'Whatever was sown/ Now fully grown,/ Whatever conceived/ Now fully leaved,/ Abounding, ablaze − / O long lion days!' written nine years ago.[16]

But there was an early Larkin on a cliff-edge, a young man who would come to be rejected, who would feel the outer black but had neither name nor answer for it. This strikes me as one of the great poems of a poet early on − that is, *about* a poet early on:

> The northern sky rose high and black
> Over the proud unfruitful sea,
> East and west the ships came back
> Happily or unhappily:
>
> But the third went wide and far
> Into an unforgiving sea
> Under a fire-spilling star,
> And it was rigged for a long journey.
> ('The North Ship: Legend', *TNS*, 302)

There is a sense in which that journey stopped, really in a way that others did not. Larkin's technical gift was apparent certainly by the 1950s, when he was beginning to speak some of his last words on things. Life ends. Things do not come up to expectations. Love fades. Sex is not so hot. Life ends. Perhaps these things have never been said better, not in this century, but blindly to elevate Larkin to greatness on the strength of polish seems likely to open a particularly pearly gate to too many callers.

Give us the ones with Us in them: 'Myxomatosis' (*TLD*, 100), 'To the Sea' (*HW*, 173), 'Sunny Prestatyn' (*TWW*, 149), or the ones that outface magnificently the huge modern falsehoods − 'Essential Beauty' (*TWW*, 144), 'Faith Healing' (*TWW*, 126); not the skilled, manipulative Variations − 'Aubade' (*CP*, 208) (which is the best poem ever written about Larkin being sad and believing nothing), 'Nothing To Be Said' (*TWW*, 138), which has, 'If, My Darling' (*TLD*, 41), which makes the assumption that the girl in question believes the 'I' to be pure as new snow inside − as if anyone thinks that about anyone − or 'Mr

Bleaney' (*TWW*, 102), which leans on words like 'Stoke' and 'Frinton'
to get the thing across – bit of a class-ridden English scam, that. But
better to leave this marvellous poet – during the decade when everyone
has to have a first say – at a moment where he knew what would survive,
or what else, apart from 'Larkin', the 'bastard' we and Balokowsky are
stuck with for an endless semester,[17] would survive:

> the dismantled Show
> Itself dies back into the area of work.
> Let it stay hidden there like strength, below
> Sale-bills and swindling; something people do,
> Not noticing how time's rolling smithy-smoke
> Shadows much greater gestures; something they
> > share
> That breaks ancestrally each year into
> Regenerate union. Let it always be there.
> > ('Show Saturday', *HW*, 199)

Dunn journeys on, restless, Dunn who really is rigged for a long
journey, Dunn whose footprints say at every point – as at the end of the
later 'Remembering Lunch' (*SKP*, 44): *'But where are you going?'* Near the
end of *Love or Nothing*, he prefigures his arrival in the Land of the
Decent, armed: 'Should I take off my glove?/ Should I cry in the streets,
or sail over the rooftops – / Silver Street, Holy Trinity, the Guildhall,
Whitefriargate – / Dropping leaflets?' ('The White Poet', *LN*, 55).

Now he is not the Decent; he is a Barbarian. Like Derek Walcott,
like Tony Harrison, he is well aware of what he looks like among the
Legislators, the white southern anglos of then and now:

> Barbarians in a garden, softness does
> Approve of who we are as it does those
> Who when we speak proclaim us barbarous
> And say we have no business with the rose.
>
> [They are]
> Afraid we'll steal their family's treasured things,
> Then hawk them – pictures, furniture and plate –
> Round the encampments of our saddle-kings.
> > ('In The Grounds', *B*, 15–16)

Here, his Lordship is hanged 'somewhere in [the] shade' of his own
beautifully landscaped property ('Gardeners', *B*), and the out-of-work
apprentice who plays *'God Save the Queen'* on an Edwardian flute/ [is] but
does not know it, destitute' ('Empires', *B*, 26).

Dunn here is finding a tribe to speak among, to speak for, in a sense
that is far from Larkin, who speaks only *of*. 'The Come-on' (*B*, 13–14) is
central to this risen feeling that the narrow path of the done thing, the
decent or civilised, the right way, as it is understood or practised by the
Establishment, is politically, artistically, distorting and oppressive.
Objective realism is suddenly not enough. This is a call to arms against
a system, or complex of interlocking systems: it is extremely
appropriate eleven years on; it is fitting, decent, now:

> To have watched the soul of my people
>   Fingered by the callous
> Enlivens the bitter ooze from my grudge . . .
>   Men dressed in prunella
> Utter credentials and their culture rules us,
>   A culture of connivance . . .
> Our level is the popular, the media,
>   The sensational columns,
> Unless we enter through a narrow gate
>   In a wall they have built
> To join them in the 'disinterested tradition'
>   Of tea, of couplets dipped
> In sherry and the decanted, portentous remark.
>   Therefore, we'll deafen them
> With the dull staccato of our typewriters.

And *Barbarians* and *St Kilda's Parliament* are intensely political books
(which is not at all to confine them: to nail the self-interested lie of the
'disinterested tradition' is nothing if not liberating), from student, 'My
scholarship of barley, secret work/ On which authority must slam its
door/ As Rome on Goth, Byzantium on Turk' ('The Student', *B*, 20) to
shipyard worker: 'They toast that city still to come/ Where truth and
justice meet/ And though they don't know where it is/ It's not on
Clydeside Street' ('Ballad of the Two Left Hands', *B*, 43). The nervous
student, the 'suitably ashamed/ Observer of the poor' ('Second-hand
Clothes', *SKP*, 43) begins to give way to a strident sense of belonging,
or striving to belong: 'Share with me, then, the sad glugs in your
bottles;/ Throw a stolen spud for me on the side embers . . .' ('An
Address on the Destitution of Scotland', *SKP*, 20).

More powerful, perhaps, is to locate such a strong dynamic of
decency – the well-lived life, the response that fits the time – in
ordinary men from as far away as possible, a remote, now uninhabitable
island:

> They are aware of what we are up to
> With our internal explorations, our
> Designs of affluence and education.
> They know us so well, and are not jealous,
> Whose be-all and end-all was an eternal
> Casual husbandry upon a toehold
> Of Europe, which, when failing, was not their fault.
>   ('St Kilda's Parliament 1879–1979', *SKP*, 14)

In the past and passion, history and politics, the 'drunken decency and sober violence' ('The Apple Tree', *SKP*, 16) of Scotland, its having something England doesn't have – a sense of the future being brighter than this, a proud, heartfelt sense, not grey novel lies – Dunn finds touchstones for how to live and how to write, whether in a present disillusionment with fellows in his trade: 'Propping up bars with them I can pretend to be as they are/ Though I no longer know what they are thinking, if ever I did . . .' (Remembering Lunch', *SKP*, 46) or from the lips of 'John Wilson in Greenock, 1786' (*SKP*, 61):

> But know, I worked, and tried,
> And hope still for a small posterity
> And, through a chink in time, to hear men say,
> That, wasting these best talents of my life,
> I fed my children and I loved my wife.

But the next City – *Elegies* – was dark and hard, queries as face-to-face as they get: how to live on with grief, how to act the civilised part, 'running out of vases' ('Thirteen Steps and the Thirteenth of March', *E*, 13), 'closing the door behind me,/ Turning the corner on a wet day in March' ('Arrangements', *E*, 17). Loss forced the poet from the natural movement he was making – out, backwards in history, wide across geography, a movement that would have to wait until *Northlight* – to an abrupt, agonising focus, shattering out of him beautiful poems. There, beyond – 'Why be discreet? A broken heart is what I have – / A pin to burst the bubble of shy poetry' ('The Stories', *E*, 58) – abstractions turn into people, some weapon-parts of poetry are revealed as as cutting as can be:

> Now there is grief the couturier, and grief
> The needlewoman mourning with her hands,
> And grief the scattered finery of life,
> The clothes she gave as keepsakes to her friends.
>   ('Empty Wardrobes', *E*, 29)

Dunn enters 'into the bedroom of the world,/ Discovering the long
night of my life' ('A Summer Night', *E*, 42), and it is where Larkin is
writing 'Aubade', where 'the mind blanks at the glare' — but what he
does next is come out of it, and travel to another place, on a fourth ship,
south . . .

> Erotic gardens promise fruit
> Nurtured from an ancestral root,
> A smile, and the clematis flowers.
> A few weeks more and south is ours!
>   ('75°', *N*, 17)

> Here, everywhere, forethought and afterthought,
> Nowhere and nothing's what I think I see,
>
> Or what I thought I thought, or saw, no if
> Or but about it, just the world I'm in.
> My heart beats back and forth across a life
> Bearing its spoon of blood like medicine.
>   ('Maggie's Corner', *N*, 54)

> Here on imagination's waterfronts
> It's even simpler: fidelity directs
> Love to its place, the eye to what it sees
> And who we live with, and the *whys* and *whens*
> That follow *ifs* and *buts*, as, on our knees,
> We hope for spirit and intelligence.
>   ('Here and There', *N*, 27)

And of course what you feel is how to live depends on how you live, but
Dunn's sheer flight from agony to *Elegies* to the verve and expanse and
joy of *Northlight* seems to be the most decent of all possible responses to
life, if one thinks that to be decent is to do the best by the life you got,
or if one thinks life worth loving or time worth having.

NOTES

1 For Larkin's collections I have, both in the body of the text and in the
   notes, followed those abbreviations employed by Anthony Thwaite in
   the *Collected Poems*, i.e.: *CP*: *Collected Poems* ed. Anthony Thwaite
   (Faber, 1988). *HW*: *High Windows* (Faber, 1974). *TLD*: *The Less
   Deceived* (The Marvell Press, 1955). *TNS*: *The North Ship* (The
   Fortune Press, 1945; Faber, 1966). *TWW*: *The Whitsun Weddings*
   (Faber, 1964). All page references are to these volumes as reprinted
   in *CP*.
2 Douglas Dunn, *Under the Influence*: Douglas Dunn on Philip Larkin
   (Edinburgh University Library, 1987), 11.

3 Ibid., 1.
4 Philip Larkin, 'After-Dinner Remarks', composed 'before June 1940', *CP*, 241.
5 Philip Larkin, 'Summer Nocturne', (first published in *The Coventrian*, April 1939), *CP*, 227.
6 Dunn, *Under the Influence*, 3.
7 Ibid., 9.
8 Ibid., 2.
9 Ibid., 11.
10 Ibid., 10.
11 Larkin, 'Vers de Société', *HW*, 181.
12 Larkin, 'This Be The Verse', *HW*, 180.
13 Larkin, 'Dockery and Son', *TWW*, 152.
14 Larkin, 'A Study of Reading Habits', *TWW*, 131.
15 Larkin, 'This Be The Verse', *HW*, 180.
16 Larkin, '"Long lion days"' composed July 1982, *CP*, 219.
17 Larkin, 'Posterity', *HW*. 170.

Five

Dunn and Politics

Sean O'Brien

This bald title might suggest — though I hope it won't — a mechanical taxonomy of Douglas Dunn's 'position' as revealed in his poems and other writings. Developments in attitude can be seen and have their place, but to think exclusively along such lines would satisfy only those inclined to deny that poetry is as political as anything else. The extraction of 'attitudes' can imply that these are externally imposed on the imagination by concerns whose proper expression belongs elsewhere — in essays and polemic — rather than in poetry; and there has been an element in the critical reception of Dunn's work which has done as much — talk of chips on shoulders and a lyrical talent under threat from ideology. I hope that what follows will indicate that such views are mistaken, and that it will do so by going some way to evoke Dunn's embracing sense of what constitutes the political.

The task is complicated by Dunn's own ambivalence towards politics, in particular towards ideology, which he appears to view as synonymous with dogma, something to be avoided by intelligence and scruple, rather than as the very climate of human affairs. This is a vexed area, and Dunn is not a political theorist, although, for instance, he is clearly versed in Marxism. In general, the evidence of his writing indicates a basic adherence to an Old Left social democratic view, at once cooperative and libertarian. There have been intervals of more radical opinion, and his concern for the nationhood of Scotland has become more evident in recent years. The merits of this 'anarchy of convictions' are, of course, debatable, but whatever Dunn's resistance to its compulsion, politics — how we are governed, how power touches us — is manifestly endemic to his work.

The work itself reveals a developing vision of the intimacy of all the varieties of experience with which it deals – among them the social life, history, art and language itself. This vision – humane, tolerant, inclusive – is the product of an interior struggle which may seem to be waged between the claims of the imagination and those of social responsibility but is in fact an attempt to resolve these allegedly competing forces. The separation of realms, which Dunn has parodically characterised as 'Social Realism' and 'Romantic Sleep'.[1] is – on the repeated evidence of his work – imaginatively unsustainable. His primary subject is people, and the facts of their lives and the larger energies which shape them will not allow his art to prefer a partial reality. Much of the strength of his work, it seems to me, emerges from this scrupulous conflict.

Terry Street, like *The Whitsun Weddings* or *The Snow Party*, now seems to have been there all the time, like the weather, which begs the question of where it came from. In 1969 it would have been easy to see it as a late variant on Movement practices; but its prehistory is more complex and instructive than this might suggest. Dunn seems to have found little to go on in Scottish poetry in English, and the fact of writing in English may have set him apart from the possibly intimidating example of MacDiarmid. In the period of *Terry Street*'s composition, the most prominent English poets were Ted Hughes and Philip Larkin. Hughes has rarely shown much interest in everyday urban life; and although Dunn has acknowledged Larkin's presence in the book (while noting the greater difficulty of keeping out Baudelaire and Laforgue),[2] Larkin's elegiac habit overrides any interest he might have in class or the actual details of the ordinary lives of working people: by temperament and status he is an external observer, whatever his sympathies. Looking further back, Dunn's response to Auden has been ambivalent,[3] though he has recorded an early enthusiasm for MacNeice.[4] In writing about the city, any anglophone poet will be touched by Eliot, and hence by Baudelaire, whom Dunn read attentively in the Sixties.[5] But if we look for Dunn's sympathies among more nearly contemporary poets, they will be found first of all in the United States – in the public forms of Lowell and Randall Jarrell, but also – and most interestingly for Dunn's early work – in the now less immediately obvious example of James Wright (*Viewpoints*, 13).[6] Lowell's influence is manifest in Dunn's work after *Terry Street* (perhaps most obviously in 'The Wealth' from *Barbarians*) and he remains an exemplary poet for him, as (at the level of temperament) does Jarrell; indeed the ambition and seriousness of the poets of Lowell's generation are his gold standard.

This openness to 'foreign poetry' is, of course, by no means unique in Dunn's generation of poets writing in Britain, but in his case it illuminates 'The Grudge', the editorial he wrote in *Stand* in the mid-Seventies, in which he commented on the position of the working-class writer:

> in the effort to secure a connection between poetics and the politics of his class — one that will be meaningful for him — he can take nothing for granted. He has next to nothing to lean back on, no assurances, no literary certainties, no literary mother or father.[7]

One advantage of this condition may be — and in Dunn's case certainly is — an avoidance of provincialism. The appeal of a patrician poet like Lowell becomes clearer, for instance, when we see that Dunn is having, in effect, to invent a context of technique and example for himself. Being, in the words of 'The Come-on', allegedly 'of the wrong world', he lays his own claim to the methods used by the 'right' one. His work is political in order to accomplish itself in the first place.

By now it would be hard to view *Terry Street* as simply 'realistic', a depiction of surfaces offered by a poet, according to one reviewer, 'like a Disney cameraman parked up a palm tree with his head disguised as a coconut, [who] has shot the stuff and got it out'.[8] It would be equally hard to agree with Neil Powell's description of Dunn as 'one of a number of provincial poets . . . whose main concern is descriptive poetry', which Powell finds accurate but 'flat and without the essential enlivening intellectual impetus'.[9] Dunn might wish he had not bothered to publish 'Winter', unfavourably cited by Powell and parodied elsewhere,[10] but the Terry Street poems as a whole bear out his irritated comment that they 'were never intended as "scenes from working-class life"', to which he added that the reason some critics saw them as such 'may be that they had never been in such a street, never mind lived in one'.[11] As Terry Eagleton remarked, 'Dunn can transcend the two major pitfalls of poetry concerned with working people — bourgeois voyeurism or sympathetic mythification.'[12] Part of Dunn's success arises from the friction between his own ambiguous status in the street — as a foreigner, an intellectual, someone for whom this is not the end of the road, who 'will be reading books elsewhere' — and the original common ground of class which makes the street knowable to him and, as he later commented, a 'surrogate' of his own native place (*Viewpoints*, 16). The combination of strangeness and familiarity, intimacy and distance, results in a troubling and unsentimental exposure of the imagination to a state of sterile constraint. The manners and rituals of the street might seem to speak for a convincing if draughty domesticity, but they mean desolation, a place by day like a 'dried-up river bed' (*TS*,

14) which after dark 'rattles with nightmares' (*TS*, 22). Though Dunn
has pointed out that he fictionalised the place, letting it work on his
imagination and *vice versa*, there is an argument (albeit ultimately
unfavourable to the imagination) that he presumes too much. Peter
Porter, later an appreciative critic of Dunn, detected a patronising
assumption 'that all these livers of circumscribed lives are helplessly
hoping for romantic expansion'[13]; but this is to neglect the exactitude
with which Dunn grasps his relation to his subject. The street is not a
moral convenience for the projection of pity, but somewhere lived in
which has its own inward effects. 'New Light on Terry Street' ends:

> there is no unrest. The dust is so fine.
> You hardly notice you have grown too old to cry out for change.
>
> (*TS*, 14)

'You' is not simply the second person but the demotic equivalent of
'one, and it appeals to the commonality of experience. Here it signals an
appalled recognition of the secret success of demoralisation, a matter to
which Dunn returns with a more personal inflection in the later 'Rough-
cast', from *Barbarians*, a poem apparently about his home village:

> Hearts, houses, do not fit
> In this sweet place of stuntedness.
> Twelve years away and I cannot
> Break out. I cannot do it.
>
> (*B*, 23–4)

This sense, neither deracinated nor at home, of lives pre-emptively
shrivelled, is hardly wishful or presumptuous. The final poem, 'A
Window Affair', is an act of self-preservation. Faced with the street's
infectious debility, Dunn reveals his own exhaustion, a state 'which
does not want to love, and does not care' (*TS*, 34). It might have been
with this in mind that in his later essay on Jarrell, Dunn commented,
'sympathy is not all that unselfish'.[14] The poems are dramatic rather
than schematised, discoveries rather than prescriptions. Intimacy and
isolation coexist, opening the imaginative space on the other side of
'descriptive' realism, and it is here that Dunn's kinship with James
Wright becomes apparent. Wright's poems of the American Midwest
move freely between realism and a condensed, peremptory, interior
reformulation prompted by symbolism and surrealism. There are
striking resemblances between the two poets' work. Wright's 'Miners',
for example, where 'The police are dragging for the bodies/ Of miners in
the black waters/ Of the suburbs'[15] may stand behind the subterranean
imagery of 'Sunday Morning Among the Houses of Terry Street' (*TS*,

23) (and, more distantly, 'The River Through the City' in *The Happier Life* (*HL*, 13)). 'Autumn Begins in Martins Ferry, Ohio'[16] or the dreamlike lunar economy of 'Having Lost My Sons, I Confront the Wreckage of the Moon: Christmas, 1960'[17] (as well, perhaps, as the example of Louis Simpson) may be glimpsed in 'From the Night-Window', where young women coming home 'trot like small horses/ And disappear into white beds/ At the edge of the night' (*TS*, 22). Wright and Dunn both came from the working class; they came late and with great seriousness to study; and a conflicted sense of their origins is central to their vocation. In his memoir of Wright, Donald Hall records that Wright felt 'the desire to make in art an alternative and improved universe. If he reviled his Ohio, he understood that Ohio made him and Ohio remained his material.'[18] Dunn reviles places and causes, not their victims, but a similar tension is maintained in his work between the 'ideal communities' (*TS*, 30) which the night suggests and the one present in the street. The contrast is inescapably political, and the most radical feature of Dunn' early work is its disclosure of the psyche of Britain's 'bad address' (*TS*, 31), not the state of its pavements.

Dunn's concentration on passivity – what people have done to them – takes the place of an explicitly political vocabulary at this stage. There are the people in the street and beyond it a vague elsewhere from which institutional and commercial powers arrive to exert their effects. George Charlton has pointed out that in this respect Dunn bears more resemblance to Orwell than Larkin,[19] but while Winston Smith may infer hope from the proletariat, the idea of the future has little purchase on Terry Street, which is a continuous present, an 'urban silence' which tells its 'lost tribe' that 'They have nothing to do with where they live' (*TS*, 32).

Dunn would not normally expect to be quoted by Margaret Thatcher, but his comment that it would be irresponsible to 'accept' British society because 'for a start, I don't believe it exists' (*OxPoe*, 46) at any rate predates her more famous utterance, though the speakers mean rather different things. He has commented that in 'The Silences' (*TS*, 32) he had in mind Britain as a whole (*Viewpoints*, 15–16): the street's particular isolation stands, paradoxically, for all the other instances. *The Happier Life* casts the net wider, to inspect a society so atomised as hardly to merit the name. Much of the best of the book is a poetry of dead ends and disconnections whose causes are sensed but invisible, like the factory over the hill in 'Emblems' (*HL*, 40) – 'a big fish without eyes' (another Wrightian instance). The strongest poems make no effort to be 'representative': what lies at the edge or the bottom is held to expose society's essential nature, which is itself a negative. Something has produced these conditions and their occupants, the drunks 'who are not good at life' (*HL*, 35), the 'radically nervous' (*HL*, 21) drawn inarticulately to fascism, the 'army of unkept appointments' (*HL*, 53) who embody 'the bad meanings we are'. The language is characteristically both plain and startling. Again, Dunn is pushing beyond a ready liberalism towards what brings its hopes in question – the experience of radical doubt which, he implies, is essential to seriousness. Those under the stone 'mean nothing' (*HL*, 53), as though 'nothing' were an active presence. A central poem is 'The Hunched' (*HL*, 38), crowded with people who 'all came back' to mind, but concluding: 'not one of them has anything at all to do with me'. This provoked the complaint from one reviewer that 'The last line is obviously begging the question, both as an intellectual conclusion, and in tone. Even if the emphatic negatives are meant ironically, their implications are inadequate to their theme.'[20] On the contrary, the comment is inadequate to the poem, faulting it for failing to meet an expectation about which it is in fact far from complacent. As in *Terry Street*, Dunn works towards an exposure of the imagination at a level where the explanatory categories – need, deprivation, inadequacy and so on – lose their power to draw the sting. This involves a kind of imaginative double-take, in which 'actual circumstances' insistently re-present themselves. It's a more difficult course than a declaration of predigested solidarity – indeed, such a declaration would be implausible for a writer who has been '*in* the *boue*' (*Viewpoints*, 22) – and in fact *The Happier Life* shows Dunn feeling the pull of quietism, summed up in the line 'The only answer is to live quietly, miles away' (*HL*, 33). Dunn has disowned the latter attitude, and *Love or Nothing* shows how and why.

Love or Nothing is an eclectic book. Its variety can be seen to grow from the poems placed at the end of *The Happier Life*. It pursues their self-consciously 'literary' approach, both in tone and by taking artistic problems for some of its subjects. It is also the book in which the struggle between aesthetics and politics (as these are vulgarly construed) is most apparent. Dunn is visibly struggling to make room to breathe, in subject (the fictive 'The House Next Door' (*LN*, 8), 'Little Rich Rhapsody' (*LN*, 7) and 'A Lost Woman' (*LN*, 46), for instance); in implied commentaries on art and his place in it ('Realisms' (*LN*, 19), 'The White Poet' (*LN*, 52); and in a formal restlessness which implies that he doesn't know his own mind. Yet within this disorder a constellation of themes (and to some extent of forms, in 'Clydesiders' (*LN*, 37), and 'Sailing with the Fleet' (*LN*, 36), for instance) can be seen emerging, leading on to *Barbarians*. They involve a placing of the self in history, by autobiography (as in 'Boys With Coats' (*LN*, 35), 'White

Fields' (*LN*, 32) and 'The Competition' (*LN*, 34) as well as a more elaborate mixture of meditation and fantasy ('Renfrewshire Traveller' (*LN*, 22)) and, at the close of the book, dry runs for the 'Barbarian Pastorals' (*B*, 13–30) in 'The Estuarial Republic' (*LN*, 61) and 'The Disguise' (*LN*, 63). The last of these is a statement of policy:

> I *am* smiling, and against you.
> There is an invective of grins, winks, fingers,
> Up the sleeves of galactic offspring.
> Through your trash go their impertinent smiles,
> Hidden by glum masks, the finest insult.

Nowadays the reader may wonder why Dunn had not openly formulated the problem (of race, class, status) and announced the grudge earlier. This is to beg the question of where a political poetry was to come *from* — something that needs to be borne in mind when the work of Dunn, Tony Harrison and others now makes such a poetry appear a necessary and inevitable feature of the contemporary. The sidelong hostility of 'The Malediction' (*LN*, 60) (ostensibly about longing for snow) and the rather willed savagery of 'The Estuarial Republic' can demonstrate the difficulty of naming what was always there — as, in a different way, do the modest, deliberately naïve childhood narratives of the more explicitly autobiographical poems. The baldness of the latter seems disempowered, while the constraint of the former suggests a degree of self-hatred which is also present in the clotted, disrupted logic of 'Renfrewshire Traveller' (*LN*, 22). These difficulties have a commentary of their own in 'Restraint' (*LN*, 58), where Dunn writes of the 'interior animal' that

> A long course in freedom
> Hurts it. It cries out
> And makes you tell lies.

One of the lessons of bourgeois culture is embarrassment – the pain and shame, for example, of the imagination faced with an alleged contradiction between its loyalties and what its aspirations seem to entail. These poems struggle to unlearn embarrassment, and they foreshadow the insistence of *Barbarians* that there is no choice to be made between loyalty and literature.

In 'The Come-on', which opens *Barbarians*, Dunn writes that in the face of class and racial prejudice 'Enchanting, beloved texts,/ Searched in for a generous mandate for/ Believing who I am,/ What I have lived and felt, might just as well/ Not exist.' Formerly, by implication, Dunn may have included himself in a univalent literature governed by a seriousness which was held to override divisions of race, class and politics. This consensual view had roots in both the apparently liberal orthodoxy of the study of English – itself a part of the allegedly 'disinterested tradition' – during Dunn's youth, and in the high-cultural internationalism of some of his literary models, those 'enchanting, beloved texts'. The fury of 'The Come-on' is that of a man and poet who finds that the allowances he has been making receive no reciprocal respect: a working-class writer may join the establishment through the 'narrow gate/ In a wall they have built', but at the cost of deracination and the continued exclusion of his own people. 'The Come-on' states openly that the practice and interpretation of literature is a site, like all others, of political conflict. Precisely what is involved is made clearer by Dunn's critical writing in the 1970s. The argument of 'The Come-on' does not concern a working-class writer's search for *acceptance*, as the bourgeois critic may suppose; instead it insists that the health of the imagination will only be served by a willingness to 'admit generosity, modify the centuries of privilege and exclusiveness upon which was erected the culture of some, and not of the many'.[21] Writing on Donald Davie and Charles Tomlinson, Dunn comments, 'when both poets touch upon definable realities, they become as "middlebrow" as Tomlinson has described Larkin. It gives me immense pleasure to say so.'[22] Of Roy Fuller he states: 'bleating about the bush in the accents of the Tory backbench . . . misrepresent[s] his politics. It is not a concern for culture . . . but a suburban ethos too much loved. He forgets that what for him is an aggravated serenity is used by the suburban classes as a source of . . . attitudinising aimed at those less complacently comfortable in this "island life"; and that process is here called "politics".'[23] The establishment is impoverished by its exclusions, and its version of seriousness is ultimately parochial: as Dunn stated elsewhere, 'How can a society exist when it's not supported by a culture?' (*OxPoe*, 46).

What prompted *Barbarians* is not explicit; but perhaps it is easier now than in 1979 to understand the book's plainness. It was firmly missed by some reviewers. Anne Stevenson, for example, read the 'expository' Barbarian Pastorals as 'warnings to himself and his friends rising on the social ladder',[24] while Edna Longley accused Dunn of choosing 'soft and well-riddled targets' and detected only occasional evidence of 'a lyrical talent waving above the ideological compulsions which threaten to submerge it.'[25] Thus liberalism. These are instructive comments. They reveal, for one thing, the Byzantine impenetrability of our class system for foreigners. Further, in Stevenson's case we see a familiar tendency to isolate the political in the personal, and in

Longley's a strange innocence about the course of history and the
efficacy of literature. Their examples illustrate Dunn's cultural
contention (i.e. that there isn't a culture), as well as the familiar
problem of the supposed centre – that it can't accommodate, or for that
matter even *recognise* realities other than its own (though to her credit, in
the same review, Longley acknowledges that 'P.J. Kavanagh's *Life Before
Death* opts so overwhelmingly for personal reverie as to make barbarism
more appealing').

Neither critic can make much of the book's historical dimension.
Dunn uses history strategically, in the service of reclamation, writing,
in effect, a history of the grudge in a series of inversions of pastoral. He
looks back to Rome, to Loamshire in 1789 and Scotland in 1820, and
he places the present in its history. A number of the poems brandish
their formality as an affront, a deliberate breaching of the 'wall'. Both
metaphor and memory, the wall is inextricably bound up with art, as
'The Grudge' indicates. It begins as the wall the poet was ordered not to
sit on as a child:

> Poetry is like that wall. There are people who think they own
> poetry. They think poetry 'serves' *them*. It doesn't; and when it
> does it is being exclusive and partial. So I have a grudge. My
> grudge is a good grudge. I can even take it out myself and sing to
> it . . .[26]

If anything, time has strengthened the claims of *Barbarians* by
demonstrating the persistence, the aggressive renewal, of what the book
opposes. In the dawn of Thatcherism, the grudge might have seemed
peculiar in its intensity, but from the perspective of late 1991, it was
clearly prophetic, as the close of 'Empires' demonstrates:

> They ruined us. They conquered continents.
> We filled their uniforms. We cruised the seas.
> We worked their mines and made their histories.
> *You work, we rule*, they said. We worked; they ruled.
> They fooled the tenements. All men were fooled.
> It still persists. It will be so, always.
> Listen. An out-of-work apprentice plays
> *God Save the Queen* on an Edwardian flute.
> He is, but does not know it, destitute.
>
> (*B*, 26)

This brilliant pessimism is as characteristic as the trenchant advocacy of
Dunn's criticism or the exultant prophecy which closes 'The Come-on'.
Barbarians rests on paradoxes. As Dunn wrote in another context, 'if
poetry offers little or nothing in the way of *praxis* . . . there is some

point in pretending that it can, for the sake of poetry and the life it expresses. To acknowledge oneself as ineffective is to eat the most terrible food of all; it is to eat your own heart. To acknowledge poetry in the same way is to commit a sin against the Holy Ghost. It is perverse, and bad.'[27] The book is an assertion couched largely in negatives. It sets straight a record whose distortions were accompanied by acts it cannot alter. It seems at times like language longing to be action; but Dunn's 'utterly civilian' disposition would forbid him the politics which might affect transformation. The 'routine sadness' he ascribes to himself in 'Stranger's Grief' (*B*, 52), his elegy for Lowell, has an historical as well as a temperamental justification. For 'the inhabitants of opposition' ('Realisms', *LN*, 20), history is 'a thousand stabs in the back'; and as Dunn commented (some years before *Barbarians*) in a discussion of Heaney, 'poetry is the perpetual lost cause, a multiracial confederacy, a republican Jacobitism'.[28] It will, proverbially now, make nothing happen, though it can imagine, in Empson's words, 'what could not possibly be there' and be the pacific equivalent of Keith Douglas's 'fight without hope'. In short, *Barbarians* makes a success of its own necessary failure.

The last poem in *Barbarians*, 'The Return', takes a walk along the now-derelict Terry Street, considering the pull of Dunn's 'anarchy of convictions' and the domestic scale out of which both eloquence and alienation grew. It suggests the potential and the obligation of poetry to refresh its capacity 'to speak of the world "as it should be" from a knowledge of the world as it is.'[29] This debate expands itself into a return, both actual and imaginative, to origins and community. The title poem of *The Happier Life* proposes and swiftly dismantles an 'uncompetitive' rural idyll dreamed up by a figure described elsewhere as 'Horace with a view/ Of the gasworks' (*HL*, 58): in *St Kilda's Parliament*, Dunn reconsiders the matter in the light of knowledge, and of Scotland. While Scotland has figured throughout his work, this is the book where it becomes the poems' primary site. As might have been expected, it is imagined as pre- and post-industrial. It is also some ways post- or extra-historical (not to mention being intermittently prelapsarian), a state of ending up which speaks for both 'destitution' (*SKP*, 19) and possibility, things as they are and the ideal community glimpsed in the title poem. The photographer looking back to St Kilda after its abandonment is at once imaginatively convinced that a people who look 'like everybody's ancestors' succeeded in their lives of 'Casual husbandry upon a toehold/ Of Europe' (*SKP*, 14) and at the same time sceptical of his perceptions: 'But who,/ At this late stage, could tell . . ?' (*SKP*, 15). 'The Harp of Renfrewshire' does similar work, negotiating between

imagination and a possible past, feeling both its remoteness and its
value as an aspiration:

> And on my map is neither wall nor fence,
> But men and women and their revenue,
> As, watching them, I utter into silence
> A granary of whispers rinsed in dew.
>
> (*SKP*, 30)

The position of all the Scottish-based work here is complex, a
simultaneous yes, no and perhaps. It must evade nostalgia while
walking ground habitually claimed by it – a fact reflected in the book's
tonal range. Dunn is drawing a fine line between directness and
sentiment – not always successfully, as though unconvinced that his
lavish particularity and formal *brio* will adequately dramatise feeling. At
times (in 'The Harp of Renfrewshire' and 'Witch-girl' (*SKP*, 22), for
example), we are in the presence of a sincerity whose scrupulous self-
education places its ultimate confidence in doubt. It's a risk Dunn has
shown himself aware of (*Viewpoints*, 18: *PD*, 30), and the most striking
moments in these poems make room for a liberating detachment, as in
'An Address on the Destitution of Scotland':

> Throw a stolen spud for me on the side-embers.
> Allow me to pull up a brick, to sit beside you
> In this nocturne of modernity . . .
>
> (*SKP*, 20)

The same bleak humour, a healthy stone's throw from the religiose, can
also be found in 'Dominies' (*SKP*, 21). There is, inevitably, a dissatisfaction underlying Dunn's efforts to suggest, albeit in a highly
specialised and qualified way, an image of community. When was it last
a plausible task for poetry to do so? Modernity is, anyway, citified, and
poetically it begins with Baudelaire. It is with his successor, Rimbaud,
that Dunn walks 'the changed fields of Inchinnan' among the JCBs in
'The Miniature Metro' (*SKP*, 77), allowing Rimbaud the good lines, for
example on the pen's relation to the plough:

> Dig with it? Tell that man he's better off
> With his pen in his ear or up his arse.

'Very well, I contradict myself,' Dunn might be saying. There is a
longing for *something* on which to ground his decency. Here, as
elsewhere, the interior debate proceeds, as his attempt to marry what
seems at times like pre-political quietism with a sense of community in
origins is outfaced by his intelligence. An agrarian world, for example,

means day-labour and poverty: 'Washing the Coins' (*SKP*, 24), with its memory of his own muddied reduction to the status of the nomadic Irish howkers, and his realisation that such distinctions of status go unrecognised by the imperial Crown for whose coins he laboured, has to be read alongside 'The Harp of Renfrewshire'. Dunn's recurrent sense of obligation to 'the real world' (not to be confused with the lies and delusions of 'common sense') is admirable: it continues to subvert his every effort to escape it. As he states in 'Second-hand Clothes', 'there's nothing to be done/ Save follow the lost shoes' (*SKP*, 43).

In 1978, Dunn wrote of Derek Mahon that 'perseverance with a social idea of poetry may have saved [him] from allowing his imagination to lose itself in the eternal and irrelevant. Instead, he has managed to form a poetic which tries realist *and* metaphysical manners, and which, in opposition to narrower poetries, tries to *include*.'[30] Dunn could hardly be unaware of the dialectical nature of this process; in some ways his work reveals it more clearly than Mahon's. 'Metaphysical' might not immediately seem a word applicable to Dunn's work, given its constant return to the material circumstances, but there are traces of it from 'Cosmologist' (*TS*, 62) onwards; and in 'Loch Music' (*SKP*, 79), for example, there is an almost Wordsworthian sense that meaning inheres in the non-human, which in turn responds to the imagination. Something of this is also arguably at work in *Elegies*. Dunn is understandably cagey about the status of the perceptions involved (*PD*, 27–8) and more concerned with what they offer the imagination than with epistemology, but the 'personal extreme' of 'Loch Music', for instance, is in itself a romantic criticism of the material desert confronted elsewhere in his work. Like the surrealist-influenced narratives of Dunn's 'Homage to Robert Desnos' (*SKP*, 72) and the feeling for mysterious coherence shared with James Wright, it *makes room*.

At no point could Dunn be accounted an unsophisticated poet. He is (*pace* Neil Powell) a stylist from the outset; but the developments occurring between *Barbarians* and *Europa's Lover*, when his formal aggression converts itself into luxuriance, are striking even by his standards, as he possesses and reimagines a vast swathe of history in the name of egalitarian and pacific civility. *Europa's Lover* is perhaps a neglected eminence in his work: it is a remarkable effort to marry *ought* with *is*. Significantly, this tropical profusion of world-historical invention accompanies Dunn's discovery of a way to write about Scotland.

Back on home ground in his more recent book, *Northlight*, the same lushness and relish are impressively in play. But they are balanced by what I would argue are the most interesting poems in the book – 'The Dark Crossroads' (N, 62) and 'Adventure's Oafs' (N, 80). These deal with occasions when the atlas of possibilities imagined from Scotland is unacknowledged. Dunn, describing himself as 'an uppity Jock without valour' (N, 63), contemplates, guiltily, regretfully, a notional revenge against the English saloon-bar moron whose 'fossilised, sinister gaiety' (N, 63) means exactly what it seems to threaten. Meanwhile the voice of 'Occult history' announces, 'You're colonised! Maybe you didn't know' (N, 81). Since *Northlight*, the political crisis arising from the poll tax has led Dunn into polemic as well as poetry. His *Counterblast* pamphlet, *Poll Tax: The Fiscal Fake* (1990), places itself firmly in a dissenting tradition. Prefacing the text with quotations from Milton and Orwell, Dunn delivers a magnificently scornful and exact denunciation of the way in which the New Right in Britain has deliberately infringed democratic principle in the effort to make itself unassailable as 'Government . . . of the Government, by the Government and for the Government' (PT, 30). The problem with Britain, from the Thatcherite viewpoint, is that it 'cost[s] too much. The country would have to get cheaper before the Government could take it seriously and treat it with respect' (PT, 24). The concentration of governmental assault on Scotland in the first place – a fact not widely grasped or even noticed in England – is evidence for his long-standing conviction that what is at stake is democracy. In a climate as virulently opposed to serious public debate as the Thatcher years, it was always unlikely that Dunn's acceptance of civic duty would be seen as such, but the pamphlet is, among other things, an effort to carry debate into the public realm: which is to say, it's as serious as all his other work. Politics may be a series of misfortunes, but in his view it's no more escapable than art. Looking back now on Dunn's work to date, we can chart the course of an imaginative struggle often brilliantly conducted, a campaign of reclamation and a bringing-to-light, the result of which is a form of public poetry whose scope and invention have few equals in the postwar period. We can wait for Dunn's new poems with the excited sense that it is most unlikely that the grudge will let either him or history sleep.

NOTES

1 Quoted by Anthony Thwaite in 'Allegiance to the Clyde', *Times Literary Supplement*, 2 October 1981. p. 1125.

2 F.G. Charlton, *Inalienable Perspectives: Douglas Dunn's Poetry 1963–83*, MA thesis, Newcastle University, 1984, p. 2.

3 See for example, Dunn's comments on Auden in 'Moral Dandies', *Encounter*, March 1973, p. 66 and in *PD*, 16.

4 In conversation with the author, September 1991.

5 Ibid.
6 Dunn has also commented, in conversation with the author, that he was introduced to Wright's work in 1962 by the poet Christopher Wiseman.
7 Editorial: 'The Grudge', *Stand*, Vol. 16, No 2 (no date), p. 5.
8 Clive James, 'Adding up the Detail', *Times Literary Supplement*, 20 November 1969, p. 1330.
9 Neil Powell, *Carpenters of Light* (Manchester, Carcanet, 1979), 128–9.
10 Teddy Hogge, *Expostulations* and Alec Pope, *The Wooden Muse* (London, 1970) p. 13, cited by Donald Davie in *Thomas Hardy and British Poetry* (London, Routledge and Kegan Paul, 1973) 48–9.
11 Quoted in P.R. King, *Nine Contemporary Poets* (London, Methuen, 1979), 221.
12 'New Poetry', *Stand*, Vol. 11, No 2, 1970, pp. 70–1.
13 Peter Porter, 'Faber and Faber Ltd.', *London Magazine*, October 1969, p. 86.
14 'An Affable Misery', *Encounter*, October 1972, p. 43.
15 James Wright, *Above the River: The Complete Poems* (Farrar, Straus and Giroux and the University of New England Press, New York (?) 1990), p. 126. This poem and the others referred to here all appeared in Wright's 1963 collection *The Branch Will Not Break*.
16 Ibid., p. 121.
17 Ibid., p. 139.
18 'Lament for a Maker', introduction to *Above the River*, xxv–xxvi.
19 Charlton, op. cit., p. 99.
20 Anne Cluysenaar, 'Reviews', *Stand*, Vol. 14, No 1, 1972, p. 87.
21 'Redundant Elegance', *Encounter*, March 1975, p. 87.
22 Ibid.
23 'Make it Old', *Encounter*, March 1976, p. 78.
24 'Poems, Dressed and Undressed', *The Listener*, 11 August 1979, p. 220.
25 'Catching Up – Poetry 1: The British', *Times Literary Supplement*, 18 January 1980, pp. 64–5.
26 *Stand*, Vol. 16, No. 4, p. 6.
27 'Make it Old', *Encounter*, May 1976, p. 77.
28 'The Speckled Hill, the Plover's Shore', *Encounter*, December 1973, p. 70.
29 Ibid., p. 76.
30 'Let the God Not Abandon Us: On the Poetry of Derek Mahon', *Stone Ferry Review*, No 2, Winter 1978, p. 10.

I am indebted to George Charlton for his help in providing bibliographical information and for the stimulus of his own writing on Dunn.

Six

Them and Uz: Douglas Dunn's Technique

Dave Smith

'I can certainly get pissed off by being referred to as Hull's "other poet"'
(*Viewpoints*, 14) Douglas Dunn told interviewer John Haffenden in
1981. A decade ago he was speaking of life and art viewed from under
the wingspread of the inimitable Philip Larkin, who had befriended
Dunn at the University of Hull. Not long ago I asked Paul Muldoon a
question about Seamus Heaney, often considered Muldoon's mentor,
and the response was altogether crisp. Poets, like sons, seldom wish to
be viewed as imitative offspring. If Douglas Dunn's poetic voice,
summed up in the pallid word *technique*, is shadowed by Philip Larkin,
that is hardly Dunn's whole story.

Nevertheless, that Larkin's style seems inescapable as a source of
Dunn's voice, Dunn himself wittily testifies in his 1987 lecture *Under
the Influence: Douglas Dunn on Philip Larkin*.[1] Dunn speaks of making his
own poems as a 'blurred xerox' of Larkin. In his older colleague's work,
Dunn found the contemporary world squeezed into a scrubbed language
with the pressured, quirky feel of human personality. Larkin's
'wonderful, panoptic, sentient, subjective realism' is surely obvious in
the early poems of *Terry Street*.

For an American reader, Dunn's choice to write a book about that
slum street in Hull already separates him from Larkin. 'I identify with
small towns and villages in Scotland,' Dunn told the *Printer's Devil*
interviewer (*PD*, 30) in 1990, a slyly understated declaration of his
poet's emblem. Larkin's world is a room, a view on the fringe of
looming Metropolitan City. Aware of the sin and mortality the City
must hold, he is drawn in passion and repelled in wisdom. Despite
occasional affirmations of the natural world, Larkin's strength does not
issue from new revelations of old grace. His power lies in the humour

and the clear forthrightness with which he, one man imaginatively adrift in those streets, confronts chimeras. Larkin's poems, in contrast to Dunn's, seem unlocated.

Dunn says of Larkin – it is almost his initial remark – 'I was never enamoured of Larkin's politics; certainly, he was impatient with mine.'[2] Yet Douglas Dunn's poems bear no political platform and his self-depiction as a leftist of the spirit is rather more yearning than card-carrying fact. From the first, Dunn's scheme has been a regionalist sensibility which affirmed the abundant, vegetative, civilian and permanent spirit whose values, though eclipsed by the waywardness of the City, might yet through appropriate song be persuaded to renew us. Seamus Heaney, in so many ways the exact counterpart of Dunn, has called himself a 'venerator', and this names the non-denominational spirit in Dunn, if it misses the social bite of his anger.

Douglas Dunn has been fascinated with issues of status, especially with the regionalist's sense of inferiority, and he has dramatised the tale of man disempowered and disenfranchised: an orphan of spirit. He asks to whom we most belong and why contemporary questions are provoked by historical discontinuity, a rupture which for poets is paralleled by uncertain form and experimentation. Dunn remarks, most significantly I think, that Larkin taught him the meaning of 'restraint and candour'.[3] Any lyric poetry arising from local, sectarian tensions risks xenophobia and sentimentality, but the journey of the orphan may lead from the status of the barbarian to that of the civilian.

Terry Street, Dunn's first collection, has the surprised and dismayed feel of a witness awakening in the Other's country. The weakness of that perspective makes the didactically inclined observer a 'village explainer', as Gertrude Stein said of Ezra Pound. Dunn has said 'didacticism is in my background', and certainly it threatens the vitality of poems early and late, but, in the image compositions of *Terry Street*, Dunn's portrait of Metropolitan City and its discontents remains remarkably fresh. His youthful technique is understandably in rebellion against metric verse and lives by his severe side-of-the-mouth tone, for he had not by then cultivated what in 'John Wilson in Greenock, 1786' he would so explicitly admire: 'the grace/ A classic metre grafts on native place' (*SKP*, 59).

Still, the craft of the *Terry Street* poems is not especially complex. Dunn's imagination took snapshots of what he has called 'characterful' scenes, minimalising plot, action and intrusive commentary but with exactly calibrated contrasts and grittily tactile details. Verbs of scrutiny dominate, yet the speaker immersed entirely in a present time seems rarely reticent in the Larkin manner. Dunn's stance may be statemental

('Here they come, the agents of rot . . .' (*TS*, 26) or nominational
('Recalcitrant motorbikes' (*TS*, 27)) or interrogative ('Where do they
go, the faces, the people seen/ In glances and longed for . . . (*TS*, 37)),
but most of the poems create from blunt diction and cataleptic rhythms
Dunn's effect of breathless discovery. While his poem typically betrays a
shadowing ancestral pentameter, its refusal of felicitous rhyme and a
chatting sentence emphasises the anger, anxiety and mounting
frustration of the anti-poetic style, the defiant anti-pastoral.

This aspect of Dunn's orphan-journey composes a suppressed erotic
fable made hip with the brass-taste of irony, cool ripostes, and
judgements spat out like headlines, as in 'From the Night-Window':

> policemen test doors.
> Footsteps become people under streetlamps.
> Drunks return from parties,
> Sounding of empty bottles and old songs.
> The young women come home,
> The pleasure in them deafens me.
> They. trot like small horses
> And disappear into white beds
> At the edge of the night.
> All windows open, this hot night,
> And the sleepless, smoking in the dark,
> Making small red lights at their mouths,
> Count the years of their marriages.
>
> (*TS*, 22)

A familiar ennui of existential wastelands emerges like the telephoned-
in smudge of life in an Edward Hopper painting. But a sort of coital
danger, electric, ready, holds the stage. Dunn may not be overtly
participant in this community but he is far from disengaged,
chronicling its simmering images in the manner of Walker Evans, the
Depression Era photographer. And he is deeply ambivalent. He admires
the power of Terry Street's men ('This masculine invisibility makes gods
of them . . .' (*TS*, 17)) but mocks the superficial culture they permit; he
shows the women fecund ('I sense beneath her blouse/ The slow expanse
of unheld breasts' (*TS*, 18)) but unloved, or unlovable as they become
gum-chewing boppers ('street tarts and their celebrating trawlermen'
(*TS*, 26)).

Where such a journey's form originates, we may speculate: at the age
of twenty-two, just married, the son of what Americans call 'working-
class' people, Dunn landed in Akron, Ohio. In 1964, America was daffy
for anything British and ready to beatle out of its insularity. Bob Dylan

proclaimed 'the times they [were] a'changin'. The feel of an infinite progressive future was acute. But change is dangerous: we watched our President blown from a limousine in Dallas; freedom rides saw neighbours openly hate each other; 50,000 of us marched off to become a gouge in black marble called Vietnam. If Hemingway truly said 'moral is what you feel good after', he should have survived the 1960s. Into that struggle of class and soul came Douglas Dunn to find Dylan was right: Humpty Dumpty looked solidly down.

The early 1960s saw an astonishing wave of first books by American poets determined to reject the tidy verse of two decades. Ginsberg, Ashbery, Creeley and Olson were only four of many so-called 'redskins' attacking the academies. If the gates held and safe verse continued to be practised, a raw polyphonic *Zeitgeist* blared from the new barbarians. Louis Simpson hinted in 1963 what lay ahead:

AMERICAN POETRY

Whatever it is, it must have
A stomach that can digest
Rubber, coal, uranium, moons, poems.

Like the shark, it contains a shoe.
It must swim for miles through the desert
Uttering cries that are almost human.

But Robert Lowell, individual custodian of the Tradition, shaking off metric restraint to write what he called a verse autobiography, spoke to the young poets. Dunn says:

> When I was in America, most of the poetry I read was American poetry – Lowell, Berryman, Jarrell and James Wright, for whose poems I've a particular fondness . . . (*Viewpoints*, 13)

Certainly, Lowell's candour in the intensely personal *Life Studies*, with its driven conscience (and consciousness), took Dunn to a poem like '"To Speak of the Woe That Is In Marriage"' where Lowell writes, 'The hot magnolia night makes us keep our bedroom windows open./ Our magnolia blossoms. Life begins to happen.' This is the erotic fable enacted by *Terry Street*: the wish for life to happen. Dunn would later give it other names:

> an aspiration towards justice: a dream of equilibrium, good order, benevolence, love, of the kind of sanity which men have it within their means to create. (*Viewpoints*, 21)

From Lowell, less so from Berryman and Jarrell, Dunn learned the power of personal narrative, the value of common experience, new ways of manipulating the English verse tradition (all that Americans had ever had, really) to make effective statements. He learned the need to seek identity in history, a lesson he would apply in *The Happier Life*, *Love or Nothing*, *Barbarians* and *St Kilda's Parliament*. But James Wright taught him the force of feeling.

American civic myth prides our country on its classless society, yet divisions of class have been and remain sharp. Akron, Ohio, is an automobile industry town, its people refugees from eastern Europe and southern American farms. Black and white, few born at the bottom rise to the top, though many bubble to the middle and lodge happily. James Wright, from shabby, working-class Martins Ferry, Ohio, escaped through the army and the GI Bill which sent him to study with poets Anthony Hecht, Randall Jarrell, John Crowe Ransom and Theodore Roethke. When he taught, his colleagues included Allen Tate, Berryman and Robert Penn Warren. His first book, *The Green Wall*, was chosen by Auden for the Yale Younger Poets Prize. It is verse to the max, echoing the Tradition of his three self-proclaimed masters: E.A. Robinson, Robert Frost and Horace. But its life lies in its subjects and the journey of the orphan of the spirit towards a renewed pietas, a culture of pastoral grace and moral brightness.

That Wright saw value in and identified himself with social outlaws — murderers, drunks, suspicious women, the poor and lonely — had its own rebellious and erotic tang which he increasingly focused in his 1960s books *The Branch Will Not Break* and *Shall We Gather At the River*. Wright's formal gifts were for the lyric tale and the image; combined, they evoked something like a quest pastoral underlain with eros, the right love in the local moment. One sees it when he climbs from his car to confront two ponies by a Minnesota country road. 'A Blessing' throws aside the Tradition for rapture:

> She is black and white, .
> Her mane falls wild on her forehead,
> And the light breeze moves me to caress her long ear
> That is delicate as the skin over a girl's wrist.
> Suddenly I realise
> That if I stepped out of my body I would break
> Into blossom.

That same discovery, eros latent, might become in a more social aspect, for Douglas Dunn, the place where transcendence, and belief of a sort, begins. He ended *Terry Street* with a poem Wright might have written in those 'deep image' days. After stating that 'There is something joyful/ In the stones today,' Dunn's 'Cosmologist' concludes,

> The back of my hand
> With its network of small veins

> Has changed to the underside of a leaf.
> If water fell on me now
> I think I would grow.

(TS, 62)

By 1973, Wright's *Two Citizens*, a collection he refused to reprint, railed at the America which produced a culture of hate, material waste and spiritual suicide. His anger turned poems from an anti-poetic to what seemed no-poetic, a formless bile juxtaposing a violated pastoral home life with travels through culture in Italy. Dunn appeared pressed by his own need to discover an identity, a culture, by moving out of the present moment. His books stiffened with rhetoric as he, like Wright, patrolled fault lines between 'Them and Uz (*PD*, 24). But the incontrovertible turn in what he calls 'stylistic habits' was backwards and down towards historical depth to complement eros. In *The Happier Life* (1972) and *Love or Nothing* (1974), he examines childhood wounds ('The Competition', 'Boys With Coats', 'Guerrillas'), Scottish locales with an increasingly mythical resonance ('Renfrewshire Traveller', 'White Fields'), and addresses poetry ('Realisms', 'Billie 'n' Me', 'The White Poet'). In 'The Disguise', Dunn poses as a saboteur who says he will give 'the finest insult' by way of 'an invective of grins, winks, fingers' (*LN*, 63). Granted a hint of bravado, he covets the local strength of shipbuilders in 'Clydesiders':

> My poems should be Clyde-built, crude and sure,
> With images of those dole-deployed
> To honour the indomitable Reds,
> Clydesiders of slant steel and angled cranes;
> A poetry of nuts and bolts, born, bred,
> Embattled by the Clyde, tight and impure.

(LN, 37)

The dichotomous chronicle of Them and Uz reaches its roots in *Barbarians* (1979) and *St Kilda's Parliament* (1981). Dunn's Scottish man now wears the lineaments of one unfairly dispossessed of rights and culture, yet one whose woes are often enough self-caused; he belongs to a regionalist life: 'That reek of roots, that tactile, lunatic aroma/ Tasting of dialect and curses sent out to work . . .' (*SKP*, 19). He accepts the stereotypical character imposed: 'I am a barbarian' (*Verse*, 28), he says, and declares a sort of war in poetic terms.[4] He will roll up his versemaking sleeves and 'beat them with decorum, with manners,/ As sly as language is' (*B*, 14). Much of this poetry seems a show of skills which has, too often, the feel of trial military manoeuvres with no apparent enemy, though a show perhaps necessary before turning the orphan's journey back to the future. Dunn's discoveries of historical analogues, the poets and musicians who *made* and kept alive links between the individual and the national soul ('The Student', 'The Musician', 'Green Breeks', 'John Wilson in Greenock, 1786' and 'Tannahill') validate both the life and art in masculine, declarative poems. He seeks to marry civil discourse to a chronicle of evils in the social fabric, an attempt both to worry out an ur-harmony and still to fix a blame.

'Tannahill' reveals Dunn's acute awareness of needing to find, even to define, *right* form. In those middle books, there are poems of protest, indictment, invitation, prayer and more — all that 'classic metre' he intended to 'graft on native place' — one feels Dunn has done what he praised Larkin for doing, amended the 'forms in order to bring them into line with the possibilities for poetic use of the language of the day'.[5] Yet his stern and unyielding contest for *status* seems less to synchronise speech and feeling as a matter of course than to plod habitually.

It is pertinent that Tannahill's suicide is emblematic of a cultural suicide which the orphaned spirit now recognises but from which as yet it sees no formal escape other than the possibilities ironically twinned in the Faber *Selected Poems* which prints 'Lamp-posts' and 'Loch Music' side by side (*SP*, 202–3). The poet, it seems, may choose the Baudelaire/ Kafka posture of abandoned drunks and dandies, the European heritage of those dimmed lights

> That lean against a wall, in a corner of
> This warehouse, bleak, municipal, leaning
> In stances of exhaustion, their arms across
> Their eyes, their brows against a bare brick wall.
>
> (*SP*. 202)

But that suicide of anonymity and ignorance is juxtaposed to a glib pastoral assertion in which 'a music settles on my eyes/ Until I hear the living moors . . .' (*SP*, 203). Was there nothing in his journey into the wilderness of history where he found a poor 'Home Lycidas' (*SKP*, 55) and (in 'The Apple Tree', *SKP*, 16) Scotland's 'coarse consent/ To drunken decency and sober violence . . .'? Heaney might have proclaimed his own archaeology of the pen, but Dunn's 'The Miniature Metro', dropped from the *Selected Poems*, nevertheless scoffs at the investment in poetry with a true barbarian's gouge: 'Dig with it? Tell that man he's better off/ With his pen in his ear or up his arse' (*SKP*, 78). Frustrations of allegiance, conflicts of violent claims on the heart, a darkly elegiac character all mark the deepest diving yet of poems which, like 'Saturday', surface with a jarring and plaintive note of realism's inevitable mortality: 'I wish it to be today, always, one hour/ On this, the pleasant side of history' (*SKP*, 36).

But it is to *St Kilda's Parliament*'s 'Galloway Motor Farm' that we look for the turning in Dunn's technique, and not so much a turning as an ease, a comfort in the traces which will make the poems speak in full heat with the unstraining grace of an athlete at peak. A Dantesque catalogue of 'byres' and 'eyesores' and 'rubbished profits' (*SKP*, 26–7) marks that contemporary monument on our planet, the automobile dump – what Americans call the junkyard. It has even given us a synonym for meanness – 'a junkyard dog'. The poem's unrhymed decasyllabic octets accept the set-piece image of our despoiled bower, and by stanza two we expect Dunn's theme of industrial abuse ('eyesores/ Cast out from progress') but we do not, quite, anticipate the firm particularity with which he articulates the whole and each *thing*. Indeed, Dunn's earliest image power lay in an ability to look at things, but less to focus them metaphorically so that the poem becomes a lens opening onto layered reality. Stanza three turns us to the disorder of an unnatural (and suicidal) bondage of thing and place:

> The chemistry of weather has installed
> Its scaffolding, from which it builds its rusts
> On the iron of a horse-drawn reaper.
> Air braces itself before stinging nettles.
> Car doors, bumpers, bonnets, mudguards, engines –
> Earth will not have them back until their steels,
> Their chromes, veneers and leathers marry with
> These stony contours as the brides of place.
>
> (*SKP*, 26)

One can scarcely imagine Larkin comfortable with such lines. There is evident here a shift in Dunn's voice from whatever unlocated and dispassionate tone remains of his first work to a poem of incremental celebration, the stance of veneration that allows Dunn to touch what he described to *The Printer's Devil* as 'previously unfamiliar dimensions of reality . . . a glimpse into life beyond known reality' (*PD*, 27–8). The shift now aligns Dunn with the more ecstatic poetries of Hopkins, Thomas, and Hughes. An American might as easily say with Frost, with James Wright. The glimpse of that other life locates it not in the future, where political progressives might, but in the back-past, before all, and the last stanza of 'Galloway Motor Farm' arrives at that beginning:

Tonight, by a steading, an iron reaper
That once outscythed the scythe
Is a silent cry of its materials,
With all its blunt blades yearning for the stone.
It has come from the yonside of invention,
From pulverable ore and foundry hammers.
Old harness rots above the rusted horsehoes.
Unborn horses graze on the back pastures.

How confident Dunn is in his gliding application of those *i* sounds, making a faint scream, and buttressed by the down-tumble of alliterative *b*s until we drum ourselves into that natural manger. The success of this poem and those to come is due to a new receptivity which accompanies the dismissal of Dunn's brief for barbarians. The orphaned spirit has connected to its line through the poems of place and the monologues giving ancestral voice to poets and musicians. Dunn recognises now that the issue is not bearding the British with craft but riding the song into self-creation. There will be poems fretting the old complaints, but the focus has altered from that of accusative discourse to that of meditation and experienced states of being. Having done his historical trooping, Dunn's vulnerability and human voice speaks less strongly, in my mind, than it should in *Europa's Lover* (1982), but it is there:

Say nothing of the attainable to me.
I am tired of morals and commerce.
Say nothing of history.
Tell me of your new dress
And of the scandal of happiness.
(*EL*, xi)

'The poems of *Elegies*,' Dunn told interviewer Bernard O'Donoghue, 'differ little if at all from earlier writing' (*OxPoe*, 48). In many respects that is accurate. The book returns to the fable of Eros and completes it. Erotic love represents the creative union of the spirit with the fecundity of place. Yet death intrudes, that ever-present reality. In the kingdom of love and death, that small town, Douglas Dunn found the liberty to do what Edgar Allan Poe and others had once advised poets: to look into the heart and write. Dunn says:

Why be discreet? A broken heart is what I have –
A pin to burst the bubble of shy poetry,
Mnemosyne revealed as what, in life, she stands for.
(*E*, 58)

Little wonder he adds in 'The Stories' that 'I loathe my bitter, scorning wit,/ This raffish sorrow artificed by stories' (*E*, 57).

Elegies is hurt poetry, the cry of the soul's violation, laden with the ache of a Dickinson or a Plath. I can think of few male poets who manage quite the intense pain, although in other contexts one might mention Herbert and Hardy. The collection chronicles the death of Dunn's wife, Lesley Balfour Dunn, from cancer – but it narrates the scald, plunge and ascension of Dunn's spirit, not least via the heroic sustenance of poetry. The life of poetry, how it can manage life from death, is the burden of *Elegies*, one sometimes carried awkwardly:

> Ours was a gentle generation, pacific,
> In love with music, art, and restaurants,
> And he with she, strolling among the canvases,
> And she with him, at concerts, coats on their laps.
>
> (*E*, 53)

Dunn's barbarians – 'Them' – may turn out to be those without the appropriate tastes while these lovers could have the better profile. 'December' is wooden, badly-written poetry, but it does reveal Dunn lifting his subject to metaphor where we may all be affected. Any elegy, and collection of such, requires convincing a reader to suffer what he will not willingly experience. The story that matters to us, however, is not the pitiful 'what happened' – it is the inner tale, the unarticulated behind what happened. Dunn's earliest image skills could not cope with that inscape, though his pictoral and narrative abilities could command the scene. Two poems into *Elegies*, we hear 'We went to Leeds for a second opinion' (*E*, 12). That drum-beat is the plot, for we know the literal outcome already. What we do not know is what language in poems can do to make us *understand* the brute reality. Repeatedly, Dunn makes the poem a contest of language and life, turning the tale into a moral of endurance and courage. His memory of his wife's sexual pleasure occasions an extensively poised sonnet, 'Tursac' (*E*, 26), in which the rituals of verse observe and contain the energies of passion, composing a 'characterful' portrait whose essential speech, brassy and bold, we arrive at in guilt. Guilt because we have, invited, spent so much time admiring the distribution of the sonnet that we realise that Dunn still writes as much out of the Tradition as of the insult which his wife's death is. How subtly, though, Dunn causes us to see the barbarians are now UZ *and* THEM.

So much might be said of the gentleness, the delicate membrane of life that Dunn holds before us and then sunders that we may fail to notice that he has, foremost, told a compelling human story in lyric moments through which he continually probes for evidence of that other 'reality'. Dunn writes, 'all my calling cannot bring her back'. And he adds in 'Listening':

> I felt I almost heard the secrets of a tree –
> The fruits falling, the birds fluttering,
> The music danced to under coloured lights.
>
> (E, 43)

This new accessibility to a world of live spirit induces strain in 'Reincarnations'.

> I feel her goodness breathe, my Lady Christ.
> Her treasured stories mourn her on their shelf,
> In spirit-air, that watchful poltergeist.
>
> (E, 44)

We wince, however true the words, when pathetically he says 'I loved my wife' (E, 33) or turns her grossly poetic in making her 'wife now to the weather' (E, 59).

Beneath these failures by sentimentality, of that restraint he has moved so far from in a poetic idiom based neither in rhetoric nor image, but in anecdote and memory, Dunn's vision is religious. The praise of Eros and Thanatos is a hymn to flesh, a testimony to the power of love, of bond, of continuity, of an *idealism* wedged against the apparent connivances with the All, as Larkin put it in 'High Windows', 'that shows/ Nothing, and is nowhere, and is endless'. The temptation to yield to that hopeless impotence rides up in these poems like a watermark, but Dunn will not turn back. He dramatises the poverty of our resources to resist and *speak off* corrosive grief in 'Reading Pascal in the Lowlands'. The father of a boy with leukaemia sits on a bench beside Dunn while the boy casts for fish. Dunn would like to avoid this intrusion and, as he says, 'I am sorry. What more is there to say?' Neither the French philosopher nor the world of Nature on this beautiful day presents an answer, but something may have been said in the poem's last moment when the father moves away from the narrator:

> He is called over to the riverbank.
> I go away, leaving the Park, walking through
> The Golf Course, and then a wood, climbing,
> And then bracken and gorse, sheep pasturage.
> From a panoptic hill I look down on
> A little town, its estuary, its bridge,
> Its houses, churches, its undramatic streets.
>
> (E, 46)

Undramatic perhaps but everything of spirit's value, this is the view of one's place continuous and nurturing in the increments as small as the syntactical units that nudge us in that stanza. We are not surprised when *Elegies* concludes with Dunn's discovery of a new love, because this poetry constantly verges not on endings but on fresh starts:

> She spoke of what I might do 'afterwards'.
> 'Go, somewhere else.' I went north to Dundee.
> Tomorrow I won't live here any more,
> Nor leave alone. *My love, say you'll come with me.*
>   'Leaving Dundee' (*E*, 64)

In *Northlight* (1988), Dunn arrives at a poetry of his own place. The charms of remarriage and fatherhood cast a warm light over his pages, but it is the austere northlight of Scottish estuaries, rocks and character that he clings to. The 'previously unfamiliar dimension' seems now available wherever he turns his attention. He composes a natural text of both spiritual and national significance ('Air-psalters and pages of stone/ Inscribed and Caledonian' (*N*, 41)); everything is related to everything else, a view which dismisses the man-privileged ravages in the name of causes. Dunn has arrived, we might say, at an ecology of the spirit, the orphan having come home, his political griefs diminished in the great systole and diastole of being. Home is what is beyond contingency and time. In 'Daylight', Dunn weds image and couplets to produce once more the little town on the hill:

> I've seen a star poised on the tip
> Of a still leaf, pure partnership
> Here makes with there and everywhere
> Between life, death and forever.
> Last night in Tayport, leaf and star
> – Still, very still – melted together
> In life's delight and woke to this
> Lucidity and genesis,
> A worldlight in the watery grey,
> Sinister, thrawn, the estuary
> A colourless mirroring stone,
> Offensive, querulous, sullen;
> And then daylight on Buddon Ness,
> Curative, clear and meaningless.
>   (*N*, 12)

Meaningless! How startling to find those ritualistic couplet chants escort not to a cloistered supernatural, but to a raw and bold natural

source of beginnings. And yet the orphan of spirit who was repelled by
Metropolitan City has come to accept the mysterious state of *is* and *was*
which pulses and counterpulses ('Holding antiquity and now/ Within
the same nocturnal vow' (*N*, 19)). He has become a public civilian,
whose cares are the stewardship of the immediate ('A city's elements,
local, exact' (*N*, 22)), bridges, apple trees, water and, not least, the
deposit bank of memory. Dunn's technique, that union of strategies, is
as garrulous as ever, landscapes ('Daylight', 'Abernethy'), intimate
asides and reminiscences ('Apples', '4/4'), dramatic monologues and
dialogic debate ('In the 1950s', 'Here and There'), memorial and elegy
('Muir's Ledgers', 'Maggie's Corner', 'An Address to Adolphe Sax in
Heaven'), even a sermonic rumination which adduces a theory of
'Rhythmical memory,/ Archival drum' (*N*, 65) that might attract the
Jungian male movement.

   Dunn's homecoming permits the poignant and elegiac note of sweet
reconciliation that most characterises Dunn the poet of the 1990s. He
gives voice to the unexpressed character of a place and our feeling for
that character. More importantly, he commands a vision of a man
drawing sustenance from the fullest resources of memory and love and
ordinary experience. The classical grace he aspired to attends the
memorial fusion of nature and man in 'December's Door', a poem about
Philip Larkin's funeral. Having taken home a sycamore leaf that has
stuck to his shoe, having left it in a book, presumably Larkin's poems,
Dunn notices 'now dust/ Dirties the page, and sinews, strong as thorn,/
Impress the paper's softer crust' (*N*, 31), becoming, it seems, not so
accidental as nearly the deliberate gift that focuses sight of that other
world. Larkin's gift had been to see and say the truths men are so
desperate for. The photographic realism of *Terry Street* is subsumed but
present in the carefully runic sway and tug of lines which have – almost
simply – the weight of an orchard's fruit that strain toward myth. In
such maturity Dunn unites the tribes of Them and Uz. So long as words
move men to resist fracture, insularity and lies, the grave lucidity of
Dunn's poem will turn a face to us that we know, as Larkin did,
contains the relentless will of things we have seen and heard and
touched and looked upon with love. Surely it is no small thing to say
Hull's other poet wrote *this*:

>   Sorrow's vernacular, its minimum,
>   A leaf brought in on someone's shoe
>   Gatecrashed the church in muffled Cottingham,
>   Being's late gift, its secret value
>   A matter of downtrodden poetry,

Diminutive, and brought to this
By luck of lyric and an unknown tree.
A passer-by was bound to notice
Crisp leaves at work when everyone had gone,
  Some fricative on paving-stones
As others flecked a winter-wrinkled lawn,
  Remote, unswept oblivions.

(N, 32)

NOTES

1 Douglas Dunn. *Under the Influence* (Edinburgh: Edinburgh University Library, 1987), 2.
2 Ibid., 1.
3 Ibid., 7.
4 Readers may note that Dunn ironically defines 'barbarians' positively (unlike the customary usage) as 'people who contest the Establishment and the degeneration of the State' (*Verse*, 28).
5 Dunn, *Under the Influence*, 3.

Seven

Writing with Light – *Elegies*

Paul Hamilton

Elegy, in the European tradition, is an aristocratic and selfish genre. It typically shows a poet profiting professionally from the demise of another person, and doing so in a manner fully appreciated only by the cognoscenti. Dunn is a democratic poet who walks the culturally small-time streets of secret villages, and hears the music in their supposedly barbarous dissonances. Rhetorically, his audiences are invited to reconvene alternative or unorthodox parliaments. However, Dunn is also a highly literary poet. He frequently employs a persona whose emotions are concentrated by having been forced through the gauze of finely wrought allusions and calculated metrics. *Elegies* questions the consistency of these allegiances. The poetic confidence to empower the supposedly less articulate or to redeem the past comes under scrutiny, particularly so because of the fraught personal circumstances which force Dunn's writing into that most self-questioning of poetic forms, the elegy.

Dunn's collection confronts a traditional crisis for the poet. But what might otherwise have been thought to be a comforting pedigree only redoubles the elegist's original anxiety that he or she might be traducing a ruinous event with poetic correctness. In this tradition, it seems that an abstract literary continuity is being repeatedly achieved at the expense of representing real loss and deprivation. As well as causing these fears, though, the elegy in English has been the vehicle *par excellence* for expressing a power to imagine radical renewal in spite of personal limitation and frailty. Fear and freedom are the two sides of elegy's coin. In two of the most prominent examples in the English canon, 'Lycidas' and 'Adonais', the compensations of Milton's Christianity and Shelley's Platonism coexist with a political conclusion, the encouraging vision of a new franchise. The horror of death, which loss of personality had provoked, is finally rewritten by the elegist as absorption into an ideal, egalitarian community transfiguring the Puritan or bourgeois individualism of the poet's day. The Christianising voice in which 'Lycidas' ends envisages a new civility, imaged in a nature all before us, extended not contracted by the sunset. Its temporality signifies potential progress, just as Lycidas's death elevated him to be a 'Genius of the shore', universally available, to warn against the aristocratic corruption of religious institutions. Shelley's 'Adonais' similarly overcomes a personal crisis by suggesting that poetry's apparently heartless survival of its mortal subjects symbolises a new polis in which all will at last receive their due, the impersonality resulting from their death rewritten as equal participation in eternity. Although Dunn's work has little to do with the sublimities of these predecessors, *Elegies* shares the political tensions of their projects. Their access of power poetically to realign the world comes from a massive loss of value, an impoverishment which poetry was powerless to prevent. Dunn's poems play through premature conclusions, inhibiting rituals and false simulacra in search of a new dispensation: the community we can be inspired to imagine just because of the sharper sense bereavement gives us of a poetry powered by an essentially Utopian impulse.

But Dunn's Utopia has always been the 'happier' rather than the 'better' life, the Aristotelian recovery of our natural purpose rather than its suspension in favour of something purer, something transcendental. Eventually we find that the Utopian solution is no solution, but is a demotic resistance to and disabused freedom from the fixed forms or 'wrongs' of grief overcome throughout these poems. From the opening one, Dunn's tear is 'dry'. When we look closer, as he did to detect the fly in his book, trapped in the literary balm he sought after his wife's death, we see with him that the tear is also 'punctuating': it draws a period to a close, but also ensures its articulation. That awful personal loss is once more reinscribed as a happier state in which we can put personal differences aside. In unsuperstitious, unsentimental, quotidian terms, 'objects implicated in my love', Dunn revives an ancient image of the best society we can have.

Literariness in *Elegies* begins with the epigraph from Carducci's 'Il Canto dell 'Amore', the conciliatory conclusion to the political satires of *Gambi ed Epodi*. With its assertion that, despite the personal evidence, 'nulla può morir', with its command to love and so share a vision of Italy's sacred future, this invocation of a communal hymn to peace takes the political turn characteristic of the elegiac tradition just sketched.[1] This is in keeping with the contemporary idea of Carducci as the heroic poet of a literary *Risorgimento*, unifying a new audience, a new Italy, alongside the politicians. But it is also important that Carducci, along with Pascoli and D'Annunzio, was later identified with a pre-modernist Italian mannerism whose Parnassian magniloquence and musicality was supposedly done away with by the clearer voices of his twentieth-century successors. No doubt this is a simplification, but the ambivalence of Carducci's reputation repeats elegiac tensions and suits Dunn's plot. For *Elegies* ventures on a path so clogged with precursors that it must start by making literariness serviceable. Occasional and detached laments, like 'Stranger's Grief' in *Barbarians* for Robert Lowell, can moot a one-off, autumnal authority, trying for a natural elegiac 'neutral as a leaf'. This is impossible for the sustained and partial *Elegies*. The poems need not be comfortable with their own allusiveness, but they have to confront it. It is as Dante that the poet stations himself in 'At Cruggleton Castle', with its Hardyesque title and setting. His palette is furnished, we hear, 'From the light in the middle of our lives' (*E*, 31); and, listening to *Elegies*, the surrounding voices sound more like the animals that barred Dante's way than useful guides. Again, though, this is to be expected of a genre which traditionally tries out inherited stances and poses before establishing with its own voice some surety of life's continuing force and value. The echoes that the poems try to leave behind are always thematic. Roethke's plangent eroticism is frequently enjoyed and placed, perhaps most strikingly in 'Writing with Light'. But the argument of that poem, I hope to show later, is far nearer the bone than anything in Roethke's cadenced loveliness. 'At Cruggleton Castle', however, seems to set out to conflate particular allusions so that they merge in the general problem of literary commemoration Dunn wants to raise. Hardy's 'At Castle Boterel' is there in the setting, as noted, but also in the focal line 'Good minutes make good days. Good days make years' (*E*, 31). We are summoned to the centre of Hardy's recollection: 'It filled but a minute. But was there ever/ A time of such quality, since or before,/ In that hill's story?' Dunn is less polemical, less confidently pessimistic about the mere ideality of things that last. Nor is he as sceptical as the narrator of 'Two in the Campagna' whom the focal line also echoes and for whom 'the good minute goes'. But he does, again as I hope to show, take on the general metaphysical question raised by Browning's poem. The yearning to apprehend infinity, to experience the miscellany of nature as if it rhymed, figures the equally impossible union that Browning's narrator desires with his partner. He wishes extravagantly 'to see with your eyes'; yet how to see with the lost vision of his lover is the primary lesson taught to the elegist of *Elegies*.

After the epigraph, we begin again between the pages of another book. In his copy of Katherine Mansfield's *Bliss and Other Stories*, the narrator finds not an immortelle but 'A pressed fly' (*E*, 9) lodged in the title-story. *Bliss* is no flowery, sentimental tale, but a pitiless indictment of a simple-minded happiness which persuades itself that it is corroborated by natural beauty. Mansfield sets a modernist impersonality against the naïvely self-indulgent heroine whose stream of consciousness the tale adopts. But *Bliss* is also a story of betrayal, of two women in competition for one unworthy man. It shows the silliness of the language normally clothing visceral, erotic dispute, and it dramatises the traumatic shock of encountering the true voice of feeling, here a ghastly, silent mouthing of 'I love you' by the erring husband to his mistress glimpsed fleetingly by the wife. In the context of *Elegies*, *Bliss* silently figures a lacerated consciousness for the dead wife as her husband callously sets off on a new life. *Elegies* as a whole, though, competes with *Bliss*'s desolate scenario. It reimagines the wife's absence not as a world now filled with her replacements, replete with guilt, but as one transformed by her new-found significance. She was the artist, the poems gradually tell us. The conventional, literary mourning voice is the naïve one, constantly mistaken, ever revised by her memory, active and potent as a result, retrieved from self-pity.

The memory of bliss as balm for bereavement is thus doomed from the start of the collection. In the same poem, the bus-ticket (a weekly with the return journey unpunched for Friday?) used as a bookmark perhaps dates the lovers' first night together after 'That day, falling in love'. But the poem digs closer to a proverbial register, immune to nostalgia. The fly in the ointment is 'a skeleton of gauze', misting the book's print and clouding any easily-remembered consolation. It is a 'Prose / Fly', challenging poetic self-sufficiency, and despite its fragility capable of provoking the new reading of life required of the narrator. If the poetry of his life has died with Lesley, that only means that the genre has changed. He has been challenged to write in a new way, to seize the opportunity of a new poetic initiative. And if literary insouciance of this kind seems unbearably buoyant, utilitarian or even cynical, nevertheless it images the more successfully the airy character which consoling offers of reparation must take on during an experience of utter loss. This art counts the cost of its seriousness. Again, poetry is made to look like Utopia, although its initial frivolity secretes the hope by which we live seriously, strive for happiness and resist impositions not necessarily as final but more inequitable than death. The elegist rejoins the social world in a particular moral and political mode.

Poetry's unbearable lightness of being, unaccountable to death, becomes its mandate for redescribing life.

Elegies has its motifs, its birds, insects, mobiles, light, dusk, blues, epiphanies. Its largest image, centring the other constellations, is 'home'. Fundamentally displaced by his wife's death, the widower is homeless until the final poem, 'Leaving Dundee' (*E*, 64), plays on his difficulties with an accomplished air. On the way there, he has dramatised the need to find the journey rather than the destination sufficient: the process of grief becomes more important than its assuagement, inspiration takes priority over consolation. He has had to balance against loss the poetically useful innovations of a grief whose intensity breaks through received rituals, emotional homeliness, to achieve original forms of commemoration. These substitute for mysticism, forestall the supernatural and affirm a lyric abundance overflowing conceptual boundaries: 'angelophanous/ Secrets. They are more than remembering,/ Larger than sentiment', announces the poet of 'Home Again' (*E*, 52). 'They' are also the beyonds of 'Pretended Homes'. Their spiritual enlargements, though, are always hedged with scepticism, even disgust. 'Cancer's no metaphor', declares 'Anniversaries' (*E*, 62), but like most of the poems has to cope with cancer's metaphorical structure: never fully at home with its subject, it is always, necessarily, at a productive remove. That aesthetic analogy gnaws, condemns and evokes desire for literal identification with the loved one, the *Liebestod* to which poetic sympathy offered an alternative. Doubt poetry, as in 'The Stories', and that hopeless gesture appears morally plausible.

> Not even that sweet light garnishing Sisyphean innocence
>   Redeems me, dedicated to the one
> Pure elegy, looking as if I like the way I am.
>   I do not; for I would rather that I could die
> In the act of giving, and prove the truth of us
>   Particular, eternal, by doing so
> Be moral at the moment of the good death, showing
>   An intimate salvation beyond the wish
> Merely to die, but to be, for once, commendable.
>
>   (*E*, 58)

The syntax of this conclusion strains under the difficulties of making room for that 'commendable'. But its strange morality is squeezed out under the pressure of poetic doubt, worry that the elegiac stance never quite escapes something disreputable, a 'raffish sorrow artificed by stories' (*E*, 57). 'The Stories' satirises the elegist's therapeutic articulations of his grief as tales of colonialist adventure far from home. Imperialism is 'the world of the stories', no longer credible, an outmoded distraction from troubles at the centre. Better admit that each new elegy in the collection is 'Sisyphean', innocent of the failure of its predecessors' attempts to raise a satisfying monument, 'the one/ Pure elegy': in a way, as 'Western Blue' has it, the elegies are 'A thousand messages beside the point' (*E*, 48), this time like relics not of imperialism but the Cold War. But, in knowing their own weakness, inauthenticity and impotence, the elegies aspire perpetually towards the 'commendable', their idealism unfailingly returning to us an image of the moral, an image of what ought to be.

Dunn's elegies, then, are repeatedly unsatisfied with their own achievements. This is their therapeutic value: the mourner accepts that his loss means that he can never describe his dead wife again. His poems work through this failure, helpless to redeem but actively mourning, positively purgative.

> 'No don't stop writing your grievous poetry.
> It will do you good, this work of your grief.
> Keep writing until there is nothing left.
> It will take time, and the years will go by.'
> ('December', *E*, 53)

The aim, though, is not simply to write the dead beloved out, to expunge her: precisely the ambition to preserve her in writing at all is what the elegist's therapeutic repetitions abandon. Such relinquishment characterises his experience of her now, and in this contemporaneity lies the means to make her live. His poems criticise any established ritual for fixing her in the past; and hand in hand with their eschewal of lapidary, memorialising techniques goes the poems' equal dissatisfaction with anything they themselves might substitute. She becomes identified with the ongoingness of poetry, with process not with product, not with a poem or collection finished and left behind, but with a constant initiative.

This aesthetic solidarity graces what would otherwise be her sheer dissolution. In terms familiar from Wordsworth and Shelley, and repeated by the Carducci epigraph, her individual subsumption by larger natural forces colludes with poetic exploratoriness and resistance to any one genre, ideology, voice or value. *St Kilda's Parliament*, Dunn's preceding collection, had been free with genre and voice, kind and character, ideologically combative but nevertheless univocal in its valuing of the poetry for which one of its heroes, John Wilson, was as single-mindedly condemned. By contrast, the dialectics of *Elegies* chart the perpetually mobile ironies required of a poetry which strives to be adequate to loss. 'Tutto trapassa e nulla può morir' − everything is transformed and nothing can die.[2] The traditional difficulty lies in making plausible the poetic confidence to rewrite death as transformation. The elegised woman is 'wife now to the weather' ('Anniversaries', E, 59). She is present in the Tayside rain which Dunn increasingly delights in, and, in *Northlight*, defends as his new-found local inspiration. Her personal effacement is thus drawn as the vehicle of her return to him, to be present in the defining novelty of his poetic awareness: 'The lights of Newport rinse in the tide,/ Then one by one disperse, as life dissolves/ Into the deity within ourselves' ('Transblucency', E, 49). For here extinction is reformulated as an existence beyond determination, discovered inwardly, 'sublime', certainly, but also 'commonplace', shared, and so a kind of social template. The last poem of *Elegies*, 'Leaving Dundee', cuts through the 'grievous artifice' of the poetic life the collection has recorded. Finally, the poet can go home, but not because he has fixed on the right place. He hears the skeins of geese 'cry/ Fanatic flightpaths up autumnal Tay,/ Instinctive, mad for home'. But he is no prisoner to that absolute nostalgia, no more than he is to gentler recollections of holidays in France, their shared sensuality: 'A lost French fantasy . . . [whose] Frenchness hurts my heart'. He can go home because home is now not a place. It is to travel no longer alone. It is *Elegies'* record of a loss confronted and reenacted as poetic originality and departure which allows him his conclusion, as free now from sentimentality as it is from superstition: 'Tomorrow I won't live here any more,/ Nor leave alone. *My love, say you'll come with me'* (E, 64).

In retrospect, then, this exhilarating freedom of movement is what the personal dissolutions have prefigured. Mortality has been insisted on. In 'The Butterfly House', there appears already to be an implicit equation between 'objects implicated in my love' and those objects' transparency to an elemental vision which, losing sight of their individual outlines, returns them to their constituents. In the poem's conceit, a geographical expansion is born of the poetic tracing of domestic ornaments and comforts back to their original raw materials. 'This room is everywhere'. But its global Incarnation expresses also the brutalities of empire and the unscrupulousness of trade, not altogether whimsically.

> This room is everywhere, in its pictures,
> Its minerals and chemistry, its woods,
> Its weeping fig, bamboos, its foreign stuffs,

That slave trade in its raw materials.
But timbers long for unfootprinted forests,
China was baked from clay, metals from earth,
And these tame plants were stolen from the ground . . .
The cruelties of comfort know no end . . .

$(E, 11)$

That butterfly lightness of spirit, wittily flitting through the means of production, eventually tells of the poet's own mortality, letting him feel 'That the large percentage of me that is water/ Is conspiring to return to the sea'. At home, waiting for his love to return, he has a presentiment of a larger home, a wider dispensation in which identity is lost but still animate, 'alive in the long room of its being'. The poem just retains its levity, that seriously 'long room' perhaps still punning on an earlier mentioned etching of Lord's Cricket Ground, but only just.

With personal disintegration comes not only mobility but also a more generous sense of community, the 'large recompense' of Lycidas. For kinship to be recognised, one need only share the condition of mortality and a greater alertness to its griefs. The implication of objects in a love which grows with loss is both everyday and profound, miscellaneous and metaphysical. Small animal existences, their simple creatureliness, bind the elegist with sympathy to their society, for 'She was the gentlest creature of them all' ('Creatures', E, 33). He commemorates the 'reasonable ark' of which Lesley can now be recognised as the 'châtelaine'. Anonymity, differences of fortune or of sex create no barriers in this new citizenry. After a chance and momentary meeting with the recently bereaved, 'It is as if we shall be friends for ever' ('Arrangements' E, 15). A tramp, 'eccentric victim', exchanges nods, and wins recognition from the mourner of their belonging to a central 'private truth', a fellowship exceeding conventional attachments, cemented in 'the giving of love' ('The Stranger', E, 25). Initially, the poet seems to resent the womanly role in which Lesley's terminal illness casts him. In 'Thirteen Steps and the Thirteenth of March', he resists 'a conspiracy of women' $(E, 14)$ which feminises him as a drudge. But, once more, he is working through the idea of remembrance, trying on a realism whose unpleasing accusatoriness will help him escape the confines both of sentimentality and of bitterness. After her death, he takes a sad delight in feeling 'As if I have become a woman hidden in me' ('Dining', E, 27). But before this, he could only resent the solicitousness and correctness of behaviour which the unbearable shamelessly prescribed for him, the 'lovely forms of foresight, prayer

and hope' with which 'Grief wrongs us so' ('The Kaleidoscope', *E*, 20).
He must be redesigned and recomposed, as if in a kaleidoscope, by the
experience of losing her. And the clues to his new shape lie not in the
proprieties but in a wider, unconventional franchise, both deeper and
less discriminating.

In 'Reading Pascal in the Lowlands' (*E*, 45), the commonalty of
ordinariness and ordinary people, the lowlands, are linked to the high
metaphysical road of Pascal, brilliant gambler in the redesigning of
souls. Pascal famously offers no solutions, no guarantees, only a better
bet in a world we cannot fully understand. The poet's reticence when
talking to the father of a child dying of leukaemia is therefore
appropriate: 'I have said/ I am sorry. What more is there to say?' The
father has 'seen the limits of time, asking "Why?"', and, like Pascal, he
knows that 'Nature is silent on that question'. So, no theology joins
them, only the unspoken, which might be faith and is certainly
recognition of their common lot, what they share in spite of cultural
difference, in spite of all difference. The father sees the poet's book and
knows him 'for a stranger'. But the drift of the poem has been to suggest
that a bond has been sealed between them, although at so basic, so
'lowland' a level as to be scarcely formulated. The father walked 'On the
beautiful grass that is bright green', and the near-tautology of colour,
green grass, shows a hunger for the ordinary to be significant, a drive
subliminal both to low Larkinesque and idealist metaphysics. A world
which answers to our needs, but in its own voice, must do so beneath
our consciousness. The style answerable to this voice must therefore be
most discreet. 'Reading Pascal in the Lowlands' matches the courteous,
unspeakable sympathy between metaphysical poet and unlettered father
to the scientific, conceptual inarticulacy of poetry. This poetry, the
analogy implies, successfully redescribes nature by making us hear its
distinctive silence as beauty. At the end, the poet heads upwards to a
visionary eminence only to discover an ordinary, small-time discourse of
uninformative but unalienable disclosures: 'A little town, its estuary, its
bridge,/ Its houses, churches, its undramatic streets'. Maybe, like
Keats, the poet has to see visionary abnegation as poetic increase, and in
that loss of self find the impersonal renewal he seeks. As in the
conclusion to 'The Clear Day' (*E*, 40), the truth to be heard 'beyond
understanding' is not apocalyptic but 'Sensible, commonplace'. In this
kind of 'Listening' (*E*, 43), the poet's sorrows can be, most ambiguously,
'murdered by aesthetics'. The relief experienced is also a kind of killing
of what had felt so personal but now gives way to a comforting sense of
natural otherness. The temptation is for this to be expressed in a
language risking animism and its fey idioms: 'I felt I almost heard the

secrets of a tree' ('Listening'). A 'beyond' which is 'sensible' and 'commonplace' is not the easy option.

We do not need the little town of Keats's ode or the *Pensées* of Pascal to shape the aesthetics of *Elegies*. A more portentous Heideggerian voice disclosing 'Being' is also, implicitly, resisted. Instead, the artistic character which the poems lend to Lesley Balfour Dunn provides the needed aesthetic guidance. Her childlessness is regretted in 'At the Edge of a Birchwood' (*E*, 38), but her defining creativity is what he strives to inherit and preserve. When a second opinion confirms that her sight is blighted with melanoma, his instinctive response is '"Why *there*? She's an artist!"' ('Second Opinion', *E*, 12). On the way to 'understand the light' ('Attics', *E*, 24) with which, like Gwen John, she wrote, are the mobiles. Mobiles are toys whose play, here, unfolds a serious purpose. The little spinning planes in 'A Silver Air Force' (*E*, 18) are 'a frivolous deterrent', obviously; but in context, scrambled in the poet's wit, they are really directed against the thought of death, 'What had to happen'. Again, they are a metaphysical tease, for they mime what they actually do, fighting the poet's fear of what will become of him after bereavement. They also simulate, in miniature, a much larger dimension. They are trial runs in coping with Pascal's 'silence éternel de ces espaces infinis [qui] m'effraie',[3] the fearful, deathly expansions which *Elegies* must try to manage with its 'white and indoor sky' ('Sandra's Mobile', *E*, 21).

Mobiles expose also, I think, a reverse fear, one expressed in 'France' (*E*, 19), a poem sitting between the others on mobiles and the kaleidoscope: the fear that life after Lesley's death will be like a mobile, a diminished, unreal simulacrum. Then, the mobile would no longer furnish symbolic access to something larger, but would signify our confinement to something smaller. In 'France', the couple stand at the window, 'And, if you saw us, then you saw a ghost/ In duplicate'. The startling, Donne-like aperçu first of all figures his loving ministrations when, doubling for her, he must have been the hands, eyes and feet of his helpless wife. Their love is expressed in all its symbiotic closeness. But the conceit also suggests that such utter devotion must to some extent unrealise him too when she is gone. The sonnet celebrates the last French holiday they never had. She says, 'I would have liked us to have gone away'. While from the poem's retrospect we know she went away, we know also from *Elegies* as a whole how difficult he found his 'floating life' ('A Summer Night', *E*, 42) in that ghostly aftermath. The figure of the mobile gathers up these ambiguities, lightly reproducing the collection's aesthetic problem. *Elegies* can safely contemplate its own project in a simplified and bijou form, unthreatened by its frivolous collapse, but still staging the fearful scene its own commemorations must surpass.

Sandra's mobile of the seagulls was given to Lesley in 'old artistic comradeship' (*E*, 21). They come alive 'On thermals of my breath', ambivalent symbol of a life perpetuated in miniature. On the night Lesley dies, the gulls turn into doves, a metamorphosis so unexplained as to symbolise their power to symbolise, their art, and thus perhaps by a higher realism to make them figure Lesley's soul. The art they share with Lesley, most fully described in 'Writing with Light', is approached through a momentary mobile.

> A *dadaiste* tomboy, she'd fill a jar
> Then hold it to the sun. The art of day
> Leapt on the shapely glass, the unfamiliar
> Blues, changes, clouds, a watery display
> That calmed and caught clear heavens in a jar.
>
> And damn the hand-washing. She'd run the tap,
> Filling her jar, then hold it to the sun.
> That contemplated water formed a trap
> To catch the sky with. Experimental fun —
> A jar, a sky, the flowing cold, a tap.
>
> (*E*, 23)

In yet another reversal, for an instant the wider spaces compress themselves within a plaything, life imitating art, tricked into forming a mobile of itself. This is 'experimental fun', but it connects up with Lesley's art or the use the elegist wants to make of it in his story of her. Writing with light is like drawing without outlines, somehow shaping in a medium usually differentiated by the shapes it is not. On the other hand, what could be simpler than photography? Photographic is so often a dismissive word in aesthetics, denoting a facile reproduction void of art, the kind criticised earlier by Dunn in a poem from *Love or Nothing*, 'I Am a Cameraman' (*LN*, 41). Writing with light, photography's Englishing, restores its extraordinariness; and that seems also to have been the aim of Lesley's art, her 'rational, surreal photography'. It is rational, firstly, to the extent that a photograph must map literally. To become aware of its 'writing', however, is once more to sense the artifice of any 'reality' and to feel the poetic impulse to describe a world not necessarily bound by it, even if its beyond can only appear 'surreal' — 'Reconjuring a world in black and white — / A pond in a box, a tabletop of sea'. The exemplary awareness of the variable frameworks within which we experience limit, definition and personal identity is then retold as the lesson Lesley inculcates — 'She taught me how to live, then how to die'. Their mutual translations, their reconceivings of themselves is what, pre-emptively, her art was about.

The response invited by Lesley's art in 'Writing with Light' is not superstitious, fey or animistic, but hard-headed. The ghosts of 'Reincarnations' (*E*, 44), 'Hush' (*E*, 63) and 'Larksong' (*E*, 39) have to be faced. After 'the coupledom of us' come the phantom limbs, or her non-existent presence 'like a half-heard religious anecdote' ('Land Love', *E*, 47). There is a workable expressivity acknowledged here, though maybe more as a poetic idiom to be visited in the spirit of Philip Larkin's 'Church Going'. Nevertheless, Dunn seems to keep in mind another of Pascal's *Pensées*. 'C'est être superstitieux, de mettre son espérance dans les formalités; mais c'est être superbe, de ne vouloir s'y soumettre.'[4] To base your hope upon ceremonies is to be superstitious, but not to want to submit to them is to be proud. The immature synaesthesia of 'A Rediscovery of Juvenilia' (*E*, 50) – '"It is like listening to a rainbow"' – comes as a cathartic long shot, but then the elegist has to 'close the book on it and start again' before the more mature, Pascalian wager can be taken up. To follow Lesley and write with light, he must have 'the heart within my eye' ('Writing with Light'), a phrase which this time faces and uses the apparently out-of-bounds subject of her melanoma. Here, cancer unignorably is a metaphor, and the aesthetic analogy is no longer repressed. To 'understand the light' is the lesson reiterated by Gwen John's painting in 'Attics', the poem following 'Writing with Light' – 'A room she dreamed, but painted by Gwen John'. The lesson has immediate practical effects.

To understand the light is to perceive in it the condition of figurative representation, the element or medium which conventionally disappears to make its subject visible. To make that condition a subject is to conjure something analogous to the way in which Lesley's effacement has been enabling for the elegist. His art is no crude profit from her death, like selling a monument. Its dissolution of boundaries of self and world in response to her death have imaged a wider community that can include her. The sun-induced melanoma that killed her, *that* terrible writing with light, has now converged on her art, an art the poet emulates, an art too generous in its acceptance of the world to be incapacitated even by the parallel of cancer. The 'Sun-coaxed horrific oncos' is a growth which measures the influence of light no less effectively than a sundial ('The Sundial', *E*, 30). So impersonal a depiction as this, though, such equanimity, is achievable only momentarily, among a host of cathartic resting-places. That ultimate impersonality is kept in focus by the temporariness of these

commemorative rituals. Paradoxically, their makeshift housing makes
the poetic departures they encourage more commemorative of the
elegiac subject, the art which characterised her and which she taught.
Dunn takes on the traditional, literary problem of elegy, but
intermittently manages to cast elegy in a contemporary mould, *her*
distinctive mould, honouring and obeying her command in happier
days: '"Write out of me, not out of what you read"' ('Tursac', *E*, 26).

Sometimes to seek the light together looks like a hopeless entrap-
ment, the fluttering of 'two windowed moths' ('Creatures', *E*, 33). But
without a superstitious religion, what is there to do in the face of
personal loss? What contemporary meanings can there be for 'my Lady
Christ' ('Reincarnations', *E*, 44)? Any accommodation, anything less
than resurrection, must initially look like settling for a lower standard
of what is to count as personal and individual. *Elegies* confronts this
objection and, I have argued, recovers for it a fundamentally political
character present but easy to overlook in the elegiac tradition. Lower can
mean wider. We have seen the poems describe a socialism of suffering,
complementing 'the socialism of pleasure' to be celebrated in
Northlight's elegy for John Brogan (*N*, 52). Once assimilated to a new,
less individualistic identity and set of values, the loved one can be seen
to have set in motion an ameliorative redescription of the world.
'Chateau d'If' (*E*, 32), a sonnet about Lesley's photographs of the
famous prison off Marseilles, shows this most succinctly. Here is none of
the political manifestoes Dunn so dislikes. The significance of the
experience recorded in the photos the sonnet describes is kept at many
removes, unabashedly indeterminate: 'I can't remember, but I can't
forget/ Our outing to the Chateau d'If'. The poem's certainty lies in its
pointedly understated belief in art's necessarily oppositional mode.
Again, the elements intrude in a picture which shows its understanding
of how to write with its own failure to contain them. Such practised
laxity is presented as conflicting with any ideology licensing political
imprisonment.

> Her photographs of white embrasures glow·
> Against impossible blue, the sea and sky
> Contemptuous of how men fortify
> The State's iniquity. I do not know
> Exactly all we talked about or did.

This art's lightness, its flâneur's stance, can look merely touristic: 'She
posed me as a blue vignette'. But, in context, its holidaymaker's
treatment of the surrounding prison is salutary. By contrast with the
Chateau, its own aesthetic enclosures or framing, 'these rectangles of

printed light', will not stand scrutiny. Their significance or reality principle, as we saw, remains far from secure. Meanings lead elsewhere, into the casual vagueness of narrative recollection the sonnet enjoys. It is through its lightness, here unbearable only to an iniquitous *gravitas*, that art lets in the light the prison tried to deny. This is a good note to end on, a summer image of a happier life; Utopian – for when will we all be tourists of oppressions that are all outmoded? – but not unrealistic, careful of its time: ' "Let's stay awhile, then take the last boat home" '.

NOTES

1 Giosue Carducci, 'Il Canto dell 'Amore' in *Poesie*, edited by Giorgio Barberi Squarotti, notes by Mario Rattori (Milan: Garanti, 1985), 224–30. Carducci's poem was published in 1877 after the defeat of the last resistance to the *Risorgimento* which had provoked the earlier satires. Among other parallels, it is striking that Carducci went on to write *Odi Barbare* whose barbarism, like Dunn's, redefines classicism, here as a return to classical metrics alien to conventional Italian verse forms.

2 *Ibid.*, 229. In his note to this line, Mario Rattori glosses 'trapassa' not as the 'happened' of some translations, but 'qui nel senso di si trasmuta, si trasforma (alussivo dell'eterno avvicendarsi delle cose)'.

3 *Oeuvres de Blaise Pascal*, edited by Leon Brunschvigg (Paris: Librairie Hachette, 1925), II, No 206.

4 *Ibid.*, No 249.

Eight

Secret Villager

Robert Crawford

While Scottish subject matter and concerns were present from Dunn's first book, and were particularly important in *Barbarians*, it is in 1981 with *St Kilda's Parliament* that the 'matter of Scotland' achieves an undisputed centrality in Dunn's shaping of an individual collection. One could argue that in the overall design of *Barbarians* the obviously Scottish poems were subordinated to the general thrust of left-wing politics. With *St Kilda's Parliament* this is no longer the case. Here is a book which centres on Scotland yet whose scope is bound to excite Scottish readers, for in some senses the volume constitutes a sustained examination and critique of Scottish culture. It not only articulates Dunn's sometimes uneasy search for a voice in which to speak for and about Scotland, it also enacts his commitment to Scotland as a political entity, a stateless nation deprived of democratic control over its own affairs. Dunn's commitment to Scotland is reinforced in his public statements of this period. Asked by John Haffenden in 1981 if he would like to go back to Scotland, Dunn replied simply, 'Yes, very much' (*Viewpoints*, 28), and in 1985 he told Bernard O'Donoghue 'My political instincts have been republican for as long as I can remember and they've always existed in relation to Scotland' (*OxPoe*, 44). Ironically, *St Kilda's Parliament* has received less attention in Scotland than might have been expected. Partly this may be explained by the fact that the book appeared in the same year as Alasdair Gray's *Lanark* which almost immediately achieved dominance in the literary arena. Partly too, this may be explained by quirks of literary politics. It is noticeable, for instance, that even in 1987 Dunn is nowhere mentioned in the twentieth-century volume of *The History of Scottish Literature*.[1] For all that, the political orientation of *St Kilda's Parliament* is unmistakable, and the volume's importance in the development of contemporary Scottish poetry would be hard to dispute.

Yet approaching this book too exclusively in terms of Scottish politics would be to do it a disservice. Elsewhere I have written about Dunn's place among an array of sophisticated 'barbarian' writers which includes Tony Harrison, Seamus Heaney, Les Murray and Derek Walcott.[2] Part of the purpose of this chapter is to look at the way Dunn 'writes Scotland' in *St Kilda's Parliament*, but in such an examination it is important to pay attention to the poetic craftsmanship of the book, its verbal artifice and the part which that plays within Dunn's development. While in his political pamphlet, *Poll Tax: The Fiscal Fake*, Dunn cannot keep poetry and politics apart, it befits the Scottish critic in particular to remember that *St Kilda's Parliament* is not a political tract but a book of poems. Moreover, it is a collection which, like much of Heaney's work, is often aware of competing impulses towards the aesthetic and the political. The work in this collection takes account of what Dunn makes quite clear in his consideration of 'The Predicament of Scottish Poetry' (1983) — that Scottish poetry often tends to be willed, programmatic, and starkly intellectual at the expense of being relaxed, verbally and imagistically hedonistic. Dunn argues for a 'purer poetry' and warns that in the Scottish cultural climate 'So much attention is concentrated on the social significance of writing, that there is little time left for anything else'. While his wish for more 'sensuously imaginative phrase-making' is sometimes problematic as regards his own work, his stance is surely salutary in a Scottish context where political considerations too easily override imaginative or poetic requirements.[3] One need only look to the Eastern Europe of Stanislaw Baranczak and Joseph Brodsky to see that it is fatal for poetry to allow its humane linguistic subtleties to be replaced by the constricting regulatory language of corporate and political cliches. Ultimately, as Baranczak has written,

> History may demonstrate by millions of examples the continuous triumph of Newspeak, a deliberate and systematic falsification of words' meanings; and yet a single good poem is enough to counter all this tampering with language by making the reader aware of the word's hidden semantic possibilities. A poet who is offended by the course of modern History doesn't even have to write political poetry to find an appropriate response to it. It's enough that he write his poems well.[4]

In *St Kilda's Parliament*, Dunn attempts both to write Scottish political poetry and to 'write well', to deploy and discover his gifts for the accurate and individual relishing of language. Sometimes this balancing act provides a peculiar energy, at other moments it becomes uneasy. Certainly it is a balancing central to most of his poetry. The poet's sensibility emerges clearly in this collection as that of the 'secret villager', the temperamental inhabitant of such communities as are described in the short stories of *Secret Villages* or in Dunn's own account of growing up in an Inchinnan which 'still held on to an essentially rural character in spite of being close to Renfrew, Paisley and Glasgow'.[5]

Though one tends to think of the 'Terry Street' poems as distinctively urban, Terry Street formed something of a self-enclosed community within Hull. It may not have been quite a 'secret village', but Dunn has said that he was attracted to it because it was 'like a village' (*Viewpoints*, 14), and because, in retrospect, Inchinnan in some ways resembled the Terry Street whose inhabitants were like 'a lost tribe'. He has admitted that 'it could be argued' that his urge to write of the innate decency of such communities has driven him over the years to write about increasingly remote 'villages', moving from Hull to St Kilda (*Verse*, 26). While the first poem in *St Kilda's Parliament* is about what was the remotest community in Scotland, that poem's full title 'St Kilda's Parliament: 1879–1979' also invites thoughts of a wider Scottish political context. For if 1879 is the year that the photograph of the remote parliament described in the poem was taken, then 1979 is the year of the Scottish Devolution Referendum in which, though a majority of those who voted supported a Scottish parliament, Scotland was denied any increased say in her own affairs. Dunn's poem also idealises a lost parliament, yet the identity of the poem's supposed speaker is problematic. While the title carries the rider, *'The photographer revisits his picture'*, in a literal sense the photographer cannot be 'revisiting his picture' after a hundred years have elapsed. We are presented then with a poem that is neither articulated by the poet in his own person, nor by any clearly identifiable intermediary, unless we think of the photographer as looking on from some afterlife. This suggestion is not absurd, for Dunn's 1977 radio play *Scotsmen by Moonlight* experiments sometimes uneasily with a possibly time-travelling Voice-of-Scotland figure, Jock Tamson, who is also in search of independence in Scotland. Both play and poem present us with an apparently authoritative voice whose identity and status are less clear than first appears. There are other uncertainties associated with the voice that produces the poem. That producer clearly knows about the twentieth-century fate of the island and addresses a late twentieth-century audience which is aware of this (or, at least, can be told about it). Yet some of the poem seems directed to an audience of that other era when a Gaelic-speaking St Kilda was an exotic tourist venue:

> Traveller, tourist with your mind set on
> Romantic Staffas and materials for
> Winter conversations, if you should go there,
> Landing at sunrise on its difficult shores,
> On St Kilda you will surely hear Gaelic
> Spoken softly like a poetry of ghosts
> By those who never were contorted by
> Hierarchies of cuisine and literacy.
>
> (*SKP*, 14)

Are these sibilant, beautiful lines addressed to those who may still literally go to St Kilda and hear Gaelic, or to those for whom St Kilda's Gaelic speakers are already dead? The poem's producer seems to mock the urge to romanticise, yet is also caught up in that yearning; it is a typical Celtic Twilight touch to hear Gaelic as 'a poetry of ghosts'. Sometimes the 'speaker' communicates in something like idiomatic late-twentieth-century spoken English; at other times the speaker's voice is much more archaically stagey and declamatory:

> after
> My many photographs of distressed cities,
> My portraits of successive elegants,
> Of the emaciated dead, the lost empires,
> Exploded fleets, and of the writhing flesh
> Of dead civilians and commercial copulations,
> That after so much of that larger franchise
> It is to this island that I return.
>
> (*SKP*, 15)

It is not always apparent how far Dunn is in control of the uncertainties manifest within the voice of this poem, or how far, if at all, the reader is intended to resolve them. Yet they contribute to the potent, sometimes subliminal memorability of a poem which, like much of this writer's work, deals with the intimate and unstable haunting of the present by the past. Moving backwards and forwards between awareness of nineteenth- and twentieth-century perspectives, the poem (like *Elegies*) deals with the painfully intimate presence of what is both beautiful and lost. The line 'To ease them from their dying babies' has a hurt immediacy where the verb 'ease' suggests a concerned, and gentle separation which will result in death. The poem's best 'phrase-making' as in the earlier sibilance of 'Whose carpentry was slowly shaped by waves' or the locally appropriate 'a diet of solan goose and eggs' or 'a toehold of Europe' exploits unusual collocations and specific vocabulary to immerse the reader in the process of life as lived by the seagoing,

bird-devouring, rock-climbing islanders. However, the fact that the
tone is constantly descriptive and explanatory also distances us even as
we are attracted – for this is a way of life that, for us, *needs* explanation.
More obviously we are positioned as outsiders by a repeated awareness of
physical and temporal distance. This poem's most intimate, wary
moment of contact is also one which emphasises (like the speaker's
being 'at my window' in *Terry Street*'s 'Young Women in Rollers' (*TS*,
29), or like 'I am a Cameraman' (*LN*, 41)) separation, an outsideness
reinforced by linguistic foreignness:

> Here I whittle time, like a dry stick,
> From sunrise to sunset, among the groans
> And sighings of a tongue I cannot speak,
> Outside a parliament, looking at them,
> As they, too, must always look at me
> Looking through my apparatus at them
> Looking.
>
> (*SKP*, 15)

Versions of the verb 'look' occur eleven times in this poem, along with
various other vision-related terms. The poem relies on placing its
subject in a fluid zone between what is actually seen and what can be
seen only in imagination. The subject matter is present to the sight (the
eye of the camera), yet it also modulates into the visionary as specific
local fact becomes potentially universal myth.

> You need only look at the faces of these men
> Standing there like everybody's ancestors,
> This flick of time I shuttered on a face.
>
> (*SKP*, 14)

Here as elsewhere, Dunn alerts us to the power of photography which
can make the past appear present. The photograph gives us a likeness of
the islanders and their parliament; we can perceive their past and its
likeness to our present (the word 'like' is also important in this poem),
but its likeness, however strong, is less than total, and so it remains at a
tantalising distance from us. The distance in this poem with its
'depopulations', 'dying', 'manacles', 'ghosts', 'failing', 'fall', 'groans'
and 'sighings' is the distance of suffering and ultimately death. The
poem ends with a line which is very much a dying fall. However close it
may seem, we are cut off from that 'remote democracy' of 1879, just as
in 1979 Scotland is cut off from its almost graspable parliament. The
poem certainly admits of this political reading, yet its elegiac, intimate,
and painful resonances extend beyond as well as into the realm of

politics, while its language covers a spectrum far wider than that of the political.

The elegiac note of this opening poem is continued in a good number of the poems which follow in *St Kilda's Paliament*. Scotland may be an 'undeclared Republic' (*SKP*, 19), but it seems destitute and lost, requiring to be called back 'From the lost ground of your dismantled lands' (*SKP*, 27). Sometimes it seems uncertain if Scotland can be called back in this way. Several of the poems are explicitly elegiac. The anger present at times in *Barbarians*, that 'harshness and indignation' in which the Dunn of the later 1970s was interested, has given way to lament.[6] Dunn adopts the Burns stanza in 'Tannahill' to tell us how

> Young dead like Leyden, Smith and Gray,
> Unread, forgotten, sternly weigh
> Against the doors of elegy
> And find them shut.
>
> (*SKP*, 53)

His own elegising pays due acknowledgement to such oppressed figures as the poets Tannahill and Wilson, as well as John Leyden, Alexander Smith and David Gray. In writing of such Scottish figures, Dunn is carrying out a project covering 'a large spectrum of the personalities, concerns and issues involved in Scottish literature – almost like a critical work' (*Viewpoints*, 27). Such a project sounds too willed, and was left incomplete. It also sounds rather academic – one should remember that for all his suspicions of academia, Dunn has worked in at least five universities. There is a positive side to this, for it allows him to mount an important revision of Scottish culture. But there is also an archival or inhibitingly elegiac cast to some of the writing. When Dunn writes in the Burns stanza or the pentameters of John Wilson, he is carrying out an act of enlivening homage, but he is also putting new wine into old bottles or (riskier still) attempting to achieve a vintage poetic tone. It is this vintage tone which sometimes vitiates his writing. For all its beauty, 'The Apple Tree' (another poem which hopes for Scottish regeneration) is spoiled by weirdly unidiomatic inversions.

> Already are
> New scriptures written by the late-arriving autumn . . .
>
> (*SKP*, 17)

This too-literary library language hints that Dunn's wished-for Scotland has an elegiac or even archaic quality. Where he urges 'Sing me your songs in the speech of timber and horse' (*SKP*, 20), he invokes a Scotland which was passing away even in his own boyhood, and it often

appears that he is summoning a country which can be present only as
elegy, a beloved lost place which he is desperate to hear and restore.

Nowhere is this more evident than in the beautiful lyric, 'The Harp
of Renfrewshire' (*SKP*, 30), when as in 'St Kilda's Parliament: 1879–
1979' Dunn is interested in the power to communicate through time
across distances greater than that of a single lifetime. Here the force
resides not in a photograph and the interpreter who is able to
'retranslate' that object into its living original, but in the place names of
Renfrewshire and the 'I' who is able to read in the map's 'one-page
book, a still/ Land-language chattered in a river's burr'. While this
poem is rich in 'phrase-making' – 'Tut-tutted discourse, time of day,
word-brose' – there is nothing stagey about it. Its beautiful locutions
are unexpected, yet just, but its syntax remains colloquially idiomatic.
Interestingly, only one actual place name appears in the poem, which
deals less with the sight of the actual than with the vision of the
elegiacally recalled.

> And on my map is neither wall or fence,
> But men and women and their revenue,
> As, watching them, I utter into silence
> A granary of whispers rinsed in dew.

That last line is redolent of the revenue-earning jobs of the villagers of
yesteryear – milling and spreading out clothes on a washing-green. It
also gestures towards hopeful beginnings – the word 'dew' having
associations of spring and morning. Yet it is predominantly elegiac,
faded. We are offered not only whispers but whispers which are made
even more evanescent by being 'rinsed' in that most passing of
phenomena – dew.

This is a poem of acutely registered transience and suffering,
delicately blending landscape and human experience in a way that
anticipates some of the landscape poetry of *Northlight*. Its sense of a
voice bonded to the land is echoed in 'Witch-girl' where again the *anima*
of Scotland is at once historical and trans-historical, dead in another
time yet faintly heard 'breathing in the wood and stone' (*SKP*, 23).
Dunn has been keen to develop a sense of animated landscape, a
landscape that seems very much part of the Romantic tradition, haunted
by mystical glimpses. If official history has banished so many of the
ordinary folk and aspiring 'barbarian' poets who mean most to Dunn,
then he comes increasingly to value the way landscape (albeit as
fleetingly as the democratic art form of photography) may preserve
glimpses of them – a secret history. Even in the title poem of *St Kilda's
Parliament* it is not only the photograph but the land itself which may

preserve secret traces of its people in 'Its archeology of hazelraw/ And footprints stratified beneath the lichen' (*SKP*, 14).

This secret Scotland which Dunn likes to discover is very much a rural Scotland, recalled through elegiac glimpses, its pastness part of its allure. Even the rare urban location in 'Green Breeks' is clearly antique − 'Edinburgh, seventeen eighty-three' (*SKP*, 47). That poem is highly crafted, yet, like the work of *Barbarians*, is suspicious of the way High Art distorts or omits vernacular life through 'The quicklime of . . . ordered literature' (*SKP*, 49), and the Green Breeks who 'nursed his lovely grudge' (*SKP*, 49) is clearly akin to the Dunn-like speaker of the apparently autobiographical 'The Competition' who confronts a rich child who will never have 'a grudge as lovely as mine' (*LN*, 34). Dunn often returns to favourite themes, and in many ways 'Green Breeks' is an extended, mature and historicised rewriting of 'The Competition'. In the present context it is worth noting that while the rural settings of other poems in *St Kilda's Parliament* are relished, lovingly described and lingered over, the urban setting of 'Green Breeks' is present only as necessary stage furniture. This is entirely consonant with Dunn's comments: 'I don't like Glasgow. Never have done, never will do . . . I grew up suspicious of Edinburgh . . . I identify with small towns and villages in Scotland' (*PD*, 30). The Scotland which emerges throughout *St Kilda's Parliament* is very much a rural Scotland, and one which is past-oriented at that. In 'Remembering Lunch', though no village name is mentioned, it is the rural and old-fashioned which is set in virtuous opposition to the slick London with its 'Manias without charm, cynicism without wit, and integrity/ Lying around so long it has begun to stink' (*SKP*, 45). This attractive poem with its lively phrasing and expansive lines is all the more likeable because of the self-mockery of the speaker who longs to wander 'well-dressed in tweeds and serviceable shoes' and is again a searcher after the land's secret history, walking

> as a schoolmaster of some reading and sensibility
> *Circa* 1930 and up to his eccentric week-end pursuits, noticing,
> Before the flood of specialists, the trace of lost peoples
> In a partly eroded mound, marks in the earth, or this and that
> Turned over with the aforementioned impermeable footwear.
>
> (*SKP*, 44)

This speaker 'In a pretence of being a John Buchan of the underdog/ With my waistcoated breast puffed against the wind' is a wry self-portrait of a man whose 'not altogether satisfactory/ Independence of mind' makes him something of a descendant of Burns's 'man of independant mind', and Burns is an important figure for Dunn (*SKP*, 46).[7] As a sophisticated barbarian, Burns anticipates the figure who walks with 'a pocketful of bread and cheese,/ My hipflask and the *Poésie* of Philippe Jaccottet' and who admires the sea's 'urbane wilderness' (*SKP*, 46). Dunn wants to combine sophistication and simplicity, yet recognises that the milieu in which he longs to do this is a dated one, a paradise of tweed waistcoats. Dunn's ironic self-awareness of his antiquarian hankerings rescues this poem, just as there is a redeeming self-consciousness in the later 'Here and There' (*N*, 26) which is in some ways a rewrite of 'Remembering Lunch'. These points are worth making because there is a danger that (particularly non-Scottish) readers will assume simply that Scotland is a rurally-based, rather dated environment, and a danger that the writer may settle for a presentation of it which relies principally on the old Scots pictorial stand-bys of landscape and couthy antiquities. Dunn at times skirts that risk. In a 1979 *Radio Times* interview he said that 'in Scotland the incursion of the new into the old is far more conspicuous; it's more behind the times than England in many ways'.[8] Dunn's 1974 essay on George Mackay Brown recognises that 'Brown, as a poet of remote island communities and unindustrial, non-urban landscapes, is at odds with the tradition of modern poetry'. Dunn's admiration for this religious poet's best work is clear, and he states that 'Nostalgia for the better community is, in my view, a valid poetic activity', yet the very attractiveness of Brown's world puts Dunn on his guard. He censures Brown for 'his rapid dismissal of The City' and detects in his work stylistic confusions, quaintness and a retrospective idealism that may at times 'have gone over the score'. Brown appears to have been an important poet for Dunn to define and refine himself against. The two writers produce work which reinforces Dunn's contention that 'Scottish imagination is obsessed with the dissection of community'.[9]

Dunn has admitted to a fascination with the Kailyard, that literature of the prettified village (*Viewpoints*, 18), and the poem 'The Miniature Metro' (*SKP*, 77) presents like 'Remembering Lunch' and 'Here and There' another conflict of values between older, rural loyalties and newer experimentations. Here a speaker who appears to be Dunn himself argues with a whisky-induced Rimbaud, and calls to his own defence Seamus Heaney, a literary ally who maintains a strong presence in Dunn's poetry. It is clear that the 'I' of the poem senses the validity of Rimbaud's point of view and his anti-elegiac appeal to 'Confront your despair with enthusiasm'. Nevertheless, it is equally apparent that Dunn sticks to his 'philosophy of departures/ In which are regretted leave-takings of things'. In the age of the word-processor, the speaker of this poem concludes,

> I wrote this on my old horse-writer.
> Old ways die hard, or do not die at all.

This Dunn with his clattering 'horse-writer' is determined to maintain a fidelity towards his childhood of the 'snort-breathed Clydesdale' (*SKP*, 19). This loyalty to his own roots, and to their value, traditions and manners no doubt contributes to his valuation of Brown whom he described during the writing of *St Kilda's Parliament* as 'one of the best poets around; a remarkably interesting poet' (*Viewpoints*, 29). Brown is noted for his hostility towards progress and modernity. The intensity of such loyalty to the past is a strength in Dunn's Heaneyesque 'Washing the Coins' (*SKP*, 24) which is among the finest poems in *St Kilda's Parliament*.

This is a poem of sharp perception – 'sideways-bolted spuds/ Fast to your ear' – and of carefully weighed rhythms – 'You moaned, complained, and learned the rules of work'. A naturalistic syntax and largely colloquial vocabulary drive the poem onwards from its immediately buttonholing first line, which sounds like part of an ongoing narrative: 'You'd start at seven, and then you'd bend your back.' One phrase sounds too grandiose and Poetic – 'turbulent collusions of the sky' – but the rest of the poem is anchored in a muddy day-to-day workplace, albeit a workplace of the past; today it is likely those potatoes would be lifted by machine. Some of the most impressive lines of the poem gain from having the absolutely clear, end-stopped simplicity of direct statement.

> It is not good to feel you have no future.
> My clotted hands turned coins to muddy copper.
> I tumbled all my coins upon our table.
> My mother ran a basin of hot water.

There is a shudder at the awareness of a bald truth in the statement of that first line, spoken as the 'I' of the poem realises he had been mistaken for one of the unloved 'bedraggled Irish' whose fate is only to exist in Scottish dirt. The lines are direct, but an artificial literariness is still vestigially present in that use of the preposition 'upon'; a real boy would be much more likely to say 'on to our table'. Nevertheless, the poem is a strong one, not only in its rhythmical drive and energetic phrasing, but also in the blend of emotions invited by its imagery. Just as the identity of the 'I' has been disguised by mud, with the result that the farmer's wife mistakes him for an Irish boy, so the identity of the

coins has been hidden by mud. Everything we know about Dunn, along
with the placing of this poem between 'Witch-girl' and 'Galloway
Motor Farm' encourages us to read this poem as being about a Scottish
'I'. The word 'Irish' suggests a possible independence from British rule,
yet in this poem any such independence is bound up with a hard,
scorned life of economic dependency. The final act of washing the
money, trying to remove the dirt from filthy lucre, has the effect of
subtly reminding the reader that the 'I' of the poem finally remains
under a hegemony which seems foreign to him. The use of the word
'English' rather than 'British' suggests this:

> And when the water settled I could see
> Two English kings among their drowned Britannias.

These are pre-decimal coins; the king's head is on the florins, the
Britannias on the old pennies. 'Drowned Britannias' suggests the
passing of Empire, a theme that recurs in Dunn's work. The poem ends
on a note of alienation, a hint of a foreign domination that may be
passing. Yet the use of money in the poem prevents us from forgetting
issues of economic dependency – these 'English kings' are after all what
supports the rural economy. And the coins, if alien, are not denied a
beauty as they emerge, royal and mythological, from the mud. This
beauty is questioned, even placed under partial erasure. Yet the ending
of this poem is also about the removal of what erases – the cleansing
from 'That residue of field caked on my money'. Dunn refuses to
oversimplify. That is one of the great virtues of his best work.

Whether or not 'Washing the Coins' is purely autobiographical, it is
another poem that is rooted in the age and sensibility of Dunn's
childhood in Inchinnan. Some of the same memories resurface in his
1978 article 'Clyde and Cheek' as are contained in his 1990 foreword to
Inchinnan Past and Present. [10] Yet, even allowing for the difference of
target-audience between the two pieces, the more restrained, less
punchy 1990 piece has a new note:

> At some point I realised that there was an older, more continuous
> Inchinnan, one that had just about disappeared but which the
> imagination could detect. It took its identity from the land.
> Northbar was a token of that antiquity, but I mean something
> even older, something indestructible, the spirit of a place that had
> been settled and cultivated for many centuries. When you're
> young, listening to birdsong in summer, when a cool breeze rushes
> through the birches, you can feel yourself glimpse beyond time,
> but feel stuck for a name to give your experience. By the time
> you're older you might call that sensation 'poetry' as I do. [11]

This is very different from Dunn's more 'barbarian' and down-to-earth 1978 memories of a childhood of 'giving up cheek' to old ladies and dodging the fares on the Erskine ferry. Dunn's later evocations of his childhood are more consciously 'poetic' in a particular sense. His use of the term '"poetry"' in the 1990 piece is bound up closely with his secret villager sensibility, a sensibility which sees and seeks in the rural or village landscape trans-historical, quasi-mystical moments and voices. This sensibility is in many ways different from that of the poems of *Terry Street*, yet it is not a betrayal of the earlier work. For the poet who says of the man with the anachronistic lawnmower in 'A Removal from Terry Street', 'I wish him grass' (*TS*, 20), seems always to have longed for the rural, for a landscape which he had known in childhood, but which later seemed alien and evaded him, in which he could be 'An example of being a part of a place' (*TS*, 55). As his 'secret villager' sensibility evolves, the search for a trans-historical voice also develops, and is seen growing in *St Kilda's Parliament* where (as elsewhere in his work) it is bound up with rural landscape and the community of the secret village. *St Kilda's Parliament* is not simply a book filled with Scottish-related poems. Dunn varies the collection with, for instance, his 'poem-films' (*SKP*, 62, 66). Yet it is the Scottish-related poems which point most clearly the course his work will take. *Elegies* continues their theme of recurrent loss, while *Northlight* develops their sense of a land-voice that is part mystical and trans-historical. While *Europa's Lover* might seem a surprising departure after *St Kilda's Parliament*, it also involves an attempt to produce a trans-historical land-voice, here a voice of Europe. Yet readers will be alert to the way in which the poem subtly articulates the notion of Scotland in Europe, without labouring that theme. That European and hedonistic sensibility of the self-proclaimed Scot, Dunn's admired Lord Byron, surely plays its part here. *Europa's Lover*, whose Lady offers thousands of years of travel 'Through my archives of sun and rain,/ My annals of rivers and earth' (*EL*, I), offers another transform of 'Witch-girl' or 'The Harp of Renfrewshire'. The poem offers us the sensibility of the secret villager writ large.

If one accepts that the most powerful, innovative and distinctive Scottish contribution to poetry in the twentieth-century takes the form of that linguistic experimentalism seen in some of John Davidson's late poetry, and in the work of MacDiarmid, Graham, Morgan and Finlay, then Dunn stands apart from this love of linguistic metamorphosis and innovation. Whatever his politics, his aesthetic is a very conservative one: quieter, more archival, despite its surface angers. His poetry, particularly the work which has grown out of *St Kilda's Parliament*, may be aligned with that of Edwin Muir, George Mackay Brown and

Andrew Young. Dunn's earliest published stories may have 'read like
attempts to write in the manner of Borges without showing the
influence', but these are not the tales of *Secret Villages*.[12] With the
exception of an admiration for some aspects of surrealism, and an
enviably extended gift for richly unusual phrases, Dunn has little or no
sympathy with the avant-garde. Norman MacCaig's poetic career has
involved more experiment than has Dunn's. This aesthetic conservatism
is an imaginative limitation, yet it is also a source of great strength.
Dunn's rich, sensuous 'phrase-making' is excelled in twentieth-century
Scottish verse only by that of MacDiarmid in the early Scots lyrics.
Compared to his verbal gifts, the language of other modern Scottish
poets seems often thin and dry. Dunn can be a demanding critic;
nowhere is he more exacting than in his selection of the poems which he
chooses to republish in his own volumes. He is a dedicated poetic
craftsman whose fundamentally elegiac sensibility is at present being
modified by a desire to write a poetry that is both celebratory and
Scottish. Dunn's secret village is now Tayport. The challenge which
faces him is how to reap the rich benefits of aesthetic conservativsm
without becoming trapped in the archives, how to go on tapping his
own deep-rooted and highly sophisticated village-voice without over-
prettifying it or doing treason to the accents of contemporary speech.

NOTES

I am grateful to Jim Kidd of St Andrews University Library for advising
me about some of Dunn's uncollected prose.

1 Cairns Craig, ed., *The History of Scottish Literature, Volume 4, The
 Twentieth Century* (Aberdeen: Aberdeen University Press, 1987).
2 Robert Crawford, *Devolving English Literature* (Oxford: Clarendon
 Press, 1992), Chapter VI.
3 Douglas Dunn, 'The Predicament of Scottish Poetry', *TLS*, 18 March
 1983, p. 273.
4 Stanisław Baranczak, *Breathing under Water and Other East European
 Essays* (Cambridge, Mass. and London: Harvard University Press,
 1990), p. 244.
5 Douglas Dunn, 'Foreword' to Anon., *Inchinnan Past and Present*
 (Inchinnan: Inchinnan Community Council, 1990), p. 2.
6 Douglas Dunn, 'Finished Fragrance: The Poems of George Mackay
 Brown', in C.B. Cox and Michael Schmidt, eds, *Poetry Nation No 2*
 (Manchester: University of Manchester Department of English,
 1974), p. 92.
7 Robert Burns, *Poems and Songs*, ed. James Kinsley (Oxford: Oxford
 University Press, 1969), p. 602 ('Song – For a' that and a' that').
8 Paul Vallely, 'Scots Accent' (interview with Dunn), *Radio Times
 (Scotland)*, 24 February – 2 March 1979, p. 17.
9 Art. cit. in note 6 above, pp. 85, 90, 86.

10 Douglas Dunn, 'Clyde and Cheek', *Vole*, Vol. 2, No 1 (October, 1978), pp. 27–9; for Inchinnan foreword, see note 5 above.
11 Art. cit. in note 5 above, p. 4.
12 Douglas Dunn, 'Poetry or Prose', *Writers' Monthly*, June 1985, p. 20.

Nine

Dunn and Dundee:
Dunn's Re-entry into Scottish Culture

W.N. Herbert

Douglas Dunn has long been Scotland's poetic ambassador to the South. Indeed, to glance at Faber's list, it sometimes seems he is our only living poet to be acknowledged in that realm. It should not be overlooked in this context that Dunn was the only Scot chosen for Morrison and Motion's *Contemporary British Poetry*. Or that the poetry selected for that influential anthology depended as heavily on *Terry Street* as on *Barbarians*.[1] In many ways we are reliant on Dunn to 'explain' Scotland to the South in terms it can comprehend (briefly, Ireland without the urgency of the Armalite). So it is that two Dunns emerge across his canon, subtly different from each other and both, one suspects, divorced from his own ideal persona. One is the poet who speaks for us (the Scots), the other is the poet who speaks to them (the English).

To his English readers, the Dunn of *Terry Street* offers an engaging portrait; the Student of English Manners in Hull, the spiritual heartland of the Movement. And indeed that volume is a brilliant piece of apprentice-work; those alienated from 'high' culture as observed by an exile in the act of acquiring the authority of that culture:

> In the culture of clothes and little philosophies,
> They only have clothes. They do not need to be seen
> Carrying a copy of *International Times*,
>
> Or the Liverpool Poets, the wish to justify their looks
> With things beyond themselves. They mix up colours,
> And somehow they are often fat and unlovely.

(TS, 13)

One weighs that 'copy of *International Times*' for a moment; is this a self-portrait? Somehow the presence of the Liverpool Poets suggests not. Dunn is too far outside, too *outwith* all this (to employ a Scotticism). His nearest companion in this style is John Davidson, the Greenock poet who was stifled artistically by the Scotland of the 1880s. He too came down South, mastered the ballad and the rondeau and the jargon of Fleet Street, then turned it on its head in the cold ironies of the *Fleet Street Eclogues*, poems which offer a kind of deconstruction of the pastoral under the impact of urban life:

> The clash of iron, and the clink of gold;
> The quack's, the beggar's whining manifold;
> The harlot's whisper, tempting men to sin;
> The voice of priests who damn each other's missions;
> The babel-tongues of foolish politicians,
> Who shout around a swaying Government;
> The groans of beasts of burden, mostly men,
> Who toil to please a thankless upper ten . . .[2]

Like Davidson, Dunn seems in *Terry Street* to be enquiring whether this is all the beauty that there is.

To a Scottish reader, however, Dunn's distinctive voice begins with *Barbarians*. Here is the master of English poetics putting his skills to what seems (to us) good use; the serious questioning of the social structure underpinnning those aesthetic principles. To be sure the references are impeccably 'high'; the Marvell of the mowing poems, the Yeats of those adamantine refrains, but this is like the Scottish forward outdribbling the English defence: it satisfies our chauvinism:

> What put me up to it, this partnership
> Of lexicon and text, these five books thieved,
> These two books borrowed, handed down, this grip
> Of mind on mind, this work? Am I deceived?
> Is literature a life proved much too good
> To have its place in our coarse neighbourhood?
> *Difficult Latin sticks in my throat*
> *And the scarecrow wears my coat.*

(B, 19)

This would appear to be an uncompromising statement of involvement, but it is clear from subsequent books that Dunn will not be forced into the role of nationalist spokesperson. In this respect it is interesting to note that the city of Dundee makes its first appearance in a book which, for its own tragic reasons, makes the poet's first clear statement of non-engagement, *Elegies*. Here Dunn ceases emphatically to be the token Scot for them or the representative Scot to us and appears as an individual, whose art has a direct purpose in a private situation: 'Then hear her in her best sardonic style:/ "Write out of me, not out of what you read" ' (*E*, 26).

The presentation of Dundee, in the last poem in that volume, is paradoxical in the extreme: 'Leaving Dundee'. Here is what commentators both Scots and English might assume to be the archetypal Dunnian city; like Hull a former whaling port, like Glasgow industrialised but in decay. The place is fretworked with little MacTerry Streets, but Dunn's immediate response is to leave. (*E*, 64).

In fact he doesn't leave, of course, but sets up house in Tayport, across the Firth of Tay, and writes *Northlight*. It is in this book, with its symbolic overtones of resettlement and reabsorption in Scottish culture, that Dunn surmounts the dialectic of Scottish poet in English verse, and presents us with a new synthesis; the British poet in Horatian mode.

Battle is engaged most directly in 'Here and There', in which an English acquaintance debates the nature of provinciality with the contented pastoralist. This echoes the situation of several of Horace's poems from the seclusion of his Sabine farm. As Horace says to his patron Maecenas:

> We don't discuss the mansions or estates of others,
> nor the latest ballet-star's technique. No, we examine
> more vital subjects which it is wrong to neglect: whether
> happiness comes to men from riches or from virtue,
> what motives make men friends – profit or rectitude;
> what is the nature of good, and what its essence.[3]

Or as Dunn says to his critical companion:

> Old friend, you're good for me, but what I want's
> Not what your southern bigotry suspects.
> Here on imagination's waterfronts
> It's even simpler: fidelity directs
> Love to its place, the eye to what it sees
> And who we live with, and the *whys* and *whens*
> That follow *ifs* and *buts*, as, on our knees,
> We hope for spirit and intelligence.

> (*N*, 27)

This pious picture is promptly interrupted by low-flying jets from RAF Leuchars, since, as for Horace, what is valuable for Dunn is not the absence of 'civilisation', but the gaining of a perspective in which to view it. This issue underlines *Northlight* as a whole; despite looking directly out on a city of one hundred and eighty thousand manic urbanites, not one poem in the volume does more than pass through Dundee and continue 'Across the broad, rain-misted, subtle Tay/ . . . to a house, a door . . .' (*E*, 64). A subtlety indeed.

This 'absence' of the urban (the strategy would be familiar to the Calvino of *Invisible Cities*) is balanced by a number of international forays. England becomes a minor theme in this relocated poetic, a kind of underworld the poet visits twice, in the elegy for Larkin and in the dismal pub of 'The Dark Crossroads':

> The thatch, the whitewash and the mullioned windows
>   Negotiating eighteenth-century trust,
> A rendezvous with ordered permanence,
>   As they might see it, crowded at the bar,
> Turning to look at me. One man goes through
>   His repertoire of 'Scotsmen I have known'.
> I'm meant to hear. The calculated voice
>   Distributes mirth, rakish jocosity
> Bred in the hearty schools of prejudice.
>   'Their place,' I warn myself. 'Leave it alone.'
> But I do this, this notional revenge . . .
>
> (N, 63)

No longer the invulnerable observer, and sounding weary with 'this notional revenge', or engagement with the other on the other's terms, the poet turns to totally foreign settings and subjects, finding in flight from Australia, for instance, confirmation of his decision to move north. In 'In-flight Entertainment' the bizarrerie of the International Date Line means the plane is flying backwards in time: 'We're all travelling from the twenty-ninth/ To the twenty-eighth' even though 'everyone's fixed to biological forwards' (*N*, 59).

The result is a sense of liberation from time's value system, in which all that is past is not necessarily worse than all that is present, and different epochs can open up a dialogue which is the hallmark of this collection. Unlike the English drinkers and the silent Scot, or the two friends in 'Here and There', who oppose without reconciliation, the ages here can communicate with and affect each other:

> High over Babylon and Nineveh,
>   Ancient astronomers observe our lights;
> Soothsayers with the troops of Alexander
>   Read our high thunder as a sacred omen . . .

Now that we're all awake, I hear a fool
Refer to down-below as Istanbul:
Where has he been for these past thousand years?

(N, 59)

Not all fools are devoid of wisdom, as Hugh MacDiarmid once ironically observed ('I hear a fool (Plotinus he is ca'd) . . .'), and Dunn's journeying can also obliterate millennia.[4] Certainly it always brings him back to Scotland, as in 'S. Frediano's' where the Tuscan saint turns out to be a Scottish missionary:

S. Frediano is Saint Finnian
Who spelled the rivers with his wand of faith,
The Ayrshire Garnoch and the streams of Down . . .

A couple . . . light candles for their dead

. . . who have yet to read
S. Frediano learned his miracles
In places they came here to be away from.

(N, 5–6)

This miracle of cultural dislocation as relocation is also performed in the Scottish poems. Though sited quite specifically in space, they revise time constantly, employing the conceit of a kind of omnipresent, in which all time is available. This lacks the conspicuous literary note struck by Eliot in the *Four Quartets*, or Seamus Heaney in *Station Island*, where a metaphysical idea is manipulated to ensure an artistic succession. Dunn's temporal dislocations focus on printless predecessors, most strikingly the Picts, whose culture was absorbed by history without a written trace bar kinglists and the occasional indecipherable inscription. Paradoxically it is this wordlessness which makes them all the more immanent:

A Pictish dialect,
Above a bridged Firth, cries
For lyric nationhood,
And horsemen, in a stone disguise,
Ride through the Pictish wood.

(N, 13)

Northlight is possessed by the intangibility of our experience of time, which Dunn manifests by his various dialects of light, wind and ruin:

Early risers pause and stare
At distances beyond their town,

And someone in a dressing-gown
Eavesdrops as mysteries discuss
Sung mornings to no human purpose.
Wordless symposia, in tongues
Informed beyond mere rights and wrongs;
Luminous discourse . . .

(N, 11)

Air-psalters and pages of stone
Inscribed and Caledonian
Under these leaf-libraries where
Melodious lost literature
Remembers itself!

(N, 14)

Of course behind these instances of 'foliated sense' there is the
inaudible tongue of the absent city; urban Scots as a variation on written
English. As Dunn puts it in 'Here and There',

My accent feels at home
In the grocer's and in Tentsmuir Forest.
Without a Scottish voice, its monostome
Dictionary, I'm a contortionist –
Tongue, teeth and larynx swallowing an R's
Frog-croak and spittle. . . .

(N, 28)

Because his voice 'feels at home', Dunn can presume to talk for whole
generations of Scots in an intimate, non-polemic manner that is quite
distinct from the angry gallery of voices he assembled in *St Kilda's
Parliament*. Unlike Robert Tannahill or John Wilson, 'The People
Before' have not suffered neglect or grinding tragedy; they have just
experienced common pleasures, common pains. The specificity of
'Preliminary moonlight on the Firth' means 'time is disobedient', and
Dunn can peer into their lives with an eroticised, compassionate eye:

Processionals of lives go by
On delicate, crisp treads;
Blurred fragrances, gently percussive,
Stir among leaves.
Top-hatted heads of firms and kitchen-maids
Visit the instincts of the eye . . .

More geese rant westward, flock by chevroned flock.
The house of us now, love, of you and me.
I turn a blacksmithed key in its lock.

Feeling its freezing metal on their hands,
These other people turned this iron key.
The lunar honey fell on Buddon Sands.

(N, 7–9)

It is with this voice, in its fullest sense of mature poetic register,
metaphysical locator of the self and metaphoric locutor for his chosen
community, that Dunn mourns Philip Larkin, his English mentor, in
'December's Door'. 'Sorrow's vernacular . . . a leaf brought in on
someone's shoe' is salvaged from the service in Hull and pressed in a
book. (N, 31–2) The leaf withers in 'book-locked winterkill . . .
printed air', recalling the anti-literary advice of Dunn's first wife:
' "Write out of me, not out of what you read." '

The poem's central image suggests that this proper vocabulary,
whether of mourning or of poetics in general, which Dunn indeed
'picked up' in Hull, can only be effective if modulated through Tay's
peculiar regenerative light. The leaf is seen

In a closed shadow, opened now, a door
    Into December's estuary
Beneath a wigged moon, it honeys the floor
    To starry oak, reflected Tay.

(N, 32)

This can restore, partially, its faded colour. This door recollects the
one at the end of *Elegies*: 'The road home trickles to a house, a door'. The
ambiguity in that journey, whether it is to the house of bereavement or
of new beginnings, casts a similarly ambiguous light on Dunn's
exclamation 'now I can't repay the debt I owe . . .'. In this light
the poem becomes both elegy to, and a strategic distancing from,
Larkin. Perhaps there is also an attempt here to separate Larkin the
individual poet from the Larkin of his successors, the Justified Little
Englander.

Dunn's allegiance, then, is with the specific note of transcendence,
the 'fricative on paving-stones' that is a part-translation of Larkin's
'awkward reverence'. In 'Muir's Ledgers' he again pinpoints a precise
moment in which time breaks down and a spiritual, if secular, essence
emerges:

Now Edwin Muir walks from the tram to be a clerk
In Renfrew where the river flows like liquid work
Past Lobnitz's, a shipyard where his writing fills
Commercial ledgers with lists of materials.

Doves on a ledge, a corner of town hall baronial,
Remind him of the future life he'll live in verses
Which, one day, he'll write, in towns other than this.

(N, 37)

Again, one pauses over the possibilities of autobiography; the depiction of Dunn's native Renfrew, and that detail 'towns other than this' (Hull? Dundee?) suggest that Muir is seen as a successor to the aggressive alter egos of earlier books. That 'liquid work' sounds a more apposite depiction of the Tay from the Dundonian bank than some of *Northlight*'s more aureate epithets. That what appeals in Muir is his spirituality is suggested by remarks made in the essay 'Dundee Law Considered as Mount Parnassus'. Commenting on the early Reformation poet John Wedderburn, author of *The Gude and Godlie Ballatis*, Dunn makes a significant digression:

> It would go too far to claim that the author of these poems synchronised the topical with the eternal, but it does seem the case that a poetic gift coincided with the spiritual impetus of a life and its times which obliged poetry to be inseparable from them. That is very unusual in Scottish poetry . . . religious verse of literary value as opposed to pietistical virtue tended to come from writers opposed to the dogmatics of Presbyterianism. Religion became the object of satire, or an orthodoxy regarding which a poet like Robert Burns could be drawn into ambiguous declarations of belief. We have to wait until the twentieth century and Andrew Young and Edwin Muir before genuine religion once again became fused with poetry.[5]

It is a difficult thing nowadays to declare oneself a religious poet, let alone a presbyterian poet: is this Dunn edging towards just such a declaration? There are several poems in *Northlight* – 'At Falkland Palace', 'Memory and Imagination' – in which Dunn takes on the role of abstracted celebrant of a near-Hopkinsian world, where everything trembles on the verge of immanence: 'Lark-sung, finch-wonderful/ Edenic circumstance, not fall', 'summer's roses stir/ Religious scents/ Into invisible/ Sniffed sacraments . . .' (N, 1, 70). This does not smack of the presbyter to me, but who knows?

Certainly, in the uncollected poems written since *Northlight*, there is a sense of the continued search for an acceptable alter ego, someone who can sustain the various aspects of the pastoral Dunn – metaphysician, latter-day Pict, householder, representative. Perhaps 'Moorlander', published in *Scotland on Sunday*, gives the clearest picture of this evasive persona:

His body aches with footsore wilderness,
Burghs, streets, firths, seasonal miles
To cities seen at night from high places.
Strath, carse, mains, bal, mearns, dun, pit, auchter,
For, easter, wester, kil, drum, inver, aber, inch −
He runs like silent ballad, rumour, or
Black water, plotting courses by
Star-fix, fragrant month, and distant farms
Whose lights chink from a curtain or a door.[6]

This sounds suspiciously like *scotus vagans* à la Kenneth White, but the focus on place names (including Pictish ones) and that deft oxymoron 'silent ballad' suggest that Dunn is being very precise in his referents (one would like to say to White, in the words of the whisky advert, 'Don't be *vagans*', though we need our ambassador to France too). The sense of linguistic energy Dunn gets from his dispossessed characters is subtly reinforced by a hint of that primordial verse form, the riddle:

They stalk him with tape-recorders,
Cameras and disappointment's notebook.
In three languages, he impersonates
Water, gersie brae, swan, laverock,
Sionnach, curlew and dobhran.
He can go as an earth-trout.
He is as hoof, paw, and stealthy wing.
He can turn into tree or rock;
In winter he sleeps as such
Camped on misfortune's moorland.

This is the Scottish Sweeney, a somewhat more robust Scholar Gipsy, as a poem in tribute to Sorley MacLean, 'Bare Ruin'd Choirs', would suggest. Here Dunn plays with the space between the three artistic languages of Scotland as a fictive landscape, somewhere where myth and fact can approach each other and, as in *Northlight*, establish a dialogue. Thus we encounter once again the language of the unrecorded event:

What happens ends up written down. It speaks
    Inaccurate events,
False anecdotes, hints, covert verbal keeks
    Into unwritten testaments.
A nationless and local thrush sang there
    Beyond all history.

> Unlettered life inscribed itself on air,
> Its song-life in a vocal tree.

These poems, ostensibly concerned with a familiar theme from *Barbarians* and *St Kilda's Parliament*, the stifled voice of the subjected past, actually appear as a series of hymns to possibility. They explore the range of the national voice through the trope of absence: 'Unhappened Homer, dream-Bard, Ossianic/ Figment . . .' ('Bare Ruin'd Choirs'), 'Gaberlunzie, half-life, national waif,/ Earth-pirate of the thistle and the thorn . . .' ('Gaberlunzie').[7]

Dunn is aware of the dangers inherent in accumulating these ideal selves; he has criticised MacDiarmid's tendency in this direction. But a brief comparison of Dunn's dispossessed 'He' with the aggrandised poet-saint of MacDiarmid's 'The Poet as Prophet' reveals the younger writer's altogether more sane approach. MacDiarmid, unable to influence Scottish political thinking directly, resorts to fictional wish-fulfilment:

> He was the marvellous embodiment
> Of the complete identification
> Of the Celtic mind with all nature and all life . . .
> The whole nation felt itself shaken
> As by an electric shock . . .[8]

Dunn, substituting compassion for sentiment, never identifies himself with his subject, taking on the quieter democratic role of witness or recorder, as in 'Past and Present':

> He is as footsteps — *Is he? Isn't he?*
> Headed through etymologies and names
> Into an unrecorded country that
> Historians don't know of. If they do
> They fear its absence of modernity,
> Its unresolved remorse, its carelessness
> With land and water . . .[9]

In a sense, this voice is the legitimate heir of Dunn's early poetry, the eye as camera he has referred to, which approaches Terry Street but does not blend (*LN*, 41; *SKP*, 13). Now its subject, as in the fine 'Poor People's Cafes' in his Counterblast pamphlet on the poll tax, is still the political underdog, but invigorated by a sense of cultural possibility (*PT*, 49–56). As he says in 'Here and There', Scotland is a 'Country in which to reconstruct a self/ From local water, timber, light and earth', in which the poet must pluck a tradition out of the air (*N*, 26).

In 'Preserve and Renovate', another uncollected poem, Dunn sets out to do precisely this; to position himself in the pastoral landscape of Protestant suburbia. An old neighbour's 'fastidious hours/ Spent tying up his border's tasteful flowers' becomes the meditative focus of the poet's strolls. As in 'The Dark Crossroads', however, the observer is in turn observed:

> He looked at me with an almost-cross surprise
> That I'd walked past his house four times today,
> And yesterday . . . my walks meant indolence
> And curiosity . . .

Dunn is able to endure this vulnerability (unlike MacDiarmid) because his own role has proven itself coherent. He is the unacknowledged representative, no longer observing from the outside because he can establish a shared culture with his subject: 'I saw in him ironic song/ Echoing my dear father'. Both those adjectives are significant; the song is 'ironic' because it is unselfconscious – the old man does not reflect upon his skill or his pride, either as limited faculties with which to judge the 'indolent' Dunn, or as representative talents his observer may esteem. The word 'dear' therefore seems to contain elements of both affection and expense. The 'elderly contempt' is the price the poet pays for a glimpse of his dead father, a fine for disobeying time:

> That is my work, though he won't understand;
> Nor could my father. It is what I do,
> This risk of feeling, that the sweet and true
> Might be preserved, presented by my hand
> Among the many others who do this
> For the same sake that is obedience to
> Time and experience, for what is due
> To being, to be life's accomplice.[10]

The tragic implication of that phrase, 'life's accomplice', which seems to reach out to Lear's 'As if we were God's spies', belies the impression this poem gives of triumphal recovery. Triumph, however, and an often comic celebration, is very much a feature of Dunn's recent poetry, and the remainder of this chapter is devoted to this theme.

Dunn has always been an amusing poet, but the first really characteristic note of his comic mode came in St Kilda's Parliament with the burlesque 'Ode to a Paperclip'. Here the sustained focus on the commonplace, the unwavering formalism of the address, the mock-pedantic thoroughness of Dunn's list of uses for this innocuous little

device, all combine into a Magritte-like vision in which reality appears
subtly redrawn:

> Ghost bullets, triple-loops, no matter what
> Inquiring minds might call your outline capsules,
> You change your shapes and will go anywhere,
> Do anything for a piece of the action.
> Immoralist! Turncoat! Mercenary!
>
> (*SKP*, 82–4)

In *Northlight*, the celebration swells to Pindarics in a lavish paean to
the heroic wartime adventures of a Dundee pigeon. 'Winkie' (the phrase
'Wee Willie' rises unbidden in the brain), a stuffed bird in Dundee's
Barrack Street Museum, the ultimate urban creature, is Dunn's
roundabout way of acknowledging Dundee. It is the only poem in the
book which actually sets itself in that city (even 'Broughty Ferry' is a
view of that suburb from Fife) (*N*, 33–6, 24–5). As such, it is a bizarre
tribute both to municipal *mores* and to Dundee's particular heritage. It
should not be forgotten that wartime adventure forms a major subject-
matter in D.C. Thomson's pulpy empire. 'Winkie' comes across as a
verse equivalent to Max Ernst's collage novels, perhaps assembled from
The Victor and *The Courier*'s fabulously couthy 'Craigie Column':

> Over Norway, its fuselage and wings on fire,
> The bomber droned down to the sea . . .
> Cupped hands released you from a rubber boat.
>   Miniature of instinct,
>   Dedicated one, your stuffed breast swells
>   With pride in your only nature!
>
>   (*N*, 33)

Shades of Magritte return in the vigorous anapaests which make up
Dunn's book review in verse on Henry Petroski's book, *The Pencil: A
History*, which appeared in the *Glasgow Herald*. The extended focus on
an inanimate object, and the displacement of reader expectation caused
by the appearance of verse in a decidedly prose context, both point to
the destabilising element in Dunn's comic mode. The emphasis on
formal metre in this context is decidedly idiosyncratic, and would
appear to have a parallel in the tactics of the American New Formalists.
A poet like Dana Gioia would talk of challenging the common
perception of poetry as redundant by revitalising traditional forms, or
those aspects of poetry with which the ordinary reader is most familiar.
Dunn's formalism absorbs this and still seems to reserve a little

surrealistic frisson to itself, as when Magritte distorts the scale of a
normal object, then restores it to a normal setting:

> Computerised reason and drafting are all very well
> But you can't pick your nose with a screen, and keyboards won't do
> When it comes to that cedary, graphite-and-alphabet smell,
> While hardware and gadgetry leave you with nothing to chew.[11]

This tendency reaches its zenith in the magnificent 'Libraries: A
Rhapsody', published in its ideal setting, the *Journal of Documentation*.
The library is a social paradox; universally reviled for its boring
attributes, staff or atmosphere, it nonetheless contains, in theory,
universal knowledge. Dedicated to systems of cataloguing and
organisation, it has nonetheless arrived at a principle for linguistic
collage: alphabetic grouping. And perhaps, for Douglas Dunn, who
worked with Philip Larkin in Hull University library, the nature of the
librarian also contains some undertone of that of the poet:

> For twenty backroom girls in Marchfield Avenue
> At the unfashionable end of the book trade
> I offer up these prayers to The Nine Muses
> Mentioning that you did not discriminate between
> Volumes by half-wits, ninnies and sparkling geniuses,
> Tables of logarithms and *The Divine Comedy*.[12]

The anecdote Dunn incorporates about Larkin is especially telling,
combining as it does the perspective of xenophobe and poet (if 'poet' can
stand here for someone able to convey a sense of the extraordinary):

> my old boss, Philip Larkin, holding a book
> Written in Indonesian, published in Djakarta,
> As if it were a toad that spoke back to him, saying
> 'Isn't it *wonderful*? That someone *understands* this?'

This is a footnote to Dunn's elegy in *Northlight*, 'December's Door',
in which the perspective of the librarian is seen as 'hazily Utopian' (*N*,
31). It established the poet's affection for and independence from his
'old boss'.

The poem ends with what sounds like a grand parody of the Homeric
hymn, which recollects Frank O'Hara's similarly lavish invocation at
the start of 'To the Film Industry in Crisis' ('Not you, lean quarterlies
and swarthy periodicals/ with your studious incursions toward the
pomposity of ants . . .').[13] The laurel goes to Dunn, however, for all
O'Hara's charm cannot disguise the fact he is reminding us of the
obvious: film stars are the gods and heroes of modern mythology. The

Scottish poet's task is harder, to point out that 'All libraries at night are sleeping giants'.

> O ye anonymous reader who marked your place
> With a rasher of bacon, will I ever forget you?
> O all ye ancient ladies once on waiting-lists
> For Pope-Hennessey's *Queen Mary*, and little boys
> Imagining armadas in Jane's *Fighting Ships*!
> Philosophies and all the -ophies! Fiction! Drama!
> Soft toys, soft core, directories, encyclopaedias!
> Romances, Westerns, 'tec-tales, purchased by the yard!
> . . . O ye Chief Librarians of Scotland in your good suits!
> Celebrities of SCONUL, ASLIB, and the *J. of Doc.*,
> Associates, Fellows, and Office Bearers of the Library Association
> Hear this! − the wheels of my retrieval system running
> On lubricants of print and permanent devotion!
>
> ('Libraries: A Rhapsody')

Obviously it is too soon to determine what the nature of Dunn's next book will be, but one can determine, from the evidence of *Northlight* and those poems which have appeared in (mainly) Scottish newspapers, an approximation of the poet's first reaction to Scotland.

The move to Tayport has coincided with a sense of deepening independence from both English and Scottish overviews of what constitutes 'British' literature, and a sense of complex responsibilities to what might be defined as Dunn's ideal community. This is no longer the urban sub-unit of Terry Street, or the vanished islanders of St Kilda's, but, to revive a title from *Love or Nothing*, 'The Estuarial Republic' (*LN*, 61). What Dunn means by this is more problematic.

Certainly it comprises the kind of small town he now lives in and with which he is most familiar. This unit in his opinion preserves what he has termed a 'quite self-conscious sense of decency' which he is anxious to commemorate and extend (*Verse*, 26). The estuarial republic also contains its pasts in the form of Pictish forebears, monastic remains and ancestors of all kinds. What it does not contain, apparently, is the urban community. The Tay Bridge, celebrated in a beautiful nocturne in *Northlight*, appears to extend into nowhere (*N*, 22). Dundee exists as a view, not a reality; as something people travel from, but, surrealistically, never to. 'Winkie', though set in Dundee, doesn't stray outside a museum.

Part of his strategy here, as I have suggested, is Horatian, in terms of establishing a distance from urban culture in order to comment upon it. And the 'invisible' city proves its presence in a number of ways throughout *Northlight*. But there is, as Dunn is only too aware, a distinction between the urbanity of a cultural centre like London or Edinburgh, and that of a city ordinarily ignored or dismissed as provincial. Dunn's recent professorship at St Andrews has added a university to his estuarial republic, but there is still a disconcerting blank on his poetic map.

There are signs, however, that this is changing. Not only the essay 'Dundee Law Considered as Mount Parnassus' but also a recent poem, 'Scott's Arks', published in the *Glasgow Herald*, suggest that this Scottish Hull may be admitted to Dunn's republic. With it may come a new and authoritative approach to the themes which have engaged both the poet's English and Scottish audiences. Certainly Dunn has become what Ted Hughes could not be, and what Seamus Heaney should not be built into, a mature British poet. That he has done this by becoming more definitively a Scottish poet should give the imaginary Southerner of 'Here and There', and behind him, London, cause for contemplation:

> A girl in service wiped the steamed-up glass
> In Broughty Ferry as a ship went by
> Out of her country and beyond her eye
> To where there were no signposts, trees or grass.
>
> Her aged daughter saw Scott's ark come home;
> And everyone loves rivers and the sense
> In flowing, change, courage, perseverance –
> Great river, cities, free and mettlesome.[14]

NOTES

1 Blake Morrison and Andrew Motion, eds, *The Penguin Book of Contemporary British Poetry* (Harmondsworth: Penguin, 1982), 50–64.

2 John Davidson, *Fleet Street Eclogues* (London: John Lane/The Bodley Head, 1896), 57.

3 Quintus Horatius Flaccus, *Serm.* 2.6.70–6, translated by Gilbert Highet in *Poets in a Landscape* (Harmondsworth: Penguin, 1959), 135–6.

4 Hugh MacDiarmid, 'To Circumjack Cencrastus', *The Complete Poems of Hugh MacDiarmid*, edited by W.R. Aitken and Michael Grieve (London: Martin Brian and O'Keeffe), I, 217.

5 Douglas Dunn, 'Dundee Law Considered as Mount Parnassus', in *Duende: A Dundee Anthology* (*Gairfish*, 4), October 1991, 20.

6 'Moorlander' in *Scotland on Sunday*, 14 October 1990, 32.

7 'Bare Ruin'd Choirs' and 'Gaberlunzie' are from the author's TS.

8 Hugh MacDiarmid, *Complete Poems*, II, 1375–6.

9 'Past and Present' in *Spectrum* (Stirling University), No. 1 (1990), 3–5.

10 'Preserve and Renovate' in *Poetry Review*, 79 (4), Winter 1989/90, 26–7.

11 Dana Gioia, 'The Poet in an Age of Prose' in *Verse*, Vol. 7, No 3, 9–15; 'Henry Petroski. *The Pencil. A History*. Faber & Faber, £14.99' in *Glasgow Herald*, 17 November 1990, 24.

12 'Libraries: A Rhapsody' in *Voices aloud: an anthology of poetry about Libraries*. ed. Bernard Young and Jonathan Davidson (Hull: Humberside Leisure Services, 1990), 55–7.

13 Frank O'Hara, 'To the Film Industry in Crisis', in *The Collected Poems of Frank O'Hara*, edited by Donald Allen (New York: Alfred A. Knopf, 1979), 232–3.

14 'Scott's Arks' in *Glasgow Herald*, 6 March 1990, 9.

Ten

Telling Short Stories

Anne Varty

'To what purpose should we trouble ourselves about the world in the moon?'[1] asks Adam Smith. The serious implication behind his facetious tone is that while moral sensibility thrives by imaginative engagement with realities to hand, this necessary and powerful aspect of the imagination must not be permitted to usurp the proper objects of moral attention. The mature moral sensibility knows when to engage and when to disengage the imagination; it does not indulge in selfish or irresponsible displacements. The explicit premiss of Smith's moral theory lies implicit behind much of Dunn's fiction. 'Humanity,' Smith announces, 'consists merely in the exquisite fellow-feeling which the spectator entertains with the sentiments of the persons principally concerned . . .'.[2] Fellow-feeling, or 'sympathy' as Smith calls it (in a definition more embracing than that permitted by Hume) is born of the imagination, and allows the spectator to enter the place of the 'persons principally concerned' or, in his profoundly literary view of life, the protagonists. Imagination generates sympathy, allows the change in perspective which brings to our living rooms the world in the moon, and on this our humanity depends. Where Smith is didactic, Dunn is demonstrative. He exercises his imagination as a moral faculty and has been consistently concerned to bring the remote into focus.

Describing how Hull affects the writer, Dunn states 'it is a town which by its nature recommends the plainly human, the seriousness of what, in more glamorous places, is taken to be ordinary', which he romanticises with a touch of Yeats, continuing that 'it leads the writer to meditate on the rag and bone shop of the heart.'[3] The combatively local concerns of his fiction are stated by the narrative voice of 'Boyfriends and Girlfriends':

places like Kelmshill – places that are minor, perhaps, but where more of the world lives than the headlines and passions of history would have us believe.[4]

That 'perhaps' warns the reader against prejudice while inviting attention to distant communities and the sense of place which is a major theme of his fiction. *Secret Villages* (Faber, 1985) the title of his first collection of stories, all but one of which have Scottish settings, reflects Dunn's commitment to this theme and its relation to the view stated in *Lanark* that 'if a city hasn't been used by an artist not even the inhabitants live there imaginatively'.[5] But 'place' for Dunn has more than a geographical connotation, for it includes also social and emotional position.

With 'The Canoes' (*SV*, 46–58) Dunn explores how an imaginative sense of place affects the inhabitants, by bringing into juxtaposition the yuppydom of the South with a backwater of the North as Peter and Rosalind Barker spend their canoeing holiday at Lochearnhead. The visitors and the locals entertain preconceived ideas about one another and all, except the local first-person narrator, have their expectations fulfilled. This generates gentle humour while it also observes in the breach a belief shared by Smith and Hume about how moral sensibility is cultivated. Both philosophers liken moral to physical vision when the spectator views things at a distance. Hume argues that

> judgement . . . corrects the inequalities of our internal emotions and perceptions . . . The same object, at a double distance, really throws on the eye a picture of but half the bulk . . . we know that on our approach to it, its image would expand on the eye, . . . the difference consists not in the object itself, but in our position with regard to it. And, indeed, without such a correction of appearances, both in internal and external sentiment, men could never think or talk steadily on any subject.[6]

It is not clear that men, in 'The Canoes', do think or talk steadily, at least not across the North-South divide which remains, despite the characters' physical proximity. Dunn exploits the narrative potential of prejudice while warning the reader against it. Both sets of people fail to adjust their vision, their insight, their sympathy according to what they see, and respond instead according to preconceptions. Lochearnhead, it seems, is being lived in too imaginatively.

'The Canoes' is a story structured by observation rather than event. The Barkers are kept at a narrative distance, being permitted only one minor occasion of direct speech (*SV*, 48), to maintain the gulf between the two tribes. Instead, 'these English Barkers' (*SV*, 55) are trailed by

the idle curiosity of the locals as they go about the business of their
holiday. Their arrival provokes the unnamed narrator's reminiscence of
other visitors; he reveals that tourist-baiting provides much sport when
the village chorus is not baiting its own members. Tourists are easy
game, they exhibit their preconceptions without reserve:

> they are a familiar sight to us, these couples, who look and behave
> as if they feel themselves to have arrived in a timeless paradise of
> water and landscape and courteous strangers in old-fashioned
> clothes. (SV, 47).

All that Magee, Muir, Munro, Young Gregor, MacMurdo, MacEachan
and 'I' have to do is to act out the drama which the visitors expect to see.
With little else to do, they have perfected their art:

> We all nodded a polite and silent good evening to them, which we
> believe is necessary, for they have heard of our courtesy, our soft-
> spoken and excellent good manners and clear speech. (SV, 48)

> a lethargic disregard for time is obligatory in these parts. Or that,
> at least, is the legend. (SV, 48)

> We turned away with the precision of a chorus line. (SV, 49)

> I treated them to one of my lugubrious waves which I am so good
> at . . . (SV, 49)

> They settled back before this recitation. (SV, 51)

> I was all for putting an end to Magee's playacting . . . (SV, 52)

Apart from the charming eccentricity of this collective bad behaviour,
the reader sees nothing romantic or timeless behind the scenes.
Lochearnhead harbours unemployment, a dwindling population, marriage strife and poverty. The only wealth is in the landscape, to which
the narrator and his companions are sensitive (SV, 47).

From the moment at which the narrator wearies in embarrassment of
Magee's playacting, the power balance changes and the Barkers are
inadvertently giving as good as they and their fellow tourists get:

> Mr and Mrs Barker looked like people of the far long ago, when,
> we are told, there was great happiness and heroism in the world.
> (SV, 53)

Following this vision, the narrator encounters the minister 'scrutinising
the loch through his spyglass' (SV, 54) and with this instrument
together they watch the couple canoeing. The act of observation, rather
than voyeuristic, is like that of a legitimate theatre audience viewing
some Ardenic episode: 'They tell me she is called Rosalind.' And the
vaguely literate minister replies, 'Now, that is a name from

Shakespeare, I believe' (*SV*, 55). The show has gone out of local control, as the narrator finds himself victim of the very art in which his community specialises. His own vision, like that of the visitors, is clouded by a false imaginative engagement with the strangers. Both sets of temporary neighbours are mutually alien; the proper channels to foster understanding do not exist. To treat life as though it were art is always morally questionable, and by indulging in this both parties exhibit, paradoxically, a failure of imagination and hence a failure of sympathy in moral terms. The reader, however, is differently placed, invited by Dunn's realism and the confessional intimacy of the narration, to treat art as though it were life. The reader therefore occupies the position of Smith's ideal spectator who 'must view them . . . from the place and with the eyes of a third person, who has no particular connection with either, and who judges with impartiality between [them]'.[7] And so it is that we respond with the proper mixed emotion to the narrator's simultaneously modest and impossible closing wish for the legendary couple to return so that he can again inhabit the 'timeless paradise' into which their presence had transformed his home. Although the Barkers are the ones to depart, it is the narrator who is left with nostalgia, made acute by the understatement of its expression as he cherishes 'the way they just followed each other about on the still water' (*SV*, 58).

The quiescent nostalgia of this narrator for his home is to be contrasted with the pathetically urgent hypocrisy of C.M. McColl in 'Kilbinnin Men' (*SV*, 111–17), or the discomfort of Kenneth Fraser in 'Fishermen' (*SV*, 158–65). The latter story, like 'The Canoes', is a first-person narrative. The protagonist is angling to recover the home of his youth, and is dismayed to discover the place receding from him with time: '[m]y wife sees the place in which I grew up as part of my memory, and therefore visits to my parents are best left to myself' (*SV*, 158). The journey back to Dargal Water is one which must be made alone, but as he sets out on a fishing trip with his brother, he discovers that it cannot be made at all. One after another, members of his former community greet him with 'You're a stranger!' (*SV*, 159), reinforced by his brother's 'You're out of touch . . .' (*SV*, 161), or the blunter 'You don't seem to know anything about this place any longer' (*SV*, 162).

Kenneth's attitude to his home exhibits the naïvely self-centred belief that nothing changes in his absence, while Dunn's submerged imagery of flux carries the implicit Heraclitean maxim that it is impossible to step into the same river twice. Kenneth's failure of imagination is painfully corrected in the course of the story which ends on the abruptly ambiguous gesture of farewell from his brother:

'All the best, then. I'll see you next time,' I said. 'Sure. All the
very best,' he said, his hand reaching out across the passenger seat.
(*SV*, 165)

Because David (who 'looks in harmony with water and weather' (*SV*,
162)) has acted as Kenneth's guide throughout the episode, and has now
pragmatically declined a sentimental invitation to join Kenneth and
their father in the pub, this gesture of courtesy, between brothers,
seems to cut the protagonist, and leave him bereft where he expects to
feel most at home.

One feature of this narrative, and also of the narrator since he is the
lens through which the local colours show, is the humorously
affectionate pleasure taken in the observation of community figures with
their eccentricities and odd habits. Ironically predominant among these
is Kenneth's keen sensitivity to the misplacement of others. Paterson,
for instance, the former alcoholic, is noticed sitting outside The Plover
'cured of drink and with no thirst for it, but irresistibly drawn to his
damaging oasis' (*SV*, 165); alternatively there is the inverted snobbery
of Dr Fullerton, the minister, who speaks 'in a homespun version of
braid Scots' (*SV*, 163) and is considered affected by the parishioners
because his social place, by birth and education, is 'higher' than his
acquired accent suggests.

Dunn's characters exhibit acute sensitivity to linguistic markers of
social status. 'All of a sudden they even started to *talk* different,'
complains Pally Gray in 'Toddle-Bonny and the Bogeyman' about the
corruption of Labour Councillors[8]; the selfishly genteel Mrs Pollock in
'Bobby's Room', with her kimono and her clichés of maternal affection
announces of Mrs Bawden that she is 'very nicely spoken' (*SV*, 79) to
clinch her acceptability, while the third-person narrator of 'Getting
Used To It' remarks of the '[biliously malicious]' Vic Nairn that he
spoke in a 'slow, emphatic pronunciation, which was that of a man with
a West-of-Scotland accent trying to speak "properly" ' (*SV*, 59). The
protagonist, Harry Boyle, shares contempt for the hypocrisy of what the
man says with the manner in which he says it.

This story is about the fluctuating social place of the individual, and
the opening detail of a token of false social mobility is apt for the
thematic exposition. Vic Nairn becomes unemployed during the story,
while Harry Boyle has already been made redundant before it begins. In
the process of adjusting to this shift in terms of economy, status and
self-respect, Boyle and his wife experience their daytime leisure as an
upward change in social hierarchy. They 'spend an hour in bed' together
regularly after lunch: 'I suppose that this is what rich people do in the
afternoon. I could get used to it', says Vera (*SV*, 65). Harry Boyle also

finds himself exchanging gender roles with his wife. Vera is the breadwinner, cleaning at the local school during the early evening, while Boyle stays at home, walks the dog, scrutinises the children and gets interested in housework: 'right now I'm into carpets and curtains. I'm a home boy' (*SV*, 65).

The younger generation of the story is already familiar with the complex mobility of status and gender in society. Alan, Boyle's seventeen-year-old son, wears an earring, coddles the dog and refuses to watch his sister perform in the school play because ' "I'm in love . . . I'm staying in to wash my hair and pine" ' (*SV*. 68). These words are said 'cynically', with adolescent self-consciousness; Alan knows he is role-playing and lives at an ironic distance from his actions. His words also mock his sister who is performing in *Twelfth Night*, as Viola. 'But most of the time I'm Cesario. And he's a man' (*SV*, 64), she explains to her baffled father. Cross-dressing on and off stage, she announces 'a woman has to show a lot more initiative than a man to get on in this country. The cards are loaded against her' (*SV*, 64). Her father can correct her mixed metaphor but is at a loss with the mixed gender construction of her utterance. The younger generation moves comfortably across the borders of differently gendered social spaces, while the older generation has to acquire this confidence by the often painful process of social and economic humiliation.

There are many instances throughout the stories, which tend to focus on 'unemancipated' rural communities, of women who wield great power, dominating their lazy or uncooperative husbands. Mrs Henderson in 'Fishermen', who chased her man 'up the street with a bread knife' (*SV*, 160); Mrs Magee in 'The Canoes', who will scatter his dinner and 'probably Magee as well, before her chickens' if he is late (*SV*, 48); Mrs Bawden in 'Bobby's Room', whose feeble husband admits 'she wears the trousers' (*SV*, 84). As Monty Gault in 'Orr Mount' says, 'why . . . do some wives pretend that their husbands are the masters of the household when it's as clear as day that they aren't?'[9] These, however, are all male glimpses of women integrated by marriage into the community. Dunn's portrayals of single or deserted women in these communities, which include one first-person narrative ('The Tennis Court', *SV*, 118–26), expose the economic, emotional and prejudicial vulnerabilities of this social group. The numerous euphemisms for illegitimate children in 'South America' and 'Twin Sets and Pickle Forks' are sufficient to show the collective judgement and embarrassment which these mothers must overcome: 'excuses', 'errors', 'infidelities', 'mistakes', 'mistake or misfortune' (*SV*, 21, 22, 25, 26, 31). Equally, Dunn's first-person female narrator of 'Tennis Court' notices how prejudice against single women is connoted by lexis: 'We are both spinsters. I do not like that word, but I am stuck with it' (SV, 120). His fiction often deals with sexually segregated communities within the larger social sphere (even 'Boyfriends and Girlfriends' uses 'and' disjunctively in the title and portrays a male audience of romance and revenge), treating sex, distinct from gender, as a place in itself, where male is as far from female as the moon from either.

The presentation of clear and profound sexual difference is brought out most fully by 'Wives in the Garden' (SV, 36–45). This story, fragrant with delicate erotic desire, addresses the male question, 'why are women so powerful?' (SV, 38), asked by Steve, the first-person narrator, on vacation with his wife Laura at the holiday home of their friends Malcolm and Henrietta Blair. Sources of female power are explored but not explained, first in the social and domestic spheres, before moving to a meditation on the private union of the marriage bond. The wives are experienced by their husbands as beings so intimately alien that watching them unseen in the garden is an act of voyeurism: 'we stepped back into the room, afraid of having been caught in the act of looking at our own wives. For some reason we had to keep it secret' (SV, 43). In the very act of observing the exclusive bond between women, and their elemental bond with the cultivated earth, the men also enact the compromised union of their own sex.

Steve is never in control of the story he narrates. It is dictated throughout by the women. As the couples settle into communal domesticity, which involves some alcohol and reminiscence, the women demand to see Steve's knees, to check how he carries his age: ' "Pull up your trousers," said Henrietta . . . "Go on, pull them up . . ." ' (SV, 39). The narrator opts to clown for the partial but unavoidable striptease, making himself even more their puppet. When the ménage moves to the beach, the men lounge while the women swim. Steve states, in the narrative present, '[f]ew arrivals of the woman you love are as contenting as seeing her run towards you across the sand, having swum, splashed and waded in the sea' (SV, 41). The passivity of the watching husbands, which the narrative voice turns into a general condition, indicates not complacent power over what they see but symbolises a pervasive submission to their women which makes the inviting approach a privilege. In this context, Malcolm remarks 'Aphrodite was a woman', with telling inaccuracy about the goddess. The implied identity between deity and woman is deliberate, as the women, mysterious and magnificent, seem to control even the ocean. ' "Did you see Henrietta slap that wave? . . . as if it'd been naughty" '

(*SV*, 41). The story abounds with examples of feminine self-containment, confidence, spontaneity and control, whether of the social matrix of memory, manners and fashion, or of the surrounding natural elements, both of which the women manipulate or defy with artless skill.

As the wives return from the garden in the closing scene, Steven transposes the conventions of mental striptease to a meditation on the privilege of the ultimately intangible marriage bond:

> Laura's tight-fitting gloves were bulged on the finger on which she wears her rings. In the dark, inside the glove, I imagined them shining with commitment and convention. Esther Reids, Sweet Williams, late cornflowers . . . were bunched in her arms. (*SV*, 44).

The apparition is now of Flora, virginal and mature at once, while his mind's eye probes what is simultaneously concealed and revealed by her clothing. He focuses not on her body but on the public token of her love for him, which is so private that it can be known even by her husband only indirectly. With the closing statement ' "I'm going to ask them what they think of us" ' (*SV*, 45), the story launches into necessary silence. Although Dunn's fiction acknowledges the fact of sexual difference, its observation is not a cause to be cultivated as an end in itself. The satirical story 'Mulwhevin'[10] indicates that sexual difference is most successfully contained by social conventions and not the condition upon which a society of the future should seek to build its conventions.

The recognition of necessary distance between the sexes does not preclude their responsibility towards one another; instead it makes imaginative sympathy more imperative. Dunn offers stories in which the social and emotional duties, concomitant with the privileges and rights implicitly described by 'Wives in the Garden', are neglected. 'South America' (*SV*, 11–28) portrays a wife, Thea, deserted by her husband for work on another continent. She maintains throughout the fifteen-year period spanned by the narrative that he should ' "come back to Scotland, Jack Docherty. Your family needs you" ' (*SV*, 12). His rejection of her claim even for financial maintenance, once he hears of the two illegitimate children which have been added to his own, leaves Thea with only occasions of public ritual as a means of address to him: the story ends with her confession that she has sent him a Christmas card. This parallels the fate of the three women (two widows and one spinster) in 'Women without Gardens' (*SV*, 127–38) who, falling outside the social matrix in virtue of their singularity, must avail themselves of the public park, not the private territory of the domestic garden, to exercise and satisfy their need for a patch to nurture. The thematically related story, 'Bobby's Room' (SV, 78–93), tells of neglected parental duty. The twelve-year-old Henry Pollock is abandoned by his grotesquely selfish mother, to live for three months in the Bawdens' boarding house, while she accompanies his father to work in the Far East. Insult is added to injury when Henry finds himself skivvying in the boarding house. But he learns incidentally how to turn weakness into strength, a modulation reflected by the exchange:

'What's a black pudding?'

'Black pudding,' Henry said, with a hesitant shrug.

'But what's it made of?'

'Hold on.' . . .

Henry came back from the kitchen. 'Blood and lights,' he said.

'I'll have two lightly poached eggs . . .' (SV, 88)

By the end of his stay there he has acquired independence which, he anticipates, will lead to his own neglect of filial duty just as the Bawdens' son Bobby, in whose room Henry symbolically sleeps, keeps his parents in ignorance of his whereabouts and activities.

In a rare comment about his fiction, Dunn stated:

You have to show things in a story . . . We consider prose the language of telling, poetry the language of showing, but in contemporary poetry you can tell as much as you show . . . Short stories are very close to the spirit of poems (Viewpoints, 32)

The dialogue cited above exemplifies the economy of Dunn's strategies for 'showing' which are as diverse as the multiplicity of things that he wants to show, all of which contribute to the priming of the reader's moral sensibility. His means of approximating the short story form and 'aura' (Viewpoints, 32) to that of poetry are integrated with, and sometimes (when they concern the patterning of resonant images, for example) even constitute, his strategies of narrative display. 'Wives in the Garden', for instance, about sexual difference and female domin-ance, is told by a male narrator who is not in control of the *fabula* (chronological content), and this in itself enacts the central point of the story. Steve is, however, in control of the *suzet*: the manner in which events are described is entirely his domain. Here the detail of what is noticed, when and how it is introduced, establishes the persuasive realism of the piece and its meaningful erotic charge. The fluid sonority of the line 'a half-melted floe of ice slid from her tilted gin' (SV, 39) echoes what it describes; the caesuras of the free direct speech ' "Your legs," said Henrietta, "are a disgrace, unlike," she said, "mine" ' (SV, 42) mimic the breathing of a swimmer. Steve's observation, in the narrative present, of 'cormorants, those black birds which fly towards the sea like caricatures of thirst' (*SV*, 36) introduces a simile which disengages the narrative flow and which, with the reader's hindsight of how the sea functions as an image in the story, implies an ironic comment about himself and Malcolm. And this story ends characteristically without closure, but with the poise and provocation of direct speech.

The techniques by which Dunn controls his fiction also control the reader's position in relation to it. 'Twin Sets and Pickle Forks' (*SV*, 29–35) provides an example of the way in which the reader's position can be shifted by alteration of narrative voice, to correspond with the change in social position of the protagonist. The story concerns Miss Frame, whose name suggests the self-contained distance which she cultivates in relation to her community, and it opens with the third-person narrative voice switching between the simple past tense to recount immediate events, and the present continuous tense to comment on the eternal truths of Arnot's Tea Room or Miss Frame's management of it and her life. The alteration of voice keeps the reader at an ironical distance. Yet from the moment at which Miss Frame's illegitimate son enters the tea room, the narrative present is silenced. Reported direct speech (transcribed in dialect) of the intrigued waitresses Maureen and Mandy, and the narrative past tense, prevail. The arch distance between reader and event is collapsed as Miss Frame's social persona and status are diminished; she is brought closer to the scrutiny and social standing of her colleagues. The girls guess what kind of family drama is taking place in front of them and exact their revenge for Miss Frame's past sins of elitism. ' "We'd like y' to know th't this makes y' just one o' the girls" ' (*SV*, 35), states Maureen smugly. The story ends by eliminating distance between reader and event in the free direct speech of Maureen, who promises not to gossip only if Miss Frame removes the silver pickle-fork from the tea room. ' "It's the pickle fork that no' everybody gets to use. It bothers me. An' that's ma price. Get rid o' it" ' (*SV*, 35). The respect that Miss Frame had commanded is to be removed together with the home-made symbol of elitism. The unmediated proximity between reader and event here quickens the reader's judgement to encourage the extra-textual conclusion that the girls' brash egalitarianism is petty and too harsh. They do not share the reader's knowledge of Miss Frame's struggle against past privation and present loneliness which earns her the reader's respect, because and not in spite of, her life as a single parent. The mobility of Dunn's reader cultivates his/her impartiality and permits reason to correct misjudgement.[11]

Modulation of the reader's position is a function of the typical structure of Dunn's stories. Almost invariably the story begins with authorial comment and ends with the direct speech (or, if the story is in the first person, with a statement in the even more immediate voice of direct thought) of one of the characters. The imagery of 'framing', explicit in 'Twin Sets' and again in 'Orr Mount' where Monty, the builder and protagonist, spends a week making window frames before either he or the reader can more than glimpse what goes on, provides an appropriate model for the structure of the stories, each of which is framed by distance. So although Dunn takes us to the heart of each local community, the narrator and reader visit from afar. The reader's approach, therefore, is a training in lucidity, where judgement is quickened by the narrative balance of objectivity with sympathy.

Dunn's most powerful methods for creating this effect are, first, in the naïve intimacy with which places and people are named, whether by characters or by narrators, and, second, in his comic control of dialogue. The first is an act which creates the reader's trust in the very moment of asking for it: 'the humpbacked sandstone bridge that carried a minor road over the Kem Burn' or ' "[b]ad news always starts in Overrigg" ' are statements which assume knowledge that the reader does not have but which give as they assume it.[12] And the reader, recognising this duality of the foreign and familiar, is, like Joan in 'Mulwhevin' when she makes her escape and jumps in a car that is heading for Dumfries, willing to be carried along by it (' "That sounds lovely," Joan said'),[13] while experiencing an insistent intuition that the reader is not really going to Dumfries and has never seen the Kem Burn. Similarly, dialogue, because it is placed within a frame of distance, is both heard and overheard by the reader. Whether it is the choric exposition of 'South America' or the salt humour of everyday conversation in 'Toddle-Bonny', the reader is perceptibly privileged to hear it. The reader's sense of shared omniscience is technically most explicit in 'Mozart's Clarinet Concerto' (SV, 71–7), where two concurrent conversations in different locations are constantly interwoven and juxtaposed without narrative explanation, becoming unified, concerto-like, at the close of the story. The readers are moved by these devices 'in imagination [to] become the very persons whose actions are represented to us'[14]; but it is, precisely 'in imagination' only, a state therefore which can exist concurrently with being ourselves. In the interplay of this duality, ethical sensibility is developed.

Even when Dunn does not deploy narrative distance from which to move the reader, as in his radio plays, the dramatic structure itself keeps the listener at a shifting distance. *The Telescope Garden* (broadcast on Radio 3, FM, 11 July 1986), by its title drawing attention to the cultivated vision of the remote, subjects the terms 'imagination' and 'vision' to scrutiny. The play, about Thomas De Quincey and his fascination for astronomy which inspires his passion for the 'locomotion of the spirit', sets the listener at a historical remove, at times playfully 'anticipating' our 'future'. De Quincey is entertained in Glasgow by Professor Nichol at the University Observatory where he marvels at the new instruments of vision: 'What a fierce new energy this telescope adds to human sight.' The play itself is the listener's instrument of vision, which juxtaposes De Quincey's astronomical quest for enhancement of 'that higher faculty of the mind, which is imagination, and which is pure', with his addiction (whether this is to laudanum or its assisted dreams is not entirely clear), constipation and domestic myopia. Unable to pay the rent, he lands in debtors' prison in Holyrood while his wife works to pay off their debts. Distraught and remorseful at news of her death, he cries 'my Margaret dead . . . and her abject, contemptible husband . . . I was not at her side, I was in this Holyrood'. De Quincey's self-indulgences are pitted throughout against Presbyterian temperance and bourgeois prejudice: each position comically modifies the other (as does the Scots versus English sniping) and together they guarantee the listener's generous impartiality.

Framed within a dream which visits De Quincey late in the play when he is alone in the telescope garden is a vision which seems to come from the 'Observatory' he had pictured earlier 'on the other side of the heavens, subjecting *us* to scrutiny': the Deity speaks:

> cleanse his vision and put new breath in his body . . . only touch not with any change his human heart, the heart that weeps and trembles.

Dunn has permitted this Deity to usurp his authorial position which, in its plea for humanity, creates vision clarified and even sanctified by feeling. His assured command of this plea is conspicuous in an age of ethical insecurity.

NOTES

1 Adam Smith, *The Theory of Moral Sentiments*, ed. D.D. Raphael and A.L. Macfie (1759; Oxford: Clarendon Press, 1976), 140. Hereafter called Smith.
2 Smith, 190–1.
3 Douglas Dunn, 'Introduction', *A Rumoured City. New poets from Hull*, ed. Douglas Dunn, Foreword by Philip Larkin (Newcastle-upon-Tyne: Bloodaxe Books, 1982), 11.
4 Douglas Dunn, 'Boyfriends and Girlfriends', *The New Yorker*, 30 December 1985, 22.
5 Alasdair Gray, *Lanark* (1981), cited in *Scotland. An Anthology*, ed. Douglas Dunn (London: HarperCollins, 1991), 98.

6 David Hume, *Enquiries Concerning Human Understanding and Concerning The Principles of Morals*, ed. L.A. Selby-Bigge, rev. P.H. Nidditch (1777; Oxford: Clarendon Press, 1974), 227–8. See also Smith, 134–5.

7 Smith, 135.

8 'Toddle-Bonny and the Bogeyman', *A Roomful of Birds. Scottish Short Stories*, intro. Deirdre Chapman (London: Collins, 1990), 61.

9 'Orr Mount', *The New Yorker* 17 September 1984, 47.

10 'Mulwhevin', *Grand Street* 6:1, Autumn 1986, 73–93.

11 Dunn's influence over the reader's place could be extensive. Smith's maxim, 'humanity is the virtue of a woman, generosity of a man' (Smith, 190), suggests that Dunn's implied reader is female. Luckily, with twentieth-century hindsight we can tell this to be a distinction based on gender and not sex.

12 'Boyfriends and Girlfriends', 24, 26.

13 'Mulwhevin', 93.

14 Smith, 75.

Eleven

'The Music inside Fruit':
Douglas Dunn and France

David Kinloch

'Men make more than one native land for themselves. There are some who feel at home in twenty corners of the world, for men are born more than once.' These words by the committed French communist writer, Paul Nizan, form one of the epigraphs to the sequence of poems by Douglas Dunn entitled *Europa's Lover*. They neatly establish a connection between France, French culture and some of the principal themes of Dunn's work. Here is a poet for whom the geographical, political and cultural identity of 'home' is important and one who has travelled widely, both literally and imaginatively, partly in order to see the familiar more clearly. He is also a poet whose work continually restates the necessity for a certain kind of rebirth. From *Terry Street* through to *Barbarians*, *St Kilda's Parliament* and beyond, we can find poems that chronicle the numbing, dehumanising effects of social deprivation and intellectual disenfranchisement, poems that implicitly and explicitly prod the reader into taking stock, reconsidering and renewing his or her ideas.

This chapter will examine Dunn's experience of one of the 'twenty corners of the world' which has nourished these themes and others. France has a privileged place among them, for it is a corner Dunn made his home in for a term, in 1972, on receipt of the Somerset Maugham award, and it is obvious from his published work that its literature has proved a constant source of stimulation. Dunn has spoken in conversation of early attempts to translate poems by Jules Laforgue, Tristan Corbière and Robert Desnos.[1] The most lasting traces of these enthusiasms are, however, original poems written 'in homage', to Laforgue and Desnos. It is significant however that Dunn's interest in French poetry does not extend to that currently being produced by his

French contemporaries. Indeed the only living French poet mentioned
by Dunn with any affection is Philippe Jaccottet.[2] Dunn has also been
drawn to what is sometimes called the 'classical' period of French
literature. This has produced the translation for radio of Racine's
Andromaque as well as an unpublished and unperformed version of
Molière's *Tartuffe*, appropriately renamed *Tartooftie*. The seriousness of
Dunn's interest in France is visible also in the way he sometimes uses
French writers to sound the opening note of a particular poem or
collection of poems by using their words as epigraphs. I have already
cited the example of *Europa's Lover*. This sequence also has an epigraph
by Albert Camus, while *Barbarians* uses Camus and Nizan in a similar
way.

It would be a mistake, however, to assume that Dunn confines his
interest to French *literature*. Indeed there is a sense in which Dunn uses
Camus, Desnos and particularly Nizan to warn against the bourgeoisifi-
cation that too exclusive an interest in literature and even literacy itself
may induce. This is a theme that is particularly strong in *Barbarians* and
St Kilda's Parliament, while it is given a poignant, personal twist in
Elegies. Indeed it is one of the saddest aspects of *Elegies* that it is in this
collection that Dunn's love for France and things French is most
audible, from its cuisine and countryside to its art and music.

This love is rather like the ambiguous sound made by:

> Those French tunes on the saxophone,
> The music inside fruit!
>
> (HL, 20)

first heard in *The Happier Life*. This music winds through the collections
of the 1970s and 1980s to emerge again, its humour intact, in 'An
Address to Adolphe Sax in Heaven' from *Northlight*. Indeed, it is as well
to listen carefully at the outset to the 'young man's alto saxophone' (HL,
60) for it reminds us that, apart from intellectual stimulation, Dunn has
derived a great deal of fun from French culture. Poems like 'Ratatouille'
(SKP, 85), 'An Address to Adolphe Sax in Heaven' (N, 71) and 'The
Country Kitchen' (N, 76) are the mark of a true Francophile,
entertaining 'divertissements' which celebrate with great panache 'The
job of slicing two good peppers thinly', 'Lovingly-chopped-up cloves of
ail' (SKP, 85) as well as 'saxophonic venery's/ Libidinous communiqués'
(N, 73). Nevertheless, they also succeed in making serious observations
in a light-hearted manner. In so doing they give some indication of the
manner in which we should listen to the French voices that echo
through Dunn's work, for they are those of the discreet, suggestive

epigraph, of humour, relaxation or remembered pleasure and rarely confront us as the cultured tones of Civilisation, although what is civil and civilised is frequently their primary concern. The sweet, sly and airy reasonableness of such poems shows us that the usefulness of some foreign cultures is the way they lie at a slight tangent to our own, the tangent of the ratatouille cook's knowing smile or the saxophone's acoustic riff. If we borrow deftly from their life and art, we may enhance our own and notice more quickly our own propensity to pomposity and the small-minded. Thus, Adolphe Sax's invention which initially 'Offended purist connoisseurs' – 'Parisian social experts feared/ the sound of sex was what they heard' (N, 71) – explodes like a small time-bomb among the snooty 'clarinets of France'. Arnold Bennett who 'thought his ear/ Affronted by the tunes of beer' (N, 74) is helpless before the rise of jazz and the 'low audiences' that 'applauded it'. The impulse of the saxophone is democratising, eroticising, the very impulse of Dunn's best poetry written in the face of bourgeois prejudice and prudishness.

That such prejudice leads men all too quickly into the type of spiritual and intellectual poverty from which the horrific mundanities of war and famine spring, is one of Dunn's chief concerns. It is present in the impish slander of 'Ratatouille' (SKP, 85) which gives short shrift to 'men who do not care to know about/ The eight ripe *pommes d'amour* their wives have need of'. These men 'Invade Afghanistan, boycott the Games,/ Call off their fixtures and prepare for war'. Dunn's envoi: 'Prepare this stew of love, and ask for more./ Quick, before it is too late. Bon appétit!' is the throwaway irony of a man who, this time at least, does not wish to run the risk of spoiling his dish by overheating it.

No such scruple ever troubled the late nineteenth-century poet Jules Laforgue, whose distinctive voice fused tones of such eclectic timbre that they gave many of his less discerning contemporaries the same kind of heartburn they were to experience on hearing Adolphe Sax's new invention. Dunn pays Laforgue the compliment of pastiche in a poem called 'The White Poet' (LN, 52–5). This is a particularly interesting poem, for it provides precisely that foreign tangent on the familiar, on home, evoked above. Terry Street and The Happier Life, Dunn's first two collections, are relatively barren ground for the chronicler of such a theme, but here, in 'The White Poet', the 'Urban flora and fauna' (TS, 21) of Terry Street are sieved through the dyspeptic gaze of a reincarnated Laforgue. Nor is it simply the Dunn of Terry Street we hear but the Larkin of 'The Whitsun Weddings', his understated realism and decorum seized upon and played one speed up on a mercurial and melodramatic gramophone. The result verges on the surreal:

All Saints, Margaret Street, a wedding in a doorway
Touted by photographers, waiting for a cab . . .
Red-brick palace, streaming, baked,
Naked in its numbered days, hallowing the weddings
Of ill-dressed parties without taxis.

And the melancholy horns! Sad, undersea
Deranged tan-tivvy, dislocated fanfare!
Driven on the North Wind, ta-ra! ta-ra!
Turning the head of the groom who stands
Like a gland ripped from a throat.

                                                   (LN, 52–3)

That last image is a literal translation of a line from Laforgue's poem
'L'Hiver qui vient' published in the *Derniers vers*,[3] and we can find some
of Laforgue's favourite symbols scattered throughout Dunn's pastiche.
Walking through the backstreets, the white poet hears 'pianos in all the
houses', 'pianos in the prim districts' which symbolise the vain
pretensions of the bourgeoisie in some of Laforgue's famous 'com-
plaintes'[4] and fulfil a similar function in the poetry of Rimbaud. As we
might expect, the moon, Laforgue's 'notre dame des soirs', floats
blithely above the pain and 'carnal typists' of 'business districts'; present
also is the Laforguian theme of abortive love, stifled in an atmosphere of
small-town consumerism and architectural ugliness. It is a rich poem
that ably catches something of Laforgue's pained self-mockery, his
'dandysme lunaire', his mastery of the superficially detached, ironic
pose.
     More importantly, perhaps, it is a good example of the growing
explicitness of what Ian Gregson has called, in an earlier chapter of the
present volume, Dunn's 'subversive dialogue with realism'.[5] In 'The
White Poet', Dunn uses the Laforguian mask as a cover for the
expression of his own disgust, his feelings of alienation before the
mediocrity of parochial, materialistic existence, those who will 'have no
truck/ With that muck/ In foreign restaurants, da-da, dum-dum'. In
this poem, the microscopic realism of Terry Street is taken for a ride on
a near-surrealist merry-go-round and made violently sick. Dunn's
'complainte' is a salutary purgative that looks towards a wider European
modernist tradition.
     Similar in this regard is 'The Deserter' (*SKP*, 72–5), subtitled
'Homage to Robert Desnos'. In his interview with John Haffenden,
Dunn described Desnos as 'one of my favourite twentieth-century poets'
(*Viewpoints*, 29), and it is clear that his preference stems from the close

juxtaposition or fusion in much of Desnos's verse of different aesthetic styles and forms which a poem like 'The White Poet' gestures towards. Dunn notes that 'Desnos often managed to write surrealist poems in rhyme and metre, which I find tremendously exciting and I think the kind of poet I'd like to be . . . is the kind Desnos was' (*Viewpoints*, 29). From this statement, we can see how the internal debate present in 'The White Poet' between realism and surrealism may be extended to take account of that between free verse, in which much early surrealist poetry was written, and traditional metrical forms. This aesthetic concern is at the heart of Dunn's introduction to his work in P.R. King's *Nine Contemporary Poets*, where he states that: 'The more I write, the more I consider an internal debate about what does or does not constitute an authentic contemporary poetic style is creative rather than disabling'.[6] In 'The Deserter', Dunn articulates this debate in a more subdued and controlled manner than in 'The White Poet'. Lines from poems by Desnos are placed at the start of the three separate but thematically linked sections. The first two use free verse to develop and comment in a relatively realistic mode heavy with symbolic connotation on images from Desnos which portray the struggle between tyranny and the oppressed. The third, however, takes a haunting, identifiably surrealist image – 'A widow, in her wedding gown, gets into the wrong train' – and develops it through five four-line stanzas of rhymed iambic tetrameters.

At the end of his interview with John Haffenden, Dunn is critical of the 'gentlemanly verse towards which poets like Philip Larkin and Amis have tended', concluding that 'I don't think they should grudge the nature of the imagination the spaciousness which it has' (*Viewpoints*, 34). Dunn's excitement at the prospect of Robert Desnos's poetry is stimulated by the tense dialogue that is instigated within individual poems between the wild 'spaciousness' of a surrealist imagination and the strict metrical control to which it is subjected. For Dunn, if not for Larkin and Amis, 'different stylistic extremes' are not seen to be incompatible.

Interestingly, some of the lines from Desnos that Dunn uses in his poem come from the collection *Fortunes* which Desnos published in 1942 and to which he appended a 'postface' where he explicitly acknowledged his own deliberate move away from the more or less uncontrolled expression of surrealist visionary experience to more disciplined forms of articulation.[7] It is relevant, too, that Desnos's changing artistic strategy develops not simply for aesthetic reasons but out of a growing concern, amid the troubled political climate of the 1930s, that his poetry should communicate to greater numbers of people. This is obviously a concern shared by the poet of *Terry Street*, *Barbarians* and *St Kilda's Parliament* and Dunn has spoken openly of his dislike for 'complacency and fellow feeling towards a few like-minded people', concluding that this is 'a failure of goodwill, if nothing else, if you don't aspire towards a larger number' (*Viewpoints*, 19).

Many of the poems with a French connection discussed so far have a vein of humour or irony running through them, and all seek in their various ways to articulate some of Dunn's central themes: the intellectual and spiritual poverty endemic to much of urban twentieth-century civilisation or the attack on bourgeois pretension and small-mindedness. Before going on to discuss some of the French influences on the more overtly political poems of *Barbarians*, it is, then, appropriate to talk briefly about Dunn's 'version' of Molière's *Tartuffe* in which the comic manner and the deflation of absurdity go hand in hand. This work has remained unrevised and unperformed due partly to the coincidence of its creation in 1985 with Liz Lochhead's extremely successful translation into Scots of the same play.[8] Dunn has said that it should be considered as a prose draft which he later intended to work up into verse and is updated to the present day. It is set 'in the upper reaches of the Scottish middle class', probably in Edinburgh, and is amusing not simply for the broad Scots of Doreen, the housekeeper, but also for those moments when Dunn's exasperation at the injustices and idiocies of modern life and art, familiar from his poetry, shines through. Tartooftie bears a remarkable similarity to a weel-kent Edinburgh impresario and is described as 'having emerged from the more squalid corners of the 1960s primed on mysticism and ready to work small miracles of opportunism on a gullible and comfortably-off public'. His first appearance is memorable, and it is intriguing to speculate what Dunn might achieve were he to impose metre on this kind of humour:

> Tartooftie (on seeing Doreen):
> Ah sister! Will you add my meditational loin-cloths to the laundry, please? I want you to wash them by hand, not in your machine. A natural wash, and light scrubbing only, for the sake of my vibrations . . .

One wonders what Rik Mayall would make of this . . .

Elsewhere, however, characters like Roderick (Molière's Cléante) give voice to Dunn's principal moral concerns, his understanding of the way men and women stoop to folly but his condemnation of extremes, his sympathy for the ordinary, decent, common man. Here is Roderick, berating Professor Morgan (Molière's Orgon) for his blindness:

> I know it's hard to be reasonable. Intelligence seems dull and plodding when it's faced with questions like 'the meaning of life'

. . . I can sympathise with the restlessness that's made you opt for an extreme. We all feel it. But extremes lead to tyranny – in a single life as well as in society.

And again, a little later:

If only you'd look around you – thousands and thousands of ordinary people, decent people, and their decency gets by against all the odds . . . None of your Dr Tartoofties for them!

Decency, 'the rights of ordinariness, the beauty of the average' (*Viewpoints*, 21) which Dunn claims he was trying to assert in *Terry Street* and which Roderick praises to Professor Morgan in *Tartooftie*, takes on a more political hue in *Barbarians*. This collection takes both its epigraphs from the work of the French novelist and essayist Paul Nizan, while the opening poem, 'The Come-on' is prefaced by a line from Albert Camus. In the interview with John Haffenden, in which Dunn proclaimed his 'Francophilia' (*Viewpoints*, 30), he stated that his 'heroes' were Desnos, Camus and Nizan. Dunn's 'Barbarian Pastorals' show why this is so.

The first poem, 'The Come-on', orchestrates an attack on the ' "professional classes" ', on 'a culture of connivance', 'Of "authority", arts of bland recoveries' and evokes the day when the proletariat 'will leap down, into the garden' (*B*, 13–14). The final lines take up the epigraph from Camus who speaks of 'the guardian, the king's son, who kept watch over the gates of the garden in which I wanted to live'. It is taken from an essay published by Camus in the *Hommage de la Nouvelle Revue Française* to André Gide in November 1951, shortly after Gide's death.[9] The connection with Gide is directly relevant to Dunn's poem and to *Barbarians* as a whole, for it is Gide himself whom Camus identifies as 'the guardian, the king's son'.[10] Here a consideration of Camus's attitude to Gide as revealed in this essay throws an interesting light on Dunn's criticism of bourgeois values, as well as giving them an extra, literary dimension that is confirmed by the chosen metre of the first poem.

Camus's essay is a delicate balancing act that demonstrates a real affection and an understanding of Gide while taking care to distinguish his own circumstances and experience of life from that of the older writer. Camus recounts how, aged sixteen, he read Gide's *Les Nourritures terrestres* with incomprehension and bewilderment. 'I found these invocations rather obscure', he writes, 'I shied away from this hymn to the goods of nature' because, he implies, he was unconvinced by the attempt of a bourgeois writer to masquerade as the sensual pagan Camus knew himself to be: 'In Algiers, at the age of sixteen, I was saturated with these riches'.[11] Interestingly, Camus ascribes his initial lack of appreciation to the fact that he was 'a young unenlightened barbarian',[12] and it is perhaps that barbarian that Dunn has loved most in Camus.

Camus goes on to describe how, later, he read Gide with much more enthusiasm but he declares that he was never his 'master': 'Gide appeared to me rather . . . as the model of the artist, the guardian, the king's son, who kept watch over the gates of the garden in which I wanted to live'.[13] The use of the word 'model' is significant, for the strategy adopted by Dunn's vengeful proletariat is to 'beat them with decorum, with manners,/ As sly as language is', to model themselves on the king's son with whom they take tea at seminars, just as Camus — although quite by chance — came to live in the apartment next to Gide for part of his life.

Camus defines the main reproach addressed to Gide's work as that 'it is distant from the anguish of our time'.[14] His own circumstances have placed him in a very different position. 'History has forced itself upon my generation. I had to take my place in the line waiting before the porch of the black years'.[15] Again, this has parallels with Dunn, who spoke in his interview with Haffenden of wishing 'that I could just simply relax and deal with the play of phenomena and experience in my imagination', of wishing to escape from the need to write about political subjects, but that he had been 'condemned to remember' (*Viewpoints*, 23).

The dialogue Dunn establishes between proletariat and bourgeois, the barbarian and the civil, the literate and illiterate, in this poem is underpinned by that between Camus and Gide. This underlines the importance of the explicitly literary dimension of the poem. It is not simply a generalised attack on bourgeois culture but asks us to imagine what happens when the 'dull staccato of our typewriters' (*B*, 14) elevates members of the lower classes up the social ladder. 'The Come-on' is written in metre because, as Dunn has said, 'the style of the book hopes to portray a gesture of affront to readers who might be expected to approve of a metrical way of writing, while finding the meaning of *Barbarians* disagreeable'. But, as we shall see, this artistic strategy has its dangers. The epigraphs from Paul Nizan make this abundantly clear.

Nizan too had strong reservations about Gide and the kind of writer he represented. As a committed communist and party activist, a close friend of Sartre and de Beauvoir, who perished in 1941 during the Nazi occupation of Paris, Nizan articulated his dislike of Gide with his customary pugnacity. In 1936, Gide was invited to the Soviet Union as one of the guests of honour at a writers' conference. On his return, he published his impressions, which struck Nizan as typical of one of the aspects of bourgeois culture which he detested most, its taste for abstractions, for philosophising, its refusal to take account of facts: 'he indulges in an extremely superficial psychological analysis of economic and social issues'.[16] It was an attack which developed his earlier criticism of bourgeois writers attracted by the 'exoticism' of proletarian subject matter. Gide was indulging in precisely that art 'of bland recoveries' which Dunn stigmatises in his poem, and it is clear from other essays by Nizan that such an art was the product of what he calls 'la . . . défaillance de l'humanisme: son isolement des hommes concrets'.[17]

The prinicipal thrust of Nizan's published work was to show how every aspect of culture was penetrated by a bourgeois, humanist ethos. 'La culture est bourgeoise ou elle n'est pas', he wrote. It is so difficult to escape the kind of insidious conditioning Dunn evokes in 'The Come-on', and, even when you yourself take up the pen, attempt to improve your lot, a form of alienation is almost inevitable. This, at least, is the final message of Nizan's novel *Antoine Bloyé*, from which Dunn took the epigraphs for *Barbarians*.[18]

One critic has written that the theme of *Antoine Bloyé* is '[the] taming of freedom, [the] socialisation of the natural man',[19] and this too is what the early poems of *Barbarians* chronicle and revolt against. Briefly, Nizan's novel traces the rise from humble origins of Antoine Bloyé through the channels of technical higher education to the rank of minor official in the railway industry. The system encourages him to gain 'qualifications' but denies him an 'education'. Thus far and no further. It is a study in frustration, in how society frequently compels us to accept the second-best, but, more importantly from Dunn's point of view, how promotion through the classes alienates you from your own kith and kin: 'Without realising it, he cut himself off from his own people . . . He thought he was merely bored, but secretly he was flattered at being included. Some forces drew him towards the bourgeoisie; other forces sought to retard his transition.' This is part of the first quotation cited by Dunn as epigraph to his collection, and it exists in tension with the political and social ambitions which the first few poems of *Barbarians* articulate and which their polished style confirms and exacerbates. The second epigraph indeed, implies that 'truth' might ultimately escape those who 'leap down into the garden': 'The truth of life was on the side of the men who returned to their houses, on the side of the men who had not "made good".' Perhaps, then, truth is more on the side of the earth itself which cries out in the poem 'Gardeners' (*B*, 17–18) against the artificial taming and cultivation of its 'nourritures terrestres'.

The ambiguous relationship that exists between the style and content of these poems, however, has given rise to some heated exchanges. In the introduction to his own work, published in *Nine Contemporary Poets*, Dunn recalls how he reacted angrily to the objections of a member of the audience at a poetry reading who declared that the early poems of *Barbarians* were 'a footling and dishonest compromise with forms associated with bourgeois culture'.[20] Dunn justified his recourse to formal metre by attacking the view that 'style' and 'art' of this nature is intrinsically bourgeois, recalling the work ethic of Clydeside and the artisan's traditional pride in his creations. At first sight, this might appear to sit a little uneasily with Dunn's other claim that the style of the book was designed 'to affront readers who might be expected to approve of a metrical way of writing'. However, Dunn's use of the verb 'approve' accurately reflects bourgeois patronage of the intelligent artisan or artist, a commonplace of western culture which the poem 'An Artist Waiting in a Country House' (*B*, 21–4) sets out to satirise.

Clarification of this misunderstanding lies in admitting that what is at stake here is in fact more complex than Dunn's adversaries have admitted. The urbanity of the early poems in *Barbarians* is neither 'footling' nor 'dishonest' but a frank admission of the compromises that sometimes have to be made when struggling to assert an independent social identity. The first epigraph from Paul Nizan makes this quite clear: 'He somehow learned how to behave, as they say'. Dunn is asking us, then, to appreciate that the superior metrical skill of these poems may be seen not only as a bourgeois weapon ironically wielded against its makers or as the product of proletarian craftsmanship but in terms of the kind of technical expertise or know-how inflicted on Antoine Bloyé by his social superiors. Here it is important to put our faith in the general tone of the first poem, 'The Come-on', for one can detect that Dunn's resentment and distaste at the 'sly language' he has to adopt are directed not only at the bourgeois masters but also at himself and his own class. The same distaste and resentment at the forced cultivation of skills which alienate rather than fulfil is present in the tragic figure of Antoine Bloyé. More explicitly, then, than in 'The White Poet', and 'The Deserter', Dunn is here conducting a sophisticated aesthetic debate about what kind of writing, what kind of culture is appropriate and possible given the political and social realities of contemporary civilisation.

One of Dunn's aims in *Barbarians* and *St Kilda's Parliament* is to show
how the individual, the domestic, the private, is often conditioned and
victimised by the more vociferous imperatives at work in the public
domain, and it is perhaps in this context that his translation of Racine's
Andromaque is best viewed.

This was commissioned for BBC radio as a companion piece to Craig
Raine's updating of the same play, performed and published under the
title *1953*.[21] Dunn's brief was to produce as faithful a translation as
possible, while Raine was accorded almost total liberty. Dunn has since
implied that in retrospect he may have had something of a raw deal
here, but in interviews he has expressed genuine pleasure at the
technical challenge posed by this kind of work. One of the many things
Racine is famous for is that of not translating well into English, and
Dunn has outlined his solutions to the principal difficulties involved.
These included accommodating as much as possible 'of Racine's literal
meaning to iambic pentameters rhyming in couplets'. Blank verse,
which Dunn describes as 'the medium of the classic English stage', was
eschewed because it meant 'Shakespeare, which means metaphor and
imagery and a kind of poetry very different from Racine's'. Dunn was
determined to rhyme because 'listening to one of his plays in French is
like listening to a rally in an invisible tennis match'.[22]

There is much to admire in this translation which reads very fluently,
sometimes too fluently. Occasionally Dunn's choice of metre forces him
to abandon single words whose specific charge is crucial to nuances of
emotion conveyed by the French and which no amount of ingenious
paraphrasing can recover. Take, for example, Andromache's first entry.
Pyrrhus engages her in conversation by asking if she is looking for him.
Andromache replies:

> I'm going to see my son. You've said I'm free
> To do this, once a day — when you see fit
> Or when it seems to *you* 'compassionate'.
> My son contains Troy, and my husband too:
> He's all I've left that I can trust as true.
> The only benefit that's left of time
> Is his embrace. I go to weep with him.
>
> (A, 11)

In French this reads as follows:

> Je passais jusqu'aux lieux ou l'on garde mon fils.
> Puisqu'une fois le jour vous souffrez que je voie
> Le seul bien qui me reste et d'Hector et de Troie,

> J'allais, seigneur, pleurer un moment avec lui:
> Je ne l'ai point encore embrassé d'aujourd'hui![23]

Dunn's translation accurately captures the dignified tone of Andromache's resentment, but it misses the curious mixture of both cunning and grief introduced into the last two lines by the astute placing of the word 'seigneur'. The deft insertion of this word breaks the pathos of the Alexandrine and elevates Pyrrhus into the extraordinary position of sharing her grief for a moment while simultaneously implicating him in the effects of his cruelty. Her last line has all the tragic actress's command of grief-stricken understatement.

Such sacrifices are inevitable when translating Racine, and it would be unfair not to give Dunn his due and recognise that overall he has made a faithful translation from the French and created a piece of persuasive drama in its own right. Particularly welcome is the careful attention he has given to speeches by those secondary characters known as 'confidents' who are so often dismissed as mere sounding boards for the principals and yet who are frequently crucial to the action and help to clarify the tragic dilemma in the minds of the audience. Dunn's handling of their speeches is crisp and convincing. Equally persuasive are Dunn's translation of Andromache's great evocation of the sack of Troy in Act III, scene 8, and Hermione's half-demented tirade before Cleone in Act IV, scene 4, as she instructs her to find Orestes and make sure he tells Pyrrhus that he dies by her hand alone.

As I have suggested, however, the interest of Dunn's translation lies not simply in its relative success or failure as a translation but in the place it fills alongside collections of poetry, many of which articulate similar themes and concerns. The pitch and tension of Racine's dramatic art derive from the painful imbrication of domestic and political concerns, the intense pressure brought to bear upon private desire and jealousy by public imperative, and the way this imperative is sometimes warped or compromised by such desire. It is no surprise, then, to discover now and again in Dunn's translation of *Andromache* lines which put one in mind of poems in *Barbarians* or *St Kilda's Parliament*. In Act I, scene 2, Pyrrhus evokes the barren countryside of Troy, pillaged and burned by a foreign empire's troops:

> Tomorrow's Troy — what will become of it?
> I see its rubbled walls and powdered char,
> An empty countryside, a blood-stained river,
> A captive boy. — It's hateful prejudice
> That conjures vengeance out of nothingness!

> (A, 8)

That final epigrammatic judgement is pure Dunn, quite literally so in fact, for the French it might have translated is absent from Racine's play.

The absence of France and the French language is a theme that lies close to the heart of Dunn's collection, *Elegies*, written after the death from cancer of his first wife Lesley. A love of France and things French was evidently one of the elements that brought them together in life and it is sadly appropriate, therefore, that the first poem in the volume, which shows us Dunn discovering a 'pressed fly' trapped between the pages of Katherine Mansfield's story 'Bliss', should contain the words 'Je ne parle pas français' (*E*, 9). The conceit which this poem develops, however, is not as simple as it first appears and has consequences for the collection as a whole. Dunn's *Elegies* is a grief-stricken lament for his dead wife but, as so often in his verse, the poems also conduct a subtle aesthetic debate about the nature of poetry itself and how it might relate to life. Indeed, one of the triumphs of *Elegies* is the way these aims cohere and Dunn makes it clear, particularly in those poems which make use of or refer to the French language or France, that the seeds of this coherence are to be found in Lesley Dunn's own personality as an artist and how it affected him as a writer.

Thus, in the first poem, an implicit parallel is drawn between the fly caught between the pages of a book and the poet's wife crushed in mid-story between the pages of the book of life. The fly's ironic epitaph: 'Je ne parle pas français' speaks to us in the accents of cruel paradox about a woman who once spoke French but no longer does, one who no longer speaks, no longer hears the confession of inability to speak a language, love of which joined her to her husband in life. This much is immediately clear, but the fly has other things to say which escape the bounds of instant communicability. In the final two lines of the poem, we discover that it is 'verbosely buried in Bliss'. Even at the very moment of its death, crawling over the printed page, it was 'de trop', verbose with life, utterly beyond language in a way that makes its epitaph, 'Je ne parle pas français', less ironic and more a simple, factual statement that testifies bluntly to the inadequacy of all language, all writing, all art before the evanescent otherness of life. As the collection develops, it becomes evident that Lesley too, was in many ways 'verbose' with life; for Dunn indeed, she was life itself, inhabiting an extralinguistic dimension – writing only with light, as one poem makes clear (*E*, 23) – which no mother-tongue could adequately articulate. It is for this reason, then, that the French language takes on such significance in the volume as a whole, a foreign medium, which, because it is so closely associated with the woman he loves, her own interests and passions, is less like a language and more like life itself. That this is so is evident from the way Dunn uses French words: appropriately in a volume about the loss of life and happiness, the words which live closest in his memory to that life steal in almost surreptitiously as echoes. Thus, in the poem 'France', the word *'jouissance'* with its untranslatable mixture of aesthetic and erotic pleasure comes at the end of a line of English nouns, each of which has tried and failed with simple dignity to capture the essence of their 'dream of France'. It lives at the very edge of the articulate, yet in the voluptuous sound of its vowels and consonants communicates all that is best and most material in life.

In 'Creatures' (*E*, 33), Dunn uses French words, their exotic strangeness, as vehicles for a ripeness of experience, a *thereness*, that he seems unable or unwilling to capture in English. A french fox is 'pure *renard'*; we hear the 'impolite/ *Belettes'*, see 'Vézère's *falaises'*, an *'hérisson'*; and Lesley is seen to be in tune with this natural landscape and life, now as sadly 'insaisissable' as the shy snakes 'she scattered milk-dipped bread' for.

Yet this talk of naturalness, of life, of the extralinguistic, must strike the reader as paradoxical, if not misguided, in the context of a volume of elegies that is noteworthy for the range of its artistic references. The resolution of this paradox lies in an understanding of the literary dimension of the unfolding tragedy. Here the sonnet, 'Tursac' (*E*, 26), is helpful. In this poem, words such as 'grace', 'wit', 'right conduct' and 'elegance', which might be associated with a certain French tradition of behaviour and culture, are used to describe his wife's style of love-making during 'those weeks of France'. A perfect harmony is achieved between life and art by such love which the poet almost spoils. Dunn recalls how he named 'that house our Thébaide/ (The literary French!)' and is gently reprimanded by his wife for doing so. Here we see the poet of decency, the recorder and defender of the modest, average man tempted by his erudition into a mild form of hubris and one which Lesley recognises as ultimately destructive of the essentially humane, life-giving impulse of true art. Dunn tries momentarily to turn his life into literature and gets his fingers slapped. She reminds him he is a poet, not a scholar: 'Write out of me, not out of what you read'. But when she dies, all that is left is 'Bliss and Other Stories', years of shared life he can only 'flick/ Through' (*E*, 9), the dry tear of a crushed fly punctuating the syntax of a sentence which records their inability to speak the language of Tursac again. The poet finds himself locked in the literary tomb of the elegy, remembering when there was another time outside literature, a time when love and life assured him that he could say no to literature. Appropriately, therefore, the very next poem in the sequence, 'Dining' (*E*, 27–8), adopts the highly literary tone and form of a Renaissance elegy. It is written with moving affection, but the way the form embalms and preserves at the same time as it celebrates speaks of a certain connivance between the facts of death and the erudite fictions of literature which appals Dunn and which he hints at in later poems like 'Listening' (*E*, 43) and 'The Stories' (*E*, 56), where he speaks of 'my sorrow murdered by aesthetics' (*E*, 43) and 'this raffish sorrow artificed by stories' (*E*, 57).

The French words of *Elegies* are, therefore, important among the elements that give this collection its curiously brittle intensity, both charming the ear with their momentary naturalness and yet at odds with the English syntax, the considered 'mots justes' of a man condemned to write when he would prefer to speak.

By tracing some – by no means all – of the French influences and voices in Dunn's work, I have tried to make its European dimension and sympathies more obvious beyond the oft-repeated preferences recorded in interviews and reviews. I have left until last, therefore, the sequence of poems which makes the imbrication of the European and the Provincial most clear. *Europa's Lover* takes a stage further the fusion of real and surreal imaginings initiated in 'The White Poet' and 'The Deserter'. Indeed, echoes of the latter poem and its borrowings from Desnos may be detected in the imagery associated with wedding-clothes which appears in a number of the poems and helps to link them together. If, however, the sequence begins by opposing Europa's 'subtle décolletage', made in Paris 'by surrealist seamstresses' to 'our provincial', 'our matronly spa' (*EL*, I), nevertheless, Europa's own discourse is characterised by a refusal to sacrifice the loved particularities of her many daughters to her own cosmopolitanism. There is room to celebrate the 'harness and smalltalk' (*EL*, IX) of a migrating tribe watering its ponies by the banks of a Scandinavian lake, just as there is room to acknowledge the courage of a small boy who might explore beyond 'toy ports of the Baltic sea' (*EL*, VIII). Such space is accorded by Europa because she is conscious that yesterday's provincial is tomorrow's cosmopolitan and vice versa and that the diverse prejudices and languages which pit them against each other are meaningful only in the context of a history they share, even if they are frequently unaware that they do so. Everything becomes clearer she suggests, in death, when 'Released from nationality/ They are fraternal/ In the hoax of afterlife,/ Snug among the alluvials/ In the republic of Europe . . .' (*EL*, XII).

Europa's vision is all-encompassing, all-accepting, chronicling the
barbarities, injustices and pleasant civilities of her nations, faithful to
her own meaning 'the open space' or 'place without a name', and her
openness is initiated by the same French sound which Dunn first asked
us to listen to in *The Happier Life*:

> 'Listen' she said — you know
> That listening tilt,
> That smile on hearing far music?
> 'These are the saxophones,
> Far away, of the Riviera.'
>
> (*EL*, I)

French literature and civilisation have provoked in Douglas Dunn
'That listening tilt' which has contributed to the unique cultural poise
of his own poetry.

NOTES

1 These remarks were made during a conversation I had with Douglas
   Dunn at his home in Tayport on 9 July 1991.
2 See 'Remembering Lunch' (*SKP*, 44–6).
3 'Et il git là, comme une glande arrachée dans un cou.' Jules Laforgue,
   Oeuvres complètes, ed. J.L. Debaure, 3 vols (Lausanne: Editions L'Age
   d'Homme, 1986) II, 246.
4 *Oeuvres complètes*, I, 517–622. Laforgue's 'Complainte à notre dame
   des soirs' is on p. 551.
5 See p. 27.
6 *Nine Contemporary Poets*, 227.
7 Robert Desnos, *Fortunes* (Paris: NRF, 1942), 165.
8 Liz Lochhead, *Tartuffe* (Edinburgh and Glasgow: Polygon/Third Eye
   Centre, 1986).
9 See Albert Camus, 'Encounters with Andre Gide' in *Selected Essays
   and Notebooks*, ed. and trans. Philip Thody, (London: Penguin,
   1979), 173–7.
10 Ibid., 175.
11 Ibid., 173.
12 Ibid., 174.
13 Ibid., 175.
14 Ibid.
15 Ibid.
16 Paul Nizan, *Pour une nouvelle culture*, textes réunis et présentés par
   Susan Suleiman (Paris: Grasset, 1971), 241. The translation is mine.
17 Ibid., 165.
18 *Antoine Bloyé* was first published by Grasset in 1933.
19 W.D. Redfern, *Paul Nizan. Committed Literature in a Conspiratorial
   World* (Princeton, NJ: Princeton University Press, 1972), 53.
20 *Nine Contemporary Poets*, 225.

21 Craig Raine, *1953* (London: Faber and Faber, 1990).
22 Interview with Douglas Dunn conducted by William Oxley, *Acumen*, April 1991, No 13, p. 9.
23 Racine, *Andromaque* (Paris: Nouveaux Classiques Larousse, 1965), 46.

Twelve

Taking Exception: Douglas Dunn's Criticism

Richard Price

Douglas Dunn is one of the few major poet-critics in Scotland. A poem about the pencil, an introduction to 'local' poetry from Humberside, introductions to anthologies of Byron and Delmore Schwartz, an academic piece on Wycherley, book reviews for *The Glasgow Herald*, and poetry reviews and round-ups for the leftish magazines *The New Statesman* and *Encounter*: these are all examples of Dunn's wide-ranging criticism. When he is interviewed, his responses usually have the precision of what it is reasonable to call a critical standpoint, too. Within this considerable range of criticism, identifiable patterns emerge.

This chapter will discuss only the following: his view of what poetry is and ought to be; his sceptical opinion of poetry which tries too hard to be something it 'ought to be'; and finally, his views of Scottish poetry past and present, views which, as we shall see, reveal a persistent ambivalence towards MacDiarmid. Only passing reference can be made here to his reviews of fiction and, indeed, non-fiction. A keen and sustained interest in new poetry and fiction from abroad surfaces in his reviewing – a widening perspective that is to be admired – but the focus in this chapter will have to be closer to home. Finally, through looking at his poetry criticism, it seems sensible to identify any underlying *technique* in just how Dunn argues, and to try and relate his critical procedure to his literary temperament (it may, of course, be the flesh of procedure on the bone of intuition).

RELAXED CREATIVITY

Stylistic indecision, failure to find the identifiable style of 'one voice', or a relaxed, open-minded approach to writing that takes forms as they come? . . . These questions can be asked of virtually any contemporary poet's work. [1]

When Dunn discerns the difference between 'stylistic indecision' and an approach to poetry that 'takes forms as they come', he makes a distinction between a willed poetry and an organic kind. Because he is writing here about Derek Mahon's poetry with particular respect to Northern Irish writing before and after Bloody Sunday, the argument here is not between a posturing and a modest poetry, it is about the effective channelling of a poet's feelings when that poet is experiencing circumstances in which he or she *cannot* 'relax'. That breezy 'open-minded approach to writing' is therefore more complicated than it looks. In his introduction to *Two Decades of Irish Writing*, Dunn had noted the intense thinking-through that writers from Ireland seem to have demanded of themselves, and he praised their ability to rise above the temptation of cruder responses. In the novels of John McGahern, for example, there is 'an absence of comfortable mannerisms and relaxations, which indicates not only seriousness of purpose, but a scrupulousness of forethought rare in contemporary English letters' (*TD*, 2). A 'scrupulousness of forethought' is not the state of relaxation Dunn seems also to require, though it may be some stage before it, so there is something ultimately more rigorous in his idea of finding creative 'comfortability'.

Dunn respects the poet who is not shrill in his or her own writing, but that does not mean that the poet's subject should be tranquillised. Indeed, it is important that the poet is profoundly alive to his subject. This is a discrimination he makes again and again in his criticism.

> Among my convictions is that it is a responsibility of a contemporary writer to be lucid and clear. Another belief is that it is culturally necessary to write for other people, not for oneself. Neither principle leads me to underrate the mysterious, those half-understood perceptions and insights which the imagination can produce, nor does the latter conviction tempt me to write for anyone in particular or for that monstrous entity known as 'the public'. [2]

If one is writing for 'other people,' especially with the view that it is 'culturally necessary' to do so, is this not writing for 'the public'? And if other people are not the public, are they then still not 'anyone in particular'?

Dunn seems to be negotiating between, in the strict sense of the word, a *mystical* understanding of the creative act and an understanding of poetry as inherently political. He believes in a socially-committed

poetry in a broad sense which is not so broad as to make no difference.
In his selection of Humberside poetry, *To Build A Bridge*, he
acknowledges that such a point of view is not the 'universal' or
'common-sense' attitude for which some confuse it. Rather it is a
particular choice and a particular meeting of form and subject:

> Many writers of my own generation have chosen an admittedly
> uneasy compromise of style, in which the traditional expectations
> of a poem are made to coexist with modernity of language,
> cleanliness of line and a fidelity to a subject matter of the here and
> now. That may be the middle ground of contemporary poetry, but
> it is not the only ground a poet can occupy [. . .][3]

His critical voice is the voice of a leftish pragmatist who will not be
pinioned by the programmatic in politics or poetry. Whether one really
can write 'taking forms as they come' I am not sure. How conscious a
choice is that 'compromise'? Dunn himself, just when he seems to be
that open-minded poet about whom he has talked, usually reminds you
that there is, nevertheless, a bottom line: 'the interesting thing about
English prosody is that its laws are so flexible you can get by on the
belief that there aren't any, although the really golden rule is that verse
should sound as if there are' (*IL*, 5). Beyond the 'form' of 'free verse',
which anyway at its best is nothing of the sort, the pruning of first
meaning necessary to conform to even a relaxed sense of rhythm and
rhyme means that, to paraphrase W.S. Graham, language is using us as
well as us using it.

When a poet is too obviously gripped by what he sees as a moralistic
tone and, perhaps relatedly, inappropriate forms, Dunn tells you about
it. The problems of political voice and of poetic formalism are therefore
key subjects in his criticism. His article on Alan Bold's poetry (in a
1979 issue of *Akros*) illustrates exactly these concerns.[4] Bold is hardly of
the stature of the other poets to which Dunn has devoted full-length
articles: he sits at some considerable distance from, say, MacCaig,
Morgan or Graham. Indeed, Dunn's earlier assessment of Bold's *A Pint
of Bitter* was this: 'Prosaic, boring, unoriginal, flat, clumsy – Mr Bold
can be all of these at practically the same time, a real one-man band.'[5]
As such, Bold is an interesting choice. Indeed Dunn is so critical of his
work, and with such embarrassing detail, that it is tempting to see the
whole article as an excuse for Dunn's revealing of what he believes to be
a widespread malaise, an excuse that is productive in the context of this
chapter. Dunn gives the impression, however, of wanting to be
sympathetic towards Bold's work, too, especially towards the end of the
article, and he identifies a kind of vulnerable honesty in Bold's career, if

not his poetry, that is 'simple, primitive and moving'. This wishing to 'do good' with his criticism is something to which I will return.

Political shouting delivered in ponderous forms: Bold's poetry exemplifies what Dunn calls 'the tragedy of commitment'. Noting MacDiarmid's influence of anger rather than of excellence, he argues that Bold's vocal political allegiance to revolutionary socialism, Bold as the chip on MacDiarmid's shoulder, seems to seek — and destroy — *un*revolutionary forms. The result is heavy-handed (and heavy-footed) poetry which is 'a long way from the innovatory surprises of Modernism, no matter how aggressive his confrontation with technique may appear'. The areas in Bold's corpus that Dunn is drawn to are those few in which Bold seems, simply, comfortable. These occur especially in Bold's later poetry — particular cases of working-class life, for instance, instead of the vague 'working-class' declarations of his earlier work. Dunn repeats the idea of 'relaxing' into writing poetry and then, summing up, he suggests that 'if he can only acquire a satisfactory idiom within which he can relax, and which would discourage deliberation and a poetry of will, he might surprise us yet'.

In Dunn's 1988 inaugural lecture as Honorary Professor in the Faculty of Arts and Social Sciences at Dundee University, *Importantly Live: Lyricism in Contemporary Poetry*, there is again his admiration for that special place where fine poets do find the right idiom, where they find the 'ability to engage with the materials of ordinary life, and then absorb them, not necessarily to transcend them, or adjust ordinariness to the mysterious or the irrational, [. . . proving . . .] that poetry begins in reality as well as in the imagination that apprehends it' (*IL*, 2). By deliberately choosing very different poets from very different backgrounds and countries (though, it has to be said, all formally fairly conservative and moderately-opinioned) — Philip Larkin, Norman MacCaig, Tony Harrison and Seamus Heaney — Dunn identifies a kind of consensus of lyricism that is defined, if it can be defined at all, by a shared willingness to re-express the misnamed commonplace. That re-expression, it is imperative to say, raises itself above the odd sweetmeats upon which intransigences of all kinds dine. An 'unembarrassed exposure of the first-person singular' underlines the confidence — a version of relaxation, perhaps — that characterises these poets' best work. (Dunn has noted elsewhere that the brilliant use of the first-person singular is what characterises the poetry of many of the greatest poets.[6]) Beating the anti-sentimentality that Dunn perceives to be as dangerous as sentimentality itself is ultimately, he has said, a rather more radical act than any exerted by the stress and clatter of 'ideological poets':

It is in these moments of writing where a poet lives at his or her most important, where words are written and spoken that in contemporary life might represent the last resource of the language, one in which we can still encounter the truthfulness that embarrasses superficial mendacity, ruthless self-interest and controversial expediency, while, at the same time, being disinterested enough not to have to admit to that or any other function. (*IL*, 16).

Dunn is far from scared of talking about the 'truthfulness' of poetry. He does not find the idea problematic in the way that certain, usually ideologically-loaded, forms of criticism famously and paradoxically have. Indeed one senses that his dislike of poets such as, for example, Ashbery (in the *Encounter* essay noted above), arises from the same distrust of the apparently clever-clever, of the 'untruthful', that is noticeable in his stark avoidance of modern literary theory.[7] In his review of Malcolm Bradbury's collection of critical essays, *No, not Bloomsbury*, he takes issue with Bradbury's assertion that 'Writing is the trade, and criticism the profession'. 'Grocers and plumbers, lawyers and brain surgeons?' Dunn asks, 'No, writing is an art, and criticism the function of its curators.'[8] His affinities are with the poets who are also critics, rather than creative theorists such as Derrida. In a review of the prose of one of his favourite poets, Robert Lowell, he notes 'It is remarkable [. . .] that so much of poets' criticism should be quite unlike that of the professors'.[9] Certainly it has been the case that by and large the understanding of what is 'great poetry' has been communicated most successfully down the years not by those in academe but by other and succeeding poets, and no less in Scotland where poets have been at times almost the *only* preservers of the poetry that has gone before them.

For Dunn, 'poetic truth' is 'poetry's exercise of freedom within its intuitive principles as these are revealed acceptably in the work of an individual poet', a phenomenon 'likely to occur when what a poet is saying is a coincidence of imagery, rhythm and meaning — the imagination made visible, audible and interesting'.[10] Poetry, in this reading, is a dynamic form because it is expressive of a poet's individuality, a definition which carries that sense again of the *radical nature* of the poem whatever technical strategy it adopts (note, though, the lovely compromise implied by 'intuitive principles'). This verity derives its freedom from the time-honoured fixing points of 'imagery, rhythm and meaning', and these, I would add, are hardly aspects of poetry that can be politicised in anything but the crudest terms (formal attempts have been made).

THE PREDICAMENT OF SCOTTISH POETRY

It should be said, because I cannot go into it much further here, that in his many reviews over the years Douglas Dunn has consistently defended Scottish literature against the wilful silences of the English literary establishment. This has meant that he has not stopped at 'quibbling' with writers he very much admires, Margaret Drabble for example, when they have marginalised, perhaps unconsciously, that which is palpably not marginal.[11] That said, Dunn's sense of barren areas of parochialism in Scottish literature is a distinguishing feature of his specific critique of Scottish poetry.

In particular, that parochialism is exemplified, ironically, by a failure to see the immediate visual possibilities of Scotland's landscapes and nature – what some might call 'parish scenes'. Whether it is an intrusive philosophising, an embarrassment about the pure joy of particular visual openings, or a yomping 'internationalism' that prefers Lenin's footnotes to a brilliant winter hare, caught, perhaps, in the green of a thaw, Scottish poets can at times push too far their gangling version of the cerebral. In his introduction to *The Poetry of Scotland*, he traces the way in which nature poetry written by Scots, even though 'Scottish writers were obviously stimulated by nature long before the vogue created by the Great Unknown' (*PS*, 11), actually always tries to talk about something else. Burns's 'settings are therefore the emplacement of events, especially amorous ones [. . .] His landscapes are humanised into backdrops for memory, friendships and recreation' (*PS*, 13), and Scott's are of course highly romanticised. It is Dunn's tacit admission of Scotland's failure to produce landscape poetry of high calibre that a significant number of poems in the anthology are written by visitors to Scotland, among them Swinburne, Auden and Eliot.

Perhaps as a revising of this view, however, and particularly in the light of the general excitement about Scottish arts and politics which has surfaced in the last ten years or so, his recent selection of prose and poetry, *Scotland: An Anthology*, is rich in scenic moments in poetry and his introduction does not notice any dearth.[12] His introduction also pays some tribute to the place of his upbringing, Renfrewshire, by recounting the spiritual history of his home village, Inchinnan, where a Celtic saint set up cell having 'sailed from Ireland on a stone'.[13] Dunn has been a poet of Renfrewshire in explicit terms through the years, and in some of his poems, such as 'The Student' (*B*, 19), 'Tannahill' (*SKP*, 52) and 'John Wilson in Greenock, 1786' (*SKP*, 57), he has been loyal to his county as a poet-critic-in-verse. His fairly long assessment of

W.S. Graham in *Aquarius* sees Graham in a Renfrewshire light, not least as a poet in conflict with the steely place of his birth, Greenock.[14]

Renfrewshire is a county where forms of villages exist still huddled round various heavy industries in differing states of decay – Linwood and the car plant, Greenock and Port Glasgow and the shipyards, even my own Bridge of Weir and its mostly long-gone tanneries. These secret villages also produce many of Glasgow's professionals and Inverclyde's IBM technicians, especially with the continuing patching of private housing estates on to the first fields outside a village. Renfrewshire is rural and industrial – 'rurban' as my geography teacher used to say – and it is tempting if insupportable to see Dunn's critical toughness, and his elegiac sensibility, as a product of that special place. Dunn pays tribute to Inchinnan as in some way typical of Scotland in the way in which its 'closeness of antiquity to the here-and-now and the not-long-gone measures a country which is a nation local to itself as well as made up of intimate, particular places. It is a patchwork of times as well as districts.'[15] Critically, he has always been willing to pay homage to the locality that he has found himself in, too, so that as well as the Hull compilations, he has recently written about the literary heritage of Dundee, the nearest city to his new home town, Tayport.[16]

Something of that celebration is conveyed in the opening of his essay on 'The Predicament of Scottish Poetry':

> A piece of 1940s' film I looked at recently in the Scottish Film Archive showed a woman in a hothouse, somewhere in the market gardens of the Clyde Valley near Lanark. It was a sunny day and she wore a white blouse with short sleeves. She raised her arms into a pool of sunlight and the lens, like the eye, could not focus on it. Her arm disappeared into white among the fruits that were unseen, unphotographed, but there.[17]

This beautiful, *exceptional* image clearly held Dunn. The statement of entrancement introduces Dunn's argument: 'how rarely such images appear in Scottish poetry, roundly evoked, described warmly but without purpose other than the design of delight or a surrender to imagination in the knowledge that by doing so a poet discovers and gives'.

It need hardly be said that this criticism of Scottish poetry is linked to Dunn's wider admiration for a relaxed and, in the profound sense of the word, *uncomplicated* lyricism. In the same essay, he writes that modern Scottish poetry 'lacks [. . .] a restful certitude'. Yet Dunn points to poets, many largely ignored now, who were 'not loud enough' to be remembered as well as they should – even Edwin Muir, William Soutar and Andrew Young (Muir and Soutar not remembered?). Taking

issue with David Daiches's assertion that cantankerousness and
antiestablishmentarianism are *typically* Scottish, he asks: 'Is that not as
much a restriction as the censorious finger-wagging of pious kirkmen,
dry moralists and life-denying respectability in general?'

Dunn develops this argument to say that these arid 'characteristics'
are, in the twentieth century, only *literary* characteristics. They can
safely be said not to relate to Scottish life as it is lived today. That they
are still so prevalent in literature is to do with the vulnerabilities of
young writers who try to find safety in a lazy tradition that is condoned
by Scotland's self-renewing waiting room of third-raters, an influenzal
tradition from which only the best escape. The tired and fortified status
of much of Lallans poetry, with few exceptions, is just another
correlative to this: 'it perpetuates all those characteristics which prevent
Scottish writers from reaching a more complete imagery.' This is
precisely what W.N. Herbert has called 'The Crisis of the Mediocre
Intellect,' a crisis which arises from a chronic misunderstanding of what
Scotland is and, indeed, of what a poet is.[18] For Dunn it is tied up with
a refusal to celebrate, genuinely celebrate. Dunn writes: 'In some ways
the largest predicament of all in Scottish writing is that there should be
a gross obstacle between a poet and "sweet feeling", mysticism and the
habits of a "soft, meditative disposition." '

Dunn's wish for an appreciative gentleness has found itself on a
collision course with the work and career of MacDiarmid. His mixed
opinion of the poet has been candidly expressed. Dunn was the guest
editor of the 1978 *Aquarius* anthology, an anthology conceived of before
Grieve's death that year, but which went to press late enough to take in
Dunn's initial reaction. That Dunn was the guest editor at all illustrates
that, of course, he has not been so foolish as to dismiss MacDiarmid out
of hand and that, indeed, he cherishes much in the poet. Dunn is
nothing if not discriminating. Lamenting the inability by and large of
Scotland to approach MacDiarmid's work with any kind of sanity,
Dunn's relatively off-the-cuff remarks have changed little in spirit in the
years since:

> Among my feelings of gratitude to MacDiarmid, of sadness that so
> great a writer should now be dead, I also feel a sense of *relief* at his
> going. This is meant to express the opposite of a lack of respect. It
> is a failure of a Scottish poet's Scottishness, his sense of who he or
> she is, and where he or she comes from – a failure of heart, and a
> failure of head – to refuse to come to terms with the full range of
> MacDiarmid's work. Without the man, we might now ignore the
> more vulgar of his discipleship. We might, if we are lucky

enough, shift MacDiarmid a little, and make room for ourselves to breathe.[19]

Dunn points to a lack in critical honesty, a critical incapacity to face up to what he sees as a fairly starkly divided pre- and post-1930 MacDiarmid: the former, a poet with very fine lyrical abilities, the latter a poet of 'overstatement, self-parody and an *unco guid* style of righteousness'. That Dunn alleges a specifically Scottish context in which to see MacDiarmid is still lacking shows his wider dissatisfaction with Scottish literary criticism in general. Tellingly, it takes MacDiarmid's legacy to corrugate Dunn's normally calmer prose:

> There is, frankly, no Scottish criticism which takes these factors into full account. We deal in personalities. In the case of MacDiarmid, we deal, self-indulgently, with a hero, with a figure who has replaced Burns as a national poet of the Scottish intelligentsia (Sweet Jesus, but how many *is* that?) if not in the minds of the people at large. A few hagiographical inroads have been made. And yet, what do they explain? Precious little.[20]

In one of history's enriching twists, Alan Bold came to Dunn's rescue: his biography of MacDiarmid Dunn has called one of 'the best examples of criticism in recent years'.[21] This is praise indeed from one so hard to please, yet when we look at Dunn's review of the book in *The Observer* a more complicated response emerges.[22] A number of barbed and relativist compliments, for instance, indicate that the spectre of MacDiarmid has not been laid to rest yet: 'Alan Bold's account comes as close as we are likely to get to the required book, at least until such time as a truce is declared on the subject's talent for posthumous controversy'; 'Bold's approach is less evasive than might have been predicted, but there are several footling errors of fact'; 'Bold [. . .] draws back from an assessment of the causes and nature of MacDiarmid's temperament – its erudite cruelty, for instance, or the attitude implicit in his poetry that his readers are on a hiding to nothing.' In the end, Dunn sounds more enthusiastic about the sheer facts that Bold has presented, the very fact of a biography appearing, than about Bold's understanding of that raw material. In substance, Dunn is nearer than might be expected, therefore, to the MacDiarmid scholars who had significant reservations about the biography. W.N. Herbert has written that Bold 'perceives only that triumph MacDiarmid read into his life, not that tragedy is implicit in the forced nature of that reading; the least MacDiarmid deserves is what he demanded of Scotland: a little independent thinking.'[23] Patrick Crotty concluded that 'Sadly, many will approach the poetry through this book and conclude that it can be safely ignored [. . .]. There will have to be a better biography, written by a scholar with an ironic affection for the poet and a dispassionate commitment to the poetry.'[24] The eminent Kenneth Buthlay had considerable reservations about Bold's understanding of MacDiarmid in earlier critical work, an apparently serious misjudgement Bold repeats in the biography – without indicating that his view is at all controversial.[25]

Could it be, therefore, that *the fact* of Bold's biography – the apparently head-on tackling of Grieve's life and works – was *in itself* the foundation Dunn had been seeking; that by at least trying to address comprehensively the problems MacDiarmid raises, Bold's book almost had to be praised in the general terms Dunn has used? Dunn's devotion of column inches to MacDiarmid's haircut, and to MacDiarmid's involvement in fascism – indeed to a surprising amount of biographical detail, rather than to analysis of the book – might indicate a wish to avoid saying anything too critical, yet a wish, too, to put an extra slant on the interpretation of MacDiarmid lacking in it. More simply, it might be an admission of MacDiarmid's obscurity as regards the readership of *The Observer*. Dunn's qualified praise (the blurb-writers for Bold's paperback were unable to quote more than three words) should be seen in the light of his persistent unhappiness with MacDiarmid's previously mostly unaddressed large and noisome inconsistencies, and it is that kind of qualification with which Dunn ends the review:

> For the first time, disinterested readers now have the information to make up their own minds about MacDiarmid. When you take into account the radical, reckless, extreme complexity of the man, that is a considerable achievement.[26]

In his introduction to *The Faber Book of Twentieth-Century Scottish Poetry*, Dunn returns to MacDiarmid as poet rather than as persona (though, rightly, he will not allow a reader to leave without a reminder that this man 'had little use for democracy').[27] Dunn is particularly interesting here in that, though identifying the *philological* enthusiasm which propels MacDiarmid's early poetry, his introductory pages on MacDiarmid peter out as MacDiarmid's Scots poetry comes to end: the later work in unbelievably eclectic English, material distinguished by a 'vocab-ism' that has more in common with the early lyrics than might at first be realised, still does not figure as any kind of achievement or even as any attempt at an achievement. In his contrasting of MacDiarmid with Burns, previous criticism suggests that Dunn's affinities lie with the latter. Again we find the clever-clever being pitted against the 'organic'. That does not mean that Burns was 'simple', but it does mean that his poetry assumed, and was even a product of, an embracing vision of humanity rather than an intellectually haughty and dismissive one. Unlike MacDiarmid's,

Rarely, if ever, do individual words in Burns's poems draw
attention to themselves as lexical splendours. Some of them may
have been unusual to Burns, but they were insured by the
experience of speech, and introduced on a balanced, colloquial
metre, and on a voice that insists on the demotic integrity of its
idiom.[28]

TAKING EXCEPTION

If one were to try to identify a particular technique which seems to
inhere in Dunn's criticism, it would be his ability to take to task, at
length, those writers he nevertheless clearly admires. In 'The Wireless
Behind the Curtain', an essay on the poetry of Iain Crichton Smith,
Dunn scrutinises the early poems in particular as if he were conducting a
post mortem on a foolish teenage biker. One recognises the Dunn who is
especially uneasy with what he sees as presumptuous political poetry
when he says of *From Bourgeois Land* (1969) that it 'assails the reader':
'Quarrelsome attitudes are allowed to take the upper hand so that the
tone becomes disdainful or hectoring more than poetically critical.'[29]

Though Dunn reviews Crichton Smith's more recent poetry
generously, again we get the feeling that, as with Bold's poetic
struggles, Crichton Smith's mistakes, his trials, his poetry's 'battered
and distracted progress' have been re-presented to be instructive: 'In
Smith's poetry there is a very distinct sensation of struggling towards a
time when his poetry can win through to the perfection of which it
dreams.'[30] This view is partly an expression of that poetic 'trope' — the
poet serving his apprenticeship, and rigorously examining procedure
and strategy. One notices, for example, that he has interpreted Norman
MacCaig's career, and that of W.S. Graham, in similar terms,
although his celebration of MacCaig's poetry has notably had few
reservations.[31]

Dunn's interpretation of Edwin Morgan's sonnets forms a culminat-
ing example of his critical technique.[32] Though praising Morgan for
using the form in a fresh way, and not trying to disguise that they are
sonnets he is using (Dunn the formalist), he nevertheless goes through
the 'Glasgow Sonnets' to illustrate just exactly what might be the
weaknesses in Morgan's poetry. In particular, he takes exception with
the poet for what he sees as not just an obviously urban perspective, but
a prejudicial one: 'Wholeheartedly urban, Morgan risks denigrating
suburb and countryside, lark, leaf and lane.'[33] This is a serious charge,
made both at a specific level about the eighth poem of Morgan's
sequence and much more widely about his poetry in general. Morgan
'disregards the possibility of how a transaction between country and

city, weekend and working week, attractive and unattractive, the natural and the industrial, might, for many, be preferable to monolithic architecture designed by an ideology infatuated with the new.'[34] But does he? Isn't it rather that Morgan has done more than any poet in the United Kingdom this century to acknowledge the complexity of urban life, even, let it be said, the *existence* in Scotland of urban life? Yet Dunn's worrying reminds one that Morgan does occasionally seem to adopt apparently indefensible stances: how, for instance, in *From the Video Box* can such a literary man appear to celebrate the burning of libraries his own erudition has in part relied on? To warm the hands of the enslaved, yes, but deliberate censorship is never far from real brutality. Or am I being too po-faced about a visual moment of delight? In the same essay, Dunn's criticism of science fiction as a potentially dangerous mode for poetry seems again to show the limitations in his view of that poetry which wants to leap away from what poetry has been before: 'as a genre, it can be argued that science fiction is often implicated in unearned overviews of actual or possible states of affairs that are too important to get wrong'.[35]

This type of chariness perhaps accounts for Dunn's failure to appreciate MacDiarmid's later work (or MacDiarmid's failure to make something capable of appreciation). Yet it is not the form or the genre, ultimately, that Dunn is concerned with, and this is what makes his criticism, like his poetry, so attractive and usually so convincing. It is the moral implication of this or that strategy which forms the basis of Dunn's criticism; the belief that poetic truth does actually reach out to people at large, though in a mysterious and perhaps ultimately elusive way. Because Dunn is willing to use his considerable intelligence to ask uncomfortable questions in a genuinely critical sense, he has contributed importantly to what has been an at times rather threadbare Scottish literary criticism this century. He has been rigorous and sane.

NOTES

1 Douglas Dunn, 'Let the God Not Abandon Us: On the Poetry of Derek Mahon' in *Stone Ferry Review* No 2, Winter 1978, 20.
2 Douglas Dunn, *Douglas Dunn* (Glasgow: National Book League, 1982), 1.
3 *To Build a Bridge*, edited by Douglas Dunn (Lincoln: Lincolnshire & Humberside Art, 1982).
4 Douglas Dunn, 'The Poetry of Alan Bold: Hammering on the Lyre' in *Akros* 14:42, December 1979, 58–76.
5 Douglas Dunn, 'Damaged Instruments' in *Encounter*, August 1971, 73.

6 Douglas Dunn, *Under the Influence* (Edinburgh: Edinburgh University Library, 1987), 4.

7 Ibid.

8 Douglas Dunn, 'Curators to the art of writing' in *The Glasgow Herald*, 16 May 1987.

9 Douglas Dunn, 'Candid critic without malice' in *The Glasgow Herald*, 20 June 1987.

10 Douglas Dunn, 'The Wireless Behind the Curtain', 1991, ts p. 2; p. 4. For published version of this piece see n. 29 below.

11 Douglas Dunn, 'England going to the dogs' in *The Glasgow Herald*, 2 May 1987.

12 *Scotland: an Anthology*, ed. Douglas Dunn (London: HarperCollins, 1991). I am grateful to HarperCollins Press Office for giving me an advance copy of this volume.

13 Ibid., p. 6.

14 Douglas Dunn, [Review of W.S. Graham's *Collected Poems 1942–1977*] in *Aquarius* No. 12, 1980, 128–34.

15 Ibid., p. 7.

16 Douglas Dunn, 'Dundee Law considered as Mount Parnassus' in *Gairfish*, No 4, Summer 1991, 17–42.

17 Douglas Dunn, 'The Predicament of Scottish Poetry', in *The Times Literary Supplement*, 18 March 1983, 273.

18 W.N. Herbert, 'The Crisis of the Mediocre Intellect' in *Severe Burns* by Robert Crawford, W.N. Herbert and David Kinloch (Oxford: Obog Books, 1986), 3.

19 Douglas Dunn, 'Douglas Dunn' in *Aquarius* No 11, 1979, 68.

20 Ibid; *MacDiarmid: Christopher Murray Grieve: A Critical Biography* (London: Paladin, 1990; originally published 1988).

21 Douglas Dunn, 'Interview with Douglas Dunn' in *Acumen* No 13, April 1991, 18.

22 Douglas Dunn, 'Out of his head' in *The Observer*, 11 September 1988, 43.

23 W.N. Herbert, 'Thorny' in *Poetry Review*, Vol. 78 No 4, Winter 1988/9, 24.

24 Patrick Crotty, 'MacDiarmid: Christopher Murray Grieve. A Critical Biography' in *Scottish Literary Journal* Supplement No 30, Spring 1989, 19.

25 Cf. Kenneth Buthlay in the introduction to Hugh MacDiarmid, *A Drunk Man Looks at the Thistle*, ed. Buthlay (Edinburgh: Scottish Academic Press, 1987), xlviii.

26 Ibid.

27 Douglas Dunn, 'Language and Liberty', [introduction to] *The Faber Book of Twentieth-Century Scottish Poetry* (London: Faber and Faber, 1992), xxiii.

28 Ibid.

29 Douglas Dunn, 'The Wireless Behind the Curtain' in Colin Nicholson, ed., *Iain Crichton Smith* (Edinburgh: Edinburgh University Press, 1992), 63.

30 Ibid.
31 Douglas Dunn, ' "As a man sees" – on Norman MacCaig's poetry' in
   Verse Vol. 7 No 2, 66.
32 Douglas Dunn, 'Morgan's Sonnets' in *About Edwin Morgan*, ed.
   Robert Crawford and Hamish Whyte (Edinburgh: Edinburgh
   University Press, 1990), 75–89.
33 Ibid., 78.
34 Ibid., 78.
35 Ibid., 85.

Thirteen

Bibliography

James Kidd

No bibliography is ever completely exhaustive or finite — least of all where the writer is still alive and well and writing. What I have attempted to do here is to list all Douglas Dunn's publications to date (December 1991), together with significant reviews of his work and the major essays and articles about him. I have also noted his literary awards, work for radio and television, most of his reviewing activities, location of his manuscripts, something of his public poetry-reading, participation in poetry festivals, cultural visits abroad etc. where these have a bearing on his publications.

The arrangement of the bibliography is as follows:

Section A: Books, pamphlets etc. by, edited by, or translated by DD.
Section B: Individual poems by DD.
Section C: Short stories by DD.
Section D: Essays and articles by DD.
Section E: Anthologies — Works by DD contained in anthologies.
Section F: Reviews by DD.
Section G: DD's work for Radio, Television and the Theatre.
Section H: Biographical-critical articles on DD.

Within each Section, the arrangement is chronological by year of publication, and alphabetical within that year.

Most of the early Manuscripts relating to *Terry Street* (1969) have been deposited in the Brynmor Jones Library at the University of Hull. Otherwise, all the manuscripts and papers are zealously retained by the author himself (*pace* librarians!).

Immersion in Dunn's work over the past six months or so prompts me to a few general conclusions. The increasing range of his work is impressive: poems, short stories, reviews and critical essays, journalism, translations, radio plays, screen-plays, verse commentaries etc. He has been conspicuously generous in supporting 'little magazines', student publications, and publishing ventures by fellow poets. His visits abroad have fostered a special rapport with fellow writers in Poland, Czechoslovakia, Hungary, Yugoslavia, France, USA, Australia etc.

His growing reputation is mirrored in his increasing participation in public poetry readings, literary festivals, conferences etc., whether giving papers or chairing sessions or judging awards. The media too are making ever greater demands on him.

What (for me) shines through it all is the integrity and high quality of his work. He is primarily a poet, and takes his vocation seriously, but not too solemnly. Despite all the well-deserved awards and honours he has been acquiring over the past few years, he remains a very humble, unassuming – and very Scottish – human being, content to plough his own furrow and thereby add considerably to the sum of human enjoyment.

Many colleagues, friends and fellow admirers of Dunn's work have helped in the compilation of this bibliography. Without Douglas himself and his unfailing generosity, helpfulness and good humour, it would have been a much more difficult task, and a far less rewarding one. I must also mention the special assistance given by George Charlton and Sean O'Brien regarding the 'uncollected poems'. And I owe a particular debt to our co-editor, Robert Crawford, without whose enthusiasm, encouragement, drive and support this whole enterprise would never have reached fruition. I should also like to acknowledge the sterling contribution made by 'my' typists both in the University Library and in the Department of English. The errors and omissions, needless to say, are all my own.

SECTION A. BOOKS, PAMPHLETS ETC. BY, EDITED BY,
OR TRANSLATED BY DOUGLAS DUNN.

1965

A1   *From the Egyptians to Einstein*: a selection of History of Science books in the
     Reference Division of the Akron Public Library. [Compiled by DD].
     Akron, Ohio: Akron Public Library, [1965], 12pp.

1969

A2   (a) *Terry Street*. London: Faber & Faber, 1969. 62 pp.

     Contents: The Clothes Pit – New Light on Terry Street – The Patricians –
     Men of Terry Street – Incident in the Shop – The Terry Street Fusiliers –
     A Removal from Terry Street – On Roofs of Terry Street – From the
     Night-Window – Sunday Morning Among the Houses of Terry Street –
     Late Night Walk Down Terry Street – After Closing Time – Winter – Ins
     and Outs – Young Women in Rollers – A Death in Terry Street – The
     Silences – A Window Affair – The Worst of All Loves – Tribute of a Legs
     Lover – The Season for Hats – Bring Out Your Dead – Close of Play –
     Horses in a Suburban Field – The Love Day – The Self-made Man – Belle
     and Beau – Insomnia on Roetzel's Island – Love Poem – End of the Oldest
     Revolution – Narcissus – A Dream of Judgement – A Dream of Random
     Love – The Ocean's Love to Ralegh – Landscape with One Figure – South
     Bank of the Humber – Passing Through – The Queen of the Belgians –
     Ships – A Poem in Praise of the British – Cosmologist.

     Notes: Scottish Arts Council Award, Spring 1970. Somerset Maugham
     Award, 1972.

     Reviews
     TLS 20 November 1969, p. 1330.
     G. Kendrick. *Phoenix* nos 6/7 (1970), pp. 137–41.

(b) – Reissued in 1986.

Review
D. Grant. *London Review of Books* 7 May 1987, p. 22.

(c) – American edition. New York: Chilmark Press, 1973.

1971
A3 *Backwaters*. London: The Review, 1971. 15pp. (Supplement to *The Review* no 25).

Contents: Alternative – Modern Love – Three Days before Term – The Friendship of Young Poets – The Sportsmen – Runners – The Hunched – After the War – The Shirt – The Philologists – Five Years Married – Backwaters – Billie 'n' Me – Up in Duggie's Room – Under the Stone.

A4 *Night*. London: Poem-of-the-Month Club, 1971.

Notes: Collected in *HL* (1972).

1972
A5 (a) *The Happier Life*. London: Faber & Faber, 1972. 72pp.

Contents: The Garden – The River Through the City – The Friendship of Young Poets – Nights of Sirius – At a Yorkshire Bus-stop – The Musical Orchard – Backwaters – Leisure No End – This Year and Next – Morning Bedroom – Supreme Death – Celtica – The Boon Companions – Night – Syndrome – Billie 'n' Me – Midweek Matinée – The Hull Sit-in – The Hunched – The Shirt – Emblems – The Sportsmen – The Happier Life – Five Years Married – Runners – The Philologists – After the War – Alternative – Modern Love – Guerrillas – Under the Stone – The New Girls – Saturday Night Function – A Faber Melancholy – Up in Duggie's Room – Bird Poet – Fixed – Spoken to by Six – The Hour.

Reviews
Iain Crichton Smith. *Glasgow Herald* 3 June 1972.
TLS 9 June 1972, p. 651.
J. Raban. *Spectator* 22 July 1972, p. 136.
P.N. Furbank. *Listener* 9 August 1972, p. 190.
R. Scruton. *Encounter* vol. 39 (September 1972), pp. 84–5.
R. Fulton. *Scottish International* September 1972, p. 32.
S.F.P. Reid. *Aberdeen University Review* vol. 45 (1972), pp. 90–3.
E. Longley. *Phoenix* no 10 (1973), pp. 93–5.

(b) – American edition. New York: Chilmark Press, 1972.

1973
A6 *Antaeus* (New York) no 12 (1973), edited by Douglas Dunn.

Notes: A special British Poetry Issue guest-edited by DD.

A7   *New poems 1972–73: a PEN anthology of contemporary poetry*, edited by
     Douglas Dunn. London: Hutchinson, 1973. 184pp.

     Notes: Includes an 'Introduction' by DD (pp. 11–13), but none of his own
     poems.

1974

A8   *A Choice of Byron's Verse*: selected with an introduction by Douglas Dunn.
     London: Faber & Faber, 1974. 161pp.

     Contents: 'Introduction' by DD (pp. 11–18).

     Reviews
     Sunday Times 19 May 1974, p. 35.
     TLS 14 June 1974, p. 647.

A9   (a) *Love or Nothing*. London : Faber & Faber, 1974. 64pp.

     Contents: Little Rich Rhapsody – The House Next Door – Winter
     Graveyard – Winter Orchard – In the Small Hotel – The Global Fidget –
     Realisms – Renfrewshire Traveller – Unlucky Mariners – Ocean – Port
     Logan and a Vision of Live Maps – The Scar – Sunday – White Fields –
     The Competition – Boys With Coats – Sailing with the Fleet –
     Clydesiders – Caledonian Moonlight – Going to Bed – I am a Cameraman
     – Ars Poetica – A Lost Woman – The Concert – The Opportunity – The
     Dilemma – The White Poet – Privacies – Variations on the Words 'Solo'
     and 'Exhaust' – Restraint – Thinking, from Birds to God – The
     Malediction – The Estuarial Republic – The Disguise.

     Notes: Geoffrey Faber Memorial Prize, May 1976.

     Reviews
     J. Fenton. *New Statesman* 6 December 1974, p. 832.
     C. Falck. *New Review* 1(9) December 1974, pp. 66–8.
     P. Ackroyd. *Spectator* 4 January 1975, p. 13.
     R. Fuller. TLS 31 January 1975, p. 107.
     H.C. Hill. *Outposts* no 104 (1975), pp. 25–7.
     A. Thwaite. *Encounter* vol. 44 (February 1975), pp. 76–7.
     B. Ruddick. *Critical Quarterly* 17 (2) 1975, p. 183.
     J. Saunders. *Lines Review* no 54 (September 1975), pp. 48–50.

     (b) – American edition. New York: Chilmark Press, 1976.

1975

A10 *Corporal Punishment*. Oxford: Sycamore Press, 1975. 1 sheet (folded).
     (Sycamore Broadsheet 21).

     Notes: A poem in three sections.

A11 *Flies on a Lampshade*: an anthology of poems by the students at Lumb Bank with the Arvon Foundation, 5th to 10th August 1975. Tutors [and edited by] Alan Brownjohn and DD. Lumb Bank: Arvon Foundation, 1975. 16pp.

Contents: Includes 'Flies on a Lampshade': a poem by DD and Saul Hyman.

A12 (a) *Two Decades of Irish Writing: a critical survey*; edited by Douglas Dunn. Cheadle: Carcanet, 1975. 260pp.

Contents: 'Introduction' by DD (pp. 1–3).

Reviews
V. Sage. *New Review* 2 (20) November 1975, pp. 71–2.
THES 30 July 1976, p. 16.

(b) – American edition. Chester Springs, PA: Dufour Editions, 1975.

1976

A13 *Delmore Schwartz. What is to be Given*; selected poems with an introduction by Douglas Dunn. Manchester: Carcanet New Press, 1976. xix, 75pp.

Contents: 'Introduction' by DD (pp. vii-xix).

Reviews
I. Howe. TLS 28 April 1978, pp. 458–9.

1978

A14 *Poetry Review* vol. 68 no 1 (April 1978). Editor: Douglas Dunn. London: Poetry Society, 1978. 70pp.

Contents: 'Introduction' by DD (pp. 3–5).

1979

A15 *Aquarius* no 11 (1979); edited by Douglas Dunn.

Contents: A special issue of the journal in honour of Hugh MacDiarmid; guest-edited by DD.

Review
P. Farnon. *New Edinburgh Review* no 47 (August 1979), p. 29.

A16 *Barbarians*. London: Faber & Faber, 1979. 59pp.

Contents: The Come-on – In the Grounds – Here be Dragons – Gardeners – The Student – An Artist Waiting in a Country House – Rough-cast –

Empires — The Wealth — Elegy for the Lost Parish — Watches of
Grandfathers — Portrait Photograph, 1915 — Alice — The Musician —
Drowning — Glasgow Schoolboys, Running Backwards — Red Buses —
Ballad of the Two Left Hands — Warriors — Lost Gloves — Stories —
Stranger's Grief — Night-Devon, Dawn-Devon — On Her Picture Left
with Him — A Late Degree — The Difficulty — Transcendence — Old
Things — Wedding — The Return.

Reviews
P. Porter. *Observer* 1 April 1979, p. 38.
B. Morrison. *New Statesman* 11 May 1979, p. 690.
E. Morgan. *New Edinburgh Review* no 46 (May 1979), pp. 29–30.
A. Brownjohn. *Encounter* vol. 52 (June 1979), pp. 68–9.
I.C. Smith. *Books in Scotland* no 6 (1979), p. 14.
C. Hope. *London Magazine* 19(8) November 1979, pp. 82–4.
J. Cassidy. *Poetry Review* 69 (2) December 1979, pp. 60–1.
E. Longley. TLS 18 January 1980, pp. 64–5.
A.A. Cleary. *Thames Poetry* 1(8) March 1980, pp. 41–9.
D. Montrose. *Honest Ulsterman* no 66 (1980), pp. 70–8.

A17   *The Poetry of Scotland*, edited by Douglas Dunn. London: Batsford, 1979.
      127pp.

Review
A. Bold. *Scotsman* (Weekend) 8 December 1979.

A18   *Poetry Supplement* compiled by Douglas Dunn for the Poetry Book Society,
      Christmas 1979. London: Poetry Book Society, 1979. [61]pp.

1981

A19   *St Kilda's Parliament*. London: Faber & Faber, 1981. 87pp.

Contents: St Kilda's Parliament — The Apple Tree — An Address on the
Destitution of Scotland — Dominies — Witch-girl — Washing the Coins —
Galloway Motor Farm — Monumental Sculptor — The Harp of
Renfrewshire — War Blinded — Savings — Spinster's Wake — Rose —
Saturday — Courting — E.A. Walton thinks of painting 'The Daydream' —
The Local — Second-hand Clothes — Remembering Lunch — Green Breeks
— Tannahill — John Wilson in Greenock, 1786 — Valerio — La Route — The
Gallery — The Deserter — Lamp-posts — The Miniature Métro — Loch
Music — Fallen among anti-Semites — Wednesday — Ode to a Paperclip —
Ratatouille.

Notes: Poetry Book Society Choice for Autumn 1981. PBS *Bulletin* no 110
(Autumn 1981) contains a background article by DD entitled 'Douglas
Dunn writes . . .' (pp. 1–2).

Awarded the Hawthornden Prize in June 1982.

Reviews

E. Longley. *New Statesman* 18 September 1981, pp. 29–30.
P. Porter. *Observer* 20 September 1981.
A. Thwaite. TLS 2 October 1981, p. 1125.
A. Bold. *Scotsman* (Weekend) 10 October 1981.
S. Conn. *New Edinburgh Review* no 56 (Winter 1981), pp. 33–4.
M. Hofmann. *Quarto* no 24 (December 1981), pp. 4–5.
D. Davis. *Listener* 7 January 1982, p. 22.
L. Lerner. *Encounter* vol. 58 (January 1982), pp. 58–9.
J. Ash. *The Artful Reporter* (Manchester) no 45 (February 1982), p. 13.
C. Rawson. *London Review of Books* 17–30 June 1982, p. 20.
K. White. *Cencrastus* no 8 (1982), pp. 44–5.
D. Montrose. *Honest Ulsterman* no 72 (1982), pp. 54–7.
A.A. Cleary. *Thames Poetry* 2 (11) 1982, pp. 40–1.
D. Gioia. *Hudson Review* 37 (Spring 1984), pp. 15–16.

1982

A20   *Douglas Dunn*. Glasgow: National Book League, [1982]. 1 sheet (folded). (Writers in Brief; no 18).

Contents: Includes 8 poems by DD: Western Blue – Attics – France – Birch Room – Listening – Lakes and Rivers – The Drying Green – Shaving a Beard.

A21   *Europa's Lover*. Newcastle-upon-Tyne: Bloodaxe, 1982. [18]pp.

Contents: One long poem in XIV numbered sections.

Reviews

A. Bold. *Scotsman* (Weekend) 20 November 1982.
C. Craig. *Cencrastus* no 15 (1983), pp. 54–5.
M. O'Neill. *Poetry Review* 73 (1) March 1983, pp. 57–60.
T. Dooley. TLS 19 August 1983, p. 886.
D. Gioia. *Hudson Review* vol. 37 (Spring 1984), pp. 16–18.

A22   *A Rumoured City: new poets from Hull*; edited by Douglas Dunn; with a foreword by Philip Larkin. Newcastle-upon-Tyne: Bloodaxe, 1982. 112pp.

Contents: 'Introduction' by DD (pp. 11–16).

Reviews

I. Crichton Smith. *Glasgow Herald* 9 August 1982, p. 4.
W. Scammell. TLS 7 January 1983, p. 17.
H. Lomas. *London Magazine* 22 (11) February 1983, pp. 73–9.

A23   *To Build a Bridge: a celebration in verse of Humberside and its Bridge*; edited by Douglas Dunn. Lincoln: Lincs & Humberside Arts, 1982. x, 45pp.

Contents: 'Introduction' by DD (pp. vii-ix).

1985

A24   *Elegies*. London: Faber & Faber, 1985. 64pp.

Contents: Re-reading Katherine Mansfield's *Bliss and Other Stories* – The Butterfly House – Second Opinion – Thirteen Steps and the Thirteenth of March – Arrangements – A Silver Air Force – France – The Kaleidoscope – Sandra's Mobile – Birch Room – Writing with Light – Attics – The Stranger – Tursac – Dining – Empty Wardrobes – The Sundial – At Cruggleton Castle – Château d'If – Creatures – Pretended Homes – At the Edge of a Birchwood – Larksong – The Clear Day – A Summer Night – Listening – Reincarnations – Reading Pascal in the Lowlands – Land Love – Western Blue – Transblucency – A Rediscovery of Juvenilia – Home Again – December – Snow Days – The Stories – Anniversaries – Hush – Leaving Dundee.

Notes: Poetry Book Society Spring Choice 1985. PBS *Bulletin* no 124 (Spring 1985) contains a background article by DD entitled 'Struggling with feeling' (p. 5). Whitbread Poetry Award, 1986. Then Whitbread Book of the Year Award, 1987.

Reviews
G.M. Brown. *Scotsman* (Weekend) 9 March 1985.
B. Morrison. TLS 5 April 1985, p. 377.
B. O'Donoghue. *Poetry Review* 75 (1) April 1985, pp. 49–50.
C. Rush. *Books in Scotland* no 18 (1985), pp. 15–16.
J. Mole. *Encounter* vol. 65 (July/August 1985), pp. 51–2.
J.P. Ward. *Poetry Wales* 21 (2) 1985, pp. 89–94.
P. Whitebrook. *Lines Review* no 97 (June 1986), pp. 43–6.
W. Bedford. *Agenda* 24 (2) 1986, pp. 76–8.
A. Hutchison. *Chapman* 43/44 (1986), pp. 174–7.
L. Rector. *Hudson Review* 39 (1986), pp. 501–15.
D. Constantine. *Argos* 7 (2) 1986, pp. 36–8.

A25   (a) *Secret Villages*. London: Faber & Faber, 1985. 170pp.

Contents: South America – Twin-sets and Pickle Forks – Wives in the Garden – The Canoes – Getting used to it – Mozart's Clarinet Concerto – Bobby's Room – The Bagpiping People – Photographs of Stanley's Grandfather – Kilbinnin Men – The Tennis Court – Women without Gardens – Something for Little Robert – Ever let the Fancy Roam – Fishermen – A Night out at the Club Harmonica.

Notes: 16 short stories previously published in *The New Yorker, Punch, and Encounter*.

Reviews

I. Murray. *Scotsman* (Weekend) 13 April 1985.

D. Porter. *Glasgow Herald* (Weekender) 20 April 1985.

D.A.N. Jones. *London Review of Books* 23 May 1985, p. 22.

V. McConnell. *Financial Times* (Weekend FT) 25 May 1985.

M. O'Neill. TLS 31 May 1985, p. 597.

D. Gifford. *Books in Scotland* no 18 (1985), pp. 7–8.

P. Whitebrook. *Lines Review* no 97 (June 1986), pp. 43–6.

(b) – Reissued as a paperback: Faber & Faber, 1986.

(c) – American edition. *Secret Villages: stories.* New York: Dodd, Mead, [1985]. 218pp.

1986

A26   *Selected Poems 1964–1983.* London: Faber & Faber, 1986. ix, 262pp.

Contents: The Clothes Pit – New Light on Terry Street – The Patricians – Men of Terry Street – Incident in the Shop – A Removal from Terry Street – On Roofs of Terry Street – From the Night-Window – Sunday Morning Among the Houses of Terry Street – After Closing Time – Winter – Young Women in Rollers – The Silences – A Window Affair – Envoi (1981) – The Worst of All Loves – Tribute of a Legs Lover – Close of Play – Horses in a Suburban Field – Love Poem – A Dream of Judgement – Landscape with One Figure – South Bank of the Humber – The Queen of the Belgians – Ships – A Poem in Praise of the British – Cosmologist – The River Through the City – The Friendship of Young Poets – Nights of Sirius – The Musical Orchard – Backwaters – Supreme Death – Billie 'n' Me – Midweek Matinée – The Hunched – Emblems – The Sportsmen – After the War – Modern Love – Guerrillas – Under the Stone – The New Girls – Saturday Night Function – The House Next Door – Winter Graveyard – Winter Orchard – In the Small Hotel – The Global Fidget – Realisms – Renfrewshire Traveller – Unlucky Mariners – White Fields – The Competition – Boys With Coats – Sailing with the Fleet – Clydesiders – Caledonian Moonlight – Going to Bed – I am a Cameraman – The Concert – The White Poet – Restraint – The Disguise – The Come-on – In the Grounds – Here be Dragons – Gardeners – The Student – Empires – The Wealth – Elegy for the Lost Parish – Watches of Grandfathers – Portrait Photograph, 1915 – The Musician – Drowning – Glasgow Schoolboys, Running Backwards – Red Buses – Ballad of the Two Left Hands – Lost Gloves – Stories – Stranger's Grief – Night-Devon, Dawn-Devon – On Her Picture Left with Him – Old Things – Wedding – The Return – St Kilda's Parliament: 1879–1979 – The Apple Tree – An Address on the Destitution of Scotland – Dominies – Witch-girl – Washing the Coins – Galloway Motor Farm – Monumental Sculptor – The Harp of Renfrewshire – War Blinded – Savings – Rose – Saturday – Courting – E.A. Walton thinks of painting 'The Daydream' – The Local – Second-hand Clothes – Remembering Lunch – Green Breeks

– Tannahill – John Wilson in Greenock, 1786 – La Route – The Gallery –
The Deserter – Lamp-posts – Loch Music – Ode to a Paperclip –
Ratatouille – Second Opinion – Thirteen Steps and the Thirteenth of
March – Arrangements – France – The Kaleidoscope – Sandra's Mobile –
Birch Room – Tursac – Empty Wardrobes – Creatures – At the Edge of a
Birchwood – The Clear Day – A Summer Night – Reincarnations –
Reading Pascal in the Lowlands – Land Love – Home Again – The Stories
– Anniversaries – Hush – Leaving Dundee.

Reviews
I. Bell. *Scotsman* (Weekend) 15 November 1986.
L. Duncan. *Glasgow Herald* (Weekender) 22 November 1986.
G. Szirtes. *Poetry Review* 76 (4) 1986, pp. 50–1.
S. Cramer. *Boston Review* (February 1987).
J. O'Neill. *Literary Review* (April 1987), p. 55.
D. Grant. *London Review of Books* 7 May 1987, p. 22.
A. Fowler. *Cencrastus* no 26 (1987), pp. 44–5.
A. Wales/J. Fenton/L.A. Murray. *Verse* 4 (2) 1987, pp. 61–3.
D. Smith. *Kenyon Review* ns 10 (1988), pp. 139–42.
M. Wood. *Parnassus: Poetry Review* 14 (1988), pp. 324–9.
S. Mulrine. *Chapman* 55/56 (1989), pp. 176–8.

1987

A27 *Under the Influence: Douglas Dunn on Philip Larkin*. Edinburgh: Edinburgh
University Library, 1987. 13pp.

Contents: Includes the poem 'December's Door' by DD (pp. 12–13).

Notes: 'This essay and poem were first presented at the annual winter
meeting of the Friends of Edinburgh University Library on 2nd
December, 1986, the first anniversary of Philip Larkin's death' . . .
Preface.

1988

A28 *December's Door* (in memoriam Philip Larkin). Cottingham: Polygon
Design, 1988. 1 poster. (Bête Noire Poster Poems; no 1).

Notes: Limited edition of 100 signed copies.

A29 *'Importantly Live': Lyricism in Contemporary Poetry*: an inaugural lecture
delivered by Douglas Dunn (Honorary Professor, Faculty of Arts and
Social Sciences, Dundee University) on 28 October 1987. [Dundee:
Dundee University, 1988]. 16pp. (Dundee University occasional papers;
1 [1988]).

A30 *National Poetry Competition '87: Prizewinners*. Chosen by Douglas Dunn,
Edna Longley and Fred d'Aguiar. London: Poetry Society, 1988. [32] pp.

Contents: Includes a brief introduction by and about DD (p. 3).

A31   *Northlight*. London: Faber & Faber, 1988. xi, 81pp.

Contents: At Falkland Palace – Love-making by Candlelight – S Frediano's – The People Before – February – Daylight – Going to Aberlemno – Abernethy – 75° – Tay Bridge – Apples – Broughty Ferry – Here and There – December's Door – Winkie – Muir's Ledgers – A House in the Country – A Snow-walk – Jig of the Week No 21 – Dieback – In the 1950s – The War in the Congo – 4/4 – Maggie's Corner – Running the East Wind – In-flight Entertainment – The Departures of Friends in Childhood – The Dark Crossroads – Memory and Imagination – An Address to Adolphe Sax in Heaven – The Country Kitchen – Tremors – The Patrol – Adventure's Oafs.

Notes: Poetry Book Society Autumn 1988 Choice. Note by DD on the background in PBS *Bulletin* no 138 (Autumn 1988), pp. 3–4.

Reviews
A. Motion. *Observer* 18 September 1988, p. 42.
I.C. Smith. *Scotland on Sunday* 18 September 1988.
E. Jennings. *Independent* 1 October 1988.
D. Profumo. *Sunday Times* 2 October 1988, p. G13.
A. Massie. *Punch* 7 October 1988, p. 63.
B. O'Donoghue. TLS 21 October 1988, p. 1181.
P. Forbes. *Listener* 1 December 1988, p. 40.
D. Kinloch. *Verse* 5 (3) 1988, pp. 69–71.
S. O'Brien. *Poetry Review* 78(4) 1988/89, pp. 45–6.
R. Crawford. *London Review of Books* 20 April 1989, pp. 22–3.
A. Riach. *Chapman* no 57 (1989), pp. 83–5.
J. Hendry. *Cencrastus* no 34 (1989), pp. 34–5.
T. Adair. *Lines Review* no 108 (1989), pp. 50–2.
C. Craig. *Scottish Literary Journal* Supplement no 32 (1990), pp. 60–4.

A32   *The Pictish Coast*. Poems by Douglas Dunn. Etchings by Norman Ackroyd. London: The Penny Press, 1988.

Notes: Limited edition of 45 numbered copies. Loose-leaf in a solander box.

The poems are selected from *Northlight* (Faber, 1988).

1989

A33   *New and Selected Poems, 1966–1988*. New York: Ecco Press, 1989. 223pp. (Ecco's Modern European Poetry series).

Contents: The Clothes Pit – New Light on Terry Street – The Patricians – Men of Terry Street – Incident in the Shop – A Removal from Terry Street – On Roofs of Terry Street – From the Night-Window – Sunday Morning Among the Houses of Terry Street – After Closing Time – Winter –

Young Women in Rollers — The Silences — A Window Affair — Envoi (1981) — The River Through the City — The Friendship of Young Poets — Nights of Sirius — The Musical Orchard — Backwaters — Supreme Death — The Hunched — Emblems — Modern Love — Winter Graveyard — Winter Orchard — In the Small Hotel — Unlucky Mariners — White Fields — Clydesiders — Caledonian Moonlight — I am a Cameraman — Restraint — The Disguise — The Come-on — In the Grounds — Here be Dragons — Gardeners — The Student — Empires — The Wealth — Elegy for the Lost Parish — Watches of Grandfathers — Portrait Photograph, 1915 — Drowning — Ballad of the Two Left Hands — Lost Gloves — Stranger's Grief — On Her Picture Left with Him — St Kilda's Parliament: 1879–1979 — The Apple Tree — An Address on the Destitution of Scotland — Witch-girl — Washing the Coins — Galloway Motor Farm — The Harp of Renfrewshire — Rose — Saturday — Courting — Second-hand Clothes — Remembering Lunch — Tannahill — Green Breeks — Ode to a Paperclip — The Deserter — Ratatouille — Loch Music — Second Opinion — Thirteen Steps and the Thirteenth of March — Arrangements — France — The Kaleidoscope — Birch Room — Writing with Light — Tursac — Empty Wardrobes — At the Edge of a Birchwood — At Cruggleton Castle — The Clear Day — A Summer Night — Reading Pascal in the Lowlands — Land Love — Home Again — The Stories — Anniversaries — Hush — Leaving Dundee — At Falkland Palace — Love-making by Candlelight — S Frediano's — The People Before — February — Daylight — 75° — Here and There — December's Door — Winkie — A House in the Country — Jig of the Week No 21 — 4/4 — In-flight Entertainment — An Address to Adolphe Sax in Heaven — The Country Kitchen.

1990

A34   *Andromache* [by] Jean Racine; translated by Douglas Dunn. London: Faber & Faber, 1990. 81pp.

Notes: This translation of Racine's *Andromaque* in rhyming couplets was commissioned by BBC Radio Scotland for a BBC Radio 3 production directed by Stewart Conn and first broadcast on 24 November 1989.

Reviews
J. Weightman. *Independent on Sunday* 18 March 1990, p. 20.
P. Reading. *Sunday Times* 25 March 1990, p. H14.
M. Ford. *London Review of Books* 14 June 1990, pp. 16–17.
J. McMillan. *Glasgow Herald* (Weekender) 11 August 1990.
P. Robinson. *English* vol. 39 (Autumn 1990), pp. 275–81.
D. McDuff. *Stand* 33 (1) Winter 1991, pp. 20–2.

A35   *The Essential Browning*; selected and with an introduction by Douglas Dunn. New York: Ecco Press, 1990. 181pp. (The Essential Poets; 13).

Contents: Includes an 'Introduction' by DD (pp. 1–12).

A36   *Poll Tax: the Fiscal Fake*. London: Chatto & Windus, 1990. 56pp. (Chatto Counterblasts; no 12).

Reviews
Times Educational Supplement 23 March 1990, p. B6.
E. Robertson. *Glasgow Herald* (Weekender) 31 March 1990.

A37   *The Topical Muse: on Contemporary Poetry*: the Kenneth Allott Lectures no 6, delivered on 22 March 1990. Liverpool: Liverpool Classical Monthly, 1990. ii, 20pp.

1991

A38   *Elegien*: in Nachdichtungen von Evelyn Schlag. Frankfurt-am-Main: Fischer, 1991. 127pp.

Notes: Parallel English text and German verse translation, together with an Afterword and Notes in German.

A39   Piotr Sommer. *Things to Translate & Other Poems*. Translated by Douglas Dunn [et al]. Newcastle upon Tyne: Bloodaxe, 1991. 63pp.

Notes: DD translated 6 of the poems [from the original Polish].

A40   *Scotland: an Anthology*; edited by Douglas Dunn. London: HarperCollins, 1991. 304pp.

Contents: Introduction (pp. 1–9) – A Strong Scotch Accent of the Mind – Haunted by Time – Nothing but Heather – Cities and Towns – Highlands and Islands – Liberty Alone – Religion – The Rowan Tree – Languages and Literature – Hospitality (and Other Potations) – Diaspora-Scots Abroad.

Reviews   .
L. Duncan. *Glasgow Herald* (Weekender) 10 August 1991.
K. Mathieson. *Scotsman* (Weekend) 10 August 1991.
A. Smith. *Scotland on Sunday* 11 August 1991.
M. Lindsay. *TLS* 16 August 1991, p. 21.
A. Bold. *Sunday Times* (Books) 25 August 1991, p. 4.

SECTION B. INDIVIDUAL POEMS BY DOUGLAS DUNN

1963

B1   'Apostate on the Rock.' *Outposts* 59 (1963), pp. 8–9.

1965

B2   'Flowers of Snow and Ice.' *Glasgow Review* 2 (2) 1965, p. 22.

1967

B3   'Anglo Saxon.' *The Listener* 27 April 1967, p. 550.

B4   'Fixed.' *London Magazine* 7 (5) August 1967, p. 60.

Later published in TLS 21 April 1972, q.v.

Collected in *HL* (1972).

B5   'Horses.' *Lines Review* no 24 (Summer 1967), p. 28.

B6   'Landlocked.' *Scottish Poetry* 2 (1967), p. 42.

B7   'Narcissus.' *The Listener* 13 July 1967, p. 44.

Collected in *TS* (1969).

B8   'Requiem for a Lost Head.' *The Listener* 27 April 1967, p. 550.

B9   'Throwing Stones into the Sea.' *Scottish Poetry* 2 (1967), p. 43.

1968

B10   'After Rain.' *Scottish Poetry* 3 (1968), p. 40.

B11   'Belle and Beau.' *New Statesman* 31 May 1968, p. 733.

Collected in *TS* (1969).

B12   'A Dream of Judgment.' *The Listener* 12 September 1968, p. 341.

Collected in *TS* (1969).

B13   'Happiness Ever After.' *Poetry Review* 59 (2) Summer 1968, p. 99.

B14   'Landscape with One Figure.' *Stand* 9 (3) 1968, p. 53.

Collected in *TS* (1969).

B15   'Love Poem.' TLS 19 December 1968, p. 1431.

Collected in *TS* (1969).

B16   'Passing Through.' *Universities' Poetry Eight* ed. H. Sergeant (1968), p. 44.

Collected in *TS* (1969).

B17   'The Playboy in the Wood.' *Scottish Poetry* 3 (1968), p. 41.

B18   'A Removal from Terry Street.' *New Statesman* 8 November 1968, p. 635.

Collected in *TS* (1969).

B19   'Stepping Out of Line.' *Poetry Review* 59 Summer 1968, p. 99.

B20   'Terry Street' [7 poems]. *London Magazine* 8 (5) August 1968, pp. 62–66.

Men of Terry Street – Incident in the Shop – Young Women in Rollers – The Terry Street Fusiliers – From the Night-Window – The Patricians – New Light on Terry Street.

All collected in *TS* (1969).

1969

B21   'After Closing Time.' *The Review* no 20 (1969), p. 37.

Collected in *TS* (1969).

B22   'Backwaters.' *New Statesman* 3 October 1969, p. 466.

Collected in *Backwaters* (1971); *HL* (1972); *SP* (1986) and *NSP* (1989).

B23   'Bring Out Your Dead.' TLS 21 August 1969, p. 926.

Collected in *TS* (1969).

B24   'The Crusader.' *London Magazine* 9 (July/August) 1969, p. 53.

B25   'The Friendship of Young Poets.' *New Statesman* 31 October 1969, p. 616.

Collected in *Backwaters* (1971); *HL* (1972); *SP* (1986) and *NSP* (1989).

B26   'Horses in a Suburban Field.' *Scottish Poetry* no 4 (1969), p. 36.

Collected in *TS* (1969).

B27   'The Love Day.' *Form* no 1 (1969), p. 18.

Collected in *TS* (1969).

B28   'The Old Boys.' *Scottish Poetry* 4 (1969), p. 37.

B29   'Poem in Praise of the British.' *New Statesman* 25 July 1969, p. 119.

Collected in *TS* (1969).

B30   'The Season for Hats.' *Form* no 1 (1969), p. 18.

Collected in *TS* (1969).

B31   'Ships.' *The Review* no 20 (1969), p. 37.

       Collected in *TS* (1969).

B32   'The Silences.' *New Statesman* 11 April 1969, p. 522.

       Collected in *TS* (1969).

B33   'Tribute of a Legs Lover.' *London Magazine* 9 (July/August) 1969, p. 54.

       Collected in *TS* (1969).

B34   'Winter.' *The Review* no 20 (1969), p. 37.

       Collected in *TS* (1969).

B35   'The Worst of all Loves.' *New Statesman* 20 June 1969, p. 878.

       Collected in *TS* (1969).

                                    1970

B36   'After the War.' *New Statesman* 4 September 1970, p. 280.

       Collected in *Backwaters* (1971); *HL* (1972) and *SP* (1986).

B37   'Alternative.' *The Review* no 23 (1970), p. 17.

       Collected in *Backwaters* (1971) and *HL* (1972).

B38   'Billie 'n' Me.' *New Statesman* 13 March 1970, p. 380.

       Collected in *Backwaters* (1971); *HL* (1972) and *SP* (1986).

B39   'Five Years Married.' *London Magazine* 9 (12) March 1970, p. 83.

       Collected in *Backwaters* (1971) and *HL* (1972).

B40   'The Hunched.' *New Statesman* 30 January 1970, p. 158.

       Collected in *Backwaters* (1971); *HL* (1972); *SP* (1986) and *NSP* (1989).

B41   'In the City of H.' *New Statesman* 23 January 1970, p. 124.

B42   'Modern Love.' *The Review* no 23 (1970), p. 16.

       Collected in *Backwaters* (1971); *HL* (1972); *SP* (1986) and *NSP* (1989).

B43   'The New Girls.' *Phoenix* nos 6/7 (1970), p. 7.

       Collected in *HL* (1972) and *SP* (1986).

B44 'The Philologists.' *The Review* no 23 (1970), p. 17.

Collected in *Backwaters* (1971) and *HL* (1972).

B45 'A Poem in Praise of the British.' *Michigan Quarterly Review* 9 (3) 1970, p. 168.

Previously published in *New Statesman* 25 July 1969, q.v.

B46 'Saturday Night Function.' *Stand* 11 (4) 1970, p. 30.

Collected in *HL* (1972) and *SP* (1986).

B47 'The Sportsmen.' *New Statesman* 27 February 1970, p. 299.

Collected in *Backwaters* (1971) and *HL* (1972).

B48 'The Suit.' *London Magazine* 9 (10) January 1970, p. 38.

B49 'Up in Duggie's Room.' *Phoenix* nos 6/7 (1970), p. 6.

Collected in *Backwaters* (1971) and *HL* (1972).

1971

B50 'The Boon Companions.' *New Statesman* 25 June 1971, p. 882.

Collected in *HL* (1972).

B51 'Emblems.' *New Statesman* 5 March 1971, p. 311.

Collected in *HL* (1972); *SP* (1986) and *NSP* (1989).

B52 'Guerrillas.' *New Statesman* 19 February 1971, p. 248.

Collected in *HL* (1972) and *SP* (1986).

B53 'The Happier Life.' TLS 23 July 1971, p. 854.

Collected in *HL* (1972).

B54 'The Hull Sit-in.' *New Statesman* 2 April 1971, p. 469.

Collected in *HL* (1972).

B55 'Morning Bedroom.' *London Magazine* 11 (3) August/September 1971, pp. 50–3.

Collected in *HL* (1972).

B56   'River through the City.' *New Statesman* 6 August 1971, p. 181.

    Collected in *HL* (1972), *SP* (1986) and *NSP* (1989).

B57   'The Shirt.' TLS 29 January 1971, p. 119.

    Collected in *Backwaters* (1971) and *HL* (1972).

B58   'Supreme Death.' *New Statesman* 16 July 1971, p. 88.

    Collected in *HL* (1972), *SP* (1986) and *NSP* (1989).

1972

B59   'Boys with Coats.' *The Listener* 2 November 1972, p. 600.

    Collected in *LN* (1974) and *SP* (1986).

B60   'Caledonian Moonlight.' *The Review* nos 29/30 (1972), pp. 84–5.

    Collected in *LN* (1974), *SP* (1986) and *NSP* (1989).

B61   'Chasing the Sun.' *New Humanist* 88 (4) August 1972, p. 157.

B62   'The Competition.' *The Listener* 2 November 1972, p. 600.

    Collected in *LN* (1974) and *SP* (1986).

B63   'A Faber Melancholy.' *Antaeus* 6 (1972), pp. 72–4.

    Collected in *HL* (1972).

B64   'Fixed.' TLS 21 April 1972, p. 440.

    Previously published in *London Magazine* 7 (5) August 1967, q.v.

B65   'The Garden.' *Encounter* vol. 38 (February 1972), p. 41.

    Collected in *HL* (1972).

B66   'The Hour.' *New Statesman* 5 May 1972, p. 606.

    Collected in *HL* (1972).

B67   'Nights of Sirius.' *New Yorker* 5 February 1972, p. 82.

    Collected in *HL* (1972), *SP* (1986) and *NSP* (1989).

B68   'Privacies.' *New Statesman* 4 February 1972, p. 149.

    Collected in *LN* (1974).

B69   'Renfrewshire Traveller.' *New Statesman* 7 January 1972, p. 23.

       Collected in *LN* (1974) and *SP* (1986).

B70   'Still Rivers, Misty Plains.' *New Humanist* 88 (4) August 1972, pp.
       157–8.

B71   'Thinking, from Birds to God.' *The Review* nos 29/30 (1972), p. 84.

       Collected in *LN* (1974).

B72   'White Fields.' *The Listener* 2 November 1972, p. 601.

       Collected in *LN* (1974), *SP* (1986) and *NSP* (1989).

B73   'Winter Orchard.' TLS 6 October 1972, p. 1190.

       Collected in *LN* (1974), *SP* (1986) and *NSP* (1989).

                                 1973
B74   'Data Hooks.' TLS 4 May 1973, p. 491.

B75   'The Disguise.' *July and August in Yorkshire* (Yorkshire Arts Association)
       vol. 3 no 11 (July 1973), p. 7.

       Collected in *LN* (1974), *SP* (1986) and *NSP* (1989).

B76   'The Emigrant.' *Wave* no 6 (1973), pp. 5–7.

B77   'The Estuarial Republic.' TLS 7 December 1973, p. 1490.

       Collected in *LN* (1974).

B78   'The Host.' *Meridian* 1 (1) Autumn 1973, p. 14.

B79   'I am a Cameraman.' *New Yorker* 2 June 1973, p. 36.

       Collected in *LN* (1974), *SP* (1986) and *NSP* (1989).

B80   'In the Marriage Bed.' *New Yorker* 16 June 1973, p. 34.

B81   'In the Small Hotel.' TLS 12 January 1973, p. 36.

       Collected in *LN* (1974), *SP* (1986) and *NSP* (1989).

B82   'A Lost Woman.' *Poetry Nation* no 1 (1973), pp. 24–5.

       Collected in *LN* (1974).

B83   'The Malediction.' *New Statesman* 27 April 1973, p. 624.

       Collected in *LN* (1974).

B84   'Ocean.' *July and August in Yorkshire* (Yorkshire Arts Association) vol. 3
       no 11 (July 1973), p. 7.

       Collected in *LN* (1974).

B85   'Przeprowadzka z Terry Street.' *Poezja* 89 (4) 1973, p. 38.

      'A Removal from Terry Street' translated into Polish verse by T. Rybowski.

B86   'Reaching the Dead.' *Meridian* 1 (1) Autumn 1973, p. 15.

B87   'Realisms.' *Phoenix* no 10 (July 1973), pp. 10–11.

      Collected in *LN* (1974) and *SP* (1986).

B88   'Sneak's Noise.' *Poems for Shakespeare 2*, ed. G. Fawcett (Globe Playhouse Trust, 1973), pp. 69–70.

B89   'Variations on the Words "Solo" and "Exhaust".' *Prospice* no 1 (1973), p. 36.

      Collected in *LN* (1974).

B90   'A Weave of Social Fabric.' *The Listener* 31 May 1973, p. 718.

B91   'Wheat Field.' *Encounter* vol. 40 (February 1973), p. 16.

B92   'The White Poet: Homage to Jules Laforgue.' *Encounter* vol. 40 (April 1973), pp. 43–5.

      Collected in *LN* (1974) and *SP* (1986).

1974

B93   'The Admiral.' *Lines Review* no 51 (December 1974), p. 21.

B94   'Against the National Character.' *Lines Review* no 51 (December 1974), pp. 25–6.

B95   'The Arbitration.' *The New Review* vol. 1 no 1 (April 1974), pp. 54–5.

B96   'Big Ears.' *London Magazine* 14(3) August/September 1974, p. 65.

B97   'Bucolics.' *Poetry Nation* no 2 (1974), p. 24.

B98   'Burning Marigolds.' *Lines Review* no 51 (December 1974), p. 22.

B99   'Captain Jamie to Captain MacMorris.' *Poems for Shakespeare 3* ed. A. Thwaite (Globe Playhouse Trust, 1974), pp. 21–2.

      Also includes 'Notes' to the poem, pp. 58–9.

B100   'Christmas Refectory.' *Wave* no 8 (1974), pp. 22–4.

B101   'The Come-On.' *The Honest Ulsterman* nos 44/45 (1974), p. 3.

      Collected in *B* (1979), *SP* (1986) and *NSP* (1989).

B102 'The Difficulty.' *Encounter* vol. 43 (October 1974), p. 28.

Collected in *B* (1979).

B103 'The Dilemma.' *Vogue* 15 September 1974, p. 93.

Includes a brief note on DD by Derek Mahon (pp. 92–3).

Collected in *LN* (1974).

B104 'The Distraction.' *Poetry Nation* no 2 (1974), pp. 23–4.

B105 'The Financial Question.' *Lines Review* no 51 (December 1974), pp. 24–5.

B106 'The Generations.' *Lines Review* no 51 (December 1974), p. 24.

B107 'The Grass.' *Lines Review* no 51 (December 1974), p. 23.

B108 'Imaginary Landscapes.' *The New Review* vol. 1 no 1 (April 1974), p. 58.

B109 'Inside Democracy.' TLS 20 December 1974, p. 1441.

B110 'The Jazz Orchestra.' *Stand* 16 (1) 1974, pp. 8–10.

B111 'Justifying the Deed.' *Wave* 8 (Spring 1974), p. 28.

B112 'The Love Orchard.' *Poetry Nation* no 2 (1974), p. 23.

B113 'A Love Poet.' *Meridian* no 5 (Autumn 1974), pp. 4–7.

B114 'Mondo Senze Gente.' *The Little Word Machine* nos 4/5 (1974), p. 31.

B115 'Music and the Revolution.' *New Statesman* 27 September 1974, p. 432.

B116 'New Roads, New Town, New Bridge.' *The New Review* vol 1 no 1 (April 1974), pp. 56–7.

B117 'The North.' *Wave* 8 (Spring 1974), p. 26.

B118 'Ode to my Desk.' *New Yorker* 20 May 1974, p. 40.

B119 'Our Lady of Coincidence.' *Hullfire* (Hull University) 11 November 1974, p. [20].

Also published in *The New Review* 2 (13) April 1975, q.v.

B120 'Philanthropy's Fruit Shop.' *Caret* nos 5/6 (1974), pp. 48–9. [A prose poem].

B121 'Provincial Russian Poem.' *Lines Review* no 51 (December 1974), p. 21.

B122 'Przeprowadzka z Terry Street.' *Wsrod Angielskich Poetow* ed. T. Rybowski (Wroclaw, 1974), p. 17.

A Polish verse translation of 'A Removal from Terry Street'.

B123 'Ragtime Midnight.' *Encounter* vol. 42 (May 1974), p. 40.

B124 'The Return.' *Poetry Supplement* compiled by Philip Larkin for the Poetry Book Society, Christmas '74 (1974), pp. [6]-[7].

Collected in *B* (1979) and *SP* (1986).

B125 'Rose War.' *Lines Review* no 51 (December 1974), pp. 22-3.

B126 'Scriptoria Furniture.' TLS 19 July 1974, p. 762.

An earlier version of Poem III of *Europa's Lover* (1982).

B127 'Socialist Nature.' *The New Review* vol. 1 no 6 (September 1974), p. 61.

B128 'Straight, No Chaser.' *The New Review* vol. 1 no 5 (August 1974), p. 10.

B129 'Stud and the Demi-monde.' *Wave* 8 (Spring 1974), p. 27.

B130 'Sunday.' *Wave* 8 (Spring 1974), p. 25.

Collected in *LN* (1974).

B131 'The Tear.' *The New Review* vol. 1 no 1 (April 1974), p. 53.

B132 'Terrible Statistics.' *Encounter* vol. 42 (January 1974), p. 60.

B133 'A Theologian and a Poet.' *Meridian* no 5 (Autumn 1974), pp. 4-7.

B134 'The Threepenny Swindle: a Story of 1952.' *Caret* nos 5/6 (1974), pp. 26-7.

B135 'To Live Humane Ideals.' *The Little Word Machine* nos 4/5 (1974), p. 30.

B136 'A Walk with an Overcoat.' *London Magazine* 14 (3) August/September 1974, p. 65.

B137 'Wedding.' *Lines Review* no 51 (December 1974), p. 27.

Collected in *B* (1979) and *SP* (1986).

B138 'What's Happening?' *Green Ginger: Hull University Literary Magazine* [no 1 (1974)], pp. 30-1.

B139 'Wives Gardening.' TLS 27 September 1974, p. 1040.

B140 'Zgarbieni Ludzie.' *Wsrod Angielskich Poetow* ed. T. Rybowski (Wroclaw, 1974), p. 16.

A Polish translation of 'Close of Play' (*TS*).

1975

B141 'An Artist Waiting in a Country House.' *Encounter* vol. 44 (April 1975), pp. 12–13.

Collected in *B* (1979).

B142 'Empire.' *Hullfire* (Hull University) no 4 (February 1975), p. [26].

B143 'Fertilities.' *Outposts* no 104 (1975), pp. 10–12.

B144 'Flies on a Lampshade.' *Flies on a Lampshade: an anthology* . . . (Lumb Bank: Arvon Poems, 1975), p. 16.

Written jointly with Saul Hyman.

B145 'The Generations.' *Scottish Poetry* 8 (1975), p. 25.

B146 'Going Home.' *Honest Ulsterman* 50 (Winter 1975), pp. 114–15.

B147 'The Grass.' *Scottish Poetry* 8 (1975), p. 26.

B148 'Morning Song.' *The New Review* vol. 2 no 15 (June 1975), p. 8.

B149 'Night Song.' *The New Review* vol. 2 no 21 (December 1975), p. 51.

B150 'Our Lady of Coincidence.' *The New Review* vol. 2 no 13 (April 1975), p. 34.

Previously published in *Hullfire* 11 November 1974, q.v.

B151 'The Public Sigh.' *Yorkshire Review* no 1 (1975), p. 38.

B152 'Receiving a Letter.' *The New Review* vol. 2 no 15 (June 1975), p. 8.

B153 'A Salutation.' TLS 3 January 1975, p. 10.

B154 'She Climbs a Hill in Awkward Boots.' *The New Review* vol. 2 no 21 (December 1975), pp. 50–1.

B155 'Stories.' *Encounter* vol. 44 (February 1975), p. 64.

Collected in *B* (1979) and *SP* (1986).

B156 'Waiting for Rain.' *New Statesman* 17 October 1975, p. 482.

B157 'The Watches of Grandfathers.' *The New Review* vol. 2 no 21 (December 1975), pp. 50–1.

Collected in *B* (1979), *SP* (1986) and *NSP* (1989).

1976

B158 'Alice.' *The New Review* vol. 3 no 32 (November 1976), p. 42.

Collected in *B* (1979).

B159 'Empires.' *Diary* (Lincolnshire and Humberside Arts) July-August 1976, p. 8.

Also published in *Niagara Magazine* no 8 (1978), q.v.

Collected in *B* (1979), *SP* (1986) and *NSP* (1989).

B160 'The Host.' *Poetry in the Seventies* ed. Trevor Kneale (Liverpool: Rondo, 1976), p. 22.

B161 'Illiteracy.' *Cracked Lookingglass* 5 (1976), p. 1.

B162 'Little Rich Rhapsody.' *Poetry in the Seventies* ed. Trevor Kneale (Liverpool: Rondo, 1976), p. 22.

Previously published in *LN* (1974).

B163 'The Mower.' *Meridian* no 10 (Autumn 1976), p. 11.

B164 'On her Picture left with Him.' *Thames Poetry* vol. 1 no 2 (1976), p. 27.

Collected in *B* (1979), *SP* (1986) and *NSP* (1989).

B165 'Power Struggles.' *Cracked Lookingglass* 5 (1976), p. 3.

B166 'Warriors.' *Encounter* vol. 46 (March 1976), p. 53.

Collected in *B* (1979).

1977

B167 'Glasgow Schoolboys, Running Backwards.' *London Magazine* 17(4) October 1977, p. 5.

Collected in *B* (1979) and *SP* (1986).

B168 'Her Walk.' *London Magazine* 17 (4) October 1977, p. 5.

B169 'Islands.' (Colpitts Poetry Cards, no 4 (1977)). In *A Colpitts Dozen* ed. David Burnett (Durham: North Gate Press, 1977–9).

B170 'Night-Devon, Dawn-Devon.' *London Magazine* 17 (5) November 1977, p. 48.

Collected in *B* (1979) and *SP* (1986).

B171 'Portrait Photograph, 1915.' *London Magazine* 17 (4) October 1977, p. 5.

Collected in *B* (1979), *SP* (1986) and *NSP* (1989).

B172 'Red Buses: "The Last Western".' *Gallimaufry* no 4 (1977), p. [16].

Collected in *B* (1979) and *SP* (1986).

1978

B173 'Candleriggs Nightmare.' *Proteus* no 4 (1978), p. 32.

B174 'Le Chemin: a poem-film, starring Jean-Paul Belmondo.' *Stone Ferry Review* no 1 (1978), pp. 15–19.

B175 'Drowning.' *Vole* 2 (1) 1978, p. 30.

Collected in *B* (1979), *SP* (1986) and *NSP* (1989).

B176 'Dry Showers.' *Stone Ferry Review* no 1 (1978), p. 13.

B177 'Elegy for the Lost Parish.' *Encounter* vol. 51 (October 1978), p. 111.

Collected in *B* (1979), *SP* (1986) and *NSP* (1989).

B178 'Empires.' *Niagara Magazine* no 8 (1978), p. 14.

Previously published in *Diary* (Lincs and Humberside Arts) July/August 1976, q.v.

B179 'Islands.' *Stone Ferry Review* no 1 (1978), p. 14.

B180 'John Wilson in Greenock, 1786.' *Akros* no 39 (December 1978), p. 109.

Collected in *SKP* (1981) and *SP* (1986).

B181 'A Late Degree.' *London Magazine* 17 (8) February 1978, pp. 28–9.

Collected in *B* (1979).

B182   'The Musician.' *Fortnight* (Belfast) no 170 (September 1978), p. 12.

      Collected in *B* (1979) and *SP* (1986).

B183   'New Nature Poetry.' *Honest Ulsterman* 58 (January/February 1978), p. 3.

B184   'No Further.' *PEN Broadsheet* no 6 (Winter 1978/9), p. 8.

B185   'Old Things.' *The New Review* vol. 4 nos 45/46 (December 1977/January 1978), p. 8.

      Collected in *B* (1979) and *SP* (1986).

B186   'The Poetry of Perception.' *Honest Ulsterman* 58 (January/February 1978), p. 4.

B187   'Potato Raid.' *Proteus* no 3 (1978), p. 41.

      Later published in *Third Eye Centre Programme* 26 April–9 June 1979, q.v.

B188   'Savings.' *Poetry Supplement* compiled by Patricia Beer for the Poetry Book Society, Christmas '78 (1978), p. 21.

      Collected in *SKP* (1981) and *SP* (1986).

B189   'Seen in the Street.' *Honest Ulsterman* 58 (January/February 1978), p. 3.

B190   'Spinster's Wake.' *Poetry Supplement* compiled by Patricia Beer for the Poetry Book Society, Christmas '78 (1978), p. 30.

      Collected in *SKP* (1981).

B191   'Stranger's Grief.' *London Magazine* 18 (1) April 1978, pp. 33–4.

      Later published in *Maxy's Journal* (Tennessee) no 2 (1979), q.v.

      Collected in *B* (1979), *SP* (1986) and NSP (1989).

B192   'The Student (Renfrewshire, 1820).' *New Edinburgh Review* no 44 (November 1978), p. 13.

      Collected in *B* (1979), *SP* (1986) and NSP (1989).

B193   'Subterranean Piss Parlour, Glasgow.' *New Edinburgh Review* no 44 (November 1978), p. 5.

B194   'Tannahill.' *Akros* no 39 (December 1978), pp. 101–9.

Collected in *SKP* (1981), *SP* (1986) and *NSP* (1989).

B195 'The Truth.' *Fortnight* (Belfast) no 170 (September 1978), p. 13.

B196 'Vita Nuova.' *PEN Broadsheet* no 6 (Winter 1978/9), p. 10.

1979
B197 'An Address to M Adolphe Sax in Heaven.' *Quarto* no 1 (October 1979), p. 12.

Collected in *N* (1988) and *NSP* (1989).

B198 'The Deserter.' *London Magazine* 18 (12) March 1979, pp. 43–5.

Collected in *SKP* (1981), *SP* (1986) and *NSP* (1989).

B199 'Dominies.' *London Magazine* 19 (8) November 1979, p. 10.

Collected in *SKP* (1981) and *SP* (1986).

B200 'E.A. Walton Thinks of Painting "The Daydream".' *Yale Literary Magazine* 148 (3) December 1979, p. 15.

Collected in *SKP* (1981) and *SP* (1986).

B201 'Fallen among Anti-Semites.' *London Magazine* 19 (8) November 1979, p. 11.

Collected in *SKP* (1981).

B202 'From the Gutter.' *New Statesman* 29 June 1979, p. 966.

B203 'Green Breeks.' *New Edinburgh Review* no 45 (February 1979), pp. 18–19.

Collected in *SKP* (1981), *SP* (1986) and *NSP* (1989).

B204 'Krajobraz z Jedna Postacia.' *Nowy Medyk* no 7 (1979), p. 9.

'Landscape with one Figure' (from *TS* (1969)) translated into Polish verse by Piotr Sommer.

B205 'The Last Salon.' *Palantir* no 12 (1979), p. 15.

B206 'The Loch Music.' *Poetry Wales* 15 (3) Winter 1979/80, pp. 41–2.

In illustration of the preceding article on 'Rhyme' (pp. 39–41).

Collected in *SKP* (1981), *SP* (1986) and *NSP* (1989).

B207 'Muses.' *Third Eye Centre Programme* 26 April–9 June 1979, p. 12.

B208 'Potato Raid.' *Third Eye Centre Programme* 26 April–9 June 1979, p. 12.

Previously published in *Proteus* no 3 (1978), q.v.

B209 'Remembering Lunch.' *Encounter* vol. 52 (January 1979), pp. 30–1.

Collected in *SKP* (1981), *SP* (1986) and *NSP* (1989).

B210 'Rose.' *New Edinburgh Review* no 47 (August 1979), p. 34.

Collected in *SKP* (1981), *SP* (1986) and *NSP* (1989).

B211 'Sky Above Beverley.' *Maxy's Journal* (Tennessee) no 3 (1979) , pp. 7–8.

B212 'Stranger's Grief.' *Maxy's Journal* (Tennessee) no 2 (1979), pp. 55–6.

Previously published in *London Magazine* 18 (1) April 1978, q.v.

B213 'Valerio.' *Poetry Review* vol. 69 no 2 (December 1979), pp. 3–6.

Collected in *SKP* (1981).

B214 'The Visitor.' *London Magazine* 19 (8) November 1979, p. 11.

B215 'The Wealth.' *Poetry Review* 68 (4) 1979, pp. 44–7.

Collected in *B* (1979), *SP* (1986) and *NSP* (1989).

B216 'Wednesday.' *London Magazine* 19 (8) November 1979, p. 10.

Collected in *SKP* (1981).

B217 'Wyniescie Swoich Zmarlych.' *Nowy Medyk* no 7 (1979), p. 9.

'Bring Out Your Dead' (from *TS* (1969)) translated into Polish verse by
Piotr Sommer.

1980

B218 'An Address to the Destitution of Scotland.' *Stand* 22 (1) 1980, p. 51.

Collected in *SKP* (1981), *SP* (1986) and *NSP* (1989).

B219 'The Apple Tree.' *Thames Poetry* 1 (8) March 1980, pp. 17–19.

Collected in *SKP* (1981), *SP* (1986) and *NSP* (1989).

B220 'Between Bus-stop and Home.' *The International Portland Review* 1980,
p. 297.

A translation of a Polish poem by Piotr Sommer.

B221   'The Gallery.' *London Review of Books* 17 April 1980, p. 4.

Collected in *SKP* (1981) and *SP* (1986).

B222   'Galloway Motor Farm.' *Helix* nos 5/6 (February/August 1980), pp. 46–7.

Collected in *SKP* (1981), *SP* (1986) and *NSP* (1989).

B223   'The Harp of Renfrewshire.' TLS 25 July 1980, p. 840.

Collected in *SKP* (1981), *SP* (1986) and *NSP* (1989).

B224   'Lamp-Posts.' TLS 11 April 1980, p. 403.

Collected in *SKP* (1981) and *SP* (1986).

B225   'The Miniature Métro.' *Megaphone* no 1 (1980), pp. 13–14.

Collected in *SKP* (1981).

B226   'Monumental Sculptor.' *Quarto* no 6 (May 1980), p. 9.

Collected in *SKP* (1981) and *SP* (1986).

B227   'Ratatouille.' *Glasgow Herald* 22 December 1980, p. 4.

Collected in *SKP* (1981), *SP* (1986) and *NSP* (1989).

B228   'Second-hand Clothes.' *New Edinburgh Review* no 50 (May 1980), p. 19.

Collected in *SKP* (1981), *SP* (1986) and *NSP* (1989).

B229   'St Kilda's Parliament: 1879–1979.' *New Yorker* 31 March 1980, p. 42.

Collected in *SKP* (1981), *SP* (1986) and *NSP* (1989).

B230   'Two Gestures.' *The International Portland Review* 1980, p. 295.

A translation of a Polish poem by Piotr Sommer.

B231   'War Blinded.' *New Statesman* 19 September 1980, p. 18.

Collected in *SKP* (1981) and *SP* (1986).

B232   'Washing the Coins.' *New Yorker* 12 May 1980, p. 75.

Collected in *SKP* (1981), *SP* (1986) and *NSP* (1989).

B233   'Witch-Girl.' *Seer* (Duncan of Jordanstone College of Art) no 3 (June 1980), p. 7.

Collected in *SKP* (1981), *SP* (1986) and *NSP* (1989).

1981

B234   'Alternatywa.' *Odra* 6 (1981), p. 44.

'Alternative' (from *Backwaters* (1971)) translated into Polish verse by Piotr Sommer.

B235   'The Butterfly House.' *Quarto* no 14 (January/February 1981), p. 20.

Collected in *E* (1985).

B236   'Courting.' *The Reaper* (Indiana) no 1 (1981), pp. 24–5.

Collected in *SKP* (1981), *SP* (1986) and *NSP* (1989).

B237   'Dining.' *Glasgow Herald* 12 August 1981, p. 8.

Collected in *E* (1985).

B238   'France.' *Encounter* vol. 57 (October 1981), p. 82.

Collected in *E* (1985), *SP* (1986) and *NSP* (1989).

B239   'The Kaleidoscope.' *Poetry Supplement* compiled by Andrew Motion for the Poetry Book Society, Christmas '81 (1981), p. [5].

Collected in *E* (1985), *SP* (1986) and *NSP* (1989).

B240   'The Local.' TLS 6 February 1981, p. 140.

Collected in *SKP* (1981) and *SP* (1986).

B241   'Muir's Ledgers.' *Outcrop* (St David's University College, Dyfed) vol. 2 (1981), p. 27.

B242   'Ode to a Paperclip.' *Bananas* no 26 (April 1981), p. 4.

Collected in *SKP* (1981), *SP* (1986) and *NSP* (1989).

B243   'Rereading Katherine Mansfield's *Bliss and Other Stories*.' *London Review of Books* 7–20 May 1981, p. 15.

Collected in *E* (1985).

B244   'Western Blue.' *London Review of Books* 5–18 November 1981, p. 8.

Later published in *Douglas Dunn: Writers in Brief no 18* (NBL, [1982]), q.v.

Collected in *E* (1985).

1982

B245   'Attics.' In *Douglas Dunn: Writers in Brief no 18* (National Book League, [1982]).

Also published in *Encounter* vol. 59 (December 1982), q.v.

Collected in *E* (1985).

B246   'Attics.' *Encounter* vol. 59 (December 1982), p. 35.

Also published in *Douglas Dunn: Writers in Brief no 18* (NBL, [1982]), q.v.

B247   'Birch Room.' *London Review of Books* 1–14 April 1982, p. 5.

Also published in *Douglas Dunn: Writers in Brief no 18* (NBL, [1982]), q.v.

Collected in *E* (1985), *SP* (1986) and *NSP* (1989).

B248   'Birch Room.' In *Douglas Dunn: Writers in Brief no 18* (National Book League, [1982]).

Also published in *London Review of Books* (April 1982), q.v.

B249   'Château d'If.' *Belfast Review* no 1 (Christmas 1982), p. 33.

Collected in *E* (1985).

B250   'Creatures.' TLS 16 April 1982, p. 442.

Collected in *E* (1985) and *SP* (1986).

B251   'December.' *New Statesman* 28 May 1982, p. 24.

Collected in *E* (1985).

B252   'The Drying Green.' In *Douglas Dunn: Writers in Brief no 18* (National Book League, [1982]).

B253   'Empty Wardrobes.' New Year *Poetry Supplement* compiled by Alan Brownjohn for the Poetry Book Society, December 1982 (1982), p. [13].

Collected in *E* (1985), *SP* (1986) and *NSP* (1989).

B254   'France.' In *Douglas Dunn: Writers in Brief no 18* (National Book League, [1982]).

Collected in *E* (1985).

B255 'Lakes and Rivers.' *Gallimaufry: Dundee University Arts Magazine* no 9 (1982), p. 7.

Also published in *Douglas Dunn: Writers in Brief* (NBL, [1982]), q.v.

B256 'Lakes and Rivers.' In *Douglas Dunn: Writers in Brief no 18* (National Book League, [1982]).

Also published in *Gallimaufry* no 9 (1982), q.v.

B257 'Listening.' *Gallimaufry: Dundee University Arts Magazine* no 9 (1982), p. 8.

Also published in *Douglas Dunn: Writers in Brief no 18* (NBL, [1982]), q.v.

Collected in *E* (1985).

B258 'Listening.' In *Douglas Dunn: Writers in Brief no 18* (National Book League, [1982]).

Also published in *Gallimaufry* no 9 (1982), q.v.

B259 'Little House.' *Glasgow Herald* (Weekender) 19 June 1982, p. 7.

B260 'Playing.' *Poetry Durham* no 1 (1982), p. 9.

B261 'Pretended Homes.' *New Statesman* 28 May 1982, p. 24.

Collected in *E* (1985).

B262 'Sandra's Mobile.' *Quarto* no 29 (June 1982), p. 9.

Collected in *E* (1985) and *SP* (1986).

B263 'Shaving a Beard.' In *Douglas Dunn: Writers in Brief no 18* (National Book League, [1982]).

B264 'The Stories.' *Thames Poetry* vol. 2 no 11 (1982), pp. 28–30.

Collected in *E* (1985), *SP* (1986) and *NSP* (1989).

B265 'A Summer Night.' *New Yorker* 6 September 1982, p. 36.

Collected in *E* (1985), *SP* (1986) and *NSP* (1989).

B266 'An Underwear Salesman in a Snowdrift.' *Gallimaufry: Dundee University Arts Magazine* no 9 (1982), pp. 7–8.

B267 'Western Blue.' In *Douglas Dunn: Writers in Brief no 18* (National Book League, [1982]).

Previously published in *London Review of Books* (November 1981), q.v.

B268 'Writing with Light.' *London Magazine* 22 (3) June 1982, p. 26.

Collected in *E* (1985) and *NSP* (1989).

1983

B269 'At Cruggleton Castle.' *London Magazine* 23 (4) July 1983, p. 5.

Collected in *E* (1985) and *NSP* (1989).

B270 'The Clear Day.' *New Yorker* 1 August 1983, p. 40.

Collected in *E* (1985), *SP* (1986) and *NSP* (1989).

B271 'Hush.' TLS 5 August 1983, p. 830.

Collected in *E* (1985), *SP* (1986) and *NSP* (1989).

B272 'In the 1950s.' *London Magazine* 23 (8) November 1983, pp. 23–5.

Collected in *N* (1988).

B273 'Land Love.' TLS 8 April 1983, p. 343.

Collected in *E* (1985), *SP* (1986), and *NSP* (1989).

B274 'Leaving Dundee.' *Poetry Review* 72 (4) January 1983, p. 10.

Collected in *E* (1985), *SP* (1986), and *NSP* (1989).

B275 'Politovsky's Letters Home.' *Encounter* vol. 61 (November 1983), pp. 50–1.

B276 'Reading Pascal in the Lowlands.' Winter *Poetry Supplement* compiled by David Harsent for the Poetry Book Society, December 1983 (1983), pp. [6]–[8].

Collected in *E* (1985).

B277 'A Rediscovery of Juvenilia.' *London Magazine* 23 (4) July 1983, p. 7.

Collected in *E* (1985).

B278 'Reincarnations.' *Encounter* vol. 60 (February 1983), p. 35.

Collected in *E* (1985) and *SP* (1986).

B279 'A Silver Air Force.' *The Observer* 24 April 1983, p. 30.

Collected in *E* (1985).

B280   'The Stranger.' *Smoke* no 19 (1983), p. [3].

Collected in *E* (1985).

B281   'The Sundial.' Winter *Poetry Supplement* compiled by David Harsent for the Poetry Book Society, December 1983 (1983), p. [8].

Collected in *E* (1985).

B282   'Transblucency.' *London Magazine* 23 (4) July 1983, p. 6.

Collected in *E* (1985).

1984

B283   'Anon's People.' *Glasgow Herald* (Weekender) 28 January 1984, p. 7.

A sequence of 13 poems:

Great Western Road 1922 – Outside the Grosvenor – Pantheon – Temptations – Pageant – St Andrews Graduates 1916 – A Mother Remembers – War Memorial – Progress Report – The Amateur Cinematographer's Daughter – An Imaginary Nation I, II and III.

B284   'The Departures of Friends in Childhood.' *Nucleus (Kangaroo Six*: literary supplement) [Armidale, NSW], 38 (8) November 1984, p. 18.

Collected in *N* (1988).

B285   'Images of Scotland.' [poem sequence]. *Glasgow Herald* (Weekender) 28 January 1984, p. 7.

B286   'In Ten Seconds.' *The Poetry of Motion*, ed. A. Bold (Mainstream, 1984), pp. 170–1.

Originally broadcast on BBC1 film *Athletes* (1983).

B287   'Running the East Wind.' *Nucleus (Kangaroo Six*: literary supplement) [Armidale, NSW], 38 (8) November 1984, p. 18.

Collected in *N* (1988).

B288   'War Blinded.' *The Armidale Express* [NSW, Australia] 2 November 1984, p. 4.

Previously published in *New Statesman* 19 September 1980, q.v.

B289   'The War in the Congo.' TLS 27 April 1984. p. 456.

Collected in *N* (1988).

1985

B290 'Abernethy.' *Verse* no 4 (1985), p. 3.

Collected in *N* (1988).

B291 'Aubade.' In *Natural Light: Portraits of Scottish Writers* by Angela Catlin (Paul Harris/Waterfront, 1985), p. 20.

B292 'Pigeons of History.' TLS 6 September 1985, p. 979.

Collected under the title 'Winkie' in *N* (1988) and *NSP* (1989).

B293 'S. Frediano's.' *New Yorker* 25 February 1985, p. 36.

Collected in *N* (1988) and *NSP* (1989).

1986

B294 'Australia.' *Cencrastus* no 23 (June–August 1986), p. 14.

B295 'The Come-on.' In *La Poésie Britannique 1970–1984* (Etudes Anglaises, 1986), pp. X–XI.

Includes a French translation entitled 'Le Leurre' by Paul Bensimon.

B296 'Dieback.' *Cencrastus* no 23 (June–August 1986), p. 14.

Collected in *N* (1988).

B297 'Reading Pascal in the Lowlands.' *Guardian* 30 January 1986.

With an explanatory introduction to the poem and its background in *Elegies* (1985).

Collected in *E* (1985).

First published in Winter *Poetry Supplement* (1983), q.v.

B298 'A Small Property.' *Cencrastus* no 23 (June–August 1986), p. 14.

1987

B299 '4/4 (i.m. John Brogan).' In *Conserving the Past – Building for the Future*: Proceedings of the 73rd Annual Conference of the Scottish Library Association, Inverness 1987, ed. C.D. Dakers (SLA, 1987), p. 54.

Collected in *N* (1988) and *NSP* (1989).

B300 '75°.' TLS 18 September 1987, p. 1023.

Collected in *N* (1988) and *NSP* (1989).

B301   'Before Dark.' *Glasgow Herald* (Weekender) 12 September 1987, p. 7.

B302   'Broughty Ferry.' *Radical Scotland* no 26 (April/May 1987), p. 39.

        Collected in *N* (1988).

B303   'The Dark Crossroads.' *Verse* 4 (2) 1987, pp. 8–9.

        Collected in *N* (1988).

B304   'Daylight.' *Verse* 4 (2) 1987, pp. 7–8.

        Also published in *Five Writers in Residence* (Duncan of Jordanstone, 1987), q.v.

        Collected in *N* (1988) and *NSP* (1989).

B305   'Daylight.' In *Five Writers in Residence 1979–1987* (Duncan of Jordanstone College of Art Dundee, 1987), pp. [22]–[23].

        Also published in *Verse* 4 (2) 1987, q.v.

B306   'December's Door.' In *Under the Influence: Douglas Dunn on Philip Larkin* (Edinburgh University Library, 1987), pp. 12–13.

        Also published in *Philip Larkin 1922–1985: a Tribute* (1988), q.v.

        Collected in *N* (1988) and *NSP* (1989).

B307   'Impéria.' *Tvorba* 39 (Kmen) 1987, p. 9.

        A Czech verse translation of 'Empires' (*B* (1979)).

B308   'Jig of the Week, no 21.' *Kenyon Review* ns 9 (1987), pp. 73–4.

        Collected in *N* (1988) and *NSP* (1989).

B309   'Memory and Imagination.' In *Memory and Imagination*: [catalogue of a Touring Exhibition shown at the Royal Scottish Academy, Edinburgh 19 December 1987 to 14 February 1988] (Scottish Arts Council, 1987), pp. [1]–[5].

        Also published in *Art International* 2 (Spring 1988), q.v.

        Collected in *N* (1988).

B310   'On an Ancient Funerary Bas-Relief . . .' In *Leopardi: a Scottis Quair*, ed. R.D.S. Jack *et al.* (EUP, 1987), pp. 62–4.

        An English verse translation of Leopardi's 'Sopra un basso rilievo antico sepolcrale . . .'

B311 'The Patrol.' In *Proof: New Writing from Lincolnshire and Humberside* 9 (2) 1987, p. 1.

Includes an introductory section on the appeal of Tayport.

Collected in *N* (1988).

B312 'The People Before.' *Numbers* 2 (Spring 1987), pp. 45–7.

Also published in *Five Writers in Residence* (Duncan of Jordanstone, 1987) q.v.

Collected in *N* (1988) and *NSP* (1989).

B313 'The People Before.' In *Five Writers in Residence 1979–1987* (Duncan of Jordanstone College of Art Dundee, 1987), pp. [20]–[22].

Also published in *Numbers* 2 (Spring 1987), q.v.

B314 'Slunecní Hodiny.' *Tvorba* 39 (Kmen) 1987, p. 9.

A Czech verse translation of 'The Sundial' (*E* (1985)).

Also published in *Kmen* 4 (1989), q.v.

B315 'Stehování z Terry Street.' *Tvorba* 39 (Kmen) 1987, p. 9.

A Czech verse translation of 'A Removal from Terry Street' (*TS* (1969)).

B316 'To Himself.' In *Leopardi: a Scottis Quair*, ed. R.D.S. Jack *et al.* (EUP, 1987), p. 57.

An English verse translation of Leopardi's 'A se stesso.'

B317 'Tremors.' In *Proof: New Writing from Lincolnshire and Humberside* 9 (2) 1987, p. 1.

Includes an introductory section on the appeal of Tayport.

Collected in *N* (1988).

1988

B318 'An Address to Adolphe Sax.' *Glasgow Herald* (Weekender) 10 September 1988, p. 25.

First published in *Quarto* no 1 (October 1979), q.v.

B319 'Adventure's Oafs.' *Glasgow Herald* (Weekender) 10 September 1988, p. 25.

Collected in *N* (1988).

B320   'December's Door.' In *Philip Larkin 1922–1985: a Tribute* ed. G.
        Hartley (Marvell Press, 1988), pp. 13–14.

        Also published in *Under the Influence* (1987), q.v.

B321   'Here and There.' *Glasgow Herald* (Weekender) 16 January 1988, p. 7.

        Also published in *Poetry Review* 78 (1) Spring 1988, q.v.

        Collected in *N* (1988) and *NSP* (1989).

B322   'Here and There.' *Poetry Review* 78 (1) Spring 1988, pp. 36–7.

        Also published in *Glasgow Herald* 16 January 1988, q.v.

B323   'A House in the Country.' TLS 10 June 1988, p. 645.

        Collected in *N* (1988) and *NSP* (1989).

B324   'In-Flight Entertainment.' *Antaeus* no 60 (Spring 1988), pp. 195–7.

        Collected in *N* (1988) and *NSP* (1989).

B325   'Memory and Imagination.' *Art International* 2 (Spring 1988), pp. 58–
        60.

        Also published in *Memory and Imagination* (Scottish Arts Council
        catalogue, 1987), q.v.

B326   'Poor People's Cafés.' *Glasgow Herald* (Weekender) 10 September 1988,
        p. 25.

B327   'The Prodigious Twins.' *The Listener* 22 December 1988, p. 58.

B328   'Sketches.' In *First and Always: Poems for Great Ormond Street Children's
        Hospital* ed. L. Sail (Faber, 1988), pp. 16–19.

B329   'A Snow-Walk.' *The New Yorick* (University of York) no 16 (Spring
        1988), p. 16.

        Collected in *N* (1988).

B330   'The World's Table.' In *Images for Africa: an Anthology of Poems and
        Illustrations*, ed. Jane Glencross (WaterAid, 1988), pp. 71–2.

1989

B331   'The Crossroads of the Birds.' *Poetry Book Society Anthology 1989–1990*,
        ed. C. Reid (1989), pp. 20–1.

B332   'Hothouse February.' In *The Orange Dove of Fiji: Poems for the World Wide Fund for Nature*, ed. Simon Rae (Hutchinson, 1989), p. 30.

B333   'Preserve and Renovate.' *Poetry Review* 79 (4) Winter 1989/90, pp. 26–7.

B334   'Slunecní Hodiny.' *Kmen* 4 (1989), p. 8.

        A Czech verse translation of 'The Sundial' (*E* (1985)).

        Also published in *Tvorba* 39 (1987), q.v.

                                    1990
B335   'Libraries: a Rhapsody.' In *Voices Aloud: an Anthology of Poetry about Libraries*, ed. Bernard Young and Jonathan Davidson (Hull: Humberside Leisure Services, 1990), pp. 55–7.

        Also published in *Aslib Information* (September 1991), q.v.

B336   'Moorlander.' *Scotland on Sunday* 14 October 1990, p. 32.

B337   'Past and Present.' *Spectrum* (Stirling University) no 1 (1990), pp. 3–5.

B338   'The Penny Gibbet.' In *The Printer's Devil: a Magazine of New Writing*, ed. Sean O'Brien and Stephen Plaice (Tunbridge Wells: South East Arts, 1990), p. 11.

B339   'Poor People's Cafés' [an extract]. The *Observer* (Scotland) 11 March 1990, p. 9.

        Previously published (in full) in *Glasgow Herald* 10 September 1988, q.v.

B340   'Queen February.' In *The Printer's Devil: a Magazine of New Writing*, ed. Sean O'Brien and Stephen Plaice (Tunbridge Wells: South-East Arts, 1990), pp. 7–10.

B341   'Saturday's Rainbow.' In *Contemporary Poets: a National Portrait Gallery Exhibition*: portraits by Peter Edwards (NPG, 1990), p. [2] [of a large folded poster].

B342   'Scott's Arks.' *Glasgow Herald* (Weekender) 6 March 1990, p. 9.

B343   'Sharp to the Point.' *Glasgow Herald* (Weekender) 17 November 1990, p. 24.

A review in verse of *The Pencil* by Henry Petroski (Faber, 1990).

1991

B344   'Between Bus Stop and Home.' In *Things to Translate & Other Poems* by Piotr Sommer (Bloodaxe Books, 1991), p. 47.

An English verse translation by DD from the Polish original.

Previously published in *International Portland Review* 1980, q.v.

B345   'A Bit More Effort, Please.' In *Things to Translate & Other Poems* by Piotr Sommer (Bloodaxe Books, 1991), p. 46.

An English verse translation by DD from the Polish original.

B346   'December.' *Estuaires: Revue Culturelle* (Luxembourg) no 14 (1991), pp. 48–51.

Includes a French translation by Serge Baudot entitled 'Décembre.'

B347   'First Sentence.' In *Things to Translate & Other Poems* by Piotr Sommer (Bloodaxe Books, 1991), p. 43.

An English verse translation by DD from the Polish original.

B348   'Libraries: a Rhapsody.' *Aslib Information* 19 (9) September 1991, p. 317.

Previously published in *Voices Aloud* (1990) q.v.

B349   'Says the Son.' In *Things to Translate & Other Poems* by Piotr Sommer (Bloodaxe Books, 1991), p. 49.

An English verse translation by DD from the Polish original.

B350   'Spanish Oranges.' *The Southern Review* 27 (2) April 1991, pp. 339–40.

B351   'This is Certain.' In *Things to Translate & Other Poems* by Piotr Sommer (Bloodaxe Books, 1991), p. 44.

An English verse translation by DD from the Polish original.

B352   'Turn over a New Leaf.' *Scotland on Sunday* 17 March 1991, p. 32.

B353   'Two Gestures.' In *Things to Translate & Other Poems* by Piotr Sommer (Bloodaxe Books, 1991), p. 48.

An English verse translation by DD from the Polish original.

SECTION C. SHORT STORIES BY DOUGLAS DUNN

1974

C1   'The Blue Gallery.' *Vogue* June 1974, pp. 43–4.

C2   'Report on a Man, Bugged with Glass Devices.' *Daily Telegraph Magazine*
10 May 1974, pp. 45–6.

1975

C3   'The Dining Club.' *Green Ginger: Hull University Literary Magazine* [no 2
(1975)], pp. 33–40.

C4   'The Flying Machine.' In *Scottish Short Stories 1975* (Collins, 1975), pp.
91–3.

1978

C5   'The Canoes.' *New Yorker* 30 October 1978, pp. 39–45.

Collected in *SV* (1985).

C6   'Nymphs and Shepherds.' *Punch* 9 August 1978, pp. 210–11.

C7   'Kilbinnin Men.' *New Yorker* 30 July 1979, pp. 24–7.

Collected in *SV* (1985).

1979

C8   'Mozart's Clarinet Concerto.' *Punch* 28 March 1979, pp. 538–40.

Collected in *SV* (1985).

C9   'Old Women Without Gardens.' *Encounter* vol. 52 (May 1979), pp. 3–9.

Collected in *SV* (1985).

C10   'Photographs of Stanley's Grandfather.' *Punch* 21 November 1979, pp.
952–4.

Collected in *SV* (1985).

C11   'Wings in the Kitchen.' *Vole* 3(1) 1979, pp. 36–9.

1980

C12   'Ask Me Another One.' *Illustrated London News* Christmas Number 1980,
pp. 67–9.

C13   'Do It Yourself.' *Punch* 26 November 1980, pp. 972–4.

C14   'Inheritors.' *London Magazine* 20 (1/2) April/May 1980, pp. 5–17.

C15   'Loose Shoes.' *Punch* 2 January 1980, pp. 24–6.

C16   'Never Say Die.' *Telegraph Sunday Magazine* 5 October 1980, pp. 105, 108, 112.

C17   'Something for Little Robert.' *New Yorker* 28 January 1980, pp. 35–40.

Collected in *SV* (1985).

C18   'Twin-sets and Pickle-forks.' *Punch* 5 November 1980, pp. 808–10.

Collected in *SV* (1985).

C19   'Wallacotts in the Snow.' *Telegraph Sunday Magazine* 27 April 1980, pp. 83, 86.

1981

C20   'Ever Let the Fancy Roam.' *Punch* 16 September 1981, pp. 472–4.

Collected in *SV* (1985).

C21   'Getting Used To It.' *New Yorker* 12 October 1981, pp. 36–41.

Collected in *SV* (1985).

C22   'The Tennis Court.' *Encounter* vol. 56 (June 1981), pp. 3–7.

Collected in *SV* (1985).

C23   'Wives in the Garden.' *Encounter* vol. 57 (November 1981), pp. 3–7.

Collected in *SV* (1985).

1982

C24   'The Fishermen.' *New Yorker* 12 April 1982, pp. 42–6.

Collected in *SV* (1985).

C25   'A Night Out at the Club Harmonica.' *New Yorker* 31 May 1982, pp. 32–3.

Collected in *SV* (1985).

1983

C26   'The Bagpiping People.' *New Yorker* 19 December 1983, pp. 42–7.

Later published in *Scottish Short Stories 1985* (Collins, 1985), q.v.

Collected in *SV* (1985).

1984

C27 'Bobby's Room.' *New Yorker* 16 January 1984, pp. 38–46.

Collected in *SV* (1985).

C28 'Orr Mount.' *New Yorker* 17 September 1984, pp. 46–56.

C29 'South America.' *New Yorker* 25 June 1984, pp. 32–40.

Later published in *Woman's Journal* (April 1985), q.v.

Collected in *SV* (1985).

1985

C30 'The Bagpiping People.' In *Scottish Short Stories 1985* (Collins, 1985), pp. 89–99.

Previously published in *New Yorker* 19 December 1983, q.v.

C31 'Boyfriends and Girlfriends.' *New Yorker* 30 December 1985, pp. 22–32.

C32 'Needlework.' *New Yorker* 19 August 1985, pp. 26–34.

C33 'South America.' *Woman's Journal* April 1985, pp. 193–211.

Previously published in *New Yorker* 25 June 1984, q.v.

1986

C34 'The Boy from Birnam.' *Grand Street* (New York) 5 (2) 1986, pp. 7–21.

C35 'Le Monde des Cornemuseurs.' *Brèves: actualité de la nouvelle* no 32 (1986), pp. 79–92.

A translation of 'The Bagpiping People' (from *SV* (1985)).

C36 'Mulwhevin.' *Grand Street* (New York) 6 (1) 1986, pp. 73–93.

C37 'The Political Piano.' *The Listener* 3 July 1986, pp. 26–9.

1990

C38 'Toddle-Bonny and the Bogeyman.' In *A Roomful of Birds: Scottish Short Stories 1990* (Collins, 1990), pp. 55–75.

SECTION D. ESSAYS AND ARTICLES BY DOUGLAS DUNN.

1962

D1 'SLA quiescent and uninspired.' Letter in *SLA News* no 56 (November/December 1962), p. 21.

1963

D2   'Contemporary literature – Aspects: East and West.' *SLA News* no 58
       (March/April 1963), pp. 17–18.

D3   '[Hours of opening].' Letter in *SLA News* no 61 (November/December
       1963), p. 3.

1964

D4   'Aberfoyle Again – Another Successful Conference.' *SLA News* no 67
       (November/December 1964), 24–7.

D5   'Little Brother is Watching.' *SLA News* no 63 (March/April 1964), p.
       13.

D6   'New Periodical – "The Glasgow Review".' *SLA News* no 64 (May/June
       1964), p. 3.

D7   'Our Future at Stake – Reorganisation of Local Government in Scotland:
       a personal (re-)view of the first report.' *SLA News* no 65 (July/August
       1964), pp. 21–4.

D8   'The Pioneers.' Letter in TLS 11 June 1964, p. 511. [On library
       holdings of 'little magazines.']

D9   'Reply to an Editorial – Light the Blue Paper and Stand Back.' *SLA
       News* no 64 (May/June 1964), pp. 10–11.

1965

D10   'Letter from America – First Impressions.' *SLA News* no 70 (May/
       August 1965), pp. 12–13.

1969

D11   'Friendship of young poets.' *New Statesman* 31 October 1969, p. 616.

1970

D12   'Hull in general. In the City of H.' *New Statesman* 23 January 1970, p.
       124.

       Review-article on *A History of the County of York, East Riding, Vol. 1*: The
       City of Kingston upon Hull, ed. K.J. Allison (Victoria County History,
       1969).

1971

D13   '[Modern poets in focus]'. Introduction by DD to his own selected
       poems in *Modern Poets in Focus: 1* ed. Dannie Abse (Corgi, 1971:
       Woburn Press, 1973), pp. 106–7.

D14 'An affable misery: on Randall Jarrell.' *Encounter* vol. 39 (October 1972), pp. 42–8.

D15 'The Sacrifice.' *Ostrich* no 6 (September 1972), pp. 30–3.

On Natalya Gorbanevskaya.

1973

D16 'The big race: Lowell's visions and revisions.' *Encounter* vol. 41 (October 1973), pp. 107–13.

Review-article on Robert Lowell's *History; For Lizzie & Harriet;* and *The Dolphin* (all Faber, 1973).

D17 'Douglas Dunn on the revalued Pound.' *Spectator* 27 January 1973, pp. 107–8.

Review-article on *Ezra Pound: the Critical Heritage* ed. E. Homburger (Routledge, 1973) and *Ezra Pound's Selected Prose* ed. W. Cookson (Faber, 1973).

Also a follow-up letter from Tom Scott in *Spectator* 10 February 1973, p. 187.

D18 'Introduction' to his edition of *New Poems 1972–73* (Hutchinson, 1973), pp. 11–13.

D19 'Poets on Poetry . . . Douglas Dunn.' *The Listener* 8 November 1973, pp. 629–30.

A report of Patrick Garland's interview with DD in the BBC1 Further Education series 'Poets on Poetry'.

1974

D20 ' "Finished fragrance": the poems of George Mackay Brown.' *Poetry Nation* 2 (1974), pp. 80–92.

D21 'Gaiety and lamentation: the defeat of John Berryman.' *Encounter* vol. 43 (August, 1974), pp. 72–7.

D22 'Introduction' to *A Choice of Byron's Verse*, selected with an introduction by DD (Faber, 1974), pp. 11–18.

1975

D23 'Editorial: The Grudge.' *Stand* 16 (4) 1975, pp. 4–6.

D24 'Horribly Rough'. *New Statesman* 29 August 1975, p. 261.

Review of an Isaac Rosenberg Exhibition at the National Book League, London, 1975.

D25   'Introduction' to *Two Decades of Irish Writing: a Critical Survey*, ed. by DD (Carcanet, 1975), pp. 1–3.

D26   'John Hawkes – a profile.' *The New Review* vol. 1 no 12 (March 1975), pp. 23–8.

D27   'Toulson, Shirley.' In *Contemporary Poets*. 2nd ed., ed. J. Vinson (St James Press, 1975), pp. 1560–2.

Reprinted in *Contemporary Poets,* 3rd ed. (1980), q.v.

1976
D28   'Dispelling the myths about cancer.' *Radio Times* (North) 23–29 October 1976, pp. 16–17.

Previewing a series of programmes on BBC Radio Humberside.

D29   'Introduction' to his edition of *Delmore Schwartz. What is to be Given* (Carcanet, 1976), pp. vii–xix.

D30   'Technique, tradition and truculence – Poetry in the 1970s.' Introduction to *Poetry in the Seventies* ed. Trevor Kneale (Liverpool: Rondo, 1976), pp. 11–14.

1977
D31   'Coteries & Commitments: "Little Magazines".' *Encounter* vol. 48 (June 1977), pp. 58–65.

Review-article on *The Little Magazines* by Ian Hamilton (Weidenfeld & Nicolson, 1977).

D32   'Traditional dangers.' *Meridian* no 11 (1977), pp. 3–4.

1978
D33   'Clyde and cheek.' *Vole* 2 (1) 1978, pp. 27–30.

D34   'Introduction' to *Poetry Review* 68 (1) April 1978, ed. by DD, pp. 3–5.

D35   ' "Let the god not abandon us": on the poetry of Derek Mahon.' *Stone Ferry Review* no 2 (Winter 1978), pp. 7–30.

1979
D36   'Autumn 1969: Terry Street.' In *Poetry Book Society: the First Twenty-Five Years, 1954–1978,* ed. Eric W. White (Poetry Book Society, 1979), pp. 46–7.

D37   'Bigger energy.' *Lincolnshire and Humberside Arts Diary* (September–October 1979), p. 6.

        On Ted Hughes.

D38   'Living out of London – VIII.' *London Magazine* 19 (5 & 6) August/September 1979, pp. 71–9.

        Personal reminiscences on his life in Hull.

        Reprinted in *Living Out of London* ed. Alan Ross (LM, 1984), q.v.

D39   'The Poetry of Alan Bold: Hammering on the Lyre'. *Akros* no 42 (December 1979), pp. 58–76.

D40   'Rhyme.' *Poetry Wales* 15 (3) Winter 1979/80, pp. 39–42.

        Including the poem 'The Loch Music' (pp. 41–2).

                                    1980

D41   'Hugh MacDiarmid: inhuman splendours.' *New Edinburgh Review* no 52 (November 1980), pp. 17–21.

        Review article on *The Age of MacDiarmid*, ed. P.H. Scott & A.C. Davis (Edinburgh: Mainstream, 1980).

        Reprinted in *New Edinburgh Review Anthology* (Polygon, 1982), q.v.

d42   'Pity the Poor Philosophers: Coward's comic genius.' *Encounter* vol. 55 (October 1980), pp. 46–51.

        Review article on *Coward Plays* ed. R. Mander & J. Mitchenson. 4 vols (Eyre Methuen, 1980).

D43   'The sea-scholar and his befriended disguises.' *Aquarius* no 12 (1980), pp. 128–34.

        Review article on W.S. Graham's *Collected Poems 1942–1977* (Faber, 1980).

D44   'Symposium: on reviewing.' *New Edinburgh Review* no 49 (February 1980), pp. 5–6.

D45   'Thuis: over de recente poëzie in Groot-Brittannië.' [In Dutch]. *Raster* (Amsterdam) 15 (1980), pp. 47–59.

D46   'Toulson, Shirley.' In *Contemporary Poets*. 3rd ed., ed. J. Vinson (Macmillan, 1980), pp. 1549–50.

Reprinted from *Contemporary Poets*, 2nd ed. (1975), q.v.

D47   'Viewpoint.' TLS 12 December 1980, p. 1411.

On poetry competitions.

Also a follow-up letter from Geoffrey Grigson in TLS 2 January 1981,
p. 11 ('Poetry Competitions').

1981

D48   'Douglas Dunn writes . . .' *Poetry Book Society Bulletin* no 110 (Autumn
1981), pp. 1–2.

An introductory note to *St Kilda's Parliament*, the Poetry Book Society
'Choice' for Autumn 1981.

D49   'Mythic parody in *The Country Wife*.' *Essays in Criticism* 31 (1981), pp.
299–319.

D50   'Scott and Scott and Scotland.' *New Edinburgh Review* no 56 (Winter
1981), pp. 28–30.

D51   'Search for meaning by workmen in the Tower of Babel.' *Glasgow Herald*
(Weekender) 3 October 1981, p. 7.

Report on the 20th International Poetry Festival, held in Struga,
Macedonia.

1982

D52   'Hugh MacDiarmid: inhuman splendours.' In *New Edinburgh Review
Anthology*, ed. James Campbell (Edinburgh: Polygon, 1982), pp. 110–
23.

First published in *New Edinburgh Review* no 52 (November 1980), q.v.

D53   'Introduction' to *A Rumoured City* ed. DD (1982), pp. 11–16.

D54   'Introduction' to *To Build a Bridge* ed. DD (1982), pp. vii–ix.

D55   'Introduction' to *Where Sky and Water Meet*: photographs of Humberside
(Lincolnshire and Humberside Arts, 1982), pp. ii–iii.

D56   'Lyric sweep of Philip Larkin.' *Glasgow Herald* (Weekender) 22 May
1982, p. 7.

An 'exclusive extract' from DD's essay published in *Larkin at Sixty* ed.
A. Thwaite (Faber and Faber, 1982).

D57   'Memoirs of the Brynmor Jones Library.' In *Larkin at Sixty* ed. A.
Thwaite (Faber and Faber, 1982), pp. 53–60.

D58 'Scottish loyalty and sacrifice.' TLS 4 June 1982, p. 610.

On 7:84 Scotland's revival of 5 plays dealing with Scottish working-class issues and characters.

1983

D59 'American notes. The periodicals, 5: *Partisan Review*.' TLS 21 October 1983, p. 1160.

D60 'Iain Crichton Smith's *Old Woman*.' *Akros* no 51 (October 1983), pp. 47–9.

D61 'Infinite Mischief : Lowell's Life.' *Encounter* vol. 61 (September/October 1983), pp. 68–76.

Review-article on *Robert Lowell: a Biography* by Ian Hamilton (Faber and Faber, 1983).

D62 'The predicament of Scottish poetry.' TLS 18 March 1983, p. 273.

D63 'A pride of prejudices: a loathing for pub gasbags.' *Glasgow Herald* 16 June 1983, p. 6.

D64 'Winkie the Pigeon and my crumbs of literary advice.' *Glasgow Herald* (Weekender) 9 July 1983, p. 7.

On his year as Fellow in Creative Writing at Dundee University.

1984

D65 'Challenge of setting archive film to words.' *Glasgow Herald* (Weekender) 28 January 1984, p. 7.

DD explains how he came to write the poems for 'Anon's People', to be broadcast in 'Spectrum', BBC Scotland on 29 January 1984.

Includes the poem-sequence 'Anon's People'.

D66 'Exile and unexile.' *Cencrastus* no 16 (Spring 1984), pp. 4–6.

D67 ' "From Hell, Hull and Halifax, may the Good Lord deliver us".' In *Living Out of London* ed. Alan Ross (LM Editions, 1984), pp. 56–64.

First published in *London Magazine* 19 (5/6) 1979, q.v.

D68 'Heaney Agonistes.' *London Magazine* 24 (8) *November* 1984, pp. 92–5.

On Seamus Heaney.

D69 'Provincialism.' *Nucleus* 38 (8) November 1984 (*Kangaroo Six*: Literary Supplement) [University of New England, Armidale NSW], p. 18.

Includes 2 poems by DD: 'Running the East Wind' – 'The Departure of Friends in Childhood'.

1985

D70   'Hart Crane.' Letter in TLS 29 March 1985, p. 357.

Refers back to DD's review in TLS 1 March 1985, p. 239.

D71   'Native talent flourishes: outstanding Scottish fiction and poetry published in 1985.' *Glasgow Herald* (Weekender) 28 December 1985, p. 11.

D72   'A no-nonsense writer draws his inspiration once more from the working-class hero.' *Glasgow Herald* (Weekender) 28 August 1985, p. 9.

On William McIlvanney and his latest work *The Big Man* (1985).

D73   'Poetry or prose? The writing life of Douglas Dunn.' *Writers' Monthly* vol. 1 no 9 (June 1985), pp. 20–2.

D74   'Regained: the light behind grief's dark veil.' *Glasgow Herald* (Weekender) 24 September 1985, p. 9.

D75   'Silenced note.' *Glasgow Herald*, 3 December 1985, p. 11.

Obituary appreciation of Philip Larkin.

D76   'Struggling with feeling.' *Poetry Book Society Bulletin* no 124 (Spring 1985), p. [5].

On the background to *Elegies* (1985).

1986

D77   'Love and Longley.' *Radio Times* (Northern Ireland) 12–18 April 1986, pp. 74–5.

On the poetry of Michael Longley, previewing 'Gallery' on BBC 1 on 13 April 1986.

D78   'Poet's affection for Clydeside.' *Glasgow Herald* 15 January 1986.

Obituary notice on W.S. Graham.

1987

D79   'Art of being a writer in residence.' *Glasgow Herald* (Weekender) 25 April 1987, p. 9.

D80   ' "Baggot Street Deserta" [by Thomas Kinsella].' *Tracks* (Dublin) no 7 (1987), pp. 14–18.

D81   'Critics' choice 1987.' *Glasgow Herald* (Weekender) 28 November 1987, p. 10.

       The New Confessions by William Boyd; *The Automatic Oracle* by Peter Porter; *The Haw Lantern* by Seamus Heaney: *The Roads of Fife* by Owen Silver.

D82   'Edwin Muir: poetry, politics and nationality.' *Radical Scotland* no 27 (June/July 1987), pp. 26–7.

D83   'Introduction' to *Duncan of Jordanstone College of Art Catalogue 1987* (Dundee, 1987), p. 5.

D84   'Introduction to *The White Bird Passes* by Jessie Kesson (Hogarth Press, 1987), pp. i–viii.

D85   'Poetry Live: an introduction and excerpt.' In *Conserving the Past – Building for the Future*: Proceedings of the 73rd Annual Conference of the Scottish Library Association, Inverness 1987, ed. C.D. Dakers (SLA, 1987), pp. 53–4.

       Includes DD's poem: '4/4'.

D86   'Prawdziwy aromat wiersze George Mackay Brown.' *Literatura na Swiecie* no 2 (1987), pp. 359–73.

       A Polish translation of the article first published in *Poetry Nation* no 2 (1974), q.v.

1988

D87   'From industry and pleasure.' TLS 26 February 1988, p. 213.

       Review article on R.L. Stevenson: *The Lantern Bearers and Other Essays* ed. Jeremy Treglown (Chatto, 1988).

D88   'NB: Scottish cadence and Scottish life.' TLS 28 October 1988, pp. 1202, 1213.

       On the modern Scottish novel.

D89   '[Note on the background to *Northlight*]'. *Poetry Book Society Bulletin* no 138 (Autumn 1988), pp. 3–4.

       Northlight was the PBS 'Choice' for Autumn 1988.

D90   'On *Terry Street* (Faber & Faber) 1969.' In *Thirty Years of the Poetry Book Society 1956–1986*, ed. Jonathan Barker (Hutchinson, 1988), p. 89.

D91   'A poet's place.' *Glasgow Herald* (Weekender) 16 January 1988, p. 7.

       Introducing his poem 'Here and There'.

D92 'Poetry of inclusion.' In *On Louis Simpson* ed. H. Lazer (University of Michigan Press, 1988), pp. 143–6.

Previously published in TLS 5 June 1981 as a review of Simpson's *Caviare at the Funeral* (1981).

D93 'The power of speech.' *The Independent* 10 June 1988, p. 12.

On public poetry readings.

D94 'Thinking about women.' TLS 3 June 1988, p. 612.

On the impact of feminism on his writing.

D95 'Well versed: the experts' expert: [current poets I admire].' *Observer Magazine* 25 September 1988, p. 17.

D96 'When one man's meat is another woman's poisson.' *Glasgow Herald* 2 September 1988, p. 11.

On his amateur vegetarianism.

1989

D97 '[4 letters to Michael Schmidt 1972, 1974, 1976].' In *Letters to an Editor*, ed. Mark Fisher (Carcanet, 1989), pp. 16–17, 18–19, 49, 83.

D98 'Books of the year.' *Glasgow Herald* (Weekender) 23 December 1989, p. 20.

D99 'Dunn in the USA: diary of a poet's transatlantic progress.' *Glasgow Herald* (Weekender) 21 October 1989, pp. 21, 23.

D100 'Foreword' to *The Modern Academic Library: Essays in Memory of Philip Larkin*, ed. Brian Dyson (Library Association, 1989), pp. vii–viii.

D101 'Lord Byron and Lord Elgin.' In *Byron and Scotland*, ed. A. Calder (EUP, 1989), pp. 86–107.

Based on a paper read at an Open University in Scotland Conference in Glasgow, January 1988.

D102 'The Pride of Fife: a poet's impressions of the Royal Kingdom.' *Departures* (American Express) July/August 1989, pp. 42–9.

1990

D103 ' "As a man sees . . ." – on Norman MacCaig's poetry.' *Verse* 7 (2) 1990, pp. 55–67.

D104 'A city discovered: Dundee.' In *The Glasgow Herald Book of Scotland*, ed. Arnold Kemp & Harry Reid (Mainstream, 1990), pp. 138–53.

D105   'The dominie of the poets.' *Scotland on Sunday* 4 November 1990, p. 37.

On Norman MacCaig.

D106   'Eclectically contemporary: Prudence Farmer award.' *New Statesman & Society* 7 September 1990, p. 43.

Award to the best poem published in NSS during the past year. DD was one of the judges.

D107   'Exposing the fiscal fake of poll tax.' *Observer* (Scotland) 11 March 1990, pp. 8–9.

D108   'First impressions, lasting memories.' *Guardian* (Review) 16 August 1990, p. 21.

Books that first made a big impression when young.

D109   'Foreword.' *Inchinnan Past and Present* (Inchinnan Community Council, 1990), pp. 2–4.

D110   'Introduction' to *The Essential Browning*: selected and with an introduction by DD. (New York: Ecco Press, 1990), pp. 1–12.

D111   'Morgan's sonnets.' In *About Edwin Morgan*, ed. Robert Crawford and Hamish Whyte (EUP, 1990), pp. 75–89.

D112   'Poetry in the '80s.' *Poetry Review* 79(4) Winter 1989/90, p. 36.

D113   'Promising poetry.' *Glasgow Herald* (Weekender), 21 April 1990, p. 27.

On the 2nd St Andrews Poetry Festival, 16–22 April 1990.

D114   'Reading between the parsnip wines.' *Scotsman* (Weekend) 29 December 1990, p. 2.

D115   ' "The Thunder of Humanity": D.J. Enright's Liberal Imagination.' In *Life by Other Means: Essays on D.J. Enright*, edited by Jacqueline Simms (OUP, 1990), pp. 74–87.

1991

D116   'Communicating through a Scots accent of the mind.' In *Edinburgh Book Festival August 1991* (a special Supplement to *The Scotsman* 9 August 1991), pp. 10–11.

Introducing excerpts from his *Scotland: an Anthology* (HarperCollins, 1991).

D117   'Definitive Dozen: DD's choice of 12 favourite lyric poems.' *Glasgow Herald* (Weekender) 13 July 1991, p. 7.

Titles only.

D118   'Dundee Law considered as Mount Parnassus.' *Gairfish* no 4 (October 1991), pp. 17–42.

D119   'Introduction' to his *Scotland: an Anthology* (HarperCollins, 1991), pp. 1–9.

D120   'Noticing such things.' *The English Review* 2 (2) Winter 1991, pp. 14–17.

D121   'Prestige prize goes to powerful story in Scots.' *Glasgow Herald* (Weekender) 4 May 1991.

Introducing James Robertsons's short story 'Empty Vessel', winner of the 1991 Sloan Prize. DD was one of the judges.

SECTION E. ANTHOLOGIES – WORKS BY DOUGLAS DUNN CONTAINED IN ANTHOLOGIES.

1967

E1   *Scottish Poetry* no 2 (Edinburgh: EUP, 1967).

'Landlocked' – 'Throwing Stones into the Sea.'

1968

E2   *Scottish Poetry* no 3 (Edinburgh: EUP, 1968).

'After Rain' – 'The Playboy in the Wood.'

1969

E3   *Poetry: Introduction 1* (Faber, 1969).

'From the Night-Window' – 'A Removal from Terry Street' – 'The Terry Street Fusiliers' – 'Sunday Morning among the Houses of Terry Street' – 'Late Night Walk Down Terry Street' – 'Young Women in Rollers' – 'The Patricians' – 'A Step out of Line' – 'Narcissus' – 'Cosmologist' – 'The Last Summer' – 'Close of Play' – 'A Dream of Judgement'.

E4   *Scottish Poetry* no 4 (Edinburgh: EUP, 1969).

'Horses in a Suburban Field' – 'The Old Boys'.

1970

E5   *Contemporary Scottish Verse 1959–1969* ed. Norman MacCaig and Alexander Scott (Calder & Boyars, 1970).

'From the Night-Window' – 'Landscape with One Figure' – 'Ships'.

1971

E6   *Corgi Modern Poets in Focus 1*, ed. by Dannie Abse (Corgi, 1971).

'The Patricians' – 'Young Women in Rollers' – 'Incident in the Shop' – 'The Worst of All Loves' – 'A Dream of Random Love' – 'A Poem in Praise of the British' – 'After the War' – 'Under the Stone' – 'The Friendship of Young Poets' – 'Backwaters'.

Also includes a brief 'Introduction' by Abse (pp. 101–5), and a 'Statement' by DD (pp. 106–7).

E7   *New Poems 1970–71* ed. A. Brownjohn, Seamus Heaney, Jon Stallworthy (Hutchinson, 1971).

'The Friendship of Young Poets.'

E8   *The Young British Poets* ed. Jeremy Robson (Chatto, 1971).

'The Hunched' – 'The Clothes Pit' – 'A Removal from Terry Street' – 'After the War' – 'A Dream of Judgement'.

1973

E9   *New Poems 1971–72*, ed. Peter Porter (Hutchinson, 1973).

'Morning Bedroom.'

E10   *Thirteen Poets*, ed. by Dannie Abse for the Poetry Book Society, Christmas 1972.

'The House Next Door.'

E11   *Modern Poets in Focus: 1* ed. Dannie Abse (Woburn Press, 1973).

A reprint of *Corgi Modern Poets in Focus* 1 (1971), q.v.

E12   *Oxford Book of Twentieth-Century English Verse* ed. Philip Larkin (OUP, 1973).

'The Clothes Pit' – 'On Roofs of Terry Street'.

E13   *Poems One Line and Longer*, ed. W. Cole (Grossman, 1973).

'A Removal from Terry Street.'

1974

E14 *Living Poets*, ed. M. Morpurgo and C. Simmons (J. Murray, 1974).

'The Hunched' – 'A Removal from Terry Street'.

E15 *New Poems 1973–74* ed. Stewart Conn (Hutchinson, 1974).

'White Fields' – 'The Competition'.

1975

E16 *Literatura na Swiecie* 51 (7) 1975.

'Terry Street' [a selection of 10 poems translated into Polish verse by Piotr Sommer].

E17 *New Poems 1975*, ed. Patricia Beer (Hutchinson, 1975).

'Stories.'

E18 *Scottish Love Poems*, ed. Antonia Fraser (Edinburgh: Canongate, 1975).

'From the Night Window.'

E19 *Scottish Poetry 8* (Cheadle: Carcanet, 1975).

'The Generations' – 'The Grass'.

E20 *Scottish Short Stories 1975* (Collins, 1975).

'The Flying Machine.'

1976

E21 *Literatura na Swiecie* no 4 (1976).

[9 poems translated into Polish verse by Piotr Sommer].

Also an interview with DD in Polish by Sommer (pp. 308–27).

E22 *Modern Scottish Poetry: an Anthology of the Scottish Renaissance, 1925–1975* ed. Maurice Lindsay (Manchester: Carcanet, 1976).

'Landscape with One Figure' – 'Ships' – 'The Love Day' – 'The New Girls'.

E23 *Nowy Wyraz* no 12 (1976).

[7 poems translated into Polish verse by Piotr Sommer].

Also an introductory article (pp. 89–92) in Polish by Sommer.

E24 *Poetry in the Seventies* ed. Trevor Kneale (Liverpool: Rondo, 1976).

'The Host' – 'Little Rich Rhapsody'.

E25 *Scottish Love Poems* ed. Antonia Fraser (Penguin, 1976).

A reprint of *Scottish Love Poems* (Canongate, 1975), q.v.

1977

E26 *Andrew Cruickshank's Scottish Bedside Book* (Johnston & Bacon, 1977).

'Warriors.'

E27 *New Poems 1977–78* ed. Gavin Ewart (Hutchinson, 1977).

'On Her Picture Left With Him.'

E28 *A Sense of Belonging: Six Scottish Poets of the Seventies*, ed. B. Murray and S. Smyth (Blackie, 1977).

'White Fields' – 'Boys with Coats' – 'The Competition' – 'After the War' – 'Ships' – 'Bring out your Dead' – 'Men of Terry Street' – 'A Removal from Terry Street' – 'Wedding' – 'The Silences'.

1978

E29 *Look North: a Collection of Writing from and about North Humberside* (Lincolnshire & Humberside Arts, 1978).

'New Light on Terry Street' – 'Sunday Morning among the Houses of Terry Street'.

E30 *Modern Scottish Short Stories*, ed. F. Urquhart and Giles Gordon (H. Hamilton, 1978).

'The Blue Gallery.'

E31 *Odra* no 6 (1978).

[3 poems translated into Polish verse by Piotr Sommer].

1980

E32 *Best of the Poetry Year: Poetry Dimension Annual* 7, ed. Dannie Abse (Robson Books, 1980).

'Portrait Photograph, 1915' – 'A Poet in Hull'.

E33 *Literatura na Swiecie* no 8 (1980).

[5 poems translated into Polish verse by Piotr Sommer].

E34 *The Oxford Book of Contemporary Verse 1945–1980* ed. D.J. Enright (OUP,
1980).

'The Patricians' – 'A Removal from Terry Street' – 'Glasgow Schoolboys,
Running Backwards' – 'After the War' – 'Warriors' – 'Remembering
Lunch' – 'The House Next Door' – 'A Dream of Judgement'.

1982

E35 *Faber Book of Modern Verse*, ed. M. Roberts. 4th ed. by Peter Porter
(Faber, 1982).

'A Removal from Terry Street' – 'The Musical Orchard' – 'Supreme
Death' – 'Emblems' – 'The Estuarial Republic'.

E36 *Firebird 1: Writing Today*, ed. T.J. Binding (Penguin/Allen Lane, 1982).

'The Canoes.'

E37 *Literatura na Swiecie* no 10 (1982).

[5 poems translated into Polish verse by Piotr Sommer].

E38 *The Penguin Book of Contemporary British Poetry* ed. Blake Morrison and
Andrew Motion (1982).

'Men of Terry Street' – 'The Clothes Pit' – 'On Roofs of Terry Street' – 'A
Removal from Terry Street' – 'Modern Love' – 'In the Small Hotel' –
'Little Rich Rhapsody' – 'An Artist Waiting in a Country House' –
'Gardeners' – 'The Come-on' – 'Empires' – 'Remembering Lunch' – 'St
Kilda's Parliament: 1879–1979'.

E39 *Problemi* (Ljubljana) 12 (1982).

'Pesmi' [a selection of 7 poems translated into Slovene verse by Denis
Poniz].

E40 *Sovremenost* (Skopje) nos 1–2 (1982).

[16 poems translated into Macedonian verse by B. Guzel].

Also a note on DD by Guzel in Macedonian (pp. 104–5).

1983

E41 *Antologia Nowej Poezji Brytyjskiej* ed. Piotr Sommer (Warsaw, 1983).

[24 poems translated into Polish verse by Piotr Sommer].

Also an Introduction on DD in Polish by Sommer (pp. 60–1).

E42   *A Book of Scottish Verse* ed. R.L. Mackie. 3rd ed. by Maurice Lindsay
        (Hale, 1983).

        'The Drying Green' – 'Listening' – 'The Harp of Renfrewshire' – 'War
        Blinded'.

E43   *Poetry 1945 to 1980*, ed. Anthony Thwaite and John Mole (Longman
        English series, 1983).

        'A Removal from Terry Street' – 'In the Grounds' – 'Stories'.

E44   *A Scottish Poetry Book* ed. Alan Bold (OUP, 1983).

        'Glasgow Schoolboys, Running Backwards.'

E45   *Scottish Short Stories 1983* (Collins, 1983).

        'A Night Out at the Club Harmonica.'

                                    1984

E46   *The Oxford Book of War Poetry* ed. Jon Stallworthy (OUP, 1984).

        'War Blinded.'

E47   *The Poetry of Motion : an Anthology of Sporting Verse*, ed. Alan Bold
        (Edinburgh: Mainstream, 1984).

        'Runners' – 'In Ten Seconds'.

E48   *Seagate II*, ed. Brenda Shaw (Durham: Taxvs, 1984).

        'The Stories' – 'On Misty Law' – 'An Underwear Salesman in a Snowdrift'
        – 'Leaving Dundee'.

                                    1985

E49   *British Poetry since 1945* ed. E. Lucie-Smith. Revised ed. (Penguin, 1985).

        'Men of Terry Street' – 'A Removal from Terry Street' – 'Young Women
        in Rollers' – 'Witch-girl'.

E50   *Me, Myself, I: an Anthology* compiled by Chas White and Christine
        Shepherd (Mary Glasgow Publications, 1985).

        'A Removal from Terry Street.'

E51   *The New Review Anthology* ed. Ian Hamilton (Heinemann, 1985).

        'The Tear' – 'The Arbitration'.

E52   *Poems in Focus* ed. Christopher Martin (OUP, 1985).

'War Blinded.'

E53   *A Second Scottish Poetry Book* ed. Alan Bold (OUP, 1985).

'Lost Gloves' – 'Savings'.

E54   *Zapisy Rozmow: Wywiady z Poetami Brytyjskimi* by Piotr Sommer (Warsaw, 1985).

[4 poems translated into Polish verse by Sommer].

1986

E55   *2 Plus 2: a Collection of International Writing* ed. James Gill, no 5 (Lausanne: Mylabris Press, 1986).

'The Departures of Friends in Childhood.'

E56   *Best Short Stories 1986*, ed. Giles Gordon and David Hughes (Heinemann, 1986).

'Needlework.'

E57   *The Faber Book of Political Verse* ed. Tom Paulin (Faber, 1986).

'Washing the Coins' – 'Green Breeks'.

E58   *London Magazine 1961–85* ed. by Alan Ross (Chatto, 1986).

'Young Women in Rollers.'

E59   *Modern Scottish Poetry: an Anthology of the Scottish Renaissance, 1925–1985*; ed. Maurice Lindsay (Hale, 1986).

'Landscape with One Figure' – 'Ships' – 'The Love Day' – 'The New Girls' – 'The Harp of Renfrewshire' – 'War Blinded'.

E60   *Twelve More Modern Scottish Poets*; ed. by Charles King and Iain Crichton Smith (Hodder, 1986).

'The Patricians' – 'The Worst of All Loves' – 'The Love Day' – 'Love Poem' – 'Landscape with One Figure' – 'The Hunched' – 'After the War' – 'Guerrillas' – 'Caledonian Moonlight' – 'Glasgow Schoolboys, Running Backwards' – 'Witch-girl' – 'Savings' – 'Leaving Dundee'.

1987

E61   *The New Review Anthology* ed. Ian Hamilton (Paladin, 1987).

A reprint of *The New Review Anthology* (Heinemann, 1985), q.v.

E62   *Poetry Book Society Anthology 1987–1988*, ed. G. Clarke (1987).

'The People Before.'

E63   *Voices of Our Kind.* 3rd ed. by Alexander Scott (Chambers, 1987).

'The Harp of Renfrewshire' – 'Loch Music' – 'Ships'.

1988

E64   *A Different Sky: a Poetry Anthology for GCSE*, ed. Peter Ellison (E. Arnold, 1988).

'On Roofs of Terry Street.'

E65   *The Direction of Poetry: an Anthology of Rhymed and Metered Verse written in the English Language since 1975*, ed. Robert Richman (Boston: Houghton Mifflin, 1988).

'Elegy for the Lost Parish' – 'War Blinded'.

E66   *Listy Klubu Pratel Poezie* (Praha, 1988).

[1 poem translated into Czech verse].

Also interview with DD in Czech (pp. 22–3).

E67   *Nagyvilag* (Budapest) no 9 (1988).

[8 poems translated into Hungarian verse by Peter Kantor].

E68   *Savremena Britanska Poezija* ed. Mario Susko and David Harsent (Sarajevo, 1988).

[5 poems translated into Serbo-Croat verse].

E69   *Thirty Years of the Poetry Book Society 1956–1986*, ed. Jonathan Barker (Hutchinson, 1988).

'Empty Wardrobes.'

E70   *Ujiras* (Budapest) no 6 (June 1988).

[7 poems translated into Hungarian verse by Peter Kantor].

1989

E71   *The Best of Scottish Poetry: an Anthology of Contemporary Scottish Verse*; ed. by Robin Bell (Edinburgh: Chambers, 1989).

'The Apple Tree' — 'Loch Music'.

E72 *Contemporary British Poetry: Patterns from the 1950s to the Present Day* by Francesco Dragosei (Milano: Principato, 1989).

'Men of Terry Street' — 'On Roofs of Terry Street' — 'Re-reading Katherine Mansfield's *Bliss and Other Stories*'.

E73 *The Devil and the Giro: Two Centuries of Scottish Stories*, ed. Carl MacDougall (Edinburgh: Canongate, 1989).

'The Canoes.'

E74 *European Poetry in Scotland: an Anthology of Translations*; ed. by Peter France and Duncan Glen (Edinburgh: EUP, 1989).

'To Himself' — 'Between Bus-stop and Home' — 'Two Gestures'.

E75 *The Hutchinson Book of Post-War British Poets*, ed. Dannie Abse (Hutchinson, 1989).

'The Patricians' — 'The Friendship of Young Poets' — 'Leaving Dundee' — 'A Snow-Walk'.

E76 *Macmillan Anthologies of English Literature* vol. 5: The Twentieth Century; ed. by Neil McEwan (Macmillan, 1989).

'The Clear Day' — 'A Summer Night'.

E77 *Ostrovy Plovouci k Severu* (Ceskoslovensky Spisovatel, 1989).

[10 poems translated into Czech verse].

E78 *Steps to Poetry: a Poetry Course for GCSE* by Paul Groves, John Griffin, Nigel Grimshaw (Longman, 1989).

'The Patricians' — 'A Removal from Terry Street' — 'Ballad of the Two Left Hands'.

E79 *Streets of Gold: Contemporary Glasgow Stories* ed. Moira Burgess and Hamish Whyte (Mainstream, 1989).

'Mozart's Clarinet Concerto.'

1990

E80 *The Faber Book of Vernacular Verse* ed. Tom Paulin (Faber, 1990).

'A Removal from Terry Street.'

E81   *Faces in a Crowd: Poems about People*, ed. Anne Harvey (Viking, 1990).

'The Worst of all Loves' – 'The Hunched'.

E82   *Panorama* (Sofia) no 2 (1990).

[4 poems translated into Bulgarian verse].

1991

E83   *Six Poètes Ecossais*, traduits par Serge Baudot (Toulon: Telo Martius, 1991).

'The Kaleidoscope' – 'December' – 'A Rediscovery of Juvenilia' – 'Thirteen Steps and the Thirteenth of March' – 'Second Opinion' – 'Re-reading Katherine Mansfield's *Bliss and Other Stories*' – 'A Summer Night' – 'Anniversaries' – 'My Diaries' – 'Hush'.

Parallel texts: English with facing French verse translation.

SECTION F. REVIEWS BY DOUGLAS DUNN

1969

F1   'Old Faithfuls.' *London Magazine* 9 (7) October 1969, pp. 101–3.

Reviews of: *Fidelities* by Vernon Watkins (Faber); *Selected Poems* Patric Dickinson (Chatto); *Root and Branch* by Jon Stallworthy (Chatto); *The Powers That Be* by J.S. Cunningham (OUP).

1970

F2   'The Great Unread.' *New Statesman* 13 November 1970, pp. 648–9.

Review of: *Sir Walter Scott: the Great Unknown* by Edgar Johnson (H. Hamilton).

F3   'In the City of H.' *New Statesman* 23 January 1970, p. 124.

Review of: *A History of the County of York, East Riding. Vol. 1: The City of Kingston upon Hull*, ed. K.J. Allison (Victoria County History).

F4   'Souvenir.' *New Statesman* 5 June 1970, p. 810.

Reviews of: *A Concise History of Scotland* by Fitzroy Maclean (Thames & Hudson); *A History of Scotland* by Rosalind Mitchison (Methuen); and *The Scottish Insurrection of 1820* by P. Berresford Ellis & Seumas Mac A'Ghobhainn (Gollancz).

1971

F5   'Damaged instruments.' *Encounter* vol. 37 August 1971, pp. 68–74.

Reviews of: *Crossing the Water* by Sylvia Plath (Faber); *Moly* by Thom Gunn (Faber); *Collected Poems* by Alan Dugan (Faber); *In the Happy Valley* by Tony Connor (OUP); *Collected Poems* by George Bruce (EUP); *Poems 1962–69* by Jeff Nuttall (Fulcrum Press); *Poems of Places and People* by George Barker (Faber); *The Moral Rocking-horse* by William Price Turner (Barrie & Jenkins); *A Pint of Bitter* by Alan Bold (Chatto); *Reminiscences of Norma* by Martin Seymour-Smith (Constable); *Penguin Modern Poets 17*: W.S. Graham, Kathleen Raine, David Gascoyne (Penguin); *Penguin Modern Poets 18*: A. Alvarez, Roy Fuller, Anthony Thwaite (Penguin); *Penguin Modern Poets 19*: John Ashbery, Lee Harwood, Tom Raworth (Penguin); *Modern Poetry in Translation*, ed. Ted Hughes & Daniel Weissbort (OUP).

F6   'Last Minstrel.' *New Statesman* 16 April 1971, pp. 533–4.

Review of: *Selected Poems of James Hogg*, ed. D.S. Mack (OUP, 1970).

F7   'Old Morality.' *New Statesman* 13 August 1971, pp. 211–12.

Review of: *Samuel Richardson* by T.C. Duncan Eaves & Ben D. Kimpel (OUP).

F8   'Snatching the bays.' *Encounter* vol. 36 (March, 1971), pp. 65–71.

Reviews of: *Notebook* by Robert Lowell (Faber); *The Complete Poems* by Elizabeth Bishop (Chatto); *Crow* by Ted Hughes (Faber); *The Last of England* by Peter Porter (OUP); *The Loiners* by Tony Harrison (LM Editions); *Selected Poems* by Iain Crichton Smith (Gollancz); *The Penguin Book of Socialist Verse*, ed. Alan Bold (Penguin); *British Poetry since 1945*, ed. Edward Lucie-Smith (Penguin).

1972

DD was a regular reviewer of both poetry and fiction for the TLS over the period 1972–4 when reviews were unsigned.

F9   'A Bridge in Minneapolis.' *Encounter* vol. 38 (May 1972), pp. 73–8.

Reviews of: *The Complete Poems* by Randall Jarrell (Faber); *Love & Fame* by John Berryman (Faber); *Scorpion and Other Poems* by Stevie Smith (Longman); *High Tide in the Garden* by Fleur Adcock (OUP); *Air and Chill Earth* by Molly Holden (Chatto); *The Estuary* by Patricia Beer (Macmillan); *Collected Poems 1958–1970* by George MacBeth (Macmillan); *The Orlando Poems* by George MacBeth (Macmillan); *Regarding Wave* by Gary Snyder (Fulcrum Press); *Breaking & Entering* by X.J. Kennedy (OUP); *The Gavin Ewart Show* by Gavin Ewart (Trigram Press); *Matrix* by Roy Fisher (Fulcrum Press); *The Cut Pages* by Roy Fisher (Fulcrum Press); *Sounds Before Sleep* by James Aitchison (Chatto); *Old Movies* by John Cotton (Chatto).

F10   'Down South.' *New Statesman* 2 June 1972, p. 756.

Reviews of: *The Mortgaged Heart* by Carson McCullers (Barrie & Jenkins); *The Shorter Novels and Stories* by Carson McCullers (Barrie & Jenkins); *Close-Up* by Len Deighton (Cape); *Judas!* by Peter Van Greenaway (Gollancz).

F11   'Holy Deadlines.' *New Statesman* 4 August 1972, p. 167.

Review of: *Samuel Johnson and the Life of Writing* by Paul Fussell (Chatto).

F12   'Ism.' *Encounter* vol. 38 (June, 1972), p. 74.

Review of: *Expressionism* by John Willett (Weidenfeld & Nicolson).

F13   'King Offa alive and dead: ten poets.' *Encounter* vol. 38 (January 1972), pp. 67–74.
Reviews of: *Winter Trees* by Sylvia Plath (Faber); *Discoveries of Bones and Stones* by Geoffrey Grigson (Macmillan); *Selected Poems* by Norman MacCaig (Chatto); *Selected Poems* by Vernon Scannell (Allison & Busby); *Mercian Hymns* by Geoffrey Hill (Deutsch); *Frost-gods* by Harold Massingham (Macmillan); *Fishermen with Ploughs* by George Mackay Brown (Chatto); *Poems New and Selected* by George Mackay Brown (Chatto); *Adventures of the Letter I* by Louis Simpson (OUP); *Ride the Nightmare* by Adrian Mitchell (Cape); *The Order of Chance* by Tom Pickard (Fulcrum Press).

F14   'MacDiarmid.' *The Spectator* 14 October 1972, pp. 585–6.

Reviews of: *The Hugh MacDiarmid Anthology* ed. M. Grieve & A. Scott (Routledge); *Lucky Poet* by Hugh MacDiarmid (Cape).

F15   'Poet and politician.' *Spectator* 5 August 1972, p. 218.

Review of: *Extravagaria* by Pablo Neruda (Cape).

F16   'Quips from the computer age.' *Spectator* 23 December 1972, p. 1010.

Reviews of: *Nobody's Business* by Penelope Gilliatt (Secker); *New Queens for Old* by Gabriel Fielding (Hutchinson); *The Story of a Non-Marrying Man* by Doris Lessing (Cape).

F17   'Strait Gate.' *New Statesman* 28 January 1972, p. 119.

Reviews of: *Mon* by Natsume Soseki (Owen); *Albert's Memorial* by David Cook (Alison/Secker); *Water with Berries* by George Lamming (Longman); *The Captains and the Kings* by Jennifer Johnston (H. Hamilton); *Zoom!* by Peter Townend (Heinemann).

F18   'To still history.' *Encounter* vol. 39 (November 1972), pp. 57–64.

Reviews of: *Lives* by Derek Mahon (OUP); *Cannibals and Missionaries* by John Fuller (Secker); *Terminal Moraine* by James Fenton (Secker); *Desert of the Lions* by Michael Schmidt (Carcanet); *Autobiography* by Adrian Henri (Cape); *After the Merrymaking* by Roger McGough (Cape); *The Irrelevant Song* by Brian Patten (Allen & Unwin); *Our Mutual Scarlet Boulevard* by Barry McSweeney (Fulcrum Press); *Celebrations* by William Plomer (Cape).

1973

F19   'Black Destinies.' *New Statesman* 25 May 1973, pp. 773–5.

Reviews of: *A Woman named Solitude* by Andre Schwarz-Bart (Secker); *They Burn the Thistles* by Yasher Kemal (Collins); *The Distance and the Dark* by Terence De Vere White (Gollancz); and *Sunday Girl* by Lee Langley (Heinemann).

F20   '*Is* poetry in the pity?.' *Ostrich* no 7 1973, pp. [25]–[27].

Review of: *Glasgow Sonnets* by Edwin Morgan (Castlelaw Press, 1972).

F21   'Mechanics of misery: poetry chronicle.' *Encounter* vol. 41 (August 1973), pp. 79–85.

Reviews of: *Collected Poems* by George Oppen (Fulcrum Press); *The White Bird* by Norman MacCaig (Chatto); *Sad Grave of an Imperial Mongoose* by Geoffrey Grigson (Macmillan); *Gloves to the Hangman* by Ted Walker (Cape); *Under the Penthouse* by Val Warner (Carcanet); *Fruits and Vegetables* by Erica Jong (Secker & Warburg); *Poetry of the Committed Individual* ed. by Jon Silkin (Gollancz).

F22   'Moral dandies.' *Encounter* vol. 40 (March 1973), pp. 66–71.

Reviews of: *Epistle to a Godson* by W.H. Auden (Faber); *Preaching to the Converted* by Peter Porter (OUP); *Dr Faust's Sea-spiral Spirit* by Peter Redgrove (Routledge); *Collected Poems* by Donald Davie (Routledge); *Love Poems and Elegies* by Iain Crichton Smith (Gollancz); *Hamlet in Autumn* by Iain Crichton Smith (Lines Review Editions); *Wintering Out* by Seamus Heaney (Faber); *An Ear to the Ground* by Stewart Conn (Hutchinson); *A Local Habitation* by Norman Nicholson (Faber); *Written on Water* by Charles Tomlinson (OUP).

F23   'Native Son.' *New Statesman* 27 July 1973, p. 125.

Review of: *My Scotland* by George MacBeth (Macmillan).

F24   'Oafish liberties: poetry chronicle.' *Encounter* vol. 40 (June 1973), pp. 57–62.

Reviews of: *Ownerless Earth: New and Selected Poems* by Michael Hamburger (Carcanet); *Warrior's Career* by Alan Brownjohn (Macmillan); *Funland* by Dannie Abse (Hutchinson); *Shrapnel* by George MacBeth (Macmillan); *Rest the Poor Struggler* by Glyn Hughes (Macmillan); *Noth* by Daniel

Hughes (Secker & Warburg); *Signs of Life* by Stanley Cook (Peterloo Poets); *The Snowing Globe* by Peter Scupham (Peterloo Poets).

F25 'The revalued Pound.' *The Spectator* 27 January 1973, pp. 107–8.

Reviews of: *Ezra Pound: the Critical Heritage* ed. E. Homburger (Routledge); and *Ezra Pound's Selected Prose* ed. W. Cookson (Faber). [A follow-up letter from Tom Scott in *Spectator*, 10 February, p. 187.]

F26 'The Speckled Hill, the Plover's Shore: Northern Irish poetry today.' *Encounter* vol. 41 (December 1973), pp. 70–6.

Reviews of: *Soundings* ed. Seamus Heaney (Blackstaff); *The Rough Field* by John Montague (Dolmen/OUP); *An Exploded View* by Michael Longley (Gollancz); *The Long Summer Still to Come* by James Simmons (Blackstaff); *Gradual Wars* by Seamus Deane (Irish UP); *New Weather* by Paul Muldoon (Faber).

F27 'Success Story.' *New Statesman* 22 June 1973, p. 932.

Reviews of: *The Malacca Cane* by Mario Soldati (Deutsch); *The Wreck of the Rat Trap* by Terence Wheeler (Macmillan); and *The Monday Rhetoric of the Love Club* by Marvin Cohen (Deutsch).

1974

F28 'All Nature.' *New Statesman* 12 April 1974, p. 522.

Review of: *The Contrary View* by Geoffrey Grigson (Macmillan).

F29 ' "Embusqué Havens": new poetry.' *Encounter* vol. 42 (April 1974), pp. 79–84.

Reviews of: *Tiny Tears* by Roy Fuller (Deutsch); *The Winter Man* by Vernon Scannell (Allison & Busby); *In Memoriam Milena* by Rodney Pybus (Chatto); *The Love Horse* by John Mole (Peterloo Poets); *Definition of a Waterfall* by John Ormond (OUP); *Mountains, Polecats, Pheasants* by Leslie Norris (Chatto).

F30 'The long and the short and the . . .: poetry chronicle.' *Encounter* vol. 42 February 1974), pp. 66–70.

Reviews of: *Powers* by Michael Fried (The Review); *After Dark* by David Harsent (OUP); *Backward into the Smoke* by Colin Falck (Carcanet); *Truce* by David Harsent (Oxford: Sycamore Press); *The Whittrick* by Edwin Morgan (Akros); *From Glasgow to Saturn* by Edwin Morgan (Carcanet); *Wi the Haill Voice* by Edwin Morgan (Carcanet); *Instamatic Poems* by Edwin Morgan (London: McKelvie); *From the Wilderness* by Alasdair Maclean (Gollancz).

F31   'Marginal salvations: new poetry.' *Encounter* vol. 43 (December 1974), pp. 72–8.

Reviews of: *Half-lives* by Erica Jong (Secker & Warburg); *Correspondences* by Anne Stevenson (OUP); *Travelling Under Glass* by Anne Stevenson (OUP); *A Strange Girl in Bright Colours* by Carol Rumens (Quartet).

F32   'Not Belonging.' *New Statesman* 19 July 1974, pp. 86–7.

Review of: *Selected Letters of Edwin Muir*, ed. P.H. Butter (Hogarth).

F33   'Secret countries: recent poetry.' *Encounter* vol. 43 (September 1974), pp. 82–7.

Reviews of: *Complete Poems* by Andrew Young (Secker & Warburg); *Collected Poems* by William Plomer (Cape); *Epistles to Several Persons* by John Fuller (Secker); *The Grey Mare Being the Better Steed* by Pete Morgan (Secker).

F34   'Stained glass.' *New Statesman* 8 November 1974, p. 656.

Review of: *Robert Louis Stevenson* by J. Pope Hennessy (Cape).

1975

F35   'Dislocations and declensions: recent poetry.' *Encounter* vol. 44 (June 1975), pp. 83–6.

Reviews of: *Prehistories* by Peter Scupham (OUP); *West of Elm* by Roger Garfitt (Carcanet); *From the White Room* by David H.W. Grubb (Liverpool: Rondo Publications); *Elsewhere* by David Selzer (Manchester: E.J. Morten); *The Country Over* by Molly Holden (Chatto).

F36   'Holy Dread.' *New Statesman* 22 August 1975, pp. 228–9.

Reviews of: *The Poet's Calling* by Robin Skelton (Heinemann); *The Burnt Child* by Edward Lucie-Smith (Gollancz).

F37   'Mañana is now: new poetry.' *Encounter* vol. 45 (November 1975), pp. 76–81.

Reviews of: *Poems since 1900*, ed. by C. Falck & Ian Hamilton (Macdonald & Janes); *North* by Seamus Heaney (Faber); *The Snow Party* by Derek Mahon (OUP); *Some Sweet Day* by Hugo Williams (OUP).

F38   'Natural disorders: new poetry.' *Encounter* vol. 44 (May 1975), pp. 73–6.

Reviews of: *The Notebooks of Robinson Crusoe* by Iain Crichton Smith (Gollancz); *The World's Room* by Norman MacCaig (Chatto); *Angles and*

Circles by Geoffrey Grigson (Gollancz); *High Island* by Richard Murphy (Faber); *Private and Confidential* by Herbert Lomas (LM Editions).

F39   'Redundant elegance: new poetry.' *Encounter* vol. 44 (March 1975), pp. 85–9.

Reviews of: *The Shires* by Donald Davie (Routledge); *The Way In* by Charles Tomlinson (OUP); *The Principle of Water* by Jon Silkin (Carcanet); *Bicycle Tyre in a Tall Tree* by George Kendrick (Carcanet).

F40   'Ways of booming: new poetry'. *Encounter* vol. 45 (September 1975), pp. 76–80.

Reviews of: *Sons of My Skin* by Peter Redgrove (Routledge); *Collected Poems, 1929–1974* by James Reeves (Heinemann,); *The Lonely Suppers of W.V. Balloon* by Christopher Middleton (Carcanet).

1976

F41   'Cradles of Cold Clay.' *Encounter* vol. 47 (August 1976), pp. 70–5.

Reviews of: *Dialogues etc.* by George Barker (Faber); *The Mountain in the Sea* by John Fuller (Secker); *Bridging Loans* by Rodney Pybus (Chatto); *The New Estate* by Ciaran Carson (Blackstaff Press); *The Nightowl's Dissection* by William Peskett (Secker); *True Life Love Stories* by Michael Foley (Blackstaff Press); *In the Distance* by Dick Davis (Anvil Press); *North Carriageway* by Paul Mills (Carcanet).

F42   'Creeping and Crawling.' *New Statesman* 14 May 1976, p. 654.

Reviews of: *The Supernatural Short Stories of RLS* ed. M. Hayes (Calder); *The Smell of Hay* by Giorgio Bassani (Weidenfeld); *The Bulgarian Exclusive* by Anthony Grey (M. Joseph).

F43   ' "Make It Old!".' *Encounter* vol. 46 (May 1976), pp. 75–81.

Reviews of: *Collected Poems* by Kenneth Allott (Secker); *Poetry of the 1930s* by A.T. Tolley (Gollancz); *From the Joke Shop* by Roy Fuller (Deutsch); *Old Damson-Face* by Bernard Gutteridge (LM Editions); *Driving West* by Patricia Beer (Gollancz); *On the Abthorpe Road* by Simon Curtis (Davis-Poynter); *A Partial Light* by John Mole (Dent).

F44   'Quotidian tasks.' *Encounter* vol. 46 (February 1976), pp. 75–9.

Reviews of: *Living in a Calm Country* by Peter Porter (OUP); *A Song of Good Life* by Alan Brownjohn (Secker); *Sad Ires* by D.J. Enright (Chatto); *Be My Guest!* by Gavin Ewart (Trigram Press); *The Loving Game* by Vernon Scannell (Robson Books).

F45   'The world and his wife: new poetry.' *Encounter* vol. 47 (November 1976), pp. 78–83.

Reviews of: *Season Songs* by Ted Hughes (Faber); *Man Lying on a Wall* by Michael Longley (Gollancz); *The Little Time-Keeper* by Jon Silkin (Carcanet); *Survivals* by Jim Howell (Peterloo Poets); *Mortal Fire* by Peter Dale (Agenda Editions).

1977

F46   'Coteries and commitments.' *Encounter* vol. 48 (June 1977), pp. 58–65.

Review of: *The Little Magazines* by Ian Hamilton (Weidenfeld & Nicolson).

F47   'A forgotten America.' *Listener* 16 June 1977, pp. 789–90.

Review of: *An Autobiographical Novel* by Kenneth Rexroth (Whittet Books).

F48   'Sad Spells: collected poetry.' *Encounter* vol. 49 (August 1977), pp. 52–6.

Reviews of: *Collected Poems 1930–1976* by Richard Eberhart (Chatto); *Collected Poems 1948–1976* by Dannie Abse (Hutchinson); *Behind the Eyes: collected poems and translations* by Edgell Rickword (Carcanet); *Here.Now.-Always* by Edwin Brock (Secker); *Song of the Battery Hen: selected poems 1959–1975* by Edwin Brock (Secker); *To the Gods the Shades: new and collected poems* by David Wright (Carcanet).

F49   'Stories from the psyche.' *Listener* 5 May 1977, p. 596.

Review of: *The Lonely Hunter: a biography of Carson McCullers* by Virginia Spencer Carr (Owen).

F50   'Unhappy families.' *London Magazine* 17(3) August/September 1977, pp. 116–20.

Reviews of: *A Quiet Life* by Beryl Bainbridge (Duckworth); *Turnstiles* by Ursula Holden (LM Editions); *Lovers and Heretics* by John Hale (Gollancz); *How to Save your own Life* by Erica Jong (Secker); *The Demon* by Hubert Selby (Boyars); *Janine* by Phillip Callow (Bodley Head).

F51   'What the tinks sing.' *Listener* 8 December 1977, pp. 757–8.

Reviews of: *Travellers' Songs from England and Scotland* ed. Ewan MacColl and Peggy Seeger (Routledge); and *Hebridean Folksongs* II ed. and tr. J.L. Campbell (OUP).

F52   'Young fools, old fools: new poetry.' *Encounter* vol. 49 (October 1977), pp. 89–94.

Reviews of: *Fan-Mail: Seven Verse Letters* by Clive James (Faber); *The Hinterland* by Peter Scupham (OUP); *Our Ship* by John Mole (Secker); *No*

Fool like an Old Fool by Gavin Ewart (Gollancz); *Tree of Strings* by Norman MacCaig (Chatto); *Rites of Passage* by Edwin Morgan (Carcanet); *The New Divan* by Edwin Morgan (Carcanet); *On the Periphery* by Veronica Forrest-Thomson (Cambridge: Street Editions); *Waking the Dead* by Alasdair Maclean (Gollancz); *A State of Justice* by Tom Paulin (Faber); *Mules* by Paul Muldoon (Faber).

1978

F53 'For the love of Lumb: new poetry.' *Encounter* vol. 50 (January 1978), pp. 78–83.

Reviews of: *Gaudete* by Ted Hughes (Faber); *From Every Chink of the Ark* by Peter Redgrove (Routledge); *Implements in their Places* by W.S. Graham (Faber); *In the Stopping Train* by Donald Davie (Carcanet).

1979

F53A 'Casino.' *Palantir* no. 12 (July 1979), pp. 47–8.

Review of: *Casino* by John Ash (Oasis Books).

F54 'His Dream, His Imitative Thievery.' *New Edinburgh Review* no 48 (November 1979), pp. 29–30.

Review of: *Creatures Tamed by Cruelty* by Ron Butlin (EUSPB).

1980

F55 'Belonging.' *The Honest Ulsterman* no 64, 1980, pp. 85–9.

Review of: *Poets from the North of Ireland* ed. Frank Ormsby (Blackstaff).

F56 'Collected Poems.' *Cencrastus* no 4 (Winter 1980–1), pp. 39–40.

Reviews of: *Collected Poems* by Robert Garioch (Carcanet/Macdonald); *A Day between Weathers* by William J. Tait (P. Harris).

F57 'Everything is susceptible.' *London Review of Books* 20 March 1980, pp. 9–10.

Reviews of: *Poems 1962–1978* by Derek Mahon (OUP); *The Echo Gate* by Michael Longley (Secker); *Poets from the North of Ireland* ed. Frank Ormsby (Blackstaff).

F58 'A Hero of the Quotidian.' *New Edinburgh Review* no 51 (August 1980), pp. 25–6.

Review of: *The Equal Skies* by Norman MacCaig (Chatto).

F59 'Hugh MacDiarmid: inhuman splendours.' *New Edinburgh Review* no 52 (November 1980), pp. 17–21.

Review of: *The Age of MacDiarmid* ed. P.H. Scott & A.C. Davis (Mainstream).

F60   'Pity the Poor Philosophers: Coward's comic genius.' *Encounter* vol. 55 (October 1980), pp. 46–51.

Review of: *Coward Plays* ed. R. Mander & J. Mitchenson. 4 vols (Eyre Methuen),

F61   'The sea-scholar and his befriended disguises.' *Aquarius* no 12 (1980), pp. 128–34.

Review of: *Collected Poems 1942–1977* by W.S. Graham (Faber).

1981

F62   'The bedside profession.' TLS 21 August 1981, p. 952.

Review of: *Way Out in the Centre* by Dannie Abse (Hutchinson).

F63   'Between order and disorder.' TLS 13 March 1981, p. 286.

Review of: *Eleven British Poets* ed. Michael Schmidt (Methuen).

F64   'Blessed beastly place.' *London Review of Books* 5–19 March 1981, pp. 22–3.

Reviews of: *Precipitous City* by T. Royle (Mainstream, 1980); *RLS: a Life Study* by Jenni Calder (H. Hamilton, 1980); *Gillespie* by J. MacDougall Hay (Canongate, 1979); *Scottish Satirical Verse* ed. Edwin Morgan (Carcanet, 1980); *Collected Poems* by Robert Garioch (Carcanet, 1980).

F65   'A free poet in the parish.' TLS 6 November 1981, p. 1289.

Review of: *Trails* by Patrick Williams (Sidgwick & Jackson).

F66   'Hebdominalia.' TLS 29 May 1981, p. 613.

Review of: *The Music of What Happens: poems from The Listener 1965–1980* ed. Derwent May (BBC Publications).

F67   'Imagining the ordinary.' TLS 3 April 1981, p. 389.

Review of: *Unplayed Music* by Carol Rumens (Secker).

F68   'The Newcastle nexus.' TLS 9 January 1981, p. 39.

Review of: *Ten North-East Poets* ed. Neil Astley (Bloodaxe).

F69   'Poetry of inclusion.' TLS 5 June 1981, p. 645.

Review of: *Caviare at the Funeral* by Louis Simpson (OUP).

F70   'The poetry of the Troubles.' TLS 31 July 1981, p. 886.

Review of: *Selected Poems 1963–1980* by Michael Longley (Wake Forest University Press).

F71   'Silence from farm and suburb.' *Poetry Review* 71(4) 1981, pp. 55–6.

Reviews of: *Identities: an anthology of West of Scotland poetry, prose and drama* ed. Geddes Thomson (Heinemann); and *Seven Poets* ed. Chris Carrell (Third Eye Centre).

F72   'Taking no chances.' TLS 24 July 1981, p. 850.

Review of: *The Gregory Awards 1980* ed. Peter Porter & Howard Sergeant (Secker).

1982

F73   'Acute accent.' *Quarto* no 26 March 1982, pp. 11–12.

Reviews of 3 Tony Harrison books: *Continuous* (Collings); *A Kumquat for John Keats* (Bloodaxe); *US Martial* (Bloodaxe).

F74   'Courtly diversions.' TLS 29 January 1982, p. 101.

Review of: *Poems 1911–1940* by F. Scott Fitzgerald (Michigan: Bruccoli Clark Books).

F75   'Elegies in Gaeldom.' TLS 13 August 1982, p. 876.

Review of: *Selected Poems 1955–1980* by Iain Crichton Smith (Edinburgh: Macdonald).

F76   'In the Vale of Tears: new fiction.' *Encounter* vol 58 January 1982, pp. 49–53.

Reviews of: *The Mosquito Coast* by Paul Theroux (Hamilton); *July's People* by Nadine Gordimer (Cape); *The Temptation of Eileen Hughes* by Brian Moore (Cape); *The Death of Men* by Allan Massie (Bodley Head); *The Comfort of Strangers* by Ian McEwan (Cape); *Who was Oswald Fish?* by A.N. Wilson (Secker); *Feelings Have Changed* by P.H. Newby (Faber); *Beyond the Pale* by William Trevor (Bodley Head).

F77   'The poet who spoke his mind.' *Sunday Times* 3 January 1982, p. 34.

Review of: *Robert Browning: the poems* ed. J. Pettigrew & T.J. Collins (Penguin).

F78   'Through furrowed brows.' TLS 8 January 1982, p. 38.

Reviews of: *In the Country of the Black Pig* by Christopher Hope (LM Editions); *Origins* by Peter Howe (Chatto); *Wall* by Roger Garfitt, Frances Horovitz, Richard Kell, Rodney Pybus (LYC Press, Brompton Cumbria).

1983

F79   'Grinding rainbows.' *London Magazine* 23 (5/6) August/September 1983, pp. 109–13.

Reviews of: *111 Poems* by Christopher Middleton (Carcanet); *The Mystery of the Charity of Charles Péguy* by Geoffrey Hill (Deutsch); *Anno Domini* by George Barker (Faber); *An Empty Room* by Leopold Staff (Bloodaxe); *Selected Poems* by Marin Sorescu (Bloodaxe).

F80   'In the arkyards.' TLS 8 July 1983, p. 732.

Review of: *Apprentice* by Tom Gallacher (H. Hamilton).

F81   'Infinite mischief: Lowell's life.' *Encounter* vol. 61 (September/October 1983), pp. 68–76.

Reviews of: *Robert Lowell: a biography* by Ian Hamilton (Faber); and *Robert Lowell: the Nihilist as Hero* by Vereen M. Bell (Harvard UP).

F82   'A piece of real.' *London Magazine* 23 (3) June 1983, pp. 74–8.

Review of: *Collected Poems* by Peter Porter (OUP).

F83   'The supernatural *frisson*.' TLS 1 April 1983, p. 324.

Review of: *Andrina and Other Stories* by George Mackay Brown (Chatto/Hogarth).

1984

F84   'The dance of discontent.' TLS 5 October 1984, p. 1124.

Reviews of: *The Exiles* by Iain Crichton Smith (Carcanet); and *The Dead Kingdom* by John Montague (OUP).

F85   'Inscriptions and snapshots.' TLS 20 January 1984, p. 54.

Reviews of: *Voyages* by George Mackay Brown (Chatto/Hogarth); and *Grafts/Takes* by Edwin Morgan (Mariscat Press).

F86   'Ordinary life.' *London Magazine* 23 (12) March 1984, pp. 92–5.

Review of: *Collected Poems 1952–83* by Alan Brownjohn (Secker).

F87   'Purgatorial pedagogy.' TLS 20 April 1984, p. 422.

Review of: *Mr Trill in Hades and other stories* by Iain Crichton Smith (Gollancz).

F88   'A quest for Clydeside.' TLS 29 June 1984, p. 736.

Review of: *Journeyman* by Tom Gallacher (H. Hamilton).

1985

F89 'Abrasive encounters.' *Glasgow Herald (Weekender)* 21 December, 1985, p. 11.

Reviews of: *V* by Tony Harrison (Bloodaxe); *Writing Home* by Hugo Williams (OUP); *Katerina Brac* by Christopher Reid (Faber).

F90 'All the options open up in a literary consummation.' *Glasgow Herald (Weekender)* 7 December 1985, p. 11.

Review of: *The Lover* by Marguerite Duras (Collins).

F91 'American version of Iris Murdoch?' *Glasgow Herald (Weekender)* 26 October 1985, p. 11.

Review of: *Men and Angels* by Mary Gordon (Cape).

F92 'Country tales austere and piercing.' *Glasgow Herald (Weekender)* 9 November 1985, p. 11.

Review of: *Where the Apple Ripens* by Jessie Kesson (Chatto).

F93 'Dutch courage.' *Glasgow Herald (Weekender)* 16 November 1985, p. 11.

Review of: *The Assault* by Harry Mulisch (Collins Harvill).

F94 'Echoes in the mind.' *Glasgow Herald (Weekender)* 30 November 1985, p. 11.

Reviews of: *The Stories of Mary Lavin, Vol. III* (Constable); *Family Likeness* by Mary Lavin (Constable).

F95 'Embracing history.' TLS 26 April 1985, p. 470.

Reviews of: *Sonnets from Scotland* by Edwin Morgan (Mariscat); *These Words: Weddings and After* by William McIlvanney (Mainstream); *Spring's Witch* by Brian McCabe (Mariscat).

F96 'Flipper at the future.' *Glasgow Herald (Weekender)* 2 November 1985, p. 11.

Review of: *Galapagos* by Kurt Vonnegut (Cape).

F97 'Grave-robbing touch to products from the literary laboratories.' *Glasgow Herald (Weekender)* 12 October 1985, p. 11.

Reviews of: *Black Venus* by Angela Carter (Chatto); and *Blood Libels* by Clive Sinclair (Allison & Busby).

F98   'Invitations to surrender.' TLS 1 March 1985, p. 239.

       Reviews of: *Complete Poems* by Hart Crane, ed. by B. Weber (Bloodaxe).
       [Also follow-up letters: 'Hart Crane' in TLS 15 March, p. 287 and 29
       March, p. 357].

F99   'Masterly psycho dramas.' *Glasgow Herald (Weekender)* 5 October 1985,
       p. 11.

       Reviews of: *The Good Apprentice* by Iris Murdoch (Chatto); *A Family
       Madness* by Thomas Keneally (Hodder).

F100   'New poetry.' *Books in Scotland* no 18 (1985), pp. 13–14.

       Reviews of: *The Poetical Works of Andrew Young* (Secker); *Selected Poems of
       Edwin Morgan* (Carcanet); *Selected Poems of Iain Crichton Smith* (Carcanet).

F101   'Patois merchant.' *Glasgow Herald (Weekender)* 28 September 1985,
       p. 11.

       Review of: *A Chancer* by James Kelman (Polygon).

F102   'The politics of hate.' *Glasgow Herald (Weekender)* 21 September 1985,
       p. 12.

       Reviews of: *The Good Terrorist* by Doris Lessing (Cape); *Gentlemen in
       England* by A.N. Wilson (H. Hamilton).

F103   'Shallow burrowing into deep waters.' *Glasgow Herald (Weekender)* 7
       September 1985, p. 11.

       Review of: *The Garish Day* by Rachel Billington (H. Hamilton).

F104   'Soul-shaking with sex.' *Glasgow Herald (Weekender)* 23 November 1985,
       p. 12.

       Review of: *The Awakening of George Darroch* by Robin Jenkins
       (Waterfront/Glasgow Herald).

F105   'Taste of truth from New York.' *Glasgow Herald (Weekender)* 14
       December 1985, p. 12.

       Review of: *Later the Same Day* by Grace Paley (Virago Press).

F106   'Time for mixed emotions.' *Glasgow Herald (Weekender)* 19 October
       1985, p. 11.

       Reviews of: *Life Goes On* by Alan Sillitoe (Granada); *The Golden Days* by
       John Braine (Methuen).

1986

F107 'American allegory.' *Glasgow Herald (Weekender)* 29 March 1986 p. 11.

Review of: *Free Agents* by Max Apple (Faber).

F108 'Apartheid punctured.' *Glasgow Herald (Weekender)* 31 May 1986, p. 11.

Review of: *The Innocents* by Carolyn Slaughter (Viking).

F109 'Blistering send-up of South-East.' *Glasgow Herald (Weekender)* 15 February 1986, p. 11.

Review of: *Redhill Rococo* by Shena Mackay (Heinemann).

F110 'Chic scandal-mongering.' *Glasgow Herald (Weekender)* 1 November, 1986, p. 12.

Review of: *Answered Prayers: the unfinished novel* by Truman Capote (Hamilton).

F111 'Class angle on a mid-life crisis.' *Glasgow Herald (Weekender)* 12 April 1986, p. 11.

Review of: *Reasonable Doubt* by Joan Lingard (H. Hamilton).

F112 'Doomed jester's tragic destiny.' *Glasgow Herald (Weekender)* 1 March 1986, p. 11.

Review of: *Carpenter's Gothic* by William Gaddis (Deutsch).

F113 'Exploring lurid limits of craving for amusement.' *Glasgow Herald (Weekender)* 26 July 1986, p. 11.

Review of: *Before the Cock Crow* by Simon Raven (Muller).

F114 'Flawed morality of power.' *Glasgow Herald (Weekender)* 25 January 1986, p. 13.

Review of: *Aspects of Feeling* by Peter Vansittart (Peter Owen).

F115 'High jinks in Switzerland.' *Glasgow Herald (Weekender)* 30 August 1986, p. 12.

Review of: *Private Accounts* by Ursula Bentley (Secker).

F116 'In whom the language lives.' *Poetry Review* 76(3) October 1986, pp. 4–6.

Review of: *Less than One* by Joseph Brodsky (Viking).

F117   'Interior insights.' *Glasgow Herald (Weekender)* 6 September 1986, p. 11.

      Review of: *A Long Weekend with Marcel Proust* by Ronald Frame (Bodley Head).

F118   'A Jewish family in decline.' *Glasgow Herald (Weekender)* 8 March 1986, p. 11.

      Review of: *The Afternoon Sun* by David Pryce-Jones (Weidenfeld & Nicolson).

F119   'Journey to nowhere.' *Glasgow Herald (Weekender)* 19 April 1986, p. 11.

      Review of: *A Vocation* by David Wheldon (Bodley Head).

F120   'Keys to sexual expertise.' *Glasgow Herald (Weekender)* 5 August 1986, p. 11.

      Review of: *The Pianoplayers* by Anthony Burgess (Hutchinson).

F121   'A literary revolution.' *Glasgow Herald (Weekender)* 10 May 1986, p. 12.

      Review of: *An Insular Possession* by Timothy Mo (Chatto).

F122   'Manoeuvres.' *The Irish Review* no 1 (1986), pp. 84–90.

      Review of: *The Faber Book of Contemporary Irish Poetry* ed. Paul Muldoon (Faber).

F123   'Master of fiction from Peru.' *Glasgow Herald (Weekender)* 11 October 1986, p. 7.

      Reviews of: *The Time of the Hero*; *The Green House*; *Aunt Julia and the Scriptwriter* (Picador); *The War of the End of the World* (Faber); *The Real Life of Alejandro Mayta* (Faber) – all by Mario Vargas Llosa.

F124   'Mood indigo in Tokyo.' *Glasgow Herald (Weekender)* 9 August 1986, p. 11.

      Review of: *Soldiers in Hiding* by Richard Wiley (Chatto).

F125   'New clothes for an emperor.' *Glasgow Herald (Weekender)* 27 September 1986, p. 11.

      Review of: *Augustus* by Allan Massie (Bodley Head).

F126   'No balm in this Gilead.' *Glasgow Herald (Weekender)* 15 March 1986, p. 11.

      Review of: *The Handmaid's Tale* by Margaret Atwood (Cape).

F127 'Overdose of reality.' *Glasgow Herald (Weekender)* 13 September 1986, p. 11.

Reviews of: *News from Nowhere* by David Caute (Hamilton); and *Innocence* by Penelope Fitzgerald (Collins).

F128 'Party mania.' *Glasgow Herald (Weekender)* 26 April 1986, p. 11.

Review of: *Gerald's Party* by Robert Coover (Heinemann); and *Queer* by William Burroughs (Picador).

F129 'Playful approach to military satire.' *Glasgow Herald (Weekender)* 12 July 1986, p. 12.

Review of: *The Shrapnel Academy* by Fay Weldon (Hodder).

F130 'Radiance of the banal.' *Glasgow Herald (Weekender)* 20 September 1986, p. 11.

Review of: *Staring at the Sun* by Julian Barnes (Cape).

F131 'Sad and radiant poet.' *Glasgow Herald (Weekender)* 11 January 1986, p. 12.

Review of: *Randall Jarrell's letters* ed. Mary Jarrell (Faber).

F132 'Satire with subversive edge.' *Glasgow Herald (Weekender)* 1 February 1986, p. 13.

Review of: *The Prick of Noon* by Peter de Vries (Gollancz).

F133 'Satirical trip to Ruritania.' *Glasgow Herald (Weekender)* 8 February 1986, p. 12.

Review of: *Nowhere* by Thomas Berger (Methuen).

F134 'Scottish contradictions'. TLS 25 July 1986, pp. 803–4.

Review of: *The Letters of Robert Burns*, ed. J.D. Ferguson, 2nd ed, by G.R. Roy (OUP, 1985).

F135 'Squalor made beautiful.' *Glasgow Herald (Weekender)* 18 January 1986, p. 11.

Reviews of: *The House of the Solitary Maggot* by James Purdy (Peter Owen); *The Adventures of Robina* by Emma Tennant (Faber); *Paradise* by Hugh Fleetwood (Hamilton).

F136 'A Sunflower in the West.' *Glasgow Herald (Weekender)* 28 June 1986, p. 11.

Review of: *Sunflower* by Rebecca West (Virago).

F137   'Trying to paint God by numbers.' *Glasgow Herald (Weekender)* 18 October 1986, p. 11.

Review of: *Roger's Version* by John Updike (Deutsch).

F138   'Uncertainty in the face of enjoyment.' *Glasgow Herald (Weekender)* 5 April 1986, p. 11.

Review of: *Memoirs of the Many in One* by Patrick White (Cape); and *The Fisher King* by Anthony Powell (Heinemann).

1987

F139   'African adversaries.' *Glasgow Herald (Weekender)* 10 October 1987, p. 11.

Review of: *Anthills of the Savannah* by Chinua Achebe (Heinemann).

F140   'Afterglow of loving.' *Glasgow Herald (Weekender)* 9 May 1987, p. 12.

Review of: *Moon Tiger* by Penelope Lively (Deutsch).

F141   'A blast from the past with Hemingway.' *Glasgow Herald (Weekender)* 7 February 1987, p. 12.

Review of: *The Garden of Eden* by Ernest Hemingway (Hamilton).

F142   'Blazing broomsticks.' *Glasgow Herald (Weekender)* 23 May 1987, p. 11.

Review of: *Witchcraft* by Nigel Williams (Faber).

F143   'Candid critic without malice.' *Glasgow Herald (Weekender)* 20 June 1987, p. 11.

Review of: *Collected Prose* by Robert Lowell (Faber).

F144   'Catching drift of sea parable.' *Glasgow Herald (Weekender)* 6 June 1987, p. 11.

Review of: *Close Quarters* by William Golding (Faber).

F145   'Critics' silver darling.' *Glasgow Herald (Weekender)* 11 July 1987, p. 11.

Review of: *The Novels of Neil M. Gunn: a critical study* by Margery McCulloch (Scottish Academic Press).

F146   'Decency takes a hard knock.' *Glasgow Herald (Weekender)* 7 March 1987, p. 12.

Review of: *B-Movie* by Stan Barstow (Joseph).

F147 'A disconcerting portrait of US.' *Glasgow Herald (Weekender)* 18 July 1987, p. 12.

Review of: *The Barracks* by Tobias Wolff (Cape).

F148 'Diverse talent.' *Punch* 26 August 1987, p. 54.

Reviews of: *The Moon Disposes* by Peter Redgrove (Secker); *In the Hall of the Saurians* by Peter Redgrove (Secker); *A Jump Start* by James Lasdun (Secker); *Cat's Whisker* by Philip Gross (Faber); *Legend of True Labour* by Simon Lapington (Secker).

F149 'England going to the dogs.' *Glasgow Herald (Weekender)* 2 May 1987, p. 11.

Review of: *The Radiant Way* by Margaret Drabble (Weidenfeld & Nicolson).

F150 'Erotic predicament of the times.' *Glasgow Herald (Weekender)* 24 October 1987, p. 11.

Review of: *More Die of Heartbreak* by Saul Bellow (Alison Press/Secker).

F151 'Goodbye happiness.' *Glasgow Herald (Weekender)* 30 May 1987, p. 14.

Review of: *Bluebeard's Egg* by Margaret Atwood (Cape).

F152 'Human wastes of Alaska.' *Glasgow Herald (Weekender)* 18 April 1987, p. 12.

Review of: *Bad Guys* by Elizabeth Arthur (Macmillan).

F153 'I am a theatre.' *Glasgow Herald (Weekender)* 14 March 1987, p. 11.

Review of: *The Counterlife* by Philip Roth (Cape).

F154 'Imagined and real.' *Glasgow Herald (Weekender)* 5 September 1987, p. 12.

Review of: *Chatterton* by Peter Ackroyd (Hamilton).

F155 'Jungle of emotions.' *Glasgow Herald (Weekender)* 27 June 1987, p. 12.

Review of: *Rainforest* by Jenny Diski (Jane/Methuen).

F156 'Life worse than it was.' *Glasgow Herald (Weekender)* 29 August 1987, p. 11.

Review of: *Dreams of Dead Women's Handbags* by Shena Mackay (Heinemann).

F157   'Losses & Landfalls: three poets.' *Encounter* vol. 69 (June 1987), pp. 50–4.

Reviews of: *Letter from Tokyo* by Anthony Thwaite (Hutchinson); *Homing* by John Mole (Secker); *The Frighteners* by Sean O'Brien (Bloodaxe).

F158   'Luckless lady of the lake.' *Glasgow Herald (Weekender)* 4 April 1987, p. 11.

Review of: *The Maid of Buttermere* by Melvyn Bragg (Hodder).

F159   'Luminous Verse.' *Punch* 24 June 1987, p. 62.

Reviews of: *The Haw Lantern* by Seamus Heaney (Faber); *Meeting the British* by Paul Muldoon (Faber); *The Ballad of the Yorkshire Ripper* by Blake Morrison (Chatto).

F160   'Mixed-up black magic.' *Glasgow Herald (Weekender)* 19 September 1987, p. 12.

Review of: *The Sadness of Witches* by Janice Elliott (Hodder).

F161   'No return from Timbuctoo.' *Glasgow Herald (Weekender)* 21 November 1987, p. 14.

Review of: *Laing* by Ann Schlee (Macmillan).

F162   'Oxford without effort.' *Glasgow Herald (Weekender)* 8 August 1987, p. 12.

Review of: *The Noonday Devil* by Alan Judd (Hutchinson).

F163   'The patter of tiny poets.' *Punch* 15 April 1987, p. 37.

Review of: *First Lines*, ed. Jon Stallworthy (Carcanet).

F164   'Politics of crime in Australia.' *Glasgow Herald (Weekender)* 21 February 1987, p. 11.

Review of: *Cassidy* by Morris West (Hodder).

F165   'Sanity punctured.' *Glasgow Herald (Weekender)* 3 May 1987, p. 11.

Review of: *The Bay of Silence* by Lisa St Aubin de Teran (Cape); and *Satyrday* by Duncan Fallowell (Macmillan).

F166   'Scot at the centre.' *Glasgow Herald (Weekender)* 12 September 1987, p. 11.

Reviews of: *The Book and the Brotherhood* by Iris Murdoch (Chatto); and *The Child in Time* by Ian McEwan (Cape).

F167 'A Scot on the loose.' *Glasgow Herald (Weekender)* 15 August 1987, p. 11.

Review of: *Whereabouts* by Alastair Reid (Canongate).

F168 'Scotland as nemesis.' *Glasgow Herald (Weekender)* 26 September 1987, p. 11.

Review of: *The New Confessions* by William Boyd (Hamilton).

F169 'Shadow of Holocaust.' *Glasgow Herald (Weekender)* 11 April 1987, p. 12.

Review of: *To the City* by Gillian Tindall (Hutchinson).

F170 'Shallow flows the don.' *Glasgow Herald (Weekender)* 21 March 1987, p. 11.

Review of: *After a Fashion* by Stanley Middleton (Hutchinson).

F171 'Stark exposures.' *Glasgow Herald (Weekender)* 4 May 1987, p. 11.

Review of: *Temporary Shelter* by Mary Gordon (Bloomsbury).

F172 'Step towards the real escape from dead-end.' *Glasgow Herald (Weekender)* 12 December 1987, p. 12.
Review of: *The New York Trilogy* by Paul Auster (Faber).

F173 'A tale of Everywoman.' *Glasgow Herald (Weekender)* 22 August 1987, p. 11.

Review of: *Her Story* by Dan Jacobson (Deutsch); and *A Friend from England* by Anita Brookner (Cape).

F174 'A teasing talent for the bizarre.' *Glasgow Herald (Weekender)* 1 August 1987, p. 11.

Review of: *Inspecting the Vaults* by Eric McCormack (Viking).

F175 'This side of parable.' *Glasgow Herald (Weekender)* 13 June 1987, p. 12.

Review of: *The Garden of the Villa Mollini* by Rose Tremain (Hamilton).

F176 'True freedom through work.' *Glasgow Herald (Weekender)* 25 April, 1987, p. 12.

Review of: *The Wrench* by Primo Levi (Joseph).

F177 'Vision of Africa.' *Glasgow Herald (Weekender)* 28 March 1987, p. 11

Review of: *A Sport of Nature* by Nadine Gordimer (Cape).

F178   'When the twain meet.' *Glasgow Herald (Weekender)* 17 October 1987, p. 12.

Review of: *Three Continents* by Ruth Prawer Jhabvala (Murray).

F179   'Williams tells it like it is . . . .' *Glasgow Herald (Weekender)* 28 February 1987, p. 11.

Review of: *The Doctor Stories* by William Carlos Williams (Faber).

F180   'World-love and enjoyments.' *Poetry Review* 77(2) 1987, PP. 44–5.

Review of: *Devotions* by Lawrence Sail (Secker).

1988

F181   'Adventures in abuse of rebel talent.' *Glasgow Herald (Weekender)* 6 August 1988, p. 10.

Review of: *Burton: a biography of Sir Richard Burton* by B. Farwell (Viking).

F182   'Against charlatanism and skulduggery.' *Glasgow Herald (Weekender)* 9 July 1988, p. 10.

Review of: *The Jacobite Challenge* ed. Eveline Cruickshanks and Jeremy Black (Donald).

F183   'Bad to worse.' *Glasgow Herald (Weekender)* 14 May 1988, p. 8.

Review of: *The Joy of Bad Verse* by Nicholas T. Parsons (Collins).

F184   'Blazing path to silence.' *Glasgow Herald (Weekender)* 21 May 1988, p. 8.

Review of: *Byron's Travels* by Allan Massie (Sidgwick & Jackson).

F185   'Caribbean Beat.' *Punch* 25 March 1988, p. 46.

Reviews of: *The Arkansas Testament* by Derek Walcott (Faber); *Archaic Figure* by Amy Clampitt (Faber); *Voice-over* by Norman MacCaig (Chatto); *Fifty Poems* by Ian Hamilton (Faber).

F186   'Casing the joint with comrade tourists.' *Glasgow Herald (Weekender)* 23 July 1988, p. 8.

Review of: *America through Russian Eyes*, Olga Hasty & Susanne Fusso, editors (Yale UP).

F187   'Charting the demise of liberal England.' *Glasgow Herald (Weekender)* 13 August 1988, p. 10.

Review of: *The Disturbance Fee* by Edward Blishen (H. Hamilton).

F188 'Chinese whisper of great things to come.' *Glasgow Herald (Weekender)* 19 March 1988, p. 11.

Review of: *Chinese Whispers* by Robert Sproat (Faber).

F189 'Confessions of an intruder in literature.' *Glasgow Herald (Weekender)* 3 September 1988, p. 18.

Review of: *James Hogg: the Growth of a Writer* by David Groves (SAP).

F190 'Deflecting ridicule by being ridiculous.' *Glasgow Herald (Weekender)* 30 July 1988, p. 8.

Review of: *That Singular Person called Lear* by Susan Chitty (Weidenfeld & Nicolson).

F191 'Evocation of white South African phobia.' *Glasgow Herald (Weekender)* 20 February 1988, p. 12.

Review of: *White Boy Running* by Christopher Hope (Secker).

F192 'From industry and pleasure.' TLS 26 February 1988, p. 213.

Review of: *The Lantern Bearers and Other Essays by R.L. Stevenson* ed. J. Treglown (Chatto).

F193 'From the video box and other epics.' *Punch* 24 June 1988, pp. 45–6.

Reviews of: *Themes on a Variation* by Edwin Morgan (Carcanet); *The Grey among the Green* by John Fuller (Chatto); *In the Hot-House* by Alan Jenkins (Chatto); *Monterey Cypress* by Lachlan Mackinnon (Chatto); *My Darling Camel* by Selima Hill (Chatto).

F194 'Gin and tears.' *Glasgow Herald (Weekender)* 16 April 1988, p. 8.

Review of: *Dorothy Parker: What fresh Hell is this?* by Marion Meade (Heinemann).

F195 'Hem lines.' *Glasgow Herald (Weekender)* 7 May 1988, p. 12.

Review of: *The Faces of Hemingway* by Denis Brian (Grafton).

F196 'In the shadow of the Nazis.' *Glasgow Herald (Weekender)* 30 January 1988, p. 11.

Review of: *Mother's Girl* by Elaine Feinstein (Hutchinson).

F197 'Injustice better to forget than to forgive.' *Glasgow Herald (Weekender)* 16 July 1988, p. 8.

Review of: *Fear No Evil* by Natan Sharansky (Weidenfeld & Nicolson).

F198   'Jacarandas and glass verandahs.' *Glasgow Herald (Weekender)* 26 March 1988, p. 12.

Review of: *Oscar and Lucinda* by Peter Carey (Faber).

F199   'Larkin's Golden Treasury.' *Punch* 21 October 1988, pp. 35–8.

Review of: *Philip Larkin: Collected Poems* ed. A. Thwaite (Marvell/Faber).

F200   'Looking with a listening eye.' *Glasgow Herald (Weekender)* 18 June 1988, p. 10.

Review of: *Letters on Cezanne* by Rainer Maria Rilke, ed. by Clara Rilke (Cape).

F201   'Man of letters who led from behind bars.' *Glasgow Herald (Weekender)* 27 August 1988, p. 10.

Review of: *Gramsci: Prison Letters* ed. Hamish Henderson (Edinburgh Review).

F202   'Mrs Pilgrim.' *Glasgow Herald (Weekender)* 30 April 1988, p. 8.

Review of: *S: a Novel* by John Updike (Deutsch).

F203   'Naked city of eight million storeys.' *Glasgow Herald (Weekender)* 9 April 1988, p. 12.

Review of: *Imperial City: the Rise and Rise of New York* by Geoffrey Moorhouse (Hodder).

F204   'Nervous life: counting the cost of poetry.' *Glasgow Herald (Weekender)* 24 September 1988, p. 20.

Reviews of: *Eliot's New Life* by Lyndall Gordon (OUP); *The letters of T.S. Eliot* Vol. 1 (Faber).

F205   'Oceans away.' *The Listener* 18 August 1988, pp. 24–5.

Reviews of: *Whale Nation* by Heathcote Williams (Cape); and *Men's Lives* by Peter Matthiesson (Collins Harvill).

F206   'Out of his head.' *Observer* 11 September 1988, p. 43.

Review of: *MacDiarmid: a Critical Biography* by Alan Bold (J. Murray).

F207   'Paging the Oracle.' *Punch* 15 January 1988, pp. 44–5.

Reviews of: *The Automatic Oracle* by Peter Porter (OUP); *Fivemiletown* by Tom Paulin (Faber); *The Sunset Maker* by Donald Justice (Anvil).

F208 'Poetic career towards this sporting life.' *Glasgow Herald (Weekender)* 4 June 1988, p. 10.

Review of: *Coastwise Lights* by Alan Ross (Collins Harvill).

F209 'The poetry says Yes.' *Irish Literary Supplement* 7(2) Fall 1988, p. 38.

Review of: *The Irish for No* by Ciaran Carson (Wake Forest UP, 1987).

F210 'Power of the poet.' *Glasgow Herald (Weekender)* 11 June 1988, p. 10.

Review of: *The Government of the Tongue* by Seamus Heaney (Faber).

F211 'Remember the poet but forget her fate.' *Glasgow Herald (Weekender)* 5 March 1988, p. 13.

Review of: *Sylvia Plath: a biography* by Linda Wagner-Martin (Chatto).

F212 'Return fire from the Irish Cruiser.' *Glasgow Herald (Weekender)* 12 March 1988, p. 11.

Review of: *Passion and Cunning, and other essays* by Conor Cruise O'Brien (Weidenfeld & Nicolson).

F213 'Ruffian brawler.' *Glasgow Herald (Weekender)* 28 May 1988, p. 10.

Review of: *Christopher Marlowe and Canterbury* by William Urry (Faber).

F214 'Shadow life.' *Glasgow Herald (Weekender)* 17 September 1988, p. 18.

Review of: *In Search of J.D. Salinger* by Ian Hamilton (Heinemann).

F215 'Short stories long on pessimism.' *Glasgow Herald (Weekender)* 20 August 1988, p. 8.

Review of: *I Can Sing, Dance, Roller-skate and Other Stories* (Collins).

F216 'Small-town tales of gentle realism.' *Glasgow Herald (Weekender)* 16 January 1988, p. 11.

Review of: *Leaving Home* by Garrison Keillor (Faber).

F217 'Stand-up, the real Defoe.' *Glasgow Herald (Weekender)* 27 February 1988, p. 11.

Review of: *The Canonisation of Daniel Defoe* by P.N. Furbank and W.R. Owens (Yale UP).

F218 'Suffering seasons and the brief Spring.' *Glasgow Herald (Weekender)* 25 June 1988, p. 10.

Review of: *Prague Farewell: a Life in Czechoslovakia 1941–68* by Heda
Margolius Kovaly (Gollancz).

F219   'The taste of the time.' TLS 2 December 1988, p. 1334.

Review of: *The Amis Anthology: a Personal Choice of English Verse*, by
Kingsley Amis (Century Hutchinson).

F220   'Towards crack-up.' *Glasgow Herald (Weekender)* 2 July 1988, p. 14.

Review of: *Tchaikovsky: a Biography* by Alan Kendall (Bodley Head).

F221   'A voice reveals another.' TLS 25 November 1988, p. 1300.

Review of: *Selected Poems of Philippe Jaccottet* trans. by Derek Mahon
(Penguin).

F222   'Waste land of youth.' *Glasgow Herald (Weekender)* 13 February 1988,
p. 11.

Review of: *The Savage and the City in the Work of T.S. Eliot* by Robert
Crawford (OUP).

F223   'Whaddaya, whaddaya.' *Glasgow Herald (Weekender)* 6 February 1988,
p. 12.

Review of: *The Bonfire of the Vanities* by Tom Wolfe (Cape).

1989

F224   'Anachronistic drift.' *Glasgow Herald (Weekender)* 20 May 1989, p. 20.

Review of: *Philip Larkin, the Marvell Press and Me* by Jean Hartley
(Carcanet).

F225   'Anger in eggshell.' *Glasgow Herald (Weekender)* 11 March 1989, p. 20.

Review of: *Dear Alec: Guinness at 75*, ed. R. Harwood (Hodder).

F226   'Awful Bitter.' *Listener* 9 March 1989, p. 31.

Review of: *A Disaffection* by James Kelman (Secker).

F227   'Bird path of an exile.' *Glasgow Herald (Weekender)* 13 May 1989, p. 20.

Reviews of: Kenneth White. *The Bird Path* [and] *Travels in the Drifting
Dawn* (both Mainstream).

F228   'Catching the viper.' *Glasgow Herald (Weekender)* 15 July 1989, p. 20.

Review of: *Congenial Spirits: the Letters of Virginia Woolf*, ed. J.T. Banks (Hogarth).

F229 'The colour of angels.' *Evening Standard* 16 March 1989.

Review of: *Mandela's Earth* by Wole Soyinka (Deutsch).

F230 'Combating the climate.' *Glasgow Herald (Weekender)* 3 June 1989, p. 20.

Review of: *The Literature of Region and Nation*, ed. R.P. Draper (Macmillan).

F231 'Common lessons of twined hard schools.' *Glasgow Herald (Weekender)* 25 March 1989, p. 18.

Review of: *My Companions in the Bleak House* by Eva Kanturkova (Quartet).

F232 'A cool frenzy for the macabre.' *Glasgow Herald (Weekender)* 24 June 1989, p. 20.

Review of: *The Paradise Motel* by Eric McCormack (Bloomsbury).

F233 'Delicacy and muscle.' *Glasgow Herald (Weekender)* 29 April 1989, p. 22.

Review of: *Sir Frederick Treves: the Extraordinary Edwardian* by Stephen Trombley (Routledge).

F234 'Disturbance puzzles.' *Glasgow Herald (Weekender)* 27 May 1989, p. 20.

Review of: *New and Collected Poems* by Richard Wilbur (Faber).

F235 'From here to modernity.' *Glasgow Herald (Weekender)* 8 April 1989, p. 20.

Review of: *A History of Our Own Times* by Ford Madox Ford (Carcanet).

F236 'Getting his jotters.' *Glasgow Herald (Weekender)* 1 July 1989, p. 20.

Review of: Dylan Thomas. *The Notebook Poems 1930–1934*, ed. R. Maud (Dent).

F237 'Goin' Dixie.' *Glasgow Herald (Weekender)* 15 April 1989, p. 20.

Review of: *A Turn in the South* by V.S. Naipaul (Viking).

F238 'The Ironworks Lady.' *Glasgow Herald (Weekender)* 4 March 1989, p. 22.

Review of: *Lady Charlotte: a Biography of the Nineteenth Century* by R. Guest & A.V. John (Weidenfeld & Nicolson).

F239   'Mattress affairs.' *Glasgow Herald (Weekender)* 11 February 1989, p. 18.

       Review of: *The Memoir of Marco Parenti: A Life in Medici Florence* by Mark
       Phillips (Heinemann).

F240   'Nemo art.' *Glasgow Herald (Weekender)* 25 February 1989, p. 18.

       Review of: *The Devil and Mr Barnes* by Howard Greenfeld (Boyars).

F241   'Nudging.' *Glasgow Herald (Weekender)* 18 February 1989, p. 18.

       Review of: *Speak Silence* by Idris Parry (Carcanet).

F242   'On the flip side.' TLS 31 March 1989, p. 344.

       Review of: *The Grown-Ups* by Victoria Glendinning (Century Hutchin-
       son).

F243   'Opinion disfigured.' *Glasgow Herald (Weekender)* 6 May 1989, p. 20.

       Review of: *The Way the Words are Taken* by Robin Fulton (Loanhead:
       Macdonald).

F244   'Past tenses.' *Glasgow Herald (Weekender)* 8 July 1989, p. 20.

       Review of: *Full Score* by Fred Urquhart, ed. G. Roberts (AUP).

F245   'Treason of thought.' *Glasgow Herald (Weekender)* 17 June 1989, p. 22.

       Review of: *The Godwins and the Shelleys* by W. St Clair (Faber).

F246   'Well versed in humanity.' *Evening Standard* 20 April 1989.

       Reviews of: *Selected Poems* by Hugo Williams (OUP); *Selected Poems* by
       David Harsent (OUP); *Blue Shoes* by Matthew Sweeney (Secker).

F247   'The wounded rose.' *Observer* 9 July 1989.

       Reviews of: *Federico Garcia Lorca* by Ian Gibson (Faber); *In the Green
       Morning: memories of Federico* by Francisco Garcia Lorca (Peter Owen).

F248   'The year of barricades.' *Glasgow Herald (Weekender)* 7 October 1989,
       p. 22.

Review of: *The Pale Companion* by Andrew Motion (Viking).

1990

F249   'Against uncertainty.' TLS 11 May 1990, p. 494.

Review of: *Radical Renfrew: Poetry from the French Revolution to the First World War* ed. Tom Leonard (Polygon).

F250   'Antipodean Calvinist.' *Glasgow Herald (Weekender)* 9 June 1990, p. 22.

Review of: *May Week Was in June* by Clive James (Cape).

F251   'Baroque prurience.' *Glasgow Herald (Weekender)* 14 July 1990, p. 22.

Review of: *Something Leather* by Alasdair Gray (Cape).

F252   'Bitter prototype.' *Glasgow Herald (Weekender)* 5 May 1990, p. 26.

Review of: *Dance of the Apprentices* by Edward Gaitens (Canongate).

F253   'Brittle comedian.' *Glasgow Herald (Weekender)* 6 October 1990, p. 24.

Review of: *Magnus Merriman* by Eric Linklater (Canongate).

F254   'An enduring neglect.' *Glasgow Herald (Weekender)* 2 June 1990, p. 24.

Review of: *Ford Madox Ford* by Alan Judd (Collins).

F255   'From Glasgow to Mercury.' *Sunday Times* 18 November 1990, p. 11.

Reviews of: *Collected Poems* by Edwin Morgan (Carcanet); and *Crossing the Border* by Edwin Morgan (Carcanet).

F256   'In the living past.' *Glasgow Herald (Weekender)* 20 October 1990, p. 22.

Review of: *Friend of My Youth* by Alice Munro (Chatto).

F257   'An interior grammar.' *Glasgow Herald (Weekender)* 14 April 1990, p. 20.

Review of: *Ground Work: Selected Poems and Essays 1970–9* by Paul Auster (Faber).

F258   'Picking a new bone.' *Glasgow Herald (Weekender)* 7 April 1990, p. 22.

Reviews of: *McGrotty and Ludmilla* by Alasdair Gray (Dog & Bone); *Blooding Mister Naylor* by Chris Boyce (Dog & Bone); and *Lord Byron's Relish* by Wilma Paterson (Dog & Bone).

F259   'Pursuit of the inedible.' *Glasgow Herald (Weekender)* 24 March 1990, p. 22.

Review of: *Moscow! Moscow!* by Christopher Hope (Heinemann).

F260   'A question of style.' *Glasgow Herald (Weekender)* 1 September 1990, p. 22.

Review of: *Brief Lives* by Anita Brookner (Cape).

F261   'Reconstructed pain.' *Glasgow Herald (Weekender)* 29 September 1990, p. 22.

Review of: *Affliction* by Russell Banks (Picador).

F262   'Roth's talking book.' *Glasgow Herald (Weekender)* 8 September 1990, p. 22.

Review of: *Deception* by Philip Roth (Cape).

F263   'Scrawled on the screen.' *Glasgow Herald (Weekender)* 16 June 1990, p. 24.

Review of: *Writers in Hollywood 1915–51* by Ian Hamilton (Heinemann).

F264   'Sharp to the point.' *Glasgow Herald (Weekender)* 17 November 1990, p. 24.

Review of: *The Pencil* by Henry Petroski (Faber). [A review in verse].

F265   'Slippery verse.' *Glasgow Herald (Weekender)* 10 November 1990, p. 24.

Review of: *Madoc: a Mystery* by Paul Muldoon (Faber).

F266   'Songs that linger on.' *Evening Standard* 13 September 1990.

Reviews of: *Selected Poems* by Ivor Gurney (OUP); *Collected Poems* by Patricia Beer (Carcanet); *Remembrance of Crimes Past* by Dannie Abse (Hutchinson); *Meeting Montaigne* by Adam Thorpe (Secker).

F267   'Stress of obsession.' *Glasgow Herald (Weekender)* 12 May 1990, p. 22.

Review of: *The Innocent* by Ian McEwan (Cape).

F268   'Third eye of insight.' *Glasgow Herald (Weekender)* 26 May 1990, p. 22.

Review of: *The Magic Flute* by Alan Spence (Canongate).

F269   'Voice in the bear-pit.' *Glasgow Herald (Weekender)* 21 July 1990, p. 22.

Review of: *Patrick White Speaks* (Cape).

F270 'Walk away.' *Glasgow Herald (Weekender)* 10 February 1990, p. 22.

Reviews of: *Collected Poems 1937–1971* by John Berryman (Faber); and *The Dream Songs* by John Berryman (Faber).

F271 'Who builds a dam?.' *Glasgow Herald (Weekender)* 3 March 1990, p. 24.

Reviews of: *Great Plains* by Ian Frazier (Faber); and *Cadillac Desert* by Marc Reisner (Secker).

1991

F272 'Commander surprised by victory.' *Glasgow Herald (Weekender)* 9 March 1991, p. 24.

Review of: *Haig's Command: a Reassessment* by Denis Winter (Viking).

F273 'Survival of passages in rhyme.' *Glasgow Herald (Weekender)* 5 January 1991, p. 20.

Reviews of: Osip Mandelstam. *Stone*, trans. by R. Lacy (Collins Harvill); and Osip Mandelstam. *The Collected Critical Prose and Letters*, ed. J. Harris (Collins Harvill).

SECTION G. DOUGLAS DUNN'S WORK FOR RADIO, TELEVISION, AND THE THEATRE.

Since the early 1970s, DD has frequently been interviewed, primarily on radio but also latterly on TV. He has contributed verse commentaries, radio plays, screenplays and numerous scripts for both radio and TV since about 1975; and given poetry readings far and wide, as well as presented, chaired and taken part in poetry programmes, both broadcast and local.

What follows is a very selective chronology of his main work in this field, particularly where it has resulted in some form of publication or review notice.

1973

G1 DD interviewed on BBC1 'Poets on Poetry' programme, 7 November 1973.

Report in *Listener* 8 November 1973, pp. 629–30.

1975

G2 'Experience Hotel' by DD *et al.*: a verse play produced by Poets' Theatre Group at the Humberside Theatre in June 1975.

Noted in *Paisley Daily Express* 26 June 1975, p. 3 [See H8].

1976

G3   Verse commentary for 'Early Every Morning' broadcast on the BBC TV series for GCSE English during October 1976.

1977

G4   Screenplay for BBC TV programme entitled 'Running', August 1977.

1978

G5   'Birds and Barbarians': a selection of new poetry broadcast on Radio Scotland on 18 April 1978.

Included part of an unpublished sequence by DD, read by himself.

G6   'Scotsmen by Moonlight', a radio play by DD broadcast on Radio Scotland 26 June 1978.

Previewed in *Radio Times* (Scotland) 24–30 June 1978, p. 12.

Reviewed by K. Rantell in *Glasgow Herald* 30 June 1978, p. 8.

1979

G7   'Ploughman's Share', a television play by DD, broadcast on BBC 1 'Play for Today' series 27 February 1979.

Previewed by P. Vallely in *Radio Times* (Scotland) 24 February–2 March 1979, p. 17. [See H19].

[See also H13 and H14].

1980

G8   'Wedderburn's Slave', a radio play by DD, broadcast on BBC Radio Scotland September 1980.

Noted in *Stand* 22 (1) 1980, p. 51.

1982

G9   'Scotsmen by Moonlight' repeated on Radio Scotland 9 February 1982.

Reviewed by D. Hearst in *Weekend Scotsman* 13 February 1982, p. 3.

1984

G10   'Anon's People', a screenplay by DD broadcast on BBC 1 Scotland in the 'Spectrum' series on 29 January 1984.

Previewed in *Glasgow Herald* (Weekender) 28 January 1984; and by E. Aitken in *Radio Times* (Scotland) 28 January–3 February 1984, p. 73.

1986

G11   'The Telescope Garden', a radio play by DD broadcast on Radio 3 on 11 July 1986.

Previewed by M. Brennan in *Radio Times* (Scotland) 5–11 July 1986, p. 91. [See H78].

1987

G12 Script by DD for Schools Programme on BBC Radio in the series 'English for S3 and S4' during the Summer of 1987.

G13 'The Telescope Garden' was repeated on Radio 3 on 12 May 1987.

1988

G14 BBC Radio Schools Broadcast in the 'English series' on 18 February 1988, in which DD 'tells his own story and reads two of his own poems.'

Previewed in TES (Scotland) 12 February 1988.

G15 'Poetry Now: 6' on Radio 3 on 2 March 1988 was compiled, scripted and presented by DD.

G16 DD read three of his own poems in the STV series 'In Verse', and was interviewed by the poet Tom Pow in the same series, Summer 1988.

G17 DD acted as chairman of a session discussing 'BBC – Golden Treasury' on BBC TV, Autumn 1988.

1989

G18 'Andromache', a radio play in verse by DD was broadcast on Radio 3 as 'The Friday Play' on 24 November 1989.

Reviewed by Allan Massie in *Sunday Times* (Scotland) 26 November 1989 [See H77].

Subsequently published as *Andromache* (Faber, 1990), q.v.

1991

G19 In Radio 3's 'Poet of the Month' series, DD talked to Clive Wilmer about his work: broadcast on 3 November 1991.

SECTION H. BIOGRAPHICAL-CRITICAL ARTICLES ON DOUGLAS DUNN (INCLUDING INTERVIEWS).

Douglas Dunn has been in *Who's Who* since 1984, and has brief entries in the following:–

Contemporary Poets of the English Language ed. R. Murphy (St James Press, 1970); *Scottish Writing and Writers* ed. N. Wilson (Ramsay Head Press, 1977); *The Macmillan Companion to Scottish Literature* by Trevor Royle (1983); *The Cambridge Guide to Literature in English* ed. Ian Ousby

(1988); *Scotland: a Literary guide* by Alan Bold (Routledge, 1989); *The Writers Directory 1992–94* 10th ed. (St James Press, 1991).

He does *not* feature in *The Oxford Companion to English Literature* 5th ed. by M. Drabble (OUP, 1985).

1964

H1   Grant, P. 'Douglas Dunn: [departure to USA].' *SLA News* no 67 (November/December 1964), p. 27.

1969

H2   'Fame has come to Terry Street.' *Hull & Yorkshire Times* 2 May 1969, p. 1.

1971

H3   Abse, D. 'Douglas Dunn.' In his edition of *Modern Poets in Focus: 1* (Corgi, 1971: Woburn Press, 1973), pp. 101–5.

1972

H4   'A happier life by far – to be a poet!' *Paisley Daily Express* 1 May 1972, p. 3.

On the publication of *The Happier Life*

H5   'Top prize for poet.' *Paisley and Renfrewshire Gazette* 28 April 1972, p. 1.

On DD winning the Somerset Maugham Prize for *Terry Street* (1969).

1974

H6   Mahon, D. 'Spotlight on poets.' *Vogue* 15 September 1974, pp. 90–4.

Includes a section on DD and his poem 'The Dilemma'.

1975

H7   Lindsay, M. 'Dunn, Douglas (Eaglesham).' In *Contemporary Poets*. 2nd ed., ed. J. Vinson (St James Press, 1975), pp. 403–5.

H8   'Well-versed in poetry.' *Paisley Daily Express* 26 June 1975, p. 3.

On DD's 'Poets' Theatre' in Hull, and its first production 'Experience Hotel' in June 1975.

1976

H9   'Douglas Dunn – Poet.' *Diary* (Lincolnshire and Humberside Arts) July–August 1976, pp. 8–9.

Also includes the poem 'Empires.'

H10   Sommer, P. 'Rozmowa z Douglasem Dunnem.' [Interview with DD – in Polish]. *Literatura na Swiecie* no 4 (1976), pp. 308–27.

Followed by a selection of 9 poems in Polish translation by Sommer (pp. 328–35).

H11   Sommer, P. 'Terry Street, czyli milosc albo nic.' *Nowy Wyraz* no 12 (1976), pp. 89–92.

Introduces a sequence of 7 poems by DD translated into Polish by Sommer (pp. 93–8).

1978

H12   Rantell, K. 'Evocative play on soldier myth.' *Glasgow Herald* 30 June 1978, p. 8.

Review of DD's first radio play 'Scotsmen by Moonlight'.

1979

H13   Banks-Smith, N. 'Television: Ploughman's Share.' *Guardian* 28 February 1979, p. 12.

A brief review of DD's BBC 1 'Play for Today' entitled 'The Ploughman's Share'.

H14   Downie, A. 'More than a "ploughman's share" of talents . . .' *Glasgow Herald* 17 February 1979, p. 8.

On DD's TV play 'The Ploughman's Share.'

H15   Dunn, D. 'Living out of London – VIII.' *London Magazine* 19 (5/6) August/September 1979, pp. 71–9.

Personal reminiscences of living in Hull.

H16   Duxbury, R. 'The poetry of Douglas Dunn.' *Akros* no 41 (August 1979), pp. 47–61.

H17   Haffenden, J. 'Douglas Dunn: a Scotsman in Hull.' *London Magazine* 19(8) November 1979, pp. 12–31.

Later collected in *Viewpoints: Poets in Conversation with John Haffenden* (Faber, 1981), pp. 11–34.

H18   King, P.R. 'Three new poets: Douglas Dunn, Tom Paulin, Paul Mills.' In his *Nine Contemporary Poets: a Critical Introduction* (Methuen, 1979), pp. 220–8.

Note. Consists largely of 'a brief account of the development of his work' in DD's own words, pp. 221–8.

H19   Vallely, P. 'Scots accent.' *Radio Times* (Scotland) 24 February–2 March 1979, p. 17.

On 'Ploughman's Share': Play for Today on BBC1 27 February 1979, DD's first play for TV.

1980

H20 Lindsay, M. 'Dunn, Douglas (Eaglesham).' In *Contemporary Poets*, 3rd ed., ed. by J. Vinson (Macmillan, 1980), pp. 403–5.

Updated version of the entry in *Contemporary Poets*, 2nd ed. (1975), q.v.

H21 'Local man will judge BBC poetry.' *The Renfrew Press* 1 August 1980, p. 9.

DD was one of the judges of the 1980 National Poetry Competition organised by the Poetry Society and BBC Radio 3.

H22 Montrose, D. 'Class is the curse of the thinking workers.' *The Honest Ulsterman* no 66 (1980), pp. 70–8.

Review article on *Barbarians* (1979).

H23 Motion, J. 'Three poets in Hull.' *University of Hull Bulletin* issue 31 (21 January 1980), pp. 1–2.

On Andrew Motion, DD and Philip Larkin, and previewing an exhibition of contemporary manuscripts in the Brynmor Jones Library in February 1980.

1981

H24 Haffenden, J. 'Douglas Dunn.' In his *Viewpoints: Poets in Conversation with John Haffenden* (LM Editions, 1981), pp. 11–34.

Previously published in *London Magazine* (November, 1979), q.v.

H25 Haffenden, J. 'Douglas Dunn.' In his *Viewpoints: Poets in Conversation with John Haffenden* (Faber, 1981), pp. 11–34.

A 'slightly modified' version of the original interview in *London Magazine* (November, 1979), q.v.

H26 Thwaite, A. 'Allegiance to the Clyde.' TLS 2 October 1981, p. 1125.

Review article on *SKP* (1981).

1982

H27 'Douglas Dunn tour for NW.' *The Artful Reporter* (Manchester) no 45 (February 1982), p. 12.

A personal introduction by DD, largely on 'why I write'.

H28 Dunn, D. *Douglas Dunn*. Glasgow: National Book League, [1982]. 1 sheet (folded) and portrait. (Writers in Brief; no 18).

H29 Young, A. 'Glittering prize for Dunn.' *Glasgow Herald* 16 June 1982, p. 4.

On the award of the Hawthornden Prize for *SKP* (1981).

1983

H30 Ash, J. 'Pleasures of invention, rigours of responsibility: some notes on the poetry of Douglas Dunn.' *P N Review* 10 (2) 1983, pp. 43–6.

H31 Dunn, D. 'Winkie the Pigeon and my crumbs of literary advice.' *Glasgow Herald* (Weekender) 9 July 1983, p. 7.

On his year as Fellow in Creative Writing at Dundee University.

H32 Sommer, P. 'Douglas Dunn (ur 1942).' In *Antologia Nowej Poezji Brytyjskiej* ed. P. Sommer (Warsaw, 1983), pp. 60–1.

1984

H33 Aitken, E. 'Return of the native.' *Radio Times* (Scotland) 28 January–3 February 1984, p. 73.

On DD's 'Anon's People' broadcast on BBC1 on 29 January 1984.

H34 Charlton, F.G. *Inalienable Perspectives: Douglas Dunn's Poetry 1963–83*. Newcastle: Newcastle University, 1984. 103 pp. [Unpublished MA thesis].

Includes an Appendix listing 'Dunn's Uncollected Poems 1963–83', pp. 100–3.

H35 Dunn, D. 'Emigré writers: exile and unexile.' *Cencrastus* no 16 (Spring 1984), pp. 4–6.

On himself.

H36 Dunn, D. ' "From Hell, Hull and Halifax, may the Good Lord deliver us".' In *Living Out of London* ed. Alan Ross (LM, 1984), pp. 56–64.

H37 Knowling, M. 'Doing just what he always wanted to do.' *The Armidale Express* (NSW, Australia) 2 November 1984, p. 4.

On DD's two months as Writer-in-Residence at the University of New England, Armidale, NSW. Includes the poem 'War Blinded'.

1985

H38 'Awards for writers: nominated for richest prize.' *Fife Herald* 15 November 1985, p. 17.

Scottish Arts Council awards for DD (& Christopher Rush); and DD's nomination for the Whitbread Prize.

H39 'Douglas Dunn talking with Robert Crawford.' *Verse* no 4 (1985), pp. 26–34.

H40 Dunn, D. 'Regained: the light behind grief's dark veil.' *Glasgow Herald* (Weekender) 24 September 1985, p. 9.

H41 Hulse, M. 'Order, benevolence, love.' *Prospice* 17 (1985), pp. 94–100.

Review article on *E* (1985) and *SV* (1985).

See also the follow-up article by L. Sail in *Prospice* 19 (1986) [H59].

H42 O'Donoghue, B. 'An interview with Douglas Dunn.' *Oxford Poetry* vol. 2 no 2 (Spring 1985), pp. 44–50.

H43 'Poetry is on menu of Hull restaurant.' *Hull Daily Mail* 7 November 1985.

Poetry readings by DD and others at Restaurant La France in Hull.

H44 Sommer, P. '[Interview with DD, in Polish]'. In *Zapisy Rozmow: Wywiady z Poetami Brytyjskimi* by Piotr Sommer (Warszawa, 1985), pp. 84–109.

H45 'Writers' who's who: Douglas Dunn.' *Books in Scotland* no 18 (1985), p. 18.

1986

H46 Bateman, D. 'Leading poet [i.e. DD] refuses to meet visiting Russian writers.' *Glasgow Herald* 22 May 1986, p. 3.

H47 Brennan, M. ' "The Telescope Garden", Friday 7.30, Radio 3: elegy to an opium eater.' *Radio Times* (Scotland) 5–11 July 1986, p. 91.

On DD's play for radio, featuring De Quincey in Glasgow.

H48 'Creative writer honoured.' *Courier and Advertiser* (Dundee) 15 April 1986, p. 4.

Reception given by Dundee University on DD's winning the Whitbread Book of the Year Award (for *Elegies* (1985)).

H49 Cubitt, K. 'Clyde-built and doing well.' *Anglo-American Spotlight* 8 (1986), pp. 50–1.

H50 Dinwoodie, R. 'Scottish poets strike seam of gold.' *Scotsman* 28 February 1986.

On MacCaig's receipt of the Queen's Gold Medal for Poetry, & DD's Whitbread Book of the Year award.

H51   'Douglas Dunn: profile.' *Times* 4 February 1986, p. 12.

H52   Dunn, D. 'Douglas Dunn'. In *Twelve More Modern Scottish Poets* ed. C. King and I.C. Smith (Hodder, 1986), pp. 115–16.

H53   Elliott, G. 'Douglas Dunn: [an interview].' *Winthrop II: the Poetry Ephemeral* 4 June 1986, pp. [11]–[12].

H54   Goff, R. 'Douglas Dunn: an interview.' *Very Green: New Arts Magazine* (Kent) Spring 1986, pp. 10–12.

H55   Hughes, G.E.H. 'Rhetoric and observation in the poetry of Douglas Dunn.' *Hiroshima Studies in English Language and Literature* 31 (1986), pp. 1–16.

H56   'Major poets reading in Hull.' *Lincolnshire & Humberside Arts Diary* January–February 1986, p. 11.

H57   Massie, A. 'Breathing old life back into poetry.' *Times* 4 February 1986, p. 12.

On the award of the Whitbread Prize to DD.

H58   Osborne, J. 'Douglas Dunn.' *Lincolnshire & Humberside Arts Diary* July–August 1986, pp. 6–7.

H59   Sail, L. 'The politics of grief.' *Prospice* 19 (1986), pp. 104–6.

A follow-up to M. Hulse's review in *Prospice* 17 (1985). [See H41]

H60   Taylor, A. 'The return of a poets' poet.' *Scotsman* 3 January 1986, p. 11.

DD on poetry, Scotland and success.

H61   Warner, V. 'Douglas Dunn.' *Dictionary of Literary Biography* vol. 40 (Detroit: Gale, 1986), pp. 103–9.

H62   'Whitbread Book of the Year prize' [for *Elegies*]. *Times* 29 January 1986, p. 1.

1987

H63   Argenti, N. 'Douglas Dunn: [a reported interview]' *Rumblesoup* (Durham/ St Andrews) no 3 (1987), pp. 21–5.

H64   Berry, S. 'Book Trust: Poetry Live readings.' *Scotsman* 7 May 1987, p. 4.

H65 Boyd, K. 'Dunn talking.' *The Chronicle: University of St Andrews Student Newspaper* 11 March 1987, p. 12.

H66 Dunn, D. 'Art of being a writer in residence.' *Glasgow Herald* (Weekender) 25 April 1987, p. 9.

At Duncan of Jordanstone College of Art, Dundee.

H67 Lee, J. 'Expansive lyricism: [interview with DD].' *Prelude: the Universities Arts Magazine* (Summer 1987), pp. [14]–[19].

H68 'University appointment.' *Courier and Advertiser* (Dundee) 22 April 1987.

DD as Honorary Visiting Professor at Dundee University's English Department.

1988

H69 'Douglas Dunn': [an interview in Czech]. *Listy Klubu Pratel Poezie* (Praha, 1988), pp. 22–3.

Also one poem translated into Czech (p. 22).

H70 Dunn, D. '[The impact of feminism on my writing].' TLS 3 June 1988, p. 612.

H71 Dunn, D. 'A poet's place' and 'Here and There' [a poem]. *Glasgow Herald (Weekender)* 16 January 1988, p. 16.

DD and Tayport.

H72 Dunn, D. 'Tricks and trikes.' *Scotsman* (Weekend) 10 September 1988, p. 1.

On childhood memories of Inchinnan.

H73 Henderson, G. 'Eventful meeting of two minds.' *Gloucestershire Echo* 13 October 1988, p. 11.

On DD and John Heath-Stubbs at the Cheltenham Festival of Literature.

H74 Macpherson, H. 'Scottish writers: Douglas Dunn.' *Scottish Book Collector* no 9 (1988), pp. 19–21.

H75 Robinson, A. 'The mastering eye: Douglas Dunn's social perceptions.' In his *Instabilities in Contemporary British Poetry* (Macmillan, 1988), pp. 82–99.

1989

H76 Macintyre, L. 'Creating a talent in writing.' *Sunday Times* (Scotland) 10 December 1989, p. 5.

On DD as Fellow in Creative Writing at St Andrews University.

H77 Massie, A. 'Outside Broadcast.' *Sunday Times* (Scotland) 26 November 1989.

A review of the Radio 3 presentation of DD's *Andromache*.

H78 Simpson, A. '[Report of a poetry reading & subsequent discussion by DD and Craig Raine at the Edinburgh Festival]'. *Glasgow Herald* 23 August 1989, p. 10.

H79 Williams, D. ' "They will not leave me, the lives of other people": the poetry of Douglas Dunn.' *Studies in Scottish Literature* 23 (1989), pp. 1–24.

1990

H80 'Douglas Dunn: interview with the Devil.' In *The Printer's Devil: a Magazine of New Writing*, ed. Sean O'Brien and Stephen Plaice (Tunbridge Wells: South East Arts, 1990), pp. 12–33.

H81 Mergenthal, S. ' "A work of grief": Douglas Dunns *Elegies* in der Tradition der englischen Elegie.' In *Amerikanistik und Anglistik*: Erlanger Forschungen, Reihe A, Bd. 52 (1990), pp. 347–63.

H82 Ogilvy, G. 'Arts are reborn in the city of Self-Discovery.' *The Observer* (Scotland) 3 June 1990, p. 7.

The current arts scene in and around Dundee.

H83 Roy, K. 'Poetic justice.' Interview with DD in *Scotland on Sunday* (Spectrum) 11 March 1990, pp. 29–30.

1991

H84 Lyon, J.M. 'The art of grief: Douglas Dunn's *Elegies*.' *English* vol. 40 (no 166) Spring 1991, pp. 47–67.

H85 Macintyre, L. 'Creative masterstroke as St Andrews uses poetic licence.' *Glasgow Herald* 27 February 1991, p. 13.

On DD's appointment to a professorship in the English Department at St Andrews University.

H86 Macintyre, L. 'Poetic justice for Dunn the rejected student.' *Glasgow Herald* 4 March 1991, p. 9.

On DD's appointment as Professor at St Andrews University.

H87 Oxley, W. 'Interview with Douglas Dunn.' *Acumen* no 13 (April 1991), pp. 9–20.

H88 Sedgwick, F. 'Dunn, Douglas (Eaglesham).' In *Contemporary Poets*, 5th ed., ed. T. Chevalier (St James Press, 1991), pp. 246–8.

About the Contributors

ROBERT CRAWFORD is Lecturer in Modern Scottish Literature in the Department of English, University of St Andrews. His most recent books are *Devolving English Literature* (OUP, 1992) and *Talkies* (Chatto, 1992).

IAN GREGSON is Lecturer in English at the University of Wales, North Division at Bangor. He is completing a book on Modernism and contemporary poetry, and writes regularly for a variety of periodicals, including the *Times Literary Supplement*.

PAUL HAMILTON is Professor of English at the University of Southampton. He is author of *Coleridge's Poetics* (Blackwell, 1983) and *Wordsworth* (Harvester, 1986).

W.N. HERBERT's study of the work of Hugh MacDiarmid, *To Circumjack MacDiarmid*, was published by OUP in 1992. He is an editor of *Gairfish*, and co-author of the Scots poetry collection, *Sharawaggi* (Polygon, 1990).

JAMES KIDD is Sub-Librarian (Cataloguing) at St Andrews University Library and has been co-compiler of the *Annual Bibliography of Scottish Literature* since its foundation.

DAVID KINLOCH is Lecturer in French at the University of Strathclyde. His most recent books are *The Thought and Art of Joseph Joubert* (OUP, 1992) and *Dustie-Fute* (Vennel Press, 1992).

GLYN MAXWELL's first collection of poems, *The Tale of the Mayor's Son* was a Poetry Book Society Choice in 1990. His critical essays have appeared in *Poetry Review* and *Verse*. In 1991 he won a Gregory Award for his poetry.

SEAN O'BRIEN's collections of poems include *The Indoor Park* (Bloodaxe, 1983), *The Frighteners* (Bloodaxe, 1987) and *HMS Glasshouse* (OUP, 1991). He has been awarded both the Somerset Maugham Award and the Cholmondeley Award.

BERNARD O'DONOGHUE teaches English at Magdalen College, Oxford. His collections of poetry include *The Weakness* (Chatto, 1991). He has recently written an essay on Dunn's fellow-student, Tom Paulin, in *The Chosen Ground*, a book of essays on Northern Irish poetry.

RICHARD PRICE is a Curator of Modern British Collections at the British Library, London, and is an editor of *Gairfish*. His critical study, *The Fabulous Matter of Fact: The Poetics of Neil M. Gunn*, was published by Edinburgh University Press in 1991.

DAVE SMITH, editor of the *Southern Review*, has received many awards, including a Guggenheim. His collections include *Dream Flights* (1981), *In the House of the Judge* (1984), *The Roundhouse Voices* (1985) and *Cuba Night* (1990).

JANE STABLER, a graduate of the universities of St Andrews and Stirling, is engaged on doctoral research at Glasgow University. Her essays and interviews have appeared in *Verse*.

ANNE VARTY is Lecturer in English and Drama at Royal Holloway and Bedford New College, London. She is author of a number of articles on Scottish literature, and of a forthcoming study of Walter Pater.

Index

Anderson, Sherwood 7, 17
Andrews, Lyman 40–1
Aquarius anthology (1978) 174, 175–6
Ash, John 30
Auden, W.H. 18, 19, 52, 54, 59, 67, 84, 173

Bakhtin, Mikhail 26, 28, 29, 30
Baranczak, Stanislaw 109
Bathgate, Lesley 13–14
Baudelaire, Charles 67, 76
Bennett, Arnold 153
Bergman, Ingmar 39
Bold, Alan: biography of MacDiarmid 176–7; poetry 170–1
Bradbury, Malcolm: *No, not Bloomsbury* 172
Brodsky, Joseph 109
Brown, George Mackay 116, 117, 119
Browning, Robert: 'Two in the Campagna' 96; *The Ring and the Book* 29
Burns, Robert 37, 116, 129, 173, 177–8
Buthlay, Kenneth 177
Byron, George Gordon, Lord 55, 119, 168

Camus, Albert 152, 157–8
Carducci, G.: 'Il Canto dell' Amore' 95–6, 99
Charlton, George 70
Classical formalism: in Dunn's poetry 37–8, 41, 42, 48
Conn, Stewart 11
Corbière, Tristan 151
Crane, Hart 7

Crotty, Patrick 176–7

Daiches, David 175
Dante Alighieri 96
Davidson, John 119; *Fleet Street Eclogues* 123
Davie, Donald 73
De La Mare, Walter 49
De Quincey, Thomas 12, 149
Derrida, Jacques 172
Desnos, Robert 27, 45, 151, 154–6, 157, 165; *Fortunes* 155
Didsbury, Peter 11, 30
Donne, John 53
Dostoevsky, F.: *The Brothers Karamazov* 28
Douglas, Keith 75
Drabble, Margaret 173
Duffy, Carol Ann 30
Dundee 13–14, 122–37, 174
Dundee University 13
Dunn, Douglas: biographical details 1–16; in America 6–8, 14; birth 2; childhood 1–5; children 14; in Dundee 13–14; education 3–4, 5, 8, 9; in France 10; Francophilia of 27; in Hull 8–13, 14; as a librarian 6, 8, 9–10; marriages 6–7, 13–14
Dunn, Douglas: works
    Andromaque, (translation of) 152, 161–3
    Barbarians 10, 45, 46–9, 57, 62, 71, 72–5, 77, 85, 113, 115, 131, 151, 152, 157–61, 156, 158, 159, 160, 162; 'An Artist Waiting in a Country House' 160; 'Ballad of the

Two Left Hands' 47, 62; 'Barbarian Pastorals' 35, 46, 47, 48, 72, 73, 157; 'Chateau d'If' 84; 'The Come-On' 29, 47, 48, 62, 68, 72–3, 74, 157; 'Empires' 61, 74; 'Gardeners' 48, 160; 'In the Grounds' 28, 48, 61; 'A Late Degree' 48–9; 'Lost Gloves' 47; 'On Her Picture Left with Him' 48; 'Red Buses' 47; 'The Return' 48, 75; 'Roughcast' 69; 'Stranger's Grief' 48, 75, 96; 'The Student' 25, 48, 62, 173; 'The Wealth' 67

Elegies 12–13, 14, 30, 32–3, 37, 45–6, 47, 48, 49, 63, 64, 77, 88–91, 94–107, 112, 124, 128, 152, 163–5; 'Anniversaries' 98, 100; 'Arrangements' 63, 101; 'At Cruggleton Castle' 96; 'At the Edge of a Birchwood' 103; 'Attics' 37, 103, 105; 'Chateau d'If' 106; 'The Clear Day' 102; 'Creatures' 38, 101, 106, 164; 'December' 99; 'Dining' 101, 165; 'Empty Wardrobes' 63; 'France' 103, 164; 'Home Again' 43, 45, 98; 'Hush' 105; 'The Kaleidoscope' 102; 'Land Love' 105; 'Larksong' 105; 'Leaving Dundee' 91, 98, 100, 124; 'Listening' 90, 102–3, 165; 'Re-reading Katherine Mansfield's *Bliss and Other Stories*' 163, 164; 'Reading Pascal in the Lowlands' 45–6, 90–1, 102; 'A Rediscovery of Juvenilia' 105; 'Reincarnations' 90, 105, 106; 'Sandra's Mobile' 103; 'Second Opinion' 103; 'A Silver Air Force' 103; 'A Summer Night' 64, 103; 'The Stories' 63, 98–9, 165; 'The Stranger' 101; 'The Sundial' 105; 'Thirteen Steps and the Thirteenth of March' 63, 101; 'Tursac' 89, 106, 164–5; 'Western Blue' 99; 'Writing with Light' 96, 104–5

Essays: 'Dundee Law Considered as Mount Parnassus' 136; 'Little Golden Rules' 2–3; 'Noticing Such Things' 49; 'The Predicament of Scottish Poetry' 174; 'The Wireless Behind the Curtain' 178

Europa's Lover 27, 55, 88, 119, 151, 152, 165–6

'The Grudge' (*Stand* editorial) 68, 74

The Happier Life 10, 35, 36–40, 41, 42, 43, 57–8, 70–1, 84, 85, 151, 153, 166; 'After the War' 36, 38, 48; 'Emblems' 70; 'Midweek Matinee' 33–4, 57, 58; 'Modern Love' 40; 'Supreme Death' 36, 37, 40; 'The Happier Life' 36, 38–9, 75; 'The Hour' 39; 'The Hunched' 30, 35, 57, 71; 'The Musical Orchard' 40; 'The River Through the City' 27, 58, 70; 'Under the Stone' 57

Importantly Live: Lyricism in Contemporary Poetry 171–2

Love or Nothing 10, 40–5, 57, 60, 71–2, 84, 85; 'Billie 'n' Me' 85; 'Boys with Coats' 42, 71, 85; 'Clydesiders' 44–5; 'The Competition' 72, 85, 115; 'The Concert' 45; 'The Disguise' 72, 85; 'The Estuarial Republic' 72, 135; 'The House Next Door' 42, 71; 'The Malediction' 72; 'I am a cameraman' 33, 104, 112; 'Little Rich Rhapsody' 40, 71; 'Ocean' 43; 'Realisms' 41–2, 71, 75, 85; 'Renfrewshire Traveller' 43–4, 72, 85; 'Restraint' 72; 'Sailing with the Fleet' 42, 44, 45, 71; 'Sunday' 44; 'White Fields' 41, 44, 71–2, 85; 'The White Poet' 27, 45, 60, 71, 85, 153–4, 155, 160, 165; 'Winter Graveyard' 42–3; 'Winter Orchard' 41, 43

Northlight 14, 41, 63, 64, 77–8, 91–2, 100, 106, 114, 119, 124–9, 130, 133, 135–6; '75°' 64; 'Abernethy' 92; 'An Address to Adolphe Sax in Heaven' 92, 152, 153; 'Adventure's Oafs' 78; 'Apples' 92; 'At Falkland Palace' 129; 'Broughty Ferry' 133; 'The Country Kitchen' 152; 'The Dark Crossroads' 78, 125, 132; 'Daylight' 91, 92; 'December's Door' 92, 128, 134; 'Here and There' 64, 92, 116, 124, 125, 127, 131, 136; 'In the 1950s' 92; 'In-flight Entertainment' 125; 'Maggie's Corner' 64, 92; 'Memory and Imagination' 129; 'Muir's Ledgers' 92, 128–9; 'Occult history' 78; 'S. Frediano's' 126; 'Winkie' 133, 135

Poll Tax: The Fiscal Fake 35, 78, 109, 131

Scotsmen by Moonlight 110

Secret Villages 110, 120, 139–48, 147; 'Bobby's Room' 143, 146; 'The Canoes' 139–41, 143; 'Fishermen' 141–2, 143; 'Getting Used to It' 142–3; 'Kilbinnin Men' 141; 'Mozart's Clarinet Concerto' 148; 'South America' 143, 148; 'The Tennis Court' 143–4; 'Twin Sets and Pickle Forks' 143, 148; 'Wives in the Garden' 144–5, 146–7; 'Women without Gardens' 145–6

Selected Poems 1964–1983 32, 35, 36, 37, 40, 43, 86

St Kilda's Parliament 10, 25–6, 41, 45, 46, 47, 62, 75–7, 84, 85–8, 108–18, 121, 131, 151, 152, 156, 161, 162; 'An Address on the Destitution of Scotland' 25, 62, 76; 'The Apple Tree' 63, 86, 113; 'The Deserter – Homage to Robert Desnos 27–8, 45, 77, 154–5, 160, 165; 'Dominies' 76; 'Galloway Motor Farm' 87–8, 118; 'Green Breeks' 46, 86, 115; 'The Harp of Renfrewshire' 75–6, 77, 114, 119; 'John Wilson in Greenock, 1786' 46, 63, 81, 86, 173; 'Lamp-posts' 86; 'Loch Music' 77, 86; 'The Miniature Metro' 76, 86, 116–17; 'Ode to a Paperclip' 132–3; 'Ratatouille' 152, 153 'Remembering Lunch' 61, 63, 115–16; 'Saturday' 87; 'Second-hand Clothes' 62, 77; 'St Kilda's Parliament: 1879–1979' 110–13, 114; 'Tannahill' 25–6, 46, 86, 108, 173; 'The Student' 86; 'Washing the Coins' 77, 117–18; 'Witch-girl' 76, 114, 118, 119

Tartooftie 152, 156–7

Terry Street 9, 17–18, 20–7, 32–8, 40–5, 46, 49, 54–6, 57, 80, 81–2, 83, 93, 151, 153, 156, 157; 'The Clothes Pit' 25; 'Cosmologist' 57, 77, 84–5; 'From the Night-Window' 70, 82; 'Incident in the Shop' 55; 'Ins and Outs' 24; 'Landscape with One Figure' 34; 'Men of Terry Street' 34; 'On Roofs of Terry Street' 57; 'The Patricians'
20–3, 24, 27, 55; 'A Poem in Praise of the British' 36; and politics 67, 68–70, 71; 'A Removal from Terry Street' 18, 29, 55, 119; as secret village 110; 'The Silences' 25, 70; 'Sunday Morning Among the Houses of Terry Street' 34, 69; 'A Window Affair' 26–7, 69; 'Winter' 17, 55, 68; 'Young Women in Rollers' 23–5, 54, 56, 112

The Telescope Garden (radio play) 12, 148–9

To Build A Bridge 170

Two Decades of Irish Writing 34, 169

Uncollected Poems: 'Boyfriends and Girlfriends' 138–9, 144; 'Libraries: A Rhapsody' 134–5; 'Moorlander' 129–30; 'Past and Present' 131; 'Preserve and Renovate' 132; 'Scott's Arks' 136

Dunn, Lesley Balfour 6–9, 10, 12–13, 89, 103

Dunn, William Douglas (Dunn's father) 2, 3, 4, 5, 12, 14

Dylan, Bob 82–3

Eagleton, Terry 47, 68

Eliot, T.S. 18, 52, 59, 67, 126, 173; *The Waste Land* 19, 29–30

Ernst, Max 133

Evans, Walker 82

Fenton, James 30

Flynn, Tony 11

formalism: in Dunn's poetry 36–7, 133–4

framing devices 21

France 10, 151–67

Frost, Robert 84, 87

Fuller, John 37

Fuller, Roy 73

Gide, André 157, 158–9

Gioia, Dana 133–4

Graham, W.S. 170, 174, 178

Gray, Alasdair: *Lanark* 108, 139

Gray, David 113

Gregson, Ian 11, 154

Griffin, Tony 11

Haffenden, John 10, 17, 23, 27, 33, 45, 46, 80, 108, 154, 155, 157, 158

Hall, Donald 70
Hamilton, Ian 10, 20
Hardy, Thomas 18, 30, 53, 57, 89; 'At
  Castle Boterel' 96
Harrison, Tony 28, 47, 61, 72, 109,
  171
Heaney, Seamus, 20, 32, 44, 75, 80,
  81, 86, 109, 116, 136, 171; 'Mid-
  Term Break' 6; *Station Island* 34,
  126
Hecht, Anthony 84
Hemingway, Ernest 83
Herbert, W.N. 175, 176
History of Scottish Literature, The 108
Hopkins, Gerard Manley 87
Horace 29, 84, 124
Houston, Douglas 11
Hughes, Ted 11, 67, 87, 136
Hull 8–13, 14, 54, 138
Hulme, T.E. 20
Hume, David 138, 139

Imagism 20–2, 24, 26–7, 30
Inchinnan (Dunn's home village) 2, 4,
  173, 174
Ireland, Dunn's visits to 6
Irish poetry 6, 35, 169

Jaccottet, Philippe 152
Jarrell, Randall 25, 67, 69, 83
John, Gwen 103, 105
Juby, Margot 11

Kavanagh, P.J. 74
Keats, John 102, 103; *Endymion* 48
King, P.R. 18, 20, 30; *Nine
  Contemporary Poets* 17, 155, 160
Kinloch, David 27

Laforgue, Jules 151, 153, 154
Lallans poetry 175
Lanark (Gray) 108, 139
Larkin, Philip 1, 42, 51–61, 64, 67,
  73, 155, 171; 'Aubade' 40, 60, 64;
  'Church Going' 105; *Collected Poems*
  18–19; 'Days' 59; 'Deceptions' 54;
  'Dublinesque' 60; Dunn on, 29;
  and Dunn in Hull, 8, 9–10,
  10–11; and Dunn's 'December's
  Door' 128, 134; 'Essential Beauty'
  60; 'The Explosion' 59–60; 'Faith
  Healing' 60; 'Going' 19; 'Here' 54,
  55; 'High Windows' 90; 'If, My
  Darling' 60; influence on Dunn 37,

40, 52, 80–1; 'Large Cool Store' 8,
  54; 'Mr Bleaney' 54, 60–1; and
  modernism 18–19, 21, 27;
  'Myxomatosis' 60; 'The North Ship:
  Legend' 60; 'Nothing To Be Said'
  60; 'Reasons for Attendance' 58;
  'Sad Steps' 19; 'Show Saturday' 61;
  'Sunny Prestatyn' 60; 'Sympathy in
  White Major' 59; 'Talking in Bed'
  51; and *Terry Street* 9, 33, 52, 57,
  67; 'The Trees' 58; 'The Whitsun
  Weddings' 19, 27, 54, 60, 67,
  153; 'To the Sea' 60; 'Toads
  Revisited' 19; 'Water' 59;
  'Wedding Wind' 19
Lewis, Sinclair 7, 17
Leyden, John 113
Lochhead, Liz 156
Longley, Edna 73–4
Longley, Michael 3, 11, 14, 34, 37
Lowell, Robert 8, 11, 44, 47, 48, 54,
  67, 68, 75, 83, 96, 172
Lowry, L.S. 34

MacCaig, Norman 11, 34, 120, 170,
  171, 178
MacDiarmid, Hugh (C.M. Grieve) 67,
  119, 120, 124, 131, 132, 168,
  171; Bold's biography of 176–7;
  Dunn's criticism of 175–7, 179
McGahern, John 169
MacLean, Sorley 34, 130
MacNeice, Louis 49, 67
Macrae, Alasdair 12
Mahon, Derek 37, 41, 45, 77, 169
Mansfield, Katherine: *Bliss and Other
  Stories* 97
Marvell, Andrew 29, 123
Maxwell, Glyn 30
Milton, John 39, 78; 'Lycidas' 94, 95,
  101
Molière: Dunn's version of *Tartuffe* 152,
  156–7
Montague, John 35
moral sensibility 138, 139
Morgan, Edwin 170, 178–9
Morrison, Blake 40, 42, 45, 122
Motion, Andrew 11, 40, 42, 45, 122
Movement, the 18, 20, 40, 42, 67
Muir, Edwin 119, 174; in Dunn's *Muir's
  Ledgers* 128–9
Muldoon, Paul 30, 32, 47, 80
'Mulwhevin' 145, 148

Murray, Les 109

Nine Contemporary Poets (King) 17, 155, 160
Nizan, Paul 151, 152, 157, 158–9, 160; Antoine Bloyé 159
novelisation, process of 29–30

O'Brien, Sean 11
O'Donoghue, Bernard 88, 108
O'Hara, Frank 134
O'Kane, Liz 6–7
'Orr Mount' 142, 148
Orwell, George 70, 78

Pascal, Blaise 102, 103, 105
Paulin, Tom 11, 47
Petch, Tony 11
Petroski, Henry: The Pencil: A History 133
photographic method of poetic observations 33–4
Poe, Edgar Allan 88
Pope, Alexander 29, 53
Porter, Peter 69
Pound, Ezra 20, 81
Powell, Neil 68, 77

Racine, Jean: Andromaque (Dunn's translation of) 152
Rahtz, Genny 11
Raine, Craig 30, 161
Ransom, John Crowe 84
Redpath, Frank 11
Reid, Christopher 30
Renfrewshire 173–4
Rimbaud, Arthur 76, 116, 154
Robinson, E.A. 84
Roethke, Theodore 84
Romantic Sleep 67

St Andrews University 4, 136
Schwartz, Delmore 168
science fiction, Dunn's criticism of 179
Scott, Sir Walter 173
Scottish poetry 34–5, 173–8
sexual differences: women portrayed by Dunn 143–6

Shelley, Percy Bysshe 99; 'Adonais' 94, 95
Simpson, Louis 70, 83
Sinclair, Iain 30
Smith, Adam 138, 139, 141
Smith, Alexander 113
Smith, Iain Crichton 178
Social Realism 67
Soutar, William 174
Stein, Gertrude 81
Stevenson, Anne 73
surrealism 27, 45, 120, 155
Swinburne, A.C. 173

Tannahill, Robert 127
Tarling, Ted 11
Tate, Allen 84
Tayport, 13–14, 120, 124, 135, 174
Thatcher, Margaret 70
Thatcher government 78
Thomas, Dylan 18, 59, 87
Thwaite, Anthony 9
'Toddle-Bonny and the Bogeyman' 142, 148
Todorov, Tzvetan 30
Tomlinson, Charles 73

United States of America: Douglas Dunn in 6–8, 14; New Formalists 133; poets 82–5

Walcott, Derek 61, 109
Wallace, Lesley Balfour see Dunn, Lesley Balfour
Warren, Robert Penn 84
Waste Land, The (Eliot) 19, 29–30
Wedderburn, John 129
White, Kenneth 130
Williams, Hugo 20
Wilson, John 113, 127
women portrayed by Dunn 143–6
Wordsworth, William 99
Wright, James 67, 69–70, 77, 83, 84–5, 87

Yeats, W.B. 18, 32, 34, 52, 123, 138
Young, Andrew 120, 129, 174